A KILLER COFFEE COZY MYSTERY COLLECTION
BOOKS 10-12
SPOONFUL OF MURDER
BARISTA BUMP-OFF
CAPPUCCINO CRIMINAL

BY
TONYA KAPPES

TONYA KAPPES
WEEKLY NEWSLETTER

Want a behind-the-scenes journey of me as a writer?
The ups and downs, new deals, book sales, giveaways and more? I share it all!
Join the exclusive Southern Sleuths private group today! Go to www.patreon.-
com/Tonyakappesbooks

As a special thank you for joining, you'll get an exclusive copy of my cross-over
short story, *A CHARMING BLEND.* Go to Tonyakappes.com and click on
subscribe at the top of the home page.

SPOONFUL OF MURDER

A KILLER COFFEE COZY MYSTERY BOOK 10

SPOONFUL OF MURDER

A Killer Coffee Mystery

Book Ten

BY
TONYA KAPPES

CHAPTER ONE

E ven after three years, it never got any easier to hear my alarm go off at four o'clock in the morning. A chill seeped through the small hole at my feet where Pepper, my schnauzer, stuck his nose out from underneath the covers.

"Can't you go in late?" My bedmate, Patrick, rolled over and tugged me into his arms. He snuggled his nose in my neck. "It's cold and snowy."

When Patrick broke the silence of the night, Pepper and Sassy jumped off the bed.

"That's the best time to be open." I gave him a quick kiss before I rolled to the edge of the bed, where I slipped my feet into my cozy slippers. "I'll stoke the fire."

Patrick was already snoring before I could slip my thick robe on over my pajamas and leave our bedroom in our small cabin.

"Okay. Okay." At the door, the tippy-tap of Sassy and Pepper's toenails clicked on the old hardwood floors.

I flipped on the light in the family room to greet the black standard poodle and grey schnauzer, Patrick's children and mine.

They bolted out the door and bounced off the porch into the deep snow. I shook my head and went to get a towel out of the laundry room so I could brush off their paws when they came back in.

They were taking their sweet time, giving me the opportunity to stoke the embers and put some more logs in the woodburning stove. The cabin was small, and the wood burner was the perfect solution to keep the chill out and heat the house quickly. We rarely had to use the gas heat.

"I'm coming."

The dogs scratched at the door.

"Are y'all hungry?"

Both of them were so well trained, they knew to stop on the towel I'd laid in front of the door so I could brush the snow off their furry feet and keep it from balling up.

The inside of the cabin was one big room with a combination kitchen and dining room. The bathroom and laundry room were located in the back, on the far right. A set of stairs led up to one big room we considered our bedroom.

"Good night, Sass." I called for her before she darted back up the stairs to go back to bed with her dad. "Just me and you."

Pepper stayed at my heels as we headed into the kitchen area, where I grabbed a quick scoop of Pepper's kibble to hold him over while I got ready for work. He would get his real breakfast there.

It was our routine, except for Sundays. Like Pepper, the Bean Hive Coffeehouse was my baby, and it was open six days a week. On Sunday after church, I spent most of the afternoon at the Bean Hive, making treats like muffins, casseroles, quiche, cookies, and really anything that I wanted to serve with the coffee.

Plus I'd been really working hard on creating my own coffee with my new roastery equipment. Creating some new Christmas blends had been a lot of fun, and I was excited to serve those this morning. The snow was going to bring in a lot of customers.

Some people might think the opposite, but residents of Honey Springs, Kentucky, loved to get together and gossip—um... talk over coffee.

Let's be clear. When someone consumed something as delicious as coffee, it warmed the body, invigorated the mind, and made one feel good. The Bean Hive created a fun atmosphere for locals to come together and enjoy a cup of coffee while catching up on the day's news, and even the tourists had found their spot there too.

They came in after a day of shopping at the boardwalk's local small businesses next to the coffeehouse to take a load off their feet and enjoy a delicious cup of coffee with a sweet treat. They also took advantage of looking at my corkboard, where the month's local activities were posted.

The board was filled with fun things for the Christmas season. I was looking forward to two events—the Christmas Pawrade, featuring a parade downtown for fur babies, and the Holiday Progressive Dinner, which was a fundraiser for Pet Palace, our local SPCA.

The progressive dinner was new this year, and I was excited about it. Anything I could do for the local animals, I was all over it.

"Slow down," I called to Pepper. He was scarfing down the kibble like it was his last meal. "I'll be back."

I talked to my four-legged companion like he understood me. Most times, I felt like he did.

If I stopped to listen, I could hear Patrick's light snoring. I smiled and flipped on the light in the laundry room, where I kept my uniform for work.

It would inevitably get coffee sloshed on it or food where I'd haphazardly swipe my hands down me, missing the apron I also wore. But it was nice to have a few long-sleeved shirts with the Bean Hive logo on them so I didn't have to think too hard about what to wear.

"You ready?"

Pepper was curled up on his bed in front of the potbelly but perked right up when he heard me get my keys off the hook that hung next to the door.

I took one good look around the cabin before I left, checking that everything was in order and nothing could set the cabin on fire, like the wood-burning stove.

A fire had happened here once. Luckily, I wasn't home, but with my world—Patrick and Sassy—inside, double checking had become part of my morning routine, since they did sleep in a little longer.

"Let's get your sweater on."

Pepper loved his little winter wear. The drive to the boardwalk wasn't too far from here, but the car would be cold, and I just couldn't bear seeing him shiver.

Based on the way he stood there waiting patiently, wagging his tail, he, too, was excited to be warm and toasty.

"There you go." The smile was stuck on my face at the sheer sight of my sweet fur baby. He'd been such a joy and companion.

The moon hung high in the sky, shining the perfect spotlight to our car. It had snowed about two feet over the past couple of days, which I loved. The snow fell at a nice steady pace that allowed just enough snow to cover the grass, trees, and tops of buildings while letting the snowplows keep the streets from getting covered and icy.

This was exactly what Honey Springs needed.

A white Christmas.

"How about some festive tunes?" I asked Pepper, who was already nestled in the passenger seat with his doggy seatbelt clipped. He sat there like a human child, staring out the window.

I flipped the radio on to our local station, which played twenty-four-seven Christmas music this time of year. Just hearing Bing sing "Rudolph" had my fingers drumming and toes tapping, creating a joy that was truly so intense that I knew it was going to be a really great day.

Even though I'd taken the curvy road from the cabin along the banks of Lake Honey Springs, I got through hearing only "Rudolph" and the hippopotamus song, the one in which the kid asked for a hippo for Christmas, before we pulled into the parking lot for the boardwalk.

Lake Honey Springs was really what brought tourists to Honey Springs. People loved to boat, fish, and rent cabins along the area, which made for great business on the boardwalk. That was where the Bean Hive Coffeehouse was located.

My dream job of owning a coffee shop came to life after I'd gotten a divorce from my college sweetheart, who turned out to be a sweetheart to many, and returned to where I'd known comfort and solace as a child.

Right into the arms of my aunt, Maxine Bloom, known around here as Maxi. Honey Springs was also where I'd gotten to visit with Patrick Cane, now my husband, when we were kids. Let's just say that we had feelings for each other from the first day I laid eyes on the scrawny kid.

Fast forward to now. We were happily married, I rented the Bean Hive Coffeehouse space from Aunt Maxi, and my ex, Kirk, was out of our life until recently.

Let's just say he was a new citizen of Honey Springs, and discussing him would require me to indulge in a lot of coffee. I'd yet to have my normal servings.

"Okay. What do you say we get our day started?" I unclipped my seat belt and then Pepper's, grabbed my bag from the back seat, and opened the door.

Pepper delighted so much in the snow. I stood on the bottom step of the stairs that led up to the boardwalk and watched him shove his nose into the snow and come up with a snowball mustache.

"Come on," I called out to him and headed up the steps.

The carriage lights along the boardwalk had twinkling lights roped around the base. The dowel rods had a light-up wreath hanging down. Even the railing of the boardwalk was covered in garland and red bows every few feet.

The Beautification Committee had really gone out of their way to make the boardwalk a new tourist destination for holiday travelers. The annual Christmas Pawrade had become super popular. In this fun little Christmas event, locals dressed up their animals, and we marched around the downtown park.

Since we started it, Christmas in Honey Springs had grown bigger and bigger. The townspeople had added a tree-lighting ceremony, Santa, and vendor booths, just to name a few.

This year, a progressive dinner was added to the list, only it was a little different than the typical progressive dinner held at people's homes. Not only was this progressive dinner meant to raise money, but it was a cool way for local businesses to showcase their shops. During the winter months, the lack of tourism made lean times for small businesses like mine and the other shops on the boardwalk.

Of course I was hosting the after-dinner coffee and desserts in my shop's honor. Aunt Maxi had been the one to really get the dinner together.

The first stop would be for cocktails down at the Watershed Restaurant, located on the lake. The appetizers were taking place at All About the Details, the shop next door to mine. The dinner portion would be hosted at Wild and Whimsy Antiques, though the food was coming from the In and Out Diner. After that, it would be my turn to provide everyone with the best coffee in Kentucky. Or at least in Honey Springs.

Today my agenda was to make as many of the desserts as possible so we only had to pull them out of the refrigerator, flip on the industrial coffee pots, and enjoy the winding down of the evening's festivities.

It didn't take long for Pepper to catch up to me and dart right on past. He knew exactly where to go and wait for me.

"You're so good." I got the coffeeshop keys out of my bag and unlocked the door.

I ran my hand up along the inside wall and felt for the light switch. The inside came to life.

A few café tables dotted the café's interior, as did two long window tables that had stools butted up to them on each side of the front door. The front of the café was a perfect spot to sit, enjoy the beautiful Lake Honey Springs, and sip on your favorite beverage.

Today would be especially gorgeous, thanks to the view of all the fresh snow lying on top of the frozen lake. This was my favorite spot in the coffeehouse, but today I was sure my spot would be glued behind the counter, making all the warm drinks for customers.

On my way back to the kitchen to get the ovens started, I knew Pepper would be ready for something to eat. Since he wasn't allowed to go into the food prep area because of health department regulations, I got a scoop of his kibble and tossed it into his bowl. He could get his belly full, lie down in his doggy bed, and take a nap while I got the coffeehouse ready for the day.

There were so many things to do. Flipping on all the industrial coffee makers was the priority. I walked behind the L-shaped counter and flipped the coffee makers on one by one before I finally walked through the swinging kitchen doors.

I loved the kitchen so much. The big workstation in the middle was perfect! I could mix, stir, add, cut, or do whatever I needed to do to get all the food made. The kitchen had a huge walk-in freezer, a big refrigerator, several shelving units that held all the dry ingredients, and a big pantry I used to store many of the bags of coffee beans I'd ordered from all over the world.

Now that I had my own roastery attached to the kitchen, I made a point of adding roasting fresh beans to my Sunday ritual.

"Yoooo-hoooo!" I heard my one and only employee call from the coffeehouse just as I turned on the ovens.

Soon the door swung open, and there stood Bunny Bowowski. Her little brown coat had great big buttons up the front, and her pillbox hat matched it perfectly. Her brown pocketbook hung from the crease of her arm and swung back and forth.

"You're here early." I was delighted to see her. Bunny was a regular at the coffeehouse when I first opened. Since she'd long been retired, she decided to help me out, which was how she became an employee.

"Floyd said he'd bring me, since he is heading out of town to visit some family this morning." She pulled the bobby pins from her short grey hair and took off the hat. With her mouth, she pulled the pins apart and slipped them on the lacy part of her hat.

"You didn't want to go?" I asked.

"Heavens no." She peeled off her coat and folded it over her arm. "If I did that, Floyd would think I wanted more than companionship. At my age, there's no way I want to take care of a man in the"—her head wobbled from side to side as she came up with a number—"ten years."

"You're going to be alive longer than ten years." I laughed and slipped the muffin tin in the oven. "I'd never figure you to be in your seventies. Ever."

"I attribute that to lots of coffee that keeps me active." She wiggled her brows. "I'll go get the rest of the duties done. I bet we're busy today. Everyone is looking forward to the progressive dinner tonight."

She left me alone in the kitchen. With Bunny being early, it would be a good time for me to get the coffee and treats down to the Cocoon Inn.

Every day, Camey Montgomery, owner of the inn, served Bean Hive Coffeehouse coffee and a breakfast-type item in the Inn's hospitality room. Sometimes if I was running a little behind on getting them to her, she'd send up her husband, Walker Peavler.

Not today. I hurried over to the workstation and grabbed three industrial coffee pots with the cantilever push arm from the shelf underneath.

"How do you think Maxine is going to take the news that All About the Details won't be able to host the appetizers?" Bunny's question caught me off guard.

"What?" I asked and stopped to see her face. "Why isn't Babette doing the appetizers?"

Babette Cliff was the owner of All About the Details. Her store was really an events venue with spectacular views of Lake Honey Springs and the little island across it.

"Fell on ice." Bunny tsked. "I told her just the other day how she needed to invest in some good snow boots to walk from the parking lot because she was going to fall in those heels." Bunny tapped her temple. "I should be reading people's fortunes. The very next day, she slipped on some black ice, and down she went."

Bunny clapped her hands together then slid them apart like one hand was the pavement and the other was Babette slipping on it.

"Broke an ankle." Bunny shook her head and headed behind the bar, where a few of the industrial pots had beeped.

I grabbed a couple of the carafes, set them aside, and replaced them with the ones for the hospitality room at the hotel.

"I think she's going to have a meltdown." Bunny gave a sly smile like she was going to love seeing Aunt Maxi in a little pickle. She walked over, got one carafe from the counter at a time, and took them over to the coffee bar.

"Who?" I asked, not sure if she was talking about Babette.

"Maxine Bloom." Bunny's smile told me she would personally love to see Aunt Maxi squirm, since they weren't the best of friends. She made her way to the end of the counter to the coffee bar.

On each side of the counter was a drink stand. One was a coffee bar with six industrial thermoses containing different blends of my specialty coffees as well as one filled with a decaffeinated blend, even though I never clearly understood the concept of decaffeinated coffee. When I first opened, Aunt Maxi made sure I understood some people drank only the unleaded stuff.

The coffee bar had everything you needed to take a coffee with you, even an honor system that let you pay and go. Honestly, I never truly took the time to see if the honor system worked. In my head and heart, I liked to believe everyone was kind and honest.

"I guess I could do the appetizers then come back for coffee." It was a mere suggestion. The last thing I wanted to do was come up with appetizers today and make sure the coffee beans I'd roasted for the special occasion were perfect.

Out of the corner of my eye, I saw Bunny tidying up everything as she went along.

During her shift, she took pride in making sure everything looked nice and presentable. *This is just like your home. You need to keep it tidy and clean,* she'd told me one time. I've never forgotten those words either.

While Bunny did the straightening and I waited for the coffee to brew for the hotel, I decided to change out the menus.

Instead of investing in a fancy menu or even menu boards that attached to the wall, I'd bought four large chalkboards that hung down from the ceiling over the L-shaped glass countertop.

The first chalkboard menu hung over the pie counter and listed the pies and cookies and their prices. The second menu hung over the tortes and quiches. The third menu, over where the L-shaped counter bent, listed the breakfast casseroles and drinks. Above the other counter, the chalkboard listed lunch options, including soups, as well as catering information.

"I better get rid of these soups if I'm going to make some mini-soup bowls for appetizers. It'll be a good night for them." I swiped the eraser across the chalk board, taking the harvest soup off the menu.

Bunny had moved on to the tea bar to get it ready for the breakfast crowd.

On the opposite end of the counter from the coffee bar stood the tea bar, which offered a nice selection of gourmet, loose-leaf, and cold teas. I'd even gotten a few antique teapots from the Wild and Whimsy Antique Shop, which happened to be the first shop on the boardwalk. If a customer came in and wanted a pot of hot tea, I could fix it for them, or they could fix their own to their taste.

I heard a knock on the window. From the outline of the silhouette, I knew exactly who was trying to wave me over.

Loretta Bebe.

"What on earth is she doing here at this hour?" Bunny glanced back.

"I don't know." I walked over to the door and decided to just flip the sign to Open. If people were milling about, I reckoned I better serve them. "I sure hope Birdie is okay."

"Get in here," I said to Loretta in a gleeful voice, but I knew something was going on to warrant a visit at this time of the morning. "You're gonna get frostbite."

"Are you kidding?" I heard Bunny mutter to herself, only it wasn't so quiet. "She's too mean to get frostbitten."

"Is Birdie okay?" I asked about Loretta's granddaughter, who had been working for me since she moved in with Loretta.

"Oh yes." Loretta kept tilting her head out the door.

"Are you waiting for someone?" I asked and looked out.

"Yes. My new helper dropped me off at the steps and is parking the car. I don't think she's ever been here, love her heart, and I told you were located in the middle of the boardwalk."

"She'll find us," I assured her and shut the door, since it was so cold out. "What's going on?"

"I heard, and I'm here." She tugged on each fingertip of her glove, gracefully slipping her hands out of each one. "I'm here to let you know that I'll be taking over," Loretta said in her slow southern drawl, not making it sound as bad as my gut told me it was.

"Taking over what?" Bunny's interest got piqued.

"The appetizer part of the progressive dinner." She sounded as nonchalant as though the decision was hers to make. "Now, before you two start in on me" —she slapped her gloves in one hand—"I know I wouldn't make no fundraiser about any animals. It's just me, but I like to give money back into our community."

"The animals are part of our community." I walked over to the coffee bar and plucked one of the stacked paper cups to fill for Loretta.

When you were the barista of a coffeehouse and had regular customers, you could make their orders in your sleep. Loretta liked her coffee with two light creamers, one vanilla creamer, and two packs of sugar.

"I am not here to argue with you, Roxanne." Loretta batted her fake lashes a few times before she took the cup from me. Instead of saying, "Thank you for fixing this amazing cup of coffee for me," she continued, "What's done is done. The fundraiser is set, and I've come to just turn the other cheek. This year." She let me know in her own subtle way that she would make sure to intervene for next year. "All under the bridge. What we have to deal with is the here and now, and right now I'm stepping up to the plate to offer my services."

The fundraiser was Aunt Maxi's, and if Aunt Maxi was here, there'd be no way in H-E-double-hockey-sticks that she'd let Loretta participate.

"Before you poo-poo the idea"—the bangles of her wrist jingled and jangled when she held up her finger to stop me from talking—"I'm going to give you my idea. Now…" She moved past me to walk deeper into the coffeehouse. "I've decided to host it at the Cocoon Hotel. I've already gotten confirmation with Camey Montgomery to use the appetizers. The only difference is that I'll be providing the appetizers instead of Babette."

"I'm gonna need to take some Tums tonight," Bunny murmured on her way past me back to the coffee bar. There, she cleaned up the leftover sprinkles of sugar that'd found their way out of their packet when I opened them to stir into Loretta's coffee.

The bell over the door dinged. A frazzled, snow-covered young woman walked in.

"Good." Loretta called to her. "You found it. Lana, Roxy, Roxy, Lana." Loretta waved a finger in introduction between us.

"Let me get you a coffee, Lana," I said to her when I noticed her shivering jawline.

When I reached for another cup, Bunny smacked my hands away.

"I'll fix it," she snapped, knowing full well that I'd make another mess she'd feel like she had to clean up.

Poor Bunny spent most of her shift cleaning up after people. I just let her do what made her happy.

"Lana, take off that coat and go stand in front of the fireplace. I'm sure Roxy is about to start one." Loretta had a way of giving orders indirectly. "I'll be right back."

Loretta excused herself to the bathroom.

"Lana, what do you like in your coffee, dear?" Bunny asked Lana.

"How did Loretta take hers?" she asked.

"Don't you mind Low-retta," Bunny said, her voice deepening on the end syllable of Loretta's name.

Loretta Bebe was somewhat hard to deal with in the community. She was a little forward and, well, bossy. She never bothered me any, but she did bother a lot of people. If it weren't for Loretta's volunteering, things would probably take a lot longer to get done around Honey Springs. She was not only the president of the Southern Women's Club but also a big member of the local church, which put you right on top of the society list, even though she did exaggerate about her year-round suntan.

Loretta claimed she was part Cherokee, and, well, that could have been true, since the Cherokee people were indigenous to Honey Springs, but it didn't coincide with her using Lisa Stalh's tanning bed a few times a week to keep her skin's pigment. And if you asked Loretta about it, she'd get all torn up. So we just brushed the subject underneath the rug like most secrets around here.

Funny thing I'd found out since I moved to Honey Springs—those really dark secrets were like dust bunnies. They found their way into the light when they lurked too long in the shadows.

"Black is good." Lana offered a sweet smile.

"Let me get a fire started." I had Lana move away from the front of the fireplace so I could throw in a starter log. "Pepper is excited." I laughed when he ran over and got into his dog bed.

"He's cute." She smiled.

"How long have you worked for Loretta?" I started some chitchat while the flame took.

Bunny walked behind the counter and tried to secretly write a text message on her phone. She wasn't foolin' me any. I'd bet she was texting Mae Belle Donovan, her partner in crime.

"A few weeks. She keeps me on my toes." Lana rubbed her hands together. "I'm there to cook and clean up a bit. She's so busy with all her volunteer work, and now she's offered to make the cheese balls."

She abruptly stopped talking when the handle of the bathroom door jiggled as if Loretta couldn't get it open.

"I bet she has." Bunny's flat voice and ticked-up brow made Lana smile even bigger. "What are y'all doing out so early?" Bunny handed Lana a cup of coffee.

"She put a call in to the owners down at the Wild and Whimsy about a piece missing from the Christmas china she'd bought from them. They told her they found it in another box and were holding it for her." Lana sipped on the coffee and took a seat on the hearth, giving me just enough space to lay a few of the seasoned pieces of firewood on the starter log.

"Where's my cup?" Loretta had joined us again, this time without her coat. She tapped her maroon fingernail on her big-faced watch. "I'm expected at Wild and Whimsy when they open, so we need to make this a quick chat."

"We are chatting?" I asked and glanced up at Bunny, who was pointing to where Loretta had set her cup down previously.

Bunny snarled and rolled her eyes.

"I know that your aunt is going to be all sort of, well, let's just be honest, shall we?" Loretta eased down on the edge of one of the couches, crossing her legs at the ankles like a good southern woman would sit.

"Nothing but around here," I said, giving the fire a little stoke with the poker.

"You and I both know Maxine has her opinions of me, and that's all fine and dandy, but she's going to have to put those out of her way for the good of the community. We need someone to take over the appetizers, and I've stepped up to the plate."

"Did Maxine ask you to do anything for the progressive dinner?" Bunny asked a question we all knew the answers to.

Loretta's shoulders peeled down from her ears, her head tilted and her face flat when she looked at Bunny.

"Maybe she wants you to enjoy it," Bunny suggested. All of us in the room, including Lana, knew the truth. Again, we were sweeping it under the rug, so to speak.

Here was the strange part. Bunny seemed to be taking up for Aunt Maxi, which told me she didn't want Loretta to do the appetizers either. I snickered.

"Anyways, I just wanted you to know that I've once again saved the event." Loretta was also good at taking credit where it wasn't hers to take. Her quirks were very entertaining to me. Not so much to Aunt Maxi.

"I guess I'm not sure where our visit this early comes in?" I asked.

"Honestly, Roxy." Loretta uncrossed her ankles and sighed, carefully putting the mug on the coffee table in front of her. "I'm going to need you to back me up because I'm sure when Maxine Bloom hears that I've had to save her once again, she'll be a little perturbed."

"And you think I can calm her down if she is? Then you don't know her too well." I snickered, knowing Aunt Maxi would fume once she got word, and trust me, she was going to get word before the sun popped up in about an hour and a half.

The faint sound of a ding caused Pepper to lift his head.

"The ovens are preheated. I've got to get some items cooked before we really open." It was my way of excusing myself.

"We have to get going anyways. Beverly is going to meet us down there so I can get that platter for one of my famous cheese balls." Loretta stood up. "Lana."

"Thanks for the coffee and the warm fire. I'll be back." Lana helped Loretta with her coat.

"I hope you do." I felt sorry for Lana. She was at Loretta's mercy.

Bunny and I walked them over to the door.

"From what I hear, Loretta can't keep a helper. How long do you think that girl will last?" Bunny asked.

"Maybe Lana will last. She's got a little gumption. I do know one thing." I watched out the door as Loretta and Lana hurried down the boardwalk. "Aunt Maxi sure is going to be mad."

"Mmm-hmmm, she sure is. And I thought this was going to be a good day." Bunny sighed, breathing into her coffee mug before she took a sip.

Unfortunately, Bunny was right. I could feel the chill in my bones.

CHAPTER TWO

No sooner did I get the mini quiches in the oven than the coffee pots went off for the Cocoon Inn.

"I'm going to run the coffee down to the inn." I slid the display case's sliding glass doors open and put the tray of quiche in it. They weren't the prettiest of displays today, but I was in a hurry.

Loretta Bebe's visit had put me behind. Luckily Bunny was able to do most things, just at a slower pace. I reckoned we weren't in a race, but I did like to be ready for the first customer of the day. It was just a professional thing I was sure I'd carried over from my days of being a lawyer.

Patrick had helped over the years to bring some spontaneity to my life.

"I've got everything all ready." Bunny walked behind the counter, straightening everything as she went.

"I'll be back soon." I grabbed my coat from the coat rack but kept my apron on, tugged my knit cap over my head, and pulled my gloves from the pocket. "Call if you need me." I patted my phone, which was in my coat pocket, then took the handles of the two industrial coffee pots.

"Don't forget these." Bunny picked up the bag of bagels and cream cheese I'd prepared for the hotel guests.

I put down one of the carafes and let Bunny slip the bag handle on my wrist before I made sure I had everything and headed out the door.

A nice brisk walk might wake me up a little more. It was already six o'clock, and the sun wouldn't make its appearance until at least seven thirty. From what I understood, it was going to be a sunny winter day.

"Roxanne Bloom Cane, is that you?"

My face squished up, and an inward groan escaped when I recognized the voice breaking the early morning's quiet from the opposite end of the way I was walking.

I turned around to find Aunt Maxi bolting down the boardwalk, snowshoes and ski poles in hand. She was running as fast as she could. Her crossbody bag was shaped like a Christmas tree with multicolored sequins sewn on, and it swung back and forth at her hip.

"What is this I hear about you letting Low-retta host the appetizers?" She huffed and took big steps. The snow flew up behind her as she got closer and closer.

"I didn't let her do anything." Oh my goodness. Loretta's main motive to come by this morning was for her to tell me and prevent me from disagreeing so she could conveniently tell people that I let her. "She came in this morning just a few minutes ago and told me. News travels fast."

"I reckon Bunny Bowowski couldn't wait for me to hear. She got on that text prayer chain quicker than a rabbit. Mae Belle Donovan texted Jean Hill, who texted Ursula Scott, who texted your mama. Thank God Penney decided to call me. I can't hardly hear my text go off, but I can hear my phone ringing."

"I just found out myself. And it's fine. It'll all be fine." Do y'all honestly think Aunt Maxi heard me? Well, no. She already had it in her head that she wanted me to know how this was going to go down. I could picture how she must have looked when she got the call from my mom.

I tried not to laugh out loud at the images of her face contorting from shock and running through various emotions until she got to anger. She was in that phase now and would probably remain there until she saw it would all work out.

"Have you tried her dips?" Aunt Maxi was on my heels as we walked along the boardwalk, making our way through the snow.

I was trying to listen to her while juggling the two coffee containers and bag and not falling on the boardwalk and ending up like Babette.

"What about that chipped beef ball?" She huffed, stuck one of the poles up underneath her armpit, and took out her cell phone. She was thumbing through it. "Here. Take a look at this." She shoved the phone up in my face.

I stopped and looked at the photo.

"That's one of her creations." She shook her head. "I am not having it at my first progressive dinner. That's why I didn't ask her. People will wonder if the dogs made the appetizers, they are so pitiful."

"'Tis the season," I chirped and started walking again.

"'Tis the season to ruin the season? Is that what you're saying?" She wasn't going to let this go. "You mean to tell me after everything you went through, all them hoops with the health department to get Pet Palace in the coffeehouse, that you're going to let one Low-retta Bebe ruin it for you? No one will donate if they taste her stuff because no one will survive."

Actually, I was a little glad we were discussing it outside rather than inside, where someone might hear us.

"Why don't you take it up with her?" I nodded forward. "She and Lana are at the Wild and Whimsy, picking up something from Beverly Teagarden."

We were almost past the Buzz In and Out Diner, which wasn't too far from the end of the boardwalk, where I was headed. Wild and Whimsy Antiques was the last shop.

"What on earth would Low-retta be up at this time?" Aunt Maxi asked, continuing to pronounce Loretta's name the way Loretta pronounced her own name.

In Loretta's slow southern drawl, it sounded more like she was saying Low-retta. It irked her so much when Aunt Maxi said her name that way. I had a feeling it was the only way Aunt Maxi would pronounce it until the progressive dinner was over.

"Let me guess." Aunt Maxi put her pole in front of me to stop me.

I turned to look at her.

Though Halloween had long passed, if I didn't know her, I would have thought she was dressed in costume. Her reddish-orange hair stuck out from underneath one of those winter hats with the flaps over the ears. She wore what she liked to call her Dolly Parton coat with many colors, like the movie based on the queen of country music. And the snowshoes were a much-exaggerated addition to the outfit. A pair of simple snow boots would've done the trick, even though Aunt Maxi had walked to the boardwalk from downtown, where she lived.

Being physical was a way of life in Honey Springs. If we didn't walk everywhere, we biked. Unless it was snowy, I rode my little bike with the basket to the Bean Hive on most days.

Honey Springs was small enough that it was more convenient to bike places than to worry about parking a car.

"She's been rambling on about that darn barn auction." Aunt Maxi's eyes glowed. "She has been itching to get in there all these years to see what's been held up in there. When I was at the Southern Women's Club last month, Jean Hill mentioned that she'd heard from Evan Rich all the contents had been bought by the Teagardens."

"Is that right?" I asked, letting it go in one ear and out the other. I happened to look into the Buzz In and Out Diner as we walked by.

Aunt Maxi was so busy telling me about the gossip she'd heard that she didn't notice Loretta sitting in a booth at the window with Lana.

"I just can't believe anything in the old barn would be so valuable." I acted as if I were interested now that I didn't want Aunt Maxi to see Loretta. Walking in the freezing cold and snow had zapped any energy I might have had, leaving none to stop a cat fight between the two women.

"You'd be surprised what people would hide back in the day." Aunt Maxi plunged the poles down into the snow, thumping her way across the boardwalk. "Looks like Loretta didn't get what she wanted. Ha!" Aunt Maxi squealed in delight when we passed the antique shop and it was sealed up tight. No lights whatsoever.

No wonder Loretta was at the diner. She must've been waiting.

"It would be one thing if Low-retta could cook, but to screw up a cheese ball takes talent."

I hated to admit it, but the words coming out of Aunt Maxi's mouth were true.

"And she's going to ruin the dinner."

"It's going to be fine." My shift had focused to just calming Aunt Maxi down.

The walk between the boardwalk and the Cocoon Hotel was literally a grassy field about the size of a football field.

The historic white mansion, built in 1841, had been in Camey's family for years. Camey had hired Cane Construction to help rebuild the old structure into an amazing hotel that was situated right on the Lake Honey Springs and kept the cozy character. The two-story white brick with the double porches across both stories was something to behold, especially during the Christmas season.

Camey had light-up garland wrapped around the huge columns in the front and draped along all the wrought iron two-story balconies.

"What are you smiling about? There's nothing good to smile about." Aunt Maxi huffed.

"Oh, I was just remembering my honeymoon night was right up there." I pointed at the balcony of the room Camey had offered Patrick and me on our wedding night during the Halloween festival a couple of years ago.

We'd planned the entire thing because Aunt Maxi and my mom were being pills about who got to do what after Patrick and I got engaged. Patrick and I pulled one over on them and the entire community when we dressed as a bride and groom for Halloween. We were really dressed for our wedding, which also took place in the hotel's hospitality room.

"My stars, Roxanne. Did you hear me about Low-retta's dips?" Aunt Maxi had moved on from the cheese balls to the dips.

"I did hear you, but what do you want me to do?" I asked and stopped shy of the front door.

"I want you to tell me why you decided to invite her to participate in the Christmas Progressive Dinner. And of all things, the hors d'oeuvres?" she cried out.

"It's not nice to exclude people, especially during the holidays." I had nothing for her but hoped throwing something about holidays and niceness in there might light a spark of kindness in her heart.

"It was my idea," Aunt Maxi grumbled. "If I wanted her to be involved, I'd have asked. It's fine if she wants to come with the rest of the community."

"It was a great idea too." I wanted to make sure she knew I recognized her efforts in getting such a fun event scheduled. "And sometimes we have to do things with people we aren't the fondest of. It's going to be after cocktails at the Watershed." I grinned. "Maybe people will be too looped up to notice how bad Loretta's dips are."

"Oh." Aunt Maxi's face froze. Her mouth slightly open, her brows lifted way up on her forehead. "You might just have something." She gnawed on her lip. "I think I'll go talk to Fiona and see if she can do some heavy pours that night. I'll catch up later."

Oh dear me. Just what we needed. A bunch of folks with too much alcohol in their systems walking around Honey Springs. Apparently, today wouldn't be as great as I thought it was going to be.

CHAPTER THREE

Camey Montgomery was busy with a customer when I dropped the items off in the hospitality room. I didn't get a chance to ask her about Loretta, but none of it really mattered. Loretta seemed dead set on hosting it, and Aunt Maxi had appeared to be good with trying to get Fiona Rosone, the bartender at the Watershed, to use a heavy hand. No doubt Aunt Maxi would entice the young lady with cash.

As much as I didn't like the idea, it was kind of funny to think Aunt Maxi would honestly condone such a thing, to get people to drink so they didn't have to taste Loretta's awful appetizers. Then again, I'd make amazing treats and coffee to help sober them up for their way home tonight.

Bunny had a handful of customers when I'd gotten back, and she seemed to be doing fine on her own. Pepper was still asleep in his bed next to the fireplace.

I slipped out of my coat and hung it on the rack next to the counter just as the bell over the coffeehouse door dinged. Pepper jumped up.

The jingle and jangle of bracelets immediately clued me in on who was bending down in the front of the shop. Sure enough, I saw the middle-aged, silver-bobbed, and highly classy Louise Carlton stand up, holding the cutest little puppy you'd ever seen.

"Oh my stars," I gushed, extending my arms out in front of me, weaving in and out of the tables to get my hands on the fur baby. "This one will go fast."

I made a pouty face, knowing there'd not be much time to spend with this week's featured animal from the Pet Palace, Honey Springs's idea of a local SPCA. Louise was the head of the program, and when I moved to Honey Springs, Pet Palace was where I thought I would go and volunteer. I did that, but Pepper also found me, and, well... I ended up taking him home, and now we were constant companions.

"Can you believe someone found this little one down by the lake? I'm so glad they were able to get her right before the snow today." Louise stroked the puppy's back while I snuggled the little one close to my neck.

"Oh, she's shivering." I frowned and tried to ignore Pepper, but he was standing on his hind legs with his front paws on my legs, nose tilted up to get a sniff.

"She's been scared since we got her." Louise got really close to the puppy and smiled, making smoochy sounds. "You're right. Puppies go fast, especially during Christmas. But she wasn't thriving in the shelter, so I thought I better let her come here and get some training from a perfect Pet Palace alumnus."

Louise's pockets were always full of treats, so when she dragged one out to give to Pepper, I wasn't surprised.

"I think he will show her the ropes really fast." I decided to put the puppy down to see what she did.

She peed. I grabbed some napkins off the nearest table and wiped it up.

"Great!" Bunny groaned. "Just what we need in case the health inspector comes in. Or maybe I can anonymously call the health inspector to tell them to check in on Low-retta's kitchen. If we don't do something, she's gonna kill someone."

Bunny took off toward the janitorial closet.

Louise paused to examine Bunny before her brows gave a quick furrow and lifted.

"Aunt Maxi has everyone in an uproar. Babette broke her ankle, so she can't participate in the progressive dinner tonight. Apparently, she called Loretta Bebe to take her place." I rolled my eyes.

"Oh." Louise's mouth formed a huge O. "Have you tasted"—she grimaced—"her food? In particular, her dips and cheese balls?"

"I heard. No, I've not tasted them, but if Babette saw fit to, then I can only assume it's for the best." I watched the puppy start to follow Pepper around.

Pepper was so good with the animals that were showcased each week. He'd been a Pet Palace superstar student and was a natural at loving all animals, even the cats Louise dropped off.

"Well, maybe she's gotten better. I know the ladies from church have started to give her the task of bringing paper plates and napkins." Louise laughed. "Don't be upset with Maxine. She's worked really hard, and I'm sure when she calms down, she'll realize it's best."

"I know you're right, but I'm the one who has to listen to her in the meantime."

"Hello, Louise." Bunny joined us with a mop. "Cute puppy, but I don't do pee."

"She's potty trained. Probably got a little too excited. How's Floyd?" Louise wasn't fooling me none. She wanted off the subject of the puppy and was smart enough to know to ask about Floyd.

"He's fair. He's gone to see some family over Christmas, so I reckon I'll be spending it here for dinner." I was happy to hear Bunny say she would come to my annual Christmas Day lunch at the Bean Hive.

Over the past few years, I'd hosted a big get-together for family and for friends who had become my family. Bunny Bowowski was definitely one of them. Even Louise came one year.

The invitation was open to anyone.

"That's wonderful that you're coming." My heart warmed right along with the inside of the coffee shop as the fire continued to pop and crackle.

"You might have more people than you think if this snowfall keeps up." Louise referred to how the snow kept falling at a steady pace.

"The more, the merrier." I couldn't help but picture all the people inside of the Bean Hive.

Patrick and I transformed the dining room of the coffeehouse to a large table with all the Christmas cheer the space could handle.

"Which reminds me to move that table out of the way." I pointed at the corner table up near the right corner. "Patrick should be stopping by with the Christmas tree. I had him go to Hill's Dairy Farm to get one from Jean."

"Oh, Jean. How is she?" Louise asked.

"I think she's doing better. Each month as a widower, she seems to be getting stronger." It was my standard reply, but I'd know better once I headed out that way to get the creamer, fresh eggs, and other things I needed to keep my promise to use only products from Honey Springs as much as I could.

The local supplies cost a little more, but the quality was something money couldn't buy. Jean Hill had the best of everything. Even flowers.

"That puppy will enjoy the fire with Pepper." Bunny had walked over, bent down, and fluffed up Pepper's doggy bed.

That got his attention away from the puppy. Pepper trotted over to his bed, and the puppy followed him.

"Would you look at that." A huge smile crossed Bunny's face. "That puppy has taken to Pepper."

"And I'm sure the little rascal won't be here long." I couldn't resist the cute puppy, not to mention her breath, which had a smell that was unmistakable and unforgettable.

I wasn't paying attention to where I was going and bumped into one of the tables, knocking off one of the cow ceramic creamer pots.

"I reckon I'm gonna just keep this out all day." Bunny huffed and stood over me with the mop, waiting for me to pick up the glass.

"Dang. That was one of my favorites."

"If you hurry down to the Wild and Whimsy, I heard Beverly picked up some good finds at that barn auction. I bet they had some." Louise had my interest piqued.

Aunt Maxi had mentioned the barn, and now, so did Louise.

"Maybe I'll run down there." I glanced up at the clock. It was a little before eight a.m. Although the Wild and Whimsy opened at ten, they were keeping Christmas hours, which meant they would open at eight for a few weeks.

"Go on. I've got the puppy and the cream." Bunny sloshed the mop right and then left.

"Thank you, Bunny. What would I do without you?" Even though she played tough sometimes, she knew I adored and appreciated her.

"You'd get along just fine," she joked, moving her attention to a customer who'd walked up to the bakery counter.

This time I took my apron off and exchanged it for my coat, hat, and gloves before I ventured back out into the snow.

The sun was barely peeking out from behind a low-hanging grey cloud. The wind skidded across Lake Honey Springs. The lapping waves crashed against the pier, slapping against the piles and echoing from underneath.

With my gloved hand, I fisted the collar of my coat a little tighter to ward off the chill before it settled into my bones.

"Two Blooms in one day," Beverly Teagarden said after I'd taken off all the layers and she recognized it was me. "Maxi was in earlier."

Beverly lifted her chin, giving me a look indicating that something was up.

"Let me guess." I pulled off my hat and brushed my hands through my black hair, shaking the ends to get the snowflakes off the bottom. My hair was naturally curly, and any bit of water would just add frizz. "She was in here looking for Loretta Bebe."

"You guessed it." Beverly and Dan had such a cute shop.

A grunting sound followed by a creaking noise came from the roof.

She walked over and looked out the door. "I sure hope that awning stays attached to the roof. I told Dan during the summer I noticed it was coming away from the building, but things piled up."

"The awning is coming off?" I asked and looked outside and then up to see the red awning flapping in time with the wind. "Oh yeah. I see it on the end."

Beverly let out a long sigh, shaking her head.

"Patrick is going to stop by the coffeehouse this morning. I'll have him stop by and see if he can do anything." It was a mere suggestion and one of those things Patrick didn't like me to do.

He was so handy, and since he owned Cane Construction, I offered up his services without asking him. He had told me a time or two not to fill his schedule with friends, but I was in the small-shop frame of mind. We all had to stick together to survive, and if he could screw in a bolt or hammer a nail or two, it was for the good of Honey Springs.

"Did Aunt Maxi find Loretta?" I asked and moseyed into the antique shop, looking around for anything that struck my fancy while Beverly and I made chitchat.

"No, but Lana was in here, going through the boxes of items Dan and I had gotten from that old barn off of Crescent Peek Road." She picked up some little box and dusted it off before she found a place for it on the other shelf filled with little boxes.

That was the thing about antiques. They always looked like they needed to be dusted. They were just old, and I definitely didn't want them for my house.

"Speaking of that old barn, did you get any cow creamers? I broke one this morning." I couldn't stop myself from walking over to one of the many Christmas trees, all of which had glittery ornaments on them.

"Let me look in the boxes in the back. There's so many." She hurried to the back of the shop.

The balls on the tree weren't bright but had more muted tones. The sequins along with some little Swarovski crystals made them shine and sparkle from the tree lights.

"I love these," I said when I heard her shuffling. "I think I'd like to purchase all of them for the tree at the Bean Hive."

"Sure! I can use this box." I didn't see Beverly, but I heard her voice and the noise of her removing the items she referred to out of the box. "I don't see any creamers in here. That doesn't mean there aren't any."

She walked back up to meet me at the tree with an empty box in her hand.

"Let me go get some bubble wrap for them." She set the box down at my feet.

"Nah. Patrick should be here any minute, so I don't want to take the time to wrap only to have to unwrap them." I started to pluck the ornaments off the tree one at a time and carefully place them in the box with Beverly's help.

"Loretta didn't get an earful, but Lana sure did from Maxi." Beverly began to tell me how Aunt Maxi begged Lana to make the appetizers. "Lana insisted Loretta wanted to do it because she'd offered."

"What did Loretta want from you anyways?" I asked just to bide time while we took down the ornaments.

"After she heard I'd gotten the bid on the old bar, she was on the phone, calling me." Beverly snorted. "Dan and I knew why she was calling before I even picked up the phone. She's been dying to get her hands on it, but it was the property of the banks, and, well, let's just say that the bank knew we would pay the price and not try to negotiate."

I could hear Loretta now, trying to get Evan to come down on the price.

"Believe you me, when she threw out a number for the china she wanted, I almost left this world. Honestly, she doesn't want anyone to make any money. I know she's been eyeballing that china for years." Beverly had my interest piqued.

"Years?" I asked. "From what I understood, the house on the property had been demolished a long, long time ago."

"It was by the family. I was a kid when they moved the items to the barn. At that time, the barn was in really good shape." She patted around her body. "Just like me," she joked. "Over time, this ol' gal has gone downhill."

"You look great. Just like one of the girls." I was talking about Savannah and Melanie, the Teagardens' daughters, who were about ten years younger than me. Both were in college. "What is so special about the china?"

"I don't think it's the actual worth as much as the memory. You see, the family who lived there were pretty well off. They would throw these huge Christmas parties. If your family got invited, it was a big deal." She had a look on her face as if she were remembering something.

"Did you get to go?" I asked.

"Yes," she gushed. "I'll never forget it. My parents had spent all the money they'd saved for the winter months to get us new clothes. It was the first time I'd ever had matching anything." The memory made her face glow. "The interior of the house was decorated from floor to ceiling with Christmas. There wasn't one single area that didn't have something. All the doorknobs even had some sort of decoration hanging from them."

"That sounds like a fairytale." I loved hearing old stories like these.

"It was. Especially for a kid. Santa came on a huge sled drawn by real reindeer." When I gave her an odd look, she nodded. "Don't ask me how, but it was amazing. And I'll never forget it. I got a doll the size of me." She laughed. "I think I still have the doll in my attic. See, it's the memories the house gave you. Loretta remembers the tablescape. It was gorgeous, so when I bought the barn, I let her buy the china. The china was full except for one piece—the serving platter. That's the one she really wants."

"What on earth happened to the family?" I had to know.

"They got older and became reclusive." She frowned and held one of the ornaments in her hand. "Too bad too. The house was really different, and none of their children lived here. They just let it sit and rot."

"They didn't want to buy back the property?" It was such a shame.

"Evan said the deed was signed over to Honey Springs. Technically, the city owns it, and I can't help but wonder if they are about to do something with the land. You know, one of those strip malls or something." Beverly told me something I sure didn't like to hear. She slipped the last ornament into the box. "Anyways, long gone are the good ol' days."

She picked up the box.

"That's a shame." I tugged my hat out of my coat pocket and pulled it back over my head.

"Maybe you'll find a creamer in one of them when you search for the platter."

"Maybe, but Loretta wants the platter now for this appetizer deal." Beverly handed me the box. "Maxine told me she'd pay me not to give it to Loretta. She even begged Lana to quit working for Loretta and come work for her. They almost got into an argument about it."

"What did Lana say?" I felt bad for her being stuck in the middle of what Aunt Maxi put her in.

"Lana at first thought Maxine was joking, but Maxine got a little huffy. Finally, Lana told her flat-out no, and it was literally a stern no." Beverly waved at the group of customers coming in. "I can't wait to see the tree tonight. Those will look great in the coffeeshop."

"How much?" I asked.

"Nothing if you can get Patrick down here to fix my awning," she called from over her shoulder as she walked away to see if the customers needed any help.

CHAPTER FOUR

Patrick and Sassy were at the Bean Hive when I got back. They were playing with the puppy.

"Let me help you with that." Patrick jumped up from the hearth and hurried over to take the box. He gave me a kiss. "What's inside?"

"The most beautiful box of glittery ornaments." I opened the top to show him. "I know I normally don't do all the glitter for the coffeehouse, but these really spoke to me, and they were free."

"Free? They look expensive." He set the box down on the small café table he'd moved without me. The Christmas tree he'd brought was wrapped up in the green netting and sitting in the tree stand, ready to be clipped open.

"If you want to call your labor expensive." I slipped that in without a care in the world, hoping he'd just go with it.

He did not.

"What do I have to fix now?" His shoulders fell.

"Oh, these are lovely." Bunny had found her way over to us and placed her hands in the box. "I think I've seen these before."

"They were in that barn the Teagardens had bought from the bank." I didn't think too much about it until Bunny's gasping gave her excitement away.

"The Seiferts' old place?" She dug down in the box, took out each ornament one at a time, and held them up to the light. "I'd heard about their Christmas

33

trees and parties but was never invited. I know Maxine was invited. She let the world know."

"Really?" I found it fascinating Aunt Maxi hadn't ever mentioned it. "I've never heard a word from her."

"She went, and I think she even had lunch with Mrs. Seifert once too." Bunny was blowing my mind.

There'd been talk of the old barn, and I was sure Aunt Maxi was there, especially when Loretta Bebe talked about it. But maybe all the gossip was just running together. Trust me, I heard everything in the coffeehouse by just walking past tables while serving coffee. Getting the hearsay all mixed up was all too possible, which was why I never repeated any of it.

Still, listening in was a lot of fun at the time.

"They are as gorgeous as I imagined. How much did this cost you?" she asked and held the silver one with the clear crystals up to the light.

"I'm thinking she negotiated some labor." Patrick put his hand on my back and gave it a slight rub.

"How did you guess?" I smiled, knowing he was fine with my little deal with Beverly even though he didn't have a clue what I'd agreed for him to do.

"Anything that makes you happy is worth it to me." He bent down and gave me a kiss.

"Pft, pft." Bunny put the ornament on the tree. "I've about had enough of that. This is a coffeehouse, not the Cocoon Hotel."

She waddled off to the coffee bar and began to straighten it while Patrick and I resumed decorating the tree.

"What was the cost?" he asked.

"The awning outside of the Wild and Whimsy is coming loose from the building. Do you think you can put a screw it in or something?" I asked as if it were just that easy.

"Or something," he muttered right before our attention was taken away from the tree and Aunt Maxi swept into the coffeehouse like the wind that followed her.

"Good afternoon, Maxine."

"Oh, Patrick, this afternoon has been much better than this morning." Her gaze slid to me subtly, letting me know I'd ruined the morning and she'd fixed it.

34

"I'm curious." I put the last ornament on the tree.

"Oh my stars." Aunt Maxi drew in an excited breath. "This looks just like a tree I've seen before." She reached her gloved hand out and extended it to the Christmas tree, her fingertips barely grazing a few of the ornaments as she swept her fingers back into her chest.

"If you're referring to the Seiferts' Christmas tree, you have seen it before. From what I understand, you went to their house a few times." I observed her movements.

"That old Bunny Bowowski has a big mouth," Aunt Maxi snarled. "Patrick, it was good seeing you. I need to get something in the refrigerator so I can take it tonight." She patted the oversized hobo bag strapped across her body. "Patrick, will I be seeing you tonight?"

"Yes, ma'am." He and Aunt Maxi embraced. "I can't wait. It's going to be fun. I've heard all the talking around town this morning."

"You have?" Her eyes fluttered open with a sparkle.

"Mmmhhh, sure have." Patrick was telling her a big lie. He knew exactly what to say to butter her up. "Whole town is excited."

"I knew it was a fantastic idea." She gave me the side eye with thin lips before they turned up on the corners and looked at Patrick. "I have a few up here." She tapped her temple before she excused herself.

"Did you see how she skipped right over my comment about the Seifert place?" I found it odd she didn't engage with me when normally she'd be all over it with some sort of tale.

"She looked busy, and she's got a lot on her plate to make sure this progressive dinner goes well. It's the first one, and she likes things just so." Patrick gave me all sorts of excuses for her while I watched her slip through the kitchen's swinging doors without so much as looking Bunny's way.

A sure sign Aunt Maxi was up to something.

It didn't matter what day or time it was. If Bunny was around, Aunt Maxi always said something snarky to her just to get Bunny's goat.

Bunny noticed it too.

We caught each other's eye and gave a little shrug.

"I think it's gorgeous and just for a little labor," I said sarcastically and wrapped my arms around Patrick's waist. I looked up and smiled.

The lines around his big brown eyes softened, and his chiseled jaw relaxed as he offered me a tender smile in return.

"Anything for you, Roxanne." He snuggled me tight, and we both stood there taking in the exquisite beauty of the ornaments.

"Next year, these just might go on our tree at home." Just as soon as I mentioned home, Pepper, Sassy and the little puppy had found the tree and sniffed all over it.

"No, no." Patrick unwrapped his arms from around me. "Where's Pepper's leash?"

"His leash is hanging up on the coat rack, and I think the puppy's is still in the bag Louise left," I said, so grateful he was going to take all three on a walk, in the snow, so I could keep working.

I moved around the coffeehouse, making sure the customers who were at the tables and on the couches were all taken care of. I asked if they needed any refills or anything else I could get them.

Patrick wrangled the three fur babies out the door.

"Tootles!" Aunt Maxi called on her way out.

I stopped at the window bar to pick up a cup and saucer from a previous customer. There, I watched Aunt Maxi stop to talk to Patrick just outside the door, where she had dropped her skiing equipment and entered the coffeehouse.

"She sure is up to something," Bunny said behind me, staring out too.

"I think I'll go look to see what she put in the refrigerator." I sighed and watched my aunt pat the little puppy before she snapped her ski poles open and slipped her feet into the snowshoes.

"Good idea." Bunny took the cup and saucer from me. "I'll clean this up while you go investigate."

"Investigate?" I laughed and headed back to the kitchen, where I found over four different cheese balls tucked into the refrigerator.

It wasn't the cheese balls that threw me or that I could clearly see what Aunt Maxi intended to do with them. I knew her so well.

No wonder she was so upbeat and happy. Her solution to her little dip problem with Loretta Bebe was to replace them with her own cheese balls and dips.

Unfortunately, it was the hand-engraved Christmas platter that stopped me in my tracks.

CHAPTER FIVE

The rest of the day went pretty smoothly. We'd seen a steady flow of customers in and out. The puppy had been picked up and held so many times that the little thing became worn out. I'd decided to put the puppy's bed behind the counter so she could get some peaceful sleep.

When Loretta's granddaughter, Birdie, showed up to work, she nearly melted over the sweet little baby's cuteness.

"Are you sure you're going to be okay tonight closing alone?" I asked Birdie, though I knew she'd closed so many times before.

"Yeah. And with her." She pointed at the puppy, now rolled over on her back, her full belly spilling over and taut. "Have a good time." Birdie had dug into a leftover morning quiche she'd gotten from the kitchen.

She was a bright young woman with a blond pixie cut, a rail-thin body, and a habit of wearing her tops hacked off midway, showing off her belly. Even the work shirts I gave her, she'd made into her own style by knotting it in the back and folding the edges over, giving a slight peek of skin.

"I will. How did your grandmawmaw's appetizers turn out?" Every time I referred to the woman as what Loretta wanted Birdie to call her, it cracked me up.

"Blah." She took another forkful of the quiche. "Awful," she said with a full mouth. "That's why I'm stuffing my face. She had me try one thing after the other, and she's just not good at making appetizers."

"The rest of her food is good." Loretta had made plenty of dishes for the church's repasts as well as items for the Southern Women's Club the handful of times they'd invited me to come to a meeting. But they were still on the fence about letting me join.

"Baked things can burn out the flavors," Birdie joked. "Not appetizers like these cheese balls and dips she insists on making."

"Between me and you…" I untied the apron from my waist and exchanged it for my coat, hat, and gloves so I could head on down to the Watershed, where the cocktails were being served for the progressive dinner's first round. "Aunt Maxi is planning on swapping out Loretta's cheese balls with her own."

I sighed then shrugged.

"I'm so glad Patrick took Pepper home this afternoon. Do you think you can take the puppy out a few times before we come back here for the after-dinner coffee?" I asked.

"Of course. And you don't have to come here right after dinner is served to get the coffee ready. Bunny left a list of things she's already done, and I can get the coffee brewing." Birdie was one in a million.

Birdie was sent to live with Loretta as a sort of punishment for acting up in her schoolwork and at home. She turned out to be a whiz in chemistry and science, which made her a great asset to the new roastery. I gave her free rein to combine and play with all the beans she wanted to and find the right composition for the best roasted cup of coffee.

She was always writing in her notepad about the beans' chemical makeup, how the combinations of beans felt in the mouth as she sipped the coffee, and how they tasted going down. Not only was she great at coming up with new ideas, but she was also amazing at upselling the customer. I was horrible at that.

I would give things away for free. Not Birdie. She was able to talk everyone into something else. Over the summer she'd worked full time, which gave Bunny some much-needed time to sleep in, and Birdie would beg me not to take orders because she said I was going to bankrupt the coffeehouse and she needed a job or Loretta would send her back home.

When she first came to work, I was a bit hesitant because Loretta had freaked me out by saying Birdie was in trouble at home, but when Birdie came to the job interview, the shop had a long line of customers.

She didn't hesitate. Though not hired, she jumped right on in and started taking orders. Little did I know she'd worked at a coffee shop before and really knew her way around without being told what to do. I hired her on the spot.

Plus, she was good with the high school crowd that came in after school every day during the school year.

"Are you going home for Christmas?" I asked Birdie, knowing her father, Elliot, really missed her.

"Nope. They are coming here. I told them I had to work." She glanced at me. "I see your look."

I leaned on the counter and rested on my elbows.

"Go on. I'm listening." She swiveled, turning her back to me.

"I, too, had a very volatile relationship with my mom." I had tried to talk to Birdie as a friend and not so much as an authority figure. She'd already had enough adults in her life telling her what to do, and no way did I understand being a mother.

However, I did know what it was like to have a mom who had expected more from me than I could give when I decided to move to Honey Springs.

"Life wasn't so rosy for me when I was your age. My dad had died, and my mom had pretty much kept Aunt Maxi and Honey Springs out of my life." It was hard to imagine now, since my mom had realized I was not going to move home after my divorce, and she ended up moving here.

"Your mom?" Birdie turned back around with the latte stirrer in her hand.

"Yep. My mom." I pushed myself up to stand and looked over my shoulder when a customer came through the door. "I guess what I'm saying is that everything will work out. You just have to be open and honest. Truthfully, it took a long time for me to learn to set boundaries. Tell them you don't want to come home and would rather they come here. But don't lie to them."

"Boundaries." She snorted. "That's what my therapist keeps telling me."

"Listen to your therapist." I walked around the counter and waited for the customer to decide what they wanted from the bakery case. "And if you want to work, you know I'll have the hours. Especially if this snow keeps up."

It went without saying that Bunny shouldn't be out in the snow and Floyd definitely didn't need to be driving her to work.

The winter months meant basically that I worked most of the hours, but I didn't mind. This was where I poured my heart and soul when I was healing from my past, and that did include my relationship with my mom.

"Speaking of moms." I touched Birdie's arm. "Do you think you can help them when they decide what they want? I'm going to go call my mom."

"Of course." She put the latte stirrer in the sink and walked over to the customers.

I disappeared into the kitchen and took my phone out of my pocket.

"Hey, Mom." I opened the refrigerator door and took out the red velvet whoopie pies I'd made for my after-dinner coffee and the dessert part of the progressive dinner. "What time are you headed over to the Watershed?"

"Honey, I'm running late. I had so many people looking at cabins to purchase. It's been crazy today." Mom's nomadic lifestyle settled in Honey Springs a couple of years ago.

She wasn't a true nomad, but after my father died, she just picked up and started to travel around. It went without saying that it was her way of dealing with my dad's death and trying to maneuver through life without him—or maybe it was even what her life without him had to be.

When she decided to become a realtor, I was a bit shocked, but honestly, she was darn good at it.

"I just finished up writing up a contract, so I'm going to be a little late. I'll probably just meet you at the, oh, what." She paused. "I'd heard Babette broke her ankle. Where are the appetizers?"

"That's a whole different story that I'll tell you over a cocktail." It was all I had to say to let her know we needed more than just a quick chat and alcohol had to be involved.

"Maxine?" she asked.

"Part of it." I laughed at the fact that Mom knew Aunt Maxi had to be involved. "Loretta jumped in to take over for Babette, so apps are now being served at the Cocoon Inn."

"Roxanne, honey, let me call you back. I've got to take this call from the lender." Mom clicked over. She knew I would be fine with her jumping off, but I really wanted to talk to her about the land being sold.

Not that it mattered, but I was always looking for a location to open another coffeehouse. I still had a lot of things to do before I could even reach the point of actually doing it. Things like market research, the demographics, and quite frankly, obtaining the money. How much would it cost to rent a space when the space I had here was from Aunt Maxi? The family discount had to be applied because she owned the Crooked Cat, the local bookstore also located on the boardwalk.

Aunt Maxi didn't mind upping Leslie's rent, though Leslie complained about it. Aunt Maxi had never once raised mine.

Still, the thought tickled my mind and piqued my interest.

"Rox?" Patrick pushed through the kitchen door. "Hey, you ready?"

"Look at you," I gushed. "You got all gussied up." I winked and walked over to kiss my handsome husband.

He'd traded in his heavy brown construction coat, jeans, and dirty old work boots for a pair of khakis and a button-down long-sleeved shirt topped by a V-neck sweater that looked like Christmas had thrown up on him.

"What on earth are you wearing?" I took a step back to get a better look at the horrible sweater.

"What? You don't like it?" He glanced down. "Sassy loved it. She sat with me while I glued on all the things Franny had picked up at the store."

Franny was Patrick's secretary.

"It's for the ugly sweater contest. They'll be judging all week for the festival, and I am going to win," he said with pride and certainty. "I even tried my hand at sewing on the lights. They are battery operated."

He turned around and lifted the back of the sweater. The wires from the twinkly lights he'd sewn on were hooked to a battery pack in his back pocket.

"The glitter was Franny's idea." He turned back around and did a little shimmy shake. The gold and silver glitter glistened when the kitchen lights hit it just right.

"It's a fabulous Christmas tree." It really wasn't, but it was adorable he'd taken the time to make a sweater.

"I did tell you about it, but you've been so preoccupied with this event that I just dropped it after you just nodded and shook your head." Patrick offered a forgiving smile. "I hope you're going to take some much-needed time during the week of Christmas."

"You know me." I reached out and touched the gold star atop the tree on his sweater. "I say I am, but then something takes my attention."

"I thought that's why you had Birdie." He knew she'd asked if she could work more hours over the holiday, but that was before I'd realized she did it only to get out of going back home to visit her parents.

"We can talk about that later." I reached up and ran my hand along the fuzz on his face.

The goatee he'd been wearing lately was nicely cut and had very defined lines. He had the cutest dimples just behind the corners of each side of his mouth that deepened when he grinned.

"Looks like you got a haircut." I ran my hair over the top of his salt-and-pepper hair, which was becoming saltier as the years went by. "Crissy?"

"Yep. I took the ferry over to the spa and exchanged some HVA duct work to heat the all-seasons room she'd insisted they weren't going to keep open." His eyes dipped. "When I reminded Crissy, she said Kirk insisted on it."

"That man." I groaned and walked over to the small office, where I'd kept some extra clothes for times when Patrick stopped for a quick supper.

I loved the smell of all the things in the coffee shop, but I didn't want to wear them like a perfume all day.

"He's just looking out for the business." He was talking about Bee Happy Resort, which Crissy Lane had opened on the island in the middle of the Honey Springs Lake.

It was really a fabulous idea.

At first.

On that small island in the middle of Lake Honey Springs, Andrew and Kayla Noro had a thriving honey business with their beehives. That island had a lot of property that was able to be developed, and Crissy Lane had been doing all that metaphysical yoga stuff that I barely understood, but she'd really thrown herself into the practice. She went as far as California to take classes and learn the business side.

She'd gotten a financial backer, who ended up being my ex-husband, Kirk, and, well, he'd been coming in and out of Honey Springs to check on his business.

It had been a thing for me. A real yucky thing. Poor Patrick had to deal with him, since Cane Construction was the contractor on the project. Only bad thing was how Crissy kept her financial backer a secret until the spa opened.

Here we were today, with what felt like Kirk having a hand in Patrick's financial dealings.

"Don't you dare do anything for Kirk for free. Not even a haircut." I left the office door just barely open while I changed my clothes in case Birdie came into the kitchen.

"Aw. It was really easy, and I don't mind helping Crissy out." Patrick was being nice, though I knew it pained him to see Kirk.

Kirk wasn't the standup guy Patrick was. Far from it. Kirk had really treated me badly. But one thing was for sure—Patrick didn't let Kirk bug him. He saw it as business, and I guessed that was where I was different as a business owner.

Many times Patrick would tell me to think like a man when it came to decisions about the coffeehouse, but I couldn't do that when it came to the customers in mind. I knew if I wanted a cozy and comfy coffeehouse, so did the people I wanted to serve, and I let my intuition guide me.

"Did you know they were going to be developing some land around here soon?" I asked Patrick and peeked my head out the crack of the office door.

"Yeah. We are putting in a bid." He sounded like his mouth was full of something.

"You better not be eating a red velvet whoopie pie," I trilled, sitting down in the office chair so I could get my boots on. "Because those are for tonight."

I grabbed my phone and headed back into the kitchen.

"No." He was licking his lips before he realized I'd seen him. He brushed the sleeve of his sweater over his mouth. "Nope." He shook his head. "Maybe one."

"Patrick Cane," I moaned. "What am I going to do with you?"

"I only want you to love me." He placed his arm around my shoulder.

"Oh, I do." I wrapped an arm around his waist, and we headed out the swinging door.

CHAPTER SIX

The Watershed was a pretty fancy restaurant for Honey Springs. It was located on the opposite of the boardwalk of the Cocoon Hotel and on the water's edge. The owners of the Watershed created the floating restaurant with special occasions in mind.

White tablecloths and amazing views of the lake set the scene. The restaurant also did charter boat dinners, in which the staff took you out on a boat and served your supper while you cruised down the lake.

Those were expensive but worth the romance in my opinion.

"Roxy! Patrick! Over here!" Crissy Lane's sun-washed blond hair was back. She was a smidgen like Aunt Maxi when it came to hair. Crissy was a beautician by trade, so when she went from her natural red to blond to whatever was on sale down at the grocery store, it didn't shock me. "I've got us a bar table." She scrunched up her nose, and the light dusting of red freckles sprinkled across her nose formed one big freckle.

She hopped up and down and pointed at the bar table up next to the bar, making her sassy uplifted set of breasts bounce in the sequined red V-neck sweater tight on her body.

I gave her the I'll-be-right-there finger gesture.

"Do you see Aunt Maxi?" I asked Patrick and looked around, seeing a lot of folks I knew and a lot I didn't.

Andrew and Kayla Noro were standing next to Crissy. Then there was Louise Carlton with Leslie Roarke. I was delighted when I saw Big Bib, the burly yet very kind ferryboat driver and owner of the marina near the hotel. He rarely left the boat dock, much less changed out of his blue mechanic jumper to attend anything.

He lifted a beer when Patrick noticed him.

"Do you mind if I go have a beer with Big Bib?" Patrick asked me before I nodded. He kissed me. "Do you want something?"

"No." I shook my head. "I'm going to go look for Aunt Maxi."

I wanted to see her for two reasons. The first was to make sure that she didn't need me to do any last-minute preparations, and the second was to tell her that I didn't approve of her switching out any sort of cheese balls. She needed to just let the evening progress.

I walked over to the end of the bar, where the waitstaff generally waited to pick up drinks orders and take them to their customers because it was the only space not taken. It was an unspoken reserved area.

"Hey, girl," Fiona Rosone called from behind the bar. She had two bottles of good ol'-fashioned Kentucky bourbon in each hand, tipped over and pouring into two glasses. "What can I get you?"

"Nothing." I shook my head and couldn't help but notice the heavy hand pour trickling over the cubes of ice. "I see Aunt Maxi got to you."

"Oh yeah." Fiona set the bottles down, grabbed two mini brown straws, and stuck one in each drink. She put them on the bar in front of Dan Teagarden in exchange for the cash he'd laid down.

He was sans Beverly and their one sweater.

Dan and I nodded at each other, since it was too loud to even try to say hello. Loretta didn't care about the crowd. She also found Dan at the bar. From afar, I watched the interaction between them.

While I watched their exchange, the people next to me were talking about the old Seifert place.

"I heard someone was living there when the bank went in to assess the property," the one person said.

"The ghost of the Seifert who doesn't want their secrets to be uncovered," the other teased and laughed. "Magically."

Magically? I wondered what that meant for a moment until I noticed Loretta's friendly walk up to Dan wasn't friendly at all.

Loretta's head was bobbling back and forth, and her mouth moved quickly as her finger pointed between him and Beverly, who did take notice of Loretta's behavior. The huge sweater hung down Beverly's entire body like a window drape.

I leaned in so I could get a better look once Beverly joined them. Dan apparently left whatever Loretta said to him up to Beverly to finish it. Beverly's face tightened. Dan walked away.

Loretta put her hands on her hips then threw them up in the air, leaving Beverly standing with Lana, both of their mouths open. Lana said something to Beverly, who then pointed a hard finger at Lana. Then Lana took off.

Fiona walked over, tapped on the cash register, and stuck the money in.

"Your Aunt Maxi—" Fiona caused me to shift my focus. "Oh yeah. She gave me a little moo-la to take good care of people tonight." She scanned the bar and let the other bartenders take the many orders flying in from customers. "Something about Loretta Bebe's awful attempt at appetizers." She laughed.

Fiona played it off, but she was good at listening. It was a bartending skill she'd really honed, and it made her super popular with the locals. Even though I rarely drank, sometimes I'd just walk down from the coffeehouse to get some fresh air and end up at a bar stool, sipping on a diet Coke and telling Fiona about my life.

It just kind of happened.

"Have you seen her?" I asked Fiona about Aunt Maxi.

"No." One of the servers hollered for Fiona, and she jerked her head down the opposite end of the bar. "Let me know if you need something." She smiled and took off.

I'd almost given up on finding Aunt Maxi as I continued to mosey around all the people. Then I ran into Alice Dee Spicer. She owned the Honey Comb Salon and Spa.

"You better get on down to the Honey Comb before this winter freeze-dries you out even more." Alice Dee plunged her hands in my thick hair, fanning it out between her fingers.

"Unless you're going to use my competition." She tweaked a brow. "I noticed Patrick has done gone to the dark side."

"Dark side?" I snorted. "Nah. We love you."

"You do realize every time you go over there, you're giving your ex money." She made a good point.

"It's all good," I lied. Of course it wasn't all good, and I hated giving Kirk Swindle any part of my income. "Call me tomorrow with your next open appointment, and I'll be there."

"Will do."

"Have you seen Aunt Maxi?" I asked, scanning the tops of the customers' heads. "It's so busy in here."

"When I got here, she was leaving with a box full of things. She said she'd be back." Alice took a sip of her cocktail. "I think it's turning out great. Everyone is in high spirits, and did you see all the ugly sweaters for the ugly sweater contest?"

"Yes. They are hilarious." So many great ideas were on display. "I had no idea there was even a contest until Patrick picked me up. I love how the Teagardens are in one big sweater."

Beverly and Dan were near the front, where the jazz band was playing "Have Yourself a Merry Little Christmas." They swayed as one in the huge sweater. The scene was cute, and now that their daughters were grown, the Teagardens seemed to be enjoying the empty-nester life.

"They're really lucky they got the old Seifert barn. That'll bring them some money they can spend on that old shop of theirs. I told them they needed to get that awning fixed before it fell down and smacked someone in the head." She reminded me to check to see if Patrick had put the screw in there or at least looked at it like I'd asked him to.

"If you'll excuse me." I wanted to continue to look around for Aunt Maxi.

The crowd in the Watershed had grown. This was a much bigger turnout than I'd anticipated, but when free food was around, people had a lot of interest.

Everyone was happy with how the progressive dinner was turning out. It was hard not to notice the laughter, chatter, and smiling faces when I looked around to find Aunt Maxi.

Locating her shouldn't be that hard. Her hair stood a mile high with that thick, strong eighties hairspray she used.

Still, she was nowhere to be seen.

I drummed my fingernails on the bar, wondering where on earth she'd gone. Then it dawned on me.

She'd gone to get those darn cheese balls out of the refrigerator at the Bean Hive!

I glanced back down the bar. Fiona was all the way down at the other end, gabbing it up with some locals. My eyes shifted to Patrick.

He'd settled down on a stool at a bar table with the Teagardens and Crissy Lane.

Now would be a perfect time to make a fast getaway, check on Aunt Maxi, or really try to get her to leave Loretta's appetizers alone and head on back.

Simple enough. Right?

I slipped out of the restaurant, pulled my phone out of my coat pocket, and texted Birdie, resisting the urge to call. This was one of those instances in which Birdie would respond quicker by text than by bothering to answer the phone.

From what I understood, it was a generational thing. But I liked to get things done, and to me, a phone call was quicker.

Apparently, I was wrong.

Me: Hey Birdie. How are things going?

It was so southern that I always started my text by asking the other person how they were, since I should just get to the point. Because wasn't that what texting was all about? Quicker and to the point.

Some footsteps caught my ear. When I turned around, Dan and Beverly Teagarden were in a heated discussion with each other and too busy to even notice me. Whatever Loretta had gotten on them about tonight must've spilled over into their personal discussion. From what I could tell from their body language, they didn't agree with each other.

Instead of paying too much attention to them, I went back to my phone and decided to hit the delete button to start my text to Birdie over. Of course everything was fine, or she would've called me.

Me: There are going to be a lot more people than I realized for the after-dinner coffee. The turnout at the Watershed is huge. Please pull out more of the whoopie pies from the freezer. No need to do anything with them yet. I'll let you know.

I watched as the three ellipses rolled.

My stomach lurched when they ghosted away.

"No response?" I held the phone to my chest, curling my hands together. The air whipping off Lake Honey Springs was frigid.

I pulled my phone back again to see if a text had rung in and I'd not heard it.

"Maybe my eardrums are frozen." I hit the screen with the pad of my finger to make it come alive.

Nothing.

I swiped the phone screen to open it and hit the messages icon.

"What can I say?" I wondered and thought I wasn't clear enough to warrant a response. I did say I'd let her know.

I pulled the phone back to my chest and walked a little ways down the boat slips of the Watershed, where the owners stored their dinner yachts for the season, and glanced across the water to the island to the Bee Farm, where Kayla and Andrew Noro had put up a big display of wood cutouts of bees wearing Santa hats. The display was all lit up so the people on the land side of the lake could see and enjoy it. The sight was so cute, but I quickly shifted my focus back to the boardwalk.

More importantly, I focused on the storefront of the Bean Hive. Instead of waiting for Birdie to text, I went ahead with my plan to walk up and see for myself if Aunt Maxi had been there.

If she'd already gotten her own appetizers, what was I going to do or say to keep her from following through with her plan?

That would be the hard part and was probably why my stomach felt a little nauseous. How could I get Aunt Maxi to change her mind about the switcheroo scheme she swore was going to save the progressive dinner?

The wind ripped around. The snow continued to fall harder and harder. As I walked around the watershed, I noticed the moon hanging low. The atmosphere felt more appropriate for a scary Halloween night than a joyful night of the Christmas season.

The feeling crept into my skin. Crawled its way to my heart. My eyes, ears, and eyes became very alert for some reason. Nothing could be going wrong.

I mean, it was Christmas, but the feeling, one I had come to know pretty well, still settled into my soul.

After living in Honey Springs for a couple of years, I felt that way when a crime was about to take place, but who in the world would commit a crime on Christmas?

Famous last words because it had happened before, but this year was different. Everyone was pulling together, except for Aunt Maxi, who seemed fairly upset and determined to change the whole appetizer portion of this progressive dinner.

Birdie, Louise Carlton, and another lady were sitting at one of the four-top café tables. The lady I didn't know was cuddling the puppy.

An open folder sat on top of the table, showing all the puppy's information. The puppy was nestled in the lady's lap, asleep with a big red bow. I glanced at Birdie, and she looked up.

"Isn't this wonderful? This lady is going to take home the puppy for Christmas. She recently lost their dogs, and she said this would be perfect for them." Joy was written all over Birdie's face.

Louise smiled too.

"I knew it wasn't going to take that long," I said. "Everyone loves a sweet little puppy."

I walked back into the kitchen so they could finish up the paperwork, but not without asking the woman to say goodbye so I could get a few more puppy kisses.

I had to be honest. I loved puppy breath, and I wanted a little sniff before she left.

With my eyes set on the industrial refrigerator, fully expecting to see Aunt Maxi's cheese balls, I gripped the handle and tugged open the door.

"Where are they?" I asked myself, bending down to look behind all the extra whoopie pies and various things that had moved to the front of the refrigerator throughout the day.

Like Patrick did, I moved my head side to side instead of physically moving things out of the way to find something. I always teased Patrick by telling him the items weren't going to jump out at him and that he had to actually move things to see all the contents of the refrigerator.

Taking my own advice, I pulled out the whoopie pies. They looked so delicious. I lifted the edge of the plastic wrap, took one out, and pushed the whole thing in my mouth.

"A good cup of coffee would be good right now," I mumbled and looked into the refrigerator.

The idea of coffee quickly left my mind when I saw Aunt Maxi's cheese balls were absent.

"Hey, what are you doing?" Birdie called. She peeked around the swinging door, her hand gripping the edge.

"I was looking for Aunt Maxi's cheese balls." I slid the whoopie pies back on the refrigerator shelf and shut the door.

"She came and got them a little bit ago. I'm surprised you didn't see her on your way into the coffeehouse." She motioned for me to come. "The puppy is leaving." She jutted her bottom lip out in a dramatic frowny face.

My stomach dropped on my way out of the kitchen. Not about the puppy but because Aunt Maxi was still carrying out her plan. Nothing good came out of Aunt Maxi's tricks. It took all of my willpower not to run back to the refrigerator and binge on the whoopie pies to push down the uneasy feeling rising inside me.

"Did she say where she was going?" I tried to keep everything as vague as possible. It was best to keep Aunt Maxi's scheme between her and me.

"Oh yeah, she said she was going to go down to the hotel and set up the appetizers because everything seemed to really be going well at the Watershed. She felt she didn't need to stay down there."

Inwardly, I sighed.

"Everything is going really well at the Watershed, which reminds me that I think we need to get some more out of the freezer just in case," I told her and let the kitchen door swing closed behind me.

The door rocked a little back and forth before it stopped.

"Yeah. I saw your text but just went ahead and did it." She let me know there was no reason to text me back, since she took care of it. "When Louise is finished with the puppy adoption, I'm going to go ahead and start setting up the banquet table. Beverly Teagarden dropped off a really cool vintage table-cloth and a couple new milkers."

"She dropped off some milkers?" I was excited to hear that.

"Yeah, on their way down to the Watershed." Birdie and I stopped at the table where Louise was packing up the contents of the puppy's file, giving the new owner all the information about bringing the puppy to the Pet Palace to get follow-up vaccines from our local vet.

"Beverly said that she opened up some boxes or something and found them and also found the cool Christmas tablecloth. She thought you might like it." Birdie reached over and scratched the little puppy's head.

The puppy jerked her head up and nipped at Birdie's finger.

Birdie had become such a great employee. I couldn't help but look at the young lady standing in front of me. She had changed so quickly over the past few weeks. Birdie had blossomed into an amazing young woman with a great head on her shoulders.

She was able to waltz in, look around, and just start doing. That was what I loved most about Birdie.

Since I'd opened the coffeehouse, I wasn't able to keep too many teenagers for the afternoon shifts. The only other one was Emily Rich, who just so happened to be a natural baker and took her talents out of Honey Springs when she graduated high school. Since then, I'd not found anyone to replace her until Loretta made Birdie walk through the door.

"If you have any questions, feel free to call me." Louise handed the woman her Pet Palace business card.

"Oh, bye, little puppy," Birdie whined and gave the puppy one last smooch. It didn't take long for Birdie to go back to typing away on her phone.

"Thank you for an amazing coffeehouse. I love it." The woman made my night.

"Thank you for coming. Are you here long?" I asked, since I didn't recognize her as a local.

"I'm here off and on. My husband does business here, and, well, this is the first time I've come with him, and I love it." She leaned in a little. The puppy was sucking on the edge of her long brown hair. "I'm trying to get him to purchase one of those cute lake cabins for a second home, but he's not buying it yet."

"Just take him around to all the shops and get a feel for how much our community is one big giant hug." I did love Honey Springs, except for Aunt Maxi's shenanigans, but no one needed to know about that.

"I hope your family enjoys her," Louise called to the woman, who was holding the puppy in her arms, the dog carrier tucked inside her elbow with the packet inside of it.

"That's a little backwards," I said over Louise's shoulder. "Shouldn't the puppy be in the carrier and the papers be in her hand?" I joked as I watched the woman head off into the cold and dark night with the puppy squirming in her arms.

"I hope she's prepared for a new baby." Louise sucked in a breath and turned around. "That was a quick one."

"I knew the puppy would go fast." I shook my head.

"Do you think you can take a senior?" Louise asked with caution in her tone. "I've got a senior cat who just needs to be loved in her final years."

"Of course." No way would I turn down any animal, young or old, from Louise.

"Great! I'll be by in the morning with her, if that's okay." Louise had bundled back up in her winter gear, including a thick scarf. "And I'll see you back at the Watershed."

I waved her off, knowing I was heading straight down the opposite end of the boardwalk to the Cocoon Hotel, where I would try one last time to talk Aunt Maxi out of switching those appetizers.

"You all good here?" I asked Birdie before I took off as well.

"Yeah, yeah. I'll have everything out and decorated for the progressive supper attendees." Birdie put her phone in the front pocket of her apron and went back to doing the regular straightening and cleaning of the tables.

The carriage lights lit up with the twinkling Christmas lights wrapped around them warmed me up inside. The seasonal flags whipped back and forth in the breeze blowing from the lake.

Though I knew time was of the essence to get to Aunt Maxi before the cocktail hour ended, I did take a minute to look in the Wild and Whimsy's display window.

Beverly had changed it since I'd seen it this morning. Inside were different antique Christmas trees with little candles clipped on the fake branches. The ornaments looked aged and chippy, a very popular style around here.

The entire display screamed the old-fashioned Christmas you'd see in old movies. I had a hunch while she was going through the boxes Birdie had mentioned, Beverly had found a lot of the Christmas items featured in the window display.

Beverly was quite smart to decide to change the display. The people attending the progressive supper would be walking past the Wild and Whimsy all night, and the display would surely capture their eyes, making them want to come to the shop tomorrow. It was an amazing marketing strategy.

The sound of tourists walking along the boardwalk drew me away from my thoughts and put me on track to get to the hotel. I'd dilly-dallied way too long, and it was time to set Aunt Maxi straight. In no way could I let her carry out her little scheme.

Every black rocking chair on the Cocoon Hotel's long southern-styled front porch was occupied. The outdoor heaters buzzed with life, and the chatter of guests filled the air. The live miniature Christmas trees dotted between the rocking chairs and the baskets filled with buffalo checked blankets were just little touches Camey added to the cozy atmosphere she was going for.

The smell of pine needles tickled my nose when I walked into the lobby. Camey wasn't at the desk when I passed by to look into the hospitality suite, where I saw Aunt Maxi hovering over the food table. Her crossbody bag was sitting on top of the table, wide open.

"Aunt Maxi!" I rushed over to her and whispered, "What are you doing in here?"

"What does it look like? I told you I wasn't going to let Low-retta get away with killing people with her awful cheese balls." Aunt Maxi wore a pair of white gloves. She carefully peeled off the plastic wrap from the Christmas platter I'd seen in my refrigerator.

"I think you need to stop this. Right now," I tried to demand, but she wasn't listening. She put Loretta's cheese balls in the plastic wrap before she shoved them down into her crossbody bag.

"I will not let her ruin my fundraiser." Aunt Maxi wasn't budging. She unwrapped another one of her cheese balls to replace one of Loretta's but stopped, took a cracker from the stack, and plunged it down into Loretta's creation.

"Here." She stuck it in my face. "You try it. If you think it's edible, then I'll leave them."

"Fair enough." I took the cracker and nibbled at the end. "Not bad." I pushed the whole cracker in my mouth. "It's good." I shrugged. Then she handed me a cracker with a sample of her chipped beef ball. "Delicious."

"You'd say that just to get me to stop," she snarled and used her hand to make me step back. She went down the line, replacing all of Loretta's appetizers with her own. "Hopefully, we will run out of this fast so we can just move on to the Buzz In and Out."

I'd seen Aunt Maxi get all bundled up in a tizzy before but never one of this magnitude. She'd taken it to a whole different level, making me question if it was really for the fundraiser or her ego.

After she ran out of her own appetizers to put out, I asked her, "Are you satisfied now?"

"I think we are finished here." She plucked the gloves off of her hands.

"Why the gloves?" I was curious.

"Because when or if Low-retta finds out I switched out her food, she will demand some sort of evidence. She's not beyond hiring out a private investigator, and I've seen it on television, where those kinds never stop at nothing to get fingerprints." Aunt Maxi sure did have an active imagination. "They go through people's trash and everything."

She had it all figured out, and I let her think whatever she needed to think because she wouldn't budge. Especially now that she'd already replaced all of Loretta's food.

"Let's get out of here before someone sees you." I tugged on her shirt.

"Fine." She strapped the crossbody bag over her shoulder on our way out of the hospitality room, but we were greeted with a host of town folks who'd come on down from the Watershed, including Loretta Bebe and Lana Woodward.

To say the next few minutes made me sweat was an understatement. Aunt Maxi and I both had perspiration bubbled up on our upper lips.

"I have to admit I was a little worried about these." Crissy Lane held the cracker filled with chipped beef up in the air and popped the entire thing in her mouth. "Loretta." Crissy stopped Loretta when she drifted past. "Where did you get the chipped beef? It's so good."

"Chipped beef?" Loretta asked, batting her long fake lashes. "I didn't have any chipped beef in my appetizers."

"I swear that's a chipped beef ball on the Christmas platter." Crissy's big mouth was going to get us in trouble.

"What Christmas platter? I didn't bring a Christmas platter because I don't have the one that matches my set." A sudden chill pervaded the air.

Loretta stormed off with Crissy in tow.

"I'm going to check on Birdie so I don't have to watch you-know-what hit the fan," I told Aunt Maxi and pulled out my phone on my way out of the hotel to text Birdie.

"You're not leaving me here." Aunt Maxi grabbed our coats and her cross-body bag off the back of the chair and headed outside with me.

"What's going on down there?" Aunt Maxi brought my attention to some flashlights down on the beach of Lake Honey Springs. Both of us stood on the front porch, pulling our coats on.

"People are probably walking the beach or something." I dismissed it and texted Birdie.

Me: I was thinking maybe you should get out another cookie sheet of whoopie pies from the freezer. I'd rather have too many than not enough.

"No one should ever walk down along the lake at night. That's dangerous, and they could die." Aunt Maxi had always been a stickler when I was a teenager and wanted to go to the lake for a party that the host shouldn't have thrown, but I was always honest with her. Most times she never let me go, and most times I snuck out.

She was right. A slip here or there could cost a life if they weren't familiar with the terrain. Lake Honey Springs was deep, and it was also freezing right now.

I heard my phone chirp back with a message.

Birdie: *I don't think you're going to need any more. Sheriff Shepard has canceled the progressive dinner.*

Me: *What? Why?*

Birdie: *Dead body found on the beach of Lake Honey Springs.*

The wind had stopped.

My gaze lay flat over the now-still water of Lake Honey Springs.

My mind was blank.

The chill had left my body.

A gust of wind swept past me. My chin curled into my shoulder, a natural response to shield my face.

"What's wrong?" Aunt Maxi asked.

"There's a body down there. The dinner is cancelled." My words caused me to shiver.

CHAPTER SEVEN

People would tell me how they'd been thinking about my coffee as soon as they got out of bed. According to them, before they even noticed, they were standing there ordering without even remembering walking down the boardwalk to get there. Or they couldn't remember their drive to the board-walk—you know, those instances when certain thoughts took over our minds, making us unavailable for the moment.

I really tried not to live like that. When customers told me these scenarios, I never judged them. I just made it a point to stay ever present.

Until now.

I could say that I'd had that moment as soon as I got Birdie's nonchalant text. Before I knew it, I was standing in the lobby of the Cocoon Hotel, looking into the hospitality suite, where Aunt Maxi had been called to have a little chat with Sheriff Spencer Shepard, the local sheriff.

After we'd found out Lana was the body someone had found on the banks of Lake Honey Springs, Loretta Bebe had also shown up. Now Camey Montgomery was consoling her in Camey's office.

"I didn't kill no one," I heard Aunt Maxi say with conviction. The type of conviction that you could tell was the truth. "Yes. I might've changed out Loretta's cheese balls, but have you tried them?" Aunt Maxi looked up at Spencer.

"You ask your mama." Aunt Maxi shook a finger. "She knows that Loretta can't mix a cheese ball. That's probably what killed that poor girl."

"Camey." I grabbed Camey when she darted past me.

"I have to get Loretta a water before she passes out." Camey brushed her bangs out of her eyes and tugged her thick scarlet hair over one shoulder.

"Fine. I'll follow you." I followed her to the Cocoon Hotel's bar. "Did Loretta give you any details?"

I hadn't seen a body or Kevin Roberts, our county coroner.

"And why is Aunt Maxi talking to Shepard?" I had so many questions and kept spitting them out at Camey as she walked around the bar to get a glass of water.

After Birdie had told me about the body, Aunt Maxi ran down to the beach to see what was going on. I went the opposite way and went to the Watershed to get Patrick, but the crowd had already dispersed because of the body, and I couldn't find him. Fiona told me a lot of the progressive supper attendees had decided to go to the lake to see for themselves what was going on.

"You know Loretta was hosting the appetizer part of the progressive dinner." She grabbed a glass and held it under the faucet. I leaned on the counter. "Maxine came in here and switched out the cheese balls. Loretta's employee..." Camey snapped her fingers a few times, trying to remember the girl's name.

"Lana," I said. I'd not seen her in there but that didn't mean anything. She could've come in when I was off doing something else. Still, it was good information to know.

"Yes. Lana came in to make sure everything was all good. She caught Maxi in there, switching out the cheese balls. When I tell you Maxine lost her marbles, I'm telling you she lost her marbles." In other words, Aunt Maxi was at the point that she had no idea what she was saying—that kind of out-of-your-head anger.

"Oh dear." I gnawed on my lip.

"Not 'oh dear.'" Camey's eyes grew, and she shut off the water. "'Oh dead' is more like it."

Immediately, I knew why Spencer had pulled Aunt Maxi into the hospitality room. He was trying to see what she knew.

"And..." Camey gulped. She stared at me with big eyes. "When Lana was coming out of the hospitality suite, she had a cracker filled with Maxine's chipped beef spread. She stuffed it in her mouth. I asked her if it was good and she 'mmhmmm'd' and 'mmmmm'd' while chewing." Camey tucked in her lips and shook her head. "I went into the hospitality room to say something to Maxine, but she wouldn't hear of it. She insisted Loretta wasn't going to ruin her, and neither was the little twit."

"She called Lana a twit?" Aunt Maxi had lost her marbles for sure, I thought but didn't say out loud. This was one of those times that my lawyer—well, ex-lawyer—instincts took over, and remaining silent with a straight face was the only option.

"She did. Then she said Lana will get her due too." Camey lifted a hand to stop me from asking more questions. "Now before you go all lawyering on me, I heard Maxine threaten the girl with my own ears. Now the girl ends up dead on the beach?"

"Did you happen to go after Lana?" I blinked a few times. "I had come down here to find Aunt Maxi, and you weren't at the desk."

"I did, but she didn't want to talk to me, so I walked around the porch to see if any of my guests needed anything." Her lips dipped. "I really wish I would've insisted Lana talk to me instead of letting her run off."

"Thanks," I said. I headed out of the bar so I could go into the hospitality room, where it was apparent Spencer knew about Aunt Maxi's switcheroo because a deputy was in there, talking to her.

"Excuse me." I gave a light rap on the opening trim around the door before I entered the hospitality room. "Do we need a lawyer here?"

"No, Roxanne. I'm fine." Aunt Maxi didn't look fine. She looked worried. Her normal upbeat personality had dulled. "I'm having a chat with Spencer here about some hearsay he wanted to ask me about. I don't need a lawyer."

"I'm right out here if you need me." I gave her a hard look before I turned around and left the room.

The only way to get to the bottom of this was to get my eyes on the crime scene. I slipped past the hospitality room and glanced in. I didn't see Spencer, Aunt Maxi, or Loretta.

The portable floodlights leading down to the beach on Lake Honey Springs told me Spencer had brought those in from the sheriff's office.

I walked down to the beach in the shadows of the large oaks on the grassy area between the hotel and the lake. The darkness that had fallen on Honey Springs enshrouded me as I observed what was going on around me.

As a lawyer, I took pride in my uncanny ability to read people and their body language. In fact, I'd aced that class in school. By the way Spencer and Kevin were standing over the body, I could see they were questioning its position. I watched them from afar before I'd had enough.

I wanted to talk to Spencer and get some answers to some questions that'd popped into my head.

How did Aunt Maxi kill her? Why would Aunt Maxi kill her? Did Aunt Maxi have any sort of mud or sediment on her shoes that would show she was at the beach? The beach sand had been brought in by the rock quarry, so there was a distinct difference. I was going to get to the bottom of it.

"Why am I not surprised you're here?" Spencer asked me as his jaw set hard. His thick neck looked to have melted into his deep chest. The spotlights made his deep-green eyes look almost black against his sandy-blond hair. "This is no time to ask all sorts of questions."

"How did she die?" I asked. It seemed like the most logical question.

My eyes drifted around him to the sheet lying on the ground and covering the body.

"From the bubbles exiting the mouth, it appears it could be poison, but we won't know for sure until the initial autopsy comes back." He gave me a flat look.

"Is Aunt Maxi your suspect?" I asked.

"Should she be?" he shot back.

"You know I'm telling you no. She had no reason to kill someone, even if it was over a cheese ball of sorts," I said, raising my voice as he tried to speak. "Now, you and I both know Aunt Maxi is a lot of things, but a killer she is not. If she is a suspect, you know I'm going to be her lawyer."

Though I didn't practice law anymore, I did keep my license up to date, and good thing I did, because at times like this, people needed some sound advice.

"I'm not taking her in, if that's what you're asking. There's not enough evidence, but I did tell her that I was going to need to question her some more." He sucked in a deep breath. "I do want to know what you know about her and Loretta."

"Is Loretta a suspect?" I just couldn't imagine that either.

"From what I understand, Loretta can be hard on her help, and that includes the victim," he said. "I know Loretta comes into the coffeehouse, and I'm guessing Lana does too."

"No. I've not seen her in there much, and when I have, they seem to be fine." I cautiously answered Spencer since he was a little more forthcoming than usual.

I continued to watch Kevin perform his usual duties. He was crouching near the body, lifting the sheet, taking notes on his clipboard, and repeating those steps a couple of times before he put the clipboard down to retrieve his camera from his bag.

The wind skimmed the top of the lake and skittered along my neck. I tucked my hands into my coat pocket and drew in my shoulders, snuggling my elbows into my sides.

"Cut to the chase, Spencer," I said through my chattering teeth. I watched the corners of his lips spill into a smile. "You and I both know you're being nice to me and even letting me stay down here."

"First off, I know you're going to nose into the situation, so it's better to just let you be and disperse any rumors that'll be floating around in about eight hours," he said.

He was right. The Bean Hive Coffeehouse would already be busy with the festival and the vendors, and the Pawrade was downtown tomorrow. When something significant occurred, even a natural death, the locals flocked to the coffeehouse to congregate with the other town folks and gossip about what happened.

"Second?" I brought my hands out of my pockets, brought them to my mouth, blew some warm breath on them, and rubbed them together vigorously.

"Doesn't Loretta's granddaughter work for you?" he asked.

"Oh, I see." My chin lifted in the air. The cold air curled around it like the grip of a cold hand. It caught my breath. "You want me to ask her questions. Things she might've seen."

"I'll make a deal with you. I'll let my thoughts about Maxine being a killer linger for a few days while you see what you can come up with about Loretta." He shrugged. "Maybe you won't come up with anything, but I'm willing to bet you'll do just about anything for Maxine."

"You're right I would, but I don't condone murdering anyone, and if you think Aunt Maxi killed someone over a cheese ball, then she's right. You should be ashamed of yourself and ask your mama about Loretta's dips. Besides, Aunt Maxi wouldn't put poison in a cheese ball for the whole town to die." It was ridiculous, if you asked me, but then again, I was a little too close to the case. "But I'll take your offer. I'll keep you posted."

"Sounds good." He slid his gaze back to Kevin, who appeared to have finished his initial assessment. Both of us watched as Kevin walked up again through the grass between the hotel and the parking lot of the boardwalk where the hearse was backed up. "I'll be in touch."

Spencer strutted off. I snarled and headed the other way, which was back to the hotel.

"Are you okay?" Camey asked me when I walked back in. The old hotel's radiator heat immediately warmed my cheeks.

"I'm fine." My body shivered. I took a few extra steps to look into the hospitality room. "Where is Aunt Maxi?" I asked when I noticed she wasn't in there anymore.

"She said she was going to go to the coffeehouse to find you. I assumed that's where you went after you hurried out of here."

"I went down to the scene. I wanted to see where Spencer's head was, and it's all over the place. Say…" I took her aside and out of the guests' earshot. "I know you said you heard Aunt Maxi and Lana having some words, but did you overhear Loretta and Lana have any confrontation?"

"They were never together. Loretta came down here and asked me if she could host it here, and as you know, I said yes. She had gotten a phone call from Lana because Lana was getting something at the Wild and Whimsy. Loretta murmured something under her breath about Beverly, but I don't want to repeat it." Camey was so nice. She never said a bad word about anyone.

"I understand you don't, but I am going to do everything I can to make sure Aunt Maxi isn't a suspect. Please let me know if you remember anything." I offered a smile. "I'll see you in the morning with coffee."

There wasn't any sense hanging around here because Aunt Maxi had left. She was who I needed to get in touch with.

My phone buzzed in my coat pocket as I was leaving. It was Patrick.

"Where are you?" Patrick asked. His voice held a little panic. "I heard there was a death or something by the lake."

"Meet me at the Bean Hive. Oh!" I walked down the steps of the hotel and took the sidewalk leading back to the boardwalk. I didn't bother to tell him how I'd gone looking for him because none of that mattered. "If you see Aunt Maxi, tell her to come there too."

"I've not seen her. It was like everyone scattered after one of the sheriff's deputies came into the Watershed to let everyone know the appetizer portion of the progressive dinner was canceled. I guess everyone was hungry and went straight to the Buzz In and Out."

"You mean the Bean Hive is still expecting people for coffee afterwards?" I was confused. I thought the supper was cancelled.

"Yeah. Spencer cancelled it, but people are hungry, so we are going to the diner to eat," he said.

"Then meet me at the diner," I told him, since I knew I had to keep my ears open. A lot of people would be there, gossiping about the murder.

I didn't know who killed Lana. One thing I knew for sure was that gossip had a wee bit of truth in it somewhere. The hard part was stripping down those tales to get to the facts and then exploring those to find the real details.

"Can you do me a favor?" I asked Patrick. "Can you stop by the Bean Hive and tell Birdie she can go home?"

"Yes. I'll see you in a few." Patrick hesitated as his last word lingered. "Roxanne, are you going to be looking into this?"

"I already have." I knew he wasn't huge on my naturally curious side about why people did what they did, but he'd come to embrace that I'd chosen practicing law for a career, and it was that type of work that made me feel like I did some real good in the world.

I hated to see anyone accused of a crime they didn't commit.

The Honey Comb Salon stood between the Wild and Whimsy and Buzz In and Out. It reminded me how I'd told Alice Dee Spicer to give me a call for the first available appointment. Well, now I was looking forward to her call, since gossip would be ablaze on all the tongues of her customers.

"Just be careful. You know I love you and worry about you." Patrick's voice cracked. I could hear the fear in his tone.

"You know I will. You also have my word that anything I do find out will go directly to Spencer." It was a promise I had to give Patrick because I had found myself at the short end of a killer's hand before, certain I was going to die.

I gripped the diner's door handle.

"You don't have to worry." I'd learned my lesson about handing over information when it was just too much for me. I wasn't too prideful and just wanted to help.

"I know," he whispered.

"I love you and see you soon." I hoped my words assured him and hung up before I swung the door open into the busy diner.

CHAPTER EIGHT

"Where have you been?" Aunt Maxi snuggled up to me in the diner booth after I'd walked in and she'd gotten my attention. Loretta Bebe was sitting across from us on the other side of the table.

I was a little shocked to see them together.

"After I saw you in the hospitality room. Ouch." My brows furrowed, and I reached down to rub my shin when Aunt Maxi stopped me from talking.

"Did you hear what happened?" Loretta leaned over the table. "Lana was killed." She fiddled with the various diamond rings on each finger.

"I was just telling Loretta how awful it is to hear this." Aunt Maxi was up to something.

"I'm sorry," I said.

"I can't believe it. She'd just started, so I didn't know her well, but she was a sweet girl. Very kind and, well, she just didn't say much. I was telling Maxine how it's good to find help these days. I should've vetted her credentials better." Loretta's eyes darted about. "I reckon it's what you get when you don't go through an agency."

"What do you mean?" I questioned the part about better credentials.

"You know the old saying." She released a long sigh. "Tell me who you run around with, and I'll tell you who you are."

"Did she hang around bad people? Like murdery people?" Was "murdery" even a word?

"She was killed, wasn't she? I think someone didn't want her alive, which means she must've done something to somebody." Loretta's lips rolled in, making it appear that she was biting down on them to stop a cry from erupting. "I should've mothered her more."

"Oh, Loretta." Aunt Maxi tsked. "You can't save them all. You're already raising Birdie."

"I know, but this poor girl. I couldn't bear going home into my house, where she helped me get all my appetizers together." Loretta blinked rapidly.

Aunt Maxi knocked me underneath the table with her foot.

"Ouch." I glared at her.

"Are you okay?" Loretta asked.

"She's fine." Aunt Maxi pinched a smile, speaking for me. "Ain't that right, Roxanne?"

"Mmhhmmm." I sucked in a breath and bent down to rub my shin. I wagged my finger between the two. "What's going on here?" I was so confused that the two of them seemed to be thick as thieves.

"Welcome to the Buzz In and Out." The waitress walked over with an order pad. "For tonight's progressive dinner, we were serving James Farley Truffle Fries, so now that the event is over, we are still offering them. What can I get you to drink?"

"Truffle fries?" My mouth watered at the sound.

"Yes. We want some," Loretta told the young lady.

"I don't know what I'm gonna do about an assistant now that..." Loretta's voice cracked, her eyes filling with tears.

"Now, now, honey. You can't help what happened to Lana." Aunt Maxi reached across the table and patted Loretta's hand. "Loretta."

My mouth opened slightly when my chin turned to look at her. My eyes narrowed. It was the second time I'd ever, and I mean ever, heard Aunt Maxi say Loretta's name without exaggerating the "low" in Low-retta. The first was a few minutes ago.

"What?" Aunt Maxi shrugged. "We are a community that needs to come together in this hour."

"Can I get—" the young waitress tried to say over Aunt Maxi and Loretta to no avail.

"I've got to get in touch with her family," Loretta said in her southern accent and sat back in the booth. She reached up and picked at the edges of her short black hair with long red fingernails. "Keel-ed. Whoever heard such?"

"And you two are in cahoots?" I asked them and gave the waitress the one-second finger.

"Roxy, me and Low—*ahem*." She cleared her throat. "Lor-etta have had our differences. But who doesn't? We don't wish death on no one." Aunt Maxi reached across the table to pat Loretta's hand. "I'm sorry I switched the appetizers."

Loretta continued to bobble her head up and down, agreeing with Aunt Maxi, something I'd never seen before.

"It's okay." Loretta batted her eyes. "We've got to stand united," Loretta added. "If we don't do something about this wave of crime, our little town will be ruined."

Wave of crime? I tried to digest what Loretta said.

"Alva, what are you doing?" James Farley had hurried over to our table, all sweaty browed, white button-down unbuttoned and a dingy apron tied around his waist. "We're a little busy."

"It's our fault." I made sure James didn't take it out on the waitress. "We were talking between our order."

"I've been waiting to get their drink order." The young woman had graciously waited for us to stop talking before interrupting us.

"Just bring us some waters," I suggested.

She nodded, took three straws out of the pocket of her apron and tossed them on the table, and went to the next one.

"I'm sorry, ladies." James threw his hands in the air. "It's hard to get good help these days."

"You're telling me. I'm not sure what I'm gonna do," Loretta cried out. "Did you hear about my poor Lana?"

"Yes. I'm sorry. She was in here the other day. Sweet gal. I'm sorry, Loretta." A huge crash came from the diner's kitchen. "I've got to go. Can't anyone do anything around here other than me?"

"Maybe we shouldn't've let James host the main portion." Aunt Maxi took the cup of water from the young waitress.

"I thought I'd bring y'all some water." She leaned over Aunt Maxi to hand me my plastic glass, which had a chipped edge. "Sorry. It was the only cup we had left."

"It's okay." I rotated it around. "I can drink from this side."

"Or you can use a straw," she suggested.

She put the other plastic cup in front of Loretta. "I'm sorry to hear about Lana. She was in here talking about the Wild and Whimsy. Something about the owners thinking she was trying to steal or something. I told her to brush it off. Rich people are funny sometimes."

The young girl shrugged.

"She said she didn't have many friends around here, since she was new. I was looking forward to having a friend around here." She gave a slight grin before frowning again.

"I can't stay here." Loretta flagged the paper napkin in the air like she was giving up. "I'm gonna have to go home and just crawl in bed." She wrapped the napkin around her finger and used her fingernail to dab the inside of her eye.

She sniffled a couple of times before she grabbed her handbag and slid out of the booth.

"I'll talk to you two tomorrow." Loretta gave a hard nod.

"Did I say something?" The young waitress's brows dipped.

"No," I assured her. "It's going to take some time. That's all."

"I'm sorry." She gave a slight shake of her head and hurried away.

I waited a good ten seconds before I started in on Aunt Maxi.

"First off, who are the other two supposed to be meeting us?" I asked about the number of people Loretta had told the waitress since she wanted the five trays of truffle fries. "Secondly, what was with all the Lor-etta stuff?" Aunt Maxi had something up her sleeve. "And do you know that Lana stuffed her face with your chipped beef ball before she..." I didn't finish my sentence. I just slid my finger across my neck.

"Hush up or someone in here is going to hear you," she scolded me.

"I know all about that. Everyone apparently heard you giving Lana the what-for in the hotel before the you-know-what." I hunkered down a little to look around the diner. I sighed and picked up the glass of water, making sure I didn't drink from the chipped rim.

Aunt Maxi leaned in a little. "I had to keep Low-retta in my sight. Keep your enemies closer." She slowly lifted her chin and slid her gaze down her nose to stare at me. "You know that saying."

"Are you saying you think Loretta really did—" I didn't have to finish the sentence for her to understand what I was asking.

Aunt Maxi sat back in the booth, folding her arms over her chest, giving me the side eye and letting me know she believed Loretta couldn't hurt Lana.

"Hey. It's crazy out there." Patrick slid in the booth where Loretta had been sitting. "What?" He looked between Aunt Maxi and me. "You two are up to something."

"We are fine. Just fine." Aunt Maxi gave the waitress a smile when the young woman set the small cardboard containers of truffle fries on the table.

"Thanks, Alva." Patrick took a few fries.

"You're welcome, Mr. Cane." Alva grinned.

My eyes darted between the two. The young girl wore a goofy smile, and her cheeks reddened.

"I see you met my wife, Roxy." He was oblivious to the smitten young girl. "Did you ask her?"

"I'm sorry." Alva turned to me. "I didn't know this was your wife."

"Rox, Alva is looking for a part-time job, and I told her you might be in the market for a new part-time hire." He continued to stuff the fries in his mouth.

"Do you want a coke, Mr. Cane? With a splash of vanilla?" She even knew his favorite fountain soda by heart.

"You know it." He looked across the table at me. "What do you say, Rox? You need some help?"

"Sure. You're more than welcome to come fill out an application," I suggested. Then she walked off.

"My oh my, that young lady is gushing all over you." Even Aunt Maxi noticed. "She had your vanilla Coke all ready for you, Patrick Cane."

"Yeah. What was that about?" I laughed.

"You two are awful. She's a little girl who waits on me and the guys most days we come in here." He ignored us. "What's on the progressive menu here?"

"Sorry, folks!" James Farley yelled from the front of the diner. "The food is gone. We appreciate you coming. Roxy, I know the supper is technically off, but do you have the whoopie pies to feed these good people?"

"I sure do," I agreed. "Come on down."

The back of my hand lightly smacked Aunt Maxi on the leg.

"Get up. Gotta go." I waited for her to scoot out. "Are you two coming?"

"We are gonna finish our fries." Patrick and Aunt Maxi were digging into the other three trays of truffle fries.

"Fine. I don't need your help," I said sarcastically.

"I can help," Alva said. "James doesn't have us clean up, so I can come lend a hand. I know you've not hired me, but I'd love to offer my services for free."

"Maybe it can be a working interview," Aunt Maxi chimed in, licking her fingers.

"Sure. Why not?" I shrugged and zipped my coat. "If it's busier than this, we are in trouble!"

CHAPTER NINE

Busy wasn't even skimming the top of what was going on at the Bean Hive Coffeehouse after James Farley had shut down the diner.

If it weren't for Alva pitching in, I'm not sure Birdie and I would've made it. By the end of the night, all three of us were exhausted.

"That's a really cool ring." Birdie walked past Alva on her way to the door to flip the sign to Closed. The lingering town folk had left after deciding they'd waited long enough for any news on Lana's actual cause of death.

"Thanks. It's an antique. I love it." Alva brought the ring up to her face and used one of her other fingers to move the ring back and forth. Whether the ring had a silver or platinum setting, I couldn't tell, but the large milkstone jewel on top was pretty large. "My mom gave it to me." She went back to wiping down all the café tables.

Sassy and Pepper played with Alva's untied shoestring trailing behind her. When I couldn't find Patrick after I'd found out about the murder, he'd gone home to check on the dogs. After he talked to me, he just brought them here, since he knew there was a great possibility we'd be here awhile.

"It's a cool ring." I finished refilling all the condiments on the coffee bar so everything would be ready to go in the morning,

No doubt there was anticipation of a big crowd who'd be here to talk about the murder.

"I don't know. I guess." She shrugged and put the towel on a tray before she walked around to gather all the little cow pitchers, reminding me that Beverly hadn't told me if she was going to see if the barn boxes had any. "Do you want me to go hand wash these?"

"No. You don't have to stay. Birdie and I've got it." I took the tray from her and gave it to Birdie when she walked back.

"It was fun working with you. Maybe we can hang sometimes," Birdie said. She disappeared into the kitchen, where she'd get started on the end-of-the-day cleaning tasks.

"If you're sure." Alva squatted and tied her shoe. Sassy kept jumping up on her arm to chew on her long hair. "You're a cutie. I wish I could have a dog."

"Come on, Sassy." Patrick clipped Sassy's leash on her while I slipped Pepper's coat on him, since I could tell Patrick was about to go home.

"Your family doesn't like pets?" I asked and walked her to the door so I could lock the door behind her.

"My landlord doesn't allow pets." She smiled. "I'm older than I look. I'm twenty-five."

"Oh gosh. I'm sorry." Alva wasn't too much younger than me. "That's a great thing. You'll always look young."

"That's what I hear. I used to come to Lake Honey Springs to vacation, and I decided to come spend the summer here and now the winter." She stuck her hand out. "It was so good to work here. Do you mind if I come back and fill out that application?"

"Yes. And I'll have some money for you for your work tonight." Paying her was the right thing to do. She'd worked really hard, and she was a natural at it.

Not too many people could just waltz in and pick up like they'd been there forever.

Granted, I had only had her pouring coffee, retrieving items from the display case, and walking around with the tray of whoopie pies for the progressive dinner's guests.

"No. I insisted on being here. It gets lonely at my apartment, and, well, I enjoyed getting to know Birdie. She seemed like a good kid." We shook hands. "Thanks, Roxy. I'll be back."

"I'll walk out with you." Patrick and the dogs came over to the door. He kissed me. "Don't be too long, and be careful driving home. It's slick out there."

The wind whipped in some of the snow that was already built up against the doorjamb.

"It's cold out there, huh." I shivered, quickly shutting the door. On my way to the back of the coffeehouse, I straightened up the chairs to the tables. "Birdie, we can just leave all this until the morning," I said and walked through the kitchen door.

"I have all the pans and coffee pots cleaned and put away." Birdie was standing over the checklist on the workstation, checking off the items as she said them. "Anything else?"

"Nope. You doing okay?" I asked. "I mean, with what happened, I'm sure it's mentally hard."

"You mean Lana?" Birdie walked over to my office, where she kept her purse and coat. "I don't know. I feel bad for Grandmawmaw because I think she really thought this one was going to stick around."

"So Lana made the cheese balls, not Loretta?" I asked to make sure I was getting my facts straight now that the progressive dinner was over and I could spend some brain cells on discerning fact from gossip.

"Yeah. She begged Grandmawmaw to let her do it because they were discussing how Maxi was upset about it. Grandmawmaw's feelings were hurt, and it was interesting how Lana turned it around and said that she could make the appetizers. She said if they tasted bad, Grandmawmaw could blame it on her, and if they were great, then Grandmawmaw could take credit." Birdie snickered. "Grandmawmaw was all over that."

"Were you there after they finished making them?" I asked and ignored the puppy crying from the other side of the swinging door.

"Yeah, it was during supper last night." Birdie sighed and buttoned her coat, pulled her knit cap down over her ears, and slipped her hands in her mittens.

"Then what did they do?" I asked.

"That's when Lana left for the night with the appetizers. She was going to take them to the hotel on her way home so Grandmawmaw could go to the antique shop to get that platter." Birdie was all bundled up and ready to tackle the cold on the way to her car.

That was interesting. Loretta had had no time to slip in any sort of poison or whatever killed Lana because, according to Birdie, Lana was there, and she took the food to the hotel. She wouldn't kill herself.

"I'm leaving. I'll see you tomorrow afternoon."

"I'll walk you out." I followed her out of the kitchen. Birdie was talking, but my mind was full of questions about how I could find out who had access to the food at the hotel.

I knew Camey didn't have security cameras, and her staff had been there for a long time.

Unless she had someone new working there.

"You know?" Birdie asked. Obviously, she'd asked me a question that I didn't even hear around my talking mind.

"Yeah." I nodded, smiled, and waved her off. "Toot to let me know you're in your car."

I watched Birdie walk down the boardwalk toward the parking lot on the side of the Watershed.

For some reason, I didn't feel like the killer was going to strike again. It seemed like Lana was the target, and I was going to focus on that.

Lana and her history.

It was going to be a good starting point.

Did she stop before she went to the hotel? Did she get any phone calls? Was she on social media?

CHAPTER TEN

"Good morning," Bunny called out. The ding over the coffeehouse door told me someone was there, though it had taken a few seconds to register.

Last night felt like a blur. Add to that a sleepless night because I was up thinking about who on earth had a motive to kill poor Lana. I had been around her for only a little while, but I was having a hard time trying to imagine what she could possibly do to make someone so mad that they murdered her.

All of that was on my mind, and based on the history of what happened around here when someone died, the coffeehouse was going to be busy.

It was going to be a long day.

I peeked out the swinging door and saw Bunny and Mae Bell.

"You back here, Roxy?" Bunny and Mae Bell Donovan were walking through the Bean Hive. "Mae Bell, here." She put her hand out. "Give me your coat."

Mae Belle and Bunny were my first real customers at the Bean Hive when I opened. They were considered regulars. They came in at the same time every day, sat at the same table, and ordered the same thing. And they looked alike. They dressed alike and liked to eat the same things.

One day I was so busy, Bunny got tired of waiting for me to top off her coffee, so she got up and topped off hers and everyone else's. That was when she hired herself.

Mm-hmmm, she hired herself, and I just went with it.

"I'm here." I walked out of the kitchen and watched the two fumble with their buttons, hats, and pocketbooks before they got all situated. "You're here really early."

"I was just coming in to help, honey. I figured we're gonna have a big crowd today, seeing what happened and all." Bunny pointed at a table off to the side for Mae Belle to sit in. Then Bunny sat down with her.

I kind of snickered because I knew she was here to listen to all the hearsay. Mae Belle, on the other hand, was in charge of the prayer chain, which was what we called gossip around here.

Unfortunately, they believed that when you gossiped on the prayer chain, it counted as praying for the people you were gossiping about.

Now, if they were talking about it while not discussing it on the prayer chain call, it was considered gossip.

See the difference?

"You're right. We are going to be busy, and I didn't get a wink of sleep, so you two are in for a very special treat this morning." The coffee pots had all brewed, so I knew the special Christmas Blend I'd roasted and ground this morning would be a tasty treat.

"Do you got some of that good breakfast casserole?" Mae Belle asked.

"That's not my treat, but I bet I can get you a slice." The walk-in freezer contained so many different casseroles I could easily pop into the oven for special occasions or even when I ran out of something else.

During the winter months, when the Bean Hive was closed on Sundays, I made as many things as possible that could be frozen for a long time without compromising the taste, smell, and look.

"WHERE'S THE PUPPY?" Bunny shifted in her chair when I brought over the coffee pot and two mugs.

"You didn't notice she was gone last night when we came back from the diner?" I poured the fresh brew in their cups.

Mae Belle picked up the cup, curled both hands around it, and took a nice long smell.

"It's the Christmas Blend."

"My favorite." Gingerly, she took a sip as if trying not to burn her mouth. "I'll take four bags." She put in her order, which wouldn't be hard to fill, since I'd roasted a large batch.

"I'll make sure Birdie holds you back a few bags." I smiled. "The puppy was adopted last minute before all of the hullabaloo."

"Can I also get me a little quiche?" Mae Belle sure was hungry this morning.

"I'll get that for you. The casserole might be a minute." The fire needed to be stoked a little before I went into the kitchen. There, I found a casserole in the freezer, slipped it into the oven, and set the timer.

Timers were so important at the Bean Hive. Many times I'd gotten caught up in a conversation with a customer and completely forgotten I'd put something in the oven, but the timer always saved me.

"Did I hear the door ding?" I carried out the tray of quiche I'd already plated and walked backwards out of the kitchen door. "Spencer."

I was taken back when Sheriff Spencer Shepard stood inside of the coffeehouse.

"Mornin', ladies." Spencer took off his cowboy hat and stuck it up under the arm of his heavy brown sheriff's coat.

He had a deputy with him.

"Can I get you two some amazing coffee and interest you in a danish?" I pointed at the display case where I'd already stocked the pastry side. "Fresh apricot danish this morning. I got the jam from Jean Hill's farm."

Everyone in Honey Springs knew Jean Hill made the best jam.

My nerves had jittered through my body at the mere sight of him being here this early. I just started babbling off all those questions.

"I'll take a coffee." He looked at the deputy. The deputy nodded. Spencer held up two fingers. "I really came in here to see if Maxine Bloom was here."

"No." I gulped and turned around to make his coffee. "Why?"

Then I spun around with their two cups of coffee, *to go*, with a fake smile on my face.

"I'm assuming she's at home in bed." I set the cups on the counter so my shaking hands didn't show.

"No. I went to her house, and she didn't answer." He picked up his coffee, and the deputy picked up the other. "I was hoping you'd know."

"I've not seen her since last night." My eyes popped open. "As a matter of fact"—I hurried around the counter and grabbed my coat—"I didn't even call her last night to see if she made it home safely."

The pounding thundered in my chest as I thought of her car lying in a ditch between here and downtown because of the slick roads last night.

"I've got to go look for her car." I shoved my arms in my coat.

"Her car was home." Spencer did make the urgency subside. A little.

"She didn't answer?" I asked.

He shook his head.

"Maybe she was still asleep."

"Nope. We walked around the house and looked into the windows, thinking she was hiding, and I didn't see anyone in there. Bed was made too."

"You obviously really want to talk to her or you wouldn't've snooped in her windows." I tried to ignore Bunny and Mae Belle, who had both moved to a closer table.

"This is very important. I mean, I know I asked you yesterday to keep your eyes and your ears open, but this is sheriff's business." He took a sip of the coffee and did that whole waiting-me-out thing he liked to do.

Waiting someone out was a classic move that was actually taught in law school. This technique was part of the art of reading body language, and right now, Spencer was trying to give me some open space to just start blabbing, since the silence was uncomfortable.

No way was I going to give in to that tactic. I'd bite my tongue off first.

"I understand that, Spencer, but does this have anything to do with Lana's murder?"

He sighed, took a drink, and continued staring over the rim of the cup, the steam curling around his nose and up in the air.

"I'm gonna shoot straight with you, Roxanne." He lifted a brow.

"Roxanne?" My head jerked back. "That's awfully formal."

"This doesn't look good for Maxi. I have eyewitnesses that say Maxine was in the hospitality room right before Lana came in. I have witnesses who say that she and Lana had a discussion, a heated discussion, at the Wild and

Whimsey Antique." The way he told all the witness accounts, the situation got worse and worse.

So much so, I closed my eyes just to hear the rest.

"I hate to tell you this, but I also have eyewitnesses who said your aunt Maxi and Loretta had words at the Buzz In and Out Diner after Maxine found out Loretta was going to host the appetizer portion of the progressive dinner." This was news to me.

I wondered when that was and how their confrontation fit in with the timeline of the murder.

"Aunt Maxi and Loretta have words practically every day. Just because they had a frank discussion doesn't mean Aunt Maxi killed Lana. Besides, we don't even know how she was killed." I tsked in hopes of covering up the negative thoughts in my head so they didn't show on my face. "Come, Spencer, we all know that."

He put his hand up then pulled out his phone. Spencer tapped the phone a few times then turned the screen for me to see.

"Do you recognize this?" It was that platter that Aunt Maxi was so proud of. The fancy one with the Christmas trees and the scalloped edges on it.

"Yes, I recognize it."

"Can you tell me who that belongs to?" he asked with full knowledge of its owner.

"Well, I think you and I both know it belongs to Aunt Maxie."

This little cat-and-mouse game was very interesting to Bunny and Mae Belle. So much so, they'd gotten up out of their seats, took the reading glasses dangling from around their necks, and glanced over Spencer's shoulders to get a gander at the photos.

Spencer looked over his shoulders, giving them the stink eye. They shuffled away to their table.

"We took all the platters from the Cocoon Hotel with the cheese balls on them. We ran preliminary tests to determine if they were tampered with." He continued to swipe the screen quickly, showing photo after photo of what I recognized as Aunt Maxi's cheese balls.

"Tampered with?" I snorted.

"Poison." He held his other hand out to the deputy. "There was some poison found on the rim of the platter you identified as Maxine's."

"Poison?" I questioned.

"Methanol, to be exact." The deputy handed him some papers. "Here is Kevin's autopsy report, where he got a methanol reading as soon as he swiped the inside of her mouth. Today will determine the state of Lana's kidneys, eyes—"

I interrupted him when I noticed Bunny and Mae Belle's expressions.

"Yeah. I know what methanol does to the body." I thought those words but didn't say them out loud. There was no need to let Bunny and Mae Belle know methanol was highly poisonous and literally turned into formaldehyde, ruining the liver, eyesight, kidneys, heart and other parts of the body, causing death.

"I'm gonna have to bring in Maxine to question her about it, and we will be getting a warrant to search her properties."

"Properties?" I asked for clarification.

"All of the shops she owns, all the rentals, her home, everything and anywhere she could be hiding something." By the way Spencer was talking, he had Aunt Maxi as good as locked up.

I started laughing, in place of crying, and rolled my eyes. "You and I both know she doesn't have a malicious bone in her body."

The deputy walked away when his phone buzzed.

Spencer pulled out his handy-dandy notebook from the pocket of his jacket.

"Witness statement number one, and I quote them overhearing Maxine say to Loretta, 'You ain't gonna ruin me. I'll ruin you first.'" He didn't even bother glancing up to see my reaction as he read the next one. "Next witness statement, and I quote, Maxine saying to Loretta, 'Just because you think you can throw your weight around the Beautification Committee doesn't mean you can throw your weight around my event. You better step out of my way or else you'll pay.'" He flipped the page.

For a split second I wanted to reach out, rip the notebook out of his hands, and run over to the fireplace so I could throw it in.

"Next witness account," he continued.

"Okay," I butted in. "I get it. So she was angry," I said and turned around so he couldn't see my face while I pretended to prepare some things for the overly busy coffeehouse in my hands. I didn't want him to see them shaking.

"You honestly think that Aunt Maxi put a smidgen of poison in the cheese ball in hopes that Lana would take a bite of that one?" I asked. "Or kill anyone?"

"I don't know if she was trying to kill Lana or Loretta." I could feel a "but" coming on. "But Lana died. So whether or not she meant to kill someone or just make someone sick doesn't matter at this point. We have a murder on our hands, and I'm following all leads and evidence."

I could count the few times I'd been without words. On one hand in fact. This was one of those times.

"I have been privy to information that Maxine had come up here and stored her food in your refrigerator. I'm guessing she couldn't figure out a way to get Loretta out of making the appetizers, so she came up with this crazy plan to switch them."

"Good guess," I muttered, pulling my lips in to stop talking.

His brows rose.

"I've also got a witness who saw her leave the Watershed, come here, and leave here with the platter and a bag in her hands." He flipped a page from his notepad. "Where she walked into the Cocoon Hotel, and they also reported seeing you there too."

I gulped and was about to break under pressure to tell him the truth.

"Sheriff," the deputy called while walking back over with the phone in his hand. "It's the warrant from the judge."

Spencer took the phone from his deputy. His finger slowly swiped up the phone screen. His eyes darted back and forth as he read the text.

"Roxanne Bloom, we are going to search the Bean Hive Coffeehouse now." He flipped the phone screen around.

"I'm going to need a copy of that before you do." Just then, my phone dinged.

"One step ahead of you." He smiled, knowing the text just hit my phone.

I raised a finger and dragged my phone out of my pocket, checking the file he'd sent. It was the warrant for the Bean Hive.

"Fine. Look around. You aren't going to find anything." I shrugged.

Spencer didn't bother acknowledging me. He and the deputy headed straight to the kitchen.

"This is good." Bunny's voice cracked, her usual born-to-worry look on her face.

"It's fine," I assured her before Spencer came back out. "See. Nothing."

"Not nothing." He shook his head. "There's just too many little spaces for us to look through, and from what I recall, you open at six a.m." He pulled his sleeve up and looked at his watch. "I'm not going to let you open this morning until the search is complete."

"Wwww…." I couldn't find the words. I blurted, "You're kidding me, right? You want me to close down my coffeehouse so you can search to see if I have poison here?" I knew good and well there was no way on earth my coffeehouse had methanol in it. "Plus, it is the busiest time for the winter season."

My mind was going faster than my mouth.

"You and I both know that a search warrant is going to take hours. So you're shutting me down when you know that our community depends solely on our small businesses, and any sales during the winter are crucial to what is going to carry us through these brutal months."

"I'm sorry, Roxy. I know you need every possible sale you can get, but I'm shutting you down until we are finished searching the premises."

I shook my head and stormed out of the way, near the fireplace where Pepper was still sleeping on his bed. He'd not been bothered one bit.

"Roxy, this is not personal." Spencer was busy opening the coffee bar's cabinet drawer, shuffling through various things I needed to refill the area. "There is a young lady that's dead. Do you understand?"

"Oh, I understand that you are wasting your time and mine while there's a killer on the loose." I gestured to the outside. "Out there, right here at Christmas, and you're going to look like you don't know what you're talking about."

I just couldn't stop my mouth. The more I paced back and forth between the front window and the fireplace, the angrier I got. Especially when I continued to hear customers tug on the door and couldn't get in because Spencer locked it.

"And if I'm correct, isn't an election year coming up, so you better watch it? Aunt Maxi has been a huge supporter of yours, and trust me, when all of this is solved and you're standing there with a different killer in cuffs, you're gonna wish this day never happened."

The sound of clapping from my backup, Mae Belle, came from the opposite side of the coffeehouse.

"Thank you, Mae Belle."

She gave me some encouragement. I tugged down the edges of the apron before shoving my hand in its pockets.

"Sheriff, there was a—" The deputy poked his head out of the kitchen door. He had on a pair of gloves and held something up in the air. "I think we found the poison."

It was a bottle of liquid with a label that read Methanol in red.

This was beginning to look a lot like a nightmare, not Christmas.

CHAPTER ELEVEN

"What do you mean you're at the sheriff's department?" Patrick asked.

"Listen, Patrick." Frustration built up inside of me. "I get one phone call, one phone call. You are my one phone call. I need you to come down here and throw some weight around to get me out."

I had no time to explain what had happened.

"I need you to come down here." It was still really early, and I knew he had to be in bed. "Patrick, get out of bed and come down here."

Spencer sat across the table from me with a stern look. I hung up the phone and gave it back to him.

"So, you want to tell me how the poison got into the shop?" Spencer asked me like it was just everyday conversation.

"I have no idea." I shrugged, shook my head, and threw my hands in the air.

"Then let's start with why you left the Watershed." He pulled out his notebook.

Again.

I glared.

He clicked the end of the pen, put it to the paper, and looked back up at me.

"I need to go to the bathroom," I said in a flat voice.

His face softened.

"What? I own a coffeehouse. I've been drinking coffee since four this morning. Small bladder."

"Go." He sighed, not bothering to tell me where to go, since I knew my way around the department from previous visits.

To say that I took my sweet time and actually did sing the alphabet song while I washed my hands was an understatement. I even remembered the words to the song from high school Spanish class, so I also sang it two languages.

"Roxy, come on out. You've had plenty of time in there," Spencer said to me from the other side of the door.

I glanced at my reflection in the mirror and thought that this was turning out to be a nightmare I'd never imagined when I woke up this morning.

"Aunt Maxi, where are you?" I whispered to myself before I pulled the door open. "All done."

"Stop right there!" the familiar voice boomed out. "Roxanne, do not say another word." Kirk appeared, swiftly crossing the department with his business card in between his middle and forefinger. "I'm Roxanne's lawyer, Kirk."

"Yeah, I know who you are." Spencer took the card. "The ambulance chaser."

"The what?" My jaw dropped, and my head twisted, chin down, to look at Kirk.

"Semantics." Kirk brushed it off. "Is Roxanne under arrest?"

"No," Spencer said.

"Get your things. Let's go," Kirk instructed me.

"She needs to answer some questions, or I'll hold her as long as the law will let me." Spencer, Kirk, and I all knew he could keep me here for at least twenty-four hours.

"What types of questions?" Kirk put his hand up to my face when I was about to say that I would answer questions if that meant I could leave.

Spencer wanted to know my whereabouts and why I left the Watershed.

"I don't know where Aunt Maxi is and what you want from me, Spencer." I honestly didn't know for sure where she was, but I had an idea.

"I want the truth, Roxy. The truth will set you free."

"Really, you couldn't come up with anything better than that?" Kirk snorted.

I rolled my eyes. I looked at him with a straight face and sat there fiddling my tongue along the edges of my teeth.

"Fine, I'll tell you what I did." I looked at Kirk. He knew that look. The one indicating he knew I was serious and needed to tell Spencer.

Kirk would intervene if needed.

"Yes, Aunt Maxi was upset. She didn't ask Loretta to be part of the progressive dinner, because Loretta doesn't care two hoots and a holler about Pet Palace." Without having to say it out loud, Spencer knew the proceeds of the progressive dinner tickets went to the Pet Palace.

"The only thing that Loretta wanted was to have her name somewhere on it, so after Babette Cliff broke her ankle, Loretta seized the opportunity to take Babette's place."

As soon as I got out of here, I would put a call in to Babette Cliff. Or better yet, go see her.

"Go on, I'm listening." Spencer tapped his pen on the pad of paper.

"Aunt Maxi came up with this grand scheme that she would just switch them. She wasn't even going to let anybody know. I was a little nervous about it. The more I thought about it, the more I wanted to tell her not to do it. I left the Watershed and found her at the Cocoon Hotel." My eyes popped open. "As a matter of fact, I had a taste of Aunt Maxi's chipped beef ball on that exact platter. She gave me a sample, and I'm alive."

I'd completely forgotten about that.

"See, she didn't poison anything." I sat up on the edge of my seat and smiled.

Then I wondered who on earth had told Spencer all of mine and Aunt Maxi's whereabouts.

I saw Birdie and the lady who adopted the puppy. Then there was Louise Carlton. Surely Louise and Birdie didn't talk to Spencer.

Did Birdie go home and tell Loretta everything that happened that night, after which Loretta called Spencer?

"Roxy?" Kirk touched my back. As a natural reaction, I jerked. "Where did you just float off to?" He laughed nervously.

"I was saying I went to the hotel in hopes that Aunt Maxi didn't switch the cheese balls. But by the time I got down there, it was too late. She had."

"Do you know what she did with them?" he asked.

"She threw them in her bag." My words caught them off guard. "Yeah, she did. She took her cheese balls out of the plastic wrap, set them on the platters, and wrapped Loretta's up in the wrap before putting them in her bag."

"What did she do with them once she left the hotel?"

"I have no idea."

"Did you see Lana?" he asked.

"Yeah, she and Loretta were standing right there, talking about what was why this, that, and the other, and someone mentioned to Loretta that the chipped beef cheese ball was delicious. Loretta looked like she had sucked the pickle and said, 'Where is it?' Because she knew that she had not made a chipped beef cheese ball." I was beginning to realize there was no way I could get Aunt Maxi out of this mess without her here.

"I didn't see Lana there." I looked at Kirk. "Lana wasn't at the Cocoon Hotel with Loretta."

"Where was she?" Spencer asked.

"I guess she was at the beach, meeting someone down there." I knew it wasn't what he wanted to hear. "I was with Aunt Maxi from the time I left the Watershed until we found out Lana was dead. I saw Lana and Loretta leave the Watershed before I did."

Even though I knew I didn't have Aunt Maxi's or Lana's timeline down or the grounds to dismiss Loretta's whereabouts, I knew I gave Spencer more and more doubt about his number-one suspect, Aunt Maxi.

"Clearly, you can see my client has been cooperating, and now we are leaving." Kirk touched my arm. "Let's go, Roxanne."

I got up.

"Roxanne? Isn't that a little formal for you two?" Spencer asked with a smirk.

"She only lets her friends call her Roxy." Kirk used my own line on me.

Kirk held the back of my chair and helped me get up. Neither of us said goodbye to Spencer or dilly-dallied on our way out of the department.

"What on earth are you doing here?" I asked through gritted teeth once we were outside and walking to the car.

"Somebody had to come get you out of here, and your husband is smart enough to know I was in town and you needed help." I wanted to smack that smile right off his face.

"Roxy, come on." Kirk opened the car door for me. "Bygones be bygones. What is it going to take for you to forget the past and move on?"

"Leave town. My town. The town I could never get you to come visit when we were…" I couldn't even bring myself to say it.

I reached for the door handle and slammed the door shut. He walked around the front of the car, shaking his head the entire way.

"I'm not gonna be able to do that quite yet." He put his keys in the ignition and turned the engine over. "I got a little business to take care of. Besides my wife." That lingered.

"Your what?" I gripped the handle of the door.

"My wife. She got a new dog. And she loves it here. So now she wants us to buy a cabin." He focused on the road back toward the Bean Hive. "Does your mom have anything for sale?"

I glared at him.

"You're married?" I blinked with disbelief. "I had no idea."

"Yeah. Roxy, if you would pay attention"—he held his hand up, showing the rubber-looking black ring on his ring finger—"when I come into the coffee shop, I have my ring on."

The jab to me was that I could never get him to wear a ring when we were married. That didn't matter now. I was thankful we were separated because I wouldn't have moved back to Honey Springs and found Patrick.

"Let's go back to your wife. Your wife got a puppy." It had to be the woman who'd come into the coffeehouse last night. "She got the puppy from the adoption program at the Bean Hive. Was she the witness Spencer was talking about who saw me at the coffeehouse?"

"She's sorry." He said it like I was just supposed to forget all about it.

"This day could not get any worse!" I yelled out loud.

"Well, it could if Spencer booked you for helping your aunt Maxi kill that poor girl."

"Honestly, Kirk, do you think Aunt Maxi would kill anyone?" I knew the question was loaded for him, but I had to bide time somehow until he got me back to the parking lot where I needed to get my car.

"When she doesn't like someone, she can be hard to deal with, and I wouldn't put anything past her." The only truth to his statement was that Aunt Maxi loved hard, but if you hurt someone she loved, well, let's say it wouldn't be pretty.

"Did you forget how she left me out in snow this deep"—he made a gesture with his hands—"when I came here with you and told me I could freeze to death?" Kirk had obviously kept a running list. "And she wouldn't care if the next time she saw me was at my funeral?" he recalled. "Don't forget the toast she gave at our wedding."

"Okay. I don't need to rehash all of that." He'd made his point.

"Patrick seems to think I can help you. You might want to listen to him." This was the one thing that made me listen.

"Fine. I will listen to Patrick," I said, my little dig getting a look from Kirk.

The rest of the ride was silent. My mind stewed on so many things that I knew I had to find Aunt Maxi first, even though I really wanted to call Babette Cliff.

"Don't go back in the coffeehouse. The sheriff still has it closed, and I'll let you know when he releases it." Kirk pulled up next to my car.

"What about Pepper?" I asked.

"Patrick came down and got him from Bunny." Kirk shifted the car in park. "And Roxy, if you find Maxine, please have her call me. Or at least call a lawyer."

Oh, I will, I thought. I'm a lawyer, or did you forget?

CHAPTER TWELVE

My phone had several texts and missed calls from Patrick. Instead of calling him back as soon as I got the notices, I knew I would need some time to process what was going on with Aunt Maxi, Lana's murder, and Patrick calling Kirk.

To say I was surprised he wasn't home when I got there was an understatement. In fact, I expected him to be there waiting for me to get home from the clink.

The two rocking chairs my grandfather had made were a perfect addition to the cabin. And I loved decorating the porch for each season.

Before I opened the cabin door, I rearranged the cute snowflake pillows in the rockers' seats. I also re-folded the buffalo checked blankets over the top rung of the deep-brown ladder-back-style rockers.

The babies were scratching at the door.

"You're always here for Mommy," I said in baby dog talk to Sassy and Pepper. Both danced eagerly on the other side to greet me. "Let's go potty."

They darted off the front porch, and I headed inside, where the warm glow of the fire illuminated the small window of the wood-burning stove. The Christmas tree lights were on, and the radio was tuned to the local station that had played around-the-clock Christmas music since the week of Thanksgiving.

Some people minded it, but I didn't. I loved anything that made my feelings of joy and happiness bubble up over the feelings that didn't serve me.

I started walking to the kitchen to retrieve a kettle of water, which I wanted to put on the wood burner so I could make some strong cowboy coffee. On my way, I glanced out the window to make sure Sassy and Pepper were doing okay. They were sniffing the snow and didn't seem to want to come inside.

I grabbed the kettle, filled it, and brought it over to the stove, where I set the kettle on top to boil. While I waited for the water to finish boiling and the dogs to come inside, I got a notepad and pen and my cup of coffee ready.

The kettle screamed just as I was getting the dogs inside. That way, I could get the coffee and a blanket and snuggle up on the couch while I drank the coffee so I could get all my thoughts on paper.

At least, it sounded like a great plan.

Patrick waltzed through the door.

"There you are." He hurried over and kneeled in front of me. "I went to the department, and they said you already left."

"Kirk came to my rescue," I said in a flat voice and took a drink from my mug.

"You're mad. I can see you're mad." Patrick eased up and sat on the edge of the couch next to me and in front of Pepper. "I did what you asked me to do."

"No. No, you didn't. I asked you to come get me, not send my ex-husband." It was clearly not the right decision, but what was done was done, and I knew I couldn't change it. "Maybe I didn't make myself clear when I said 'you.'"

"Roxy, what was I going to do? Have a fistfight with Spencer and throw you over my shoulder to take you out of there? No. I needed a lawyer, and trust me when I say Kirk was the last one on my list." Patrick made me smile.

"I'm sorry. I should've known you tried everyone, but do you know how humiliating it is for me to let him help me?" I asked and looked away.

"You care about what others think?" Patrick looked surprised. "I don't. I wanted you out of there so you could get to Maxine and figure out what happened. And open the coffeehouse."

"I don't know where she is." I sighed and patted Pepper as he got up to move, since Patrick had inched back a little. "I'm sorry I got upset about Kirk. He was just a topper to a bad day so far."

Patrick put his arm around and snuggled me tight. I told him what had happened as I sipped on my coffee.

"She's in a cabin." He told me about Aunt Maxi. "With Penney."

"Wait." I pushed out of his embrace and curled a leg up under me, sitting up a little taller with my hand wrapped around my mug. "How do you know where she is?"

"Penney called me. She said Maxi left her phone at Maxi's house because she didn't want the sheriff to track her." He reached out and put his hands on my legs. "Get your coat. I'll take you there."

"You two stay here," I told the pups dancing at the door to go with us. "We will be back soon."

"They don't care." Patrick flipped them a treat from his coat pocket.

We kept treats all over us, our cars, the house, everywhere we could.

"You okay?" Patrick asked when he noticed I'd stopped chatting.

"Yeah. My stomach has been funny." I didn't tell him that I'd eaten one of Loretta's crackers because Aunt Maxi had shoved it in my mouth before she had me taste hers. Now that I knew Lana was poisoned, I felt a wee bit of fear that maybe my little cracker had a little residue of poison on it, which was what made me queasy.

"Let's put on some Christmas music." Patrick flipped on the radio when we pulled out of the driveway, going toward town.

"Under normal circumstances, I'd really be enjoying this snow squall and music." I sighed and watched the snow not only start again but fall all around in huge, heavy flakes.

"The roads were getting slick again, so I'm going to drive pretty slow." Patrick had both hands on the wheel.

I hummed along to the radio and let him concentrate. Though my mouth beat to the music, my mind was focused on what I was going to say to Aunt Maxi when I saw her.

We made our way into downtown Honey Springs, which was only a five-minute drive on a non-snowy day and a ten-minute drive today.

Downtown was a gorgeous small town. Central Park was smack dab in the middle of it. Around it was a sidewalk, and different sidewalks led to the middle of the park, where a big white gazebo stood. Most of Honey Springs's small-town festivals were held in the park. And I couldn't wait for spring to come back because I missed going to the farmers' market. Today Central Park was lined with Christmas trees. Each one had a different colored strand of lights, and the line to visit Santa Claus, who was sitting in the gazebo, was all the way out of the park and around the sidewalk.

The smiles and cheer on the people's faces made me realize not everyone was aware of or as engrossed in Lana's murder as I was.

"You okay?" Patrick broke the silence.

"Yes." I stared at the dim carriage lights dotting all the downtown sidewalks. They glowed through the snowfall and made a gorgeous picture. It was almost as pretty as the vivid memory of the colorful flowers and daffodils that I knew were hiding underneath the snow and would pop up soon to let us know spring was coming.

The courthouse was in the middle of Main Street with a beautiful view of the park.

There was a medical building where the dentist, optometrist, podiatrist, and good old-fashioned medical doctors were located.

And the theater was near the library, which was across from the bank where Emily's dad was president.

Even the old theater looked great. It was a typical small-town theater with exposed light bulbs going all the way around the marquee, which was lit up atop the building. The place had double doors and a small glass cashier window, where a member of the theater committee would sit and sell tickets for the show. The theater company did four shows a year, and those coincided with the seasons. Since we were still in the winter season, the winter show was called *The Night Before Presents*, a funnier skit on the real Christmas story.

"I wanted to go see that with Mom and Aunt Maxi," I said as we passed.

"And you will. Let's just get through one day at a time." He was trying to be uplifting, but one day at a time would lead us right up to Christmas, which was only a few days away.

"Do you think she did it?" he asked.

My face said it all.

"I was just asking."

"Of course I don't."

"There's a 'but' coming." He knew me all too well.

"There's a lot of eyewitnesses that saw and heard Aunt Maxi arguing with

Lana and Loretta, which, as you know, makes it seem like she's guilty. A lot of angry chatter." I didn't need to tell him what was being said because I knew he could imagine. "Then there's the whole finding the methanol bottle at the coffeehouse."

"Do you have any idea how that got there?" he asked.

"Good question. No. The only people with keys to the coffeehouse are me, Aunt Maxi, Bunny, you, and Birdie." All the people I loved and trusted. "Only one of them is being accused of murder and had access to hide the bottle there."

"Which brings me back to this: do you think Maxi did it?"

"Why would you ask me again?" I was a little fit to be tied with his questioning.

"All the evidence points to it." He shrugged and turned left on Crescent Peck Road.

"Isn't this the same street the old Seifert barn is on?" I asked.

"Yeah. Why?" He pointed out the windshield. "It's right over the ridge. You'll see that old barn coming up. I was hoping to ask the Teagardens if I could purchase the old barn wood. You wouldn't believe how many people ask me to use reclaimed barn wood as an accent wall."

"Can we pull in there?" I asked, watching the side of the road as we drove over the ridge where the old barn came into focus.

"I guess we can. What's with the old barn?" he asked.

"I don't know. I just know Aunt Maxi had gotten the platter the sheriff is holding for evidence from the Teagardens, who bought the contents of the barn from the bank." I held on when he turned down the gravel road. The gravel was a little icier than the road.

"I'm not following." He geared the truck down so it'd grip the gravel better.

"It could be a long shot, but when I was looking around for Aunt Maxi at the Watershed, I overheard a couple of people saying they'd heard someone was living in the old barn. If that's the case, maybe someone was upset with Aunt Maxi and Loretta for taking the china or even the Teagardens for buying the contents of the barn." The idea sounded silly now that I said it out loud. "Then there's the whole ghost thing."

"Like the Ghost of Christmas Past?" He snorted, and when I didn't reciprocate, he glanced at me. "You're kidding, right?"

"I don't kid about murder, especially when someone I love is the number-one suspect." When he put the truck in park, I flung the door open.

There was a No Trespassing sign on the barn, which had seen much better days.

Patrick led the way and slipped between two broken planks with his handy flashlight clicked on.

"It looks pretty stable in here." He shot the flashlight around and shined it on the ceiling beams. "It doesn't look like anything is left." The light darted around.

A twinkle of something shiny cut the darkness. Patrick pointed the light toward it.

"Oh, man." He found delight in what was sparkling. "I'd love to have that."

We walked over, and he used the flashlight to expose a creepy-looking clown sign that read Let The Magic Begin.

"No, we do not want that," I stated and wagged my finger at it. "That's weird."

"No. It's great. You know the old theater downtown? Well, when I was a kid, the Seiferts did their magic shows there. I loved them."

"Magical," I whispered. "That's what those two people were joking about when they mentioned a ghost and something being magical."

"Probably." He ran his hand along the sign, getting the loose dirt off. "It's a bit creepy now that I look at it. But it was so much a part of our lives here before the boardwalk became a big deal. Didn't you ever go to one of their shows when you visited with your dad?"

"No. I don't think so. Or not that I remember." I shook my head.

"Even at those fancy Christmas parties, Mr. Seifert would do a Christmas magic show, from what I'd heard." He turned the light around and fluttered it all over the barn's interior. "It doesn't look to me like anyone was living here."

"Probably not now. So I guess my theory about someone mad at Aunt Maxi and Loretta for the china was way off." I knew I was reaching for any reason why someone would kill Lana and, in my opinion, blackmail either Loretta or Aunt Maxi.

CHAPTER THIRTEEN

Not only did Mom have Aunt Maxi in the secluded cabin, but Loretta Bebe of all people was also with them.

"What do you mean, Kirk got you out of prison?" Aunt Maxi's disapproval showed in the full range of emotions scrolling over her face. First it was shock, then it was anger, then it went back to surprise.

"What was I supposed to do?" Patrick asked. He walked over to the kitchen counter, where the cabin's coffee pot dinged finished. He took a few mugs off the hooks that hung on the wall. Patrick ran each one under the water faucet before he started to pour each of us a cup and put it on the table. "She needed a lawyer other than herself, and he just popped into my head."

"He got me sprung." I shrugged, knowing time spent on Kirk wasn't going to get us anywhere.

"After what all he did to you, he better help you out." Mom was the one person in my life who was close to Kirk when we'd gotten married.

And when I announced we were getting divorced, she wanted me to forgive and forget. Oh, I've forgiven him now, but the forgetting was a little hard to do.

"Forget about him." I waved off the conversation. "I'm here because you really do need to turn yourself in to the department for questioning."

"I will do no such thing." Aunt Maxi's reaction made the already tense situation rise an octave.

"You running off and hiding like this doesn't look good." I reached over and held her hand in mine. "Do you think I'm going to let him keep you?"

"I think he'd try." She drew her hand out from underneath mine and laid them in her lap.

"I think we can make a plan. Here is what I know." I fiddled with the handle of the mug. "Lana was poisoned with methanol."

Mom, Loretta, and Aunt Maxi gasped.

"Oh, dear me," Loretta cried out and put her face in her hands. "Who would do such a thing?" Her fingers parted, her eyeball between them as she looked at Aunt Maxi.

"You better cover up that eyeball before I poke it," Aunt Maxi snarled. "I didn't do anything to her. Where on earth would I find methanol?"

"When Spencer searched the Bean Hive..." I could tell by their reactions they didn't know that bit of information either. "Yes. They served me a search warrant and ended up finding a bottle of methanol in the kitchen."

"That means whoever killed Lana was planting evidence." Mom was always pretty good at solving the murders I had to try while I was in college as an assistant. She lived for when I came home to visit and could get me to talk about the cases.

"Right, and I have a solid alibi, but Aunt Maxi's story has some holes that Spencer would like filled in because apparently Aunt Maxi and Lana"—I moved my head to face Loretta—"and Loretta had some words between them."

"They were just words. Not poison." Loretta gave Aunt Maxi a solid Baptist nod. The kind that told us she had Aunt Maxi's back.

"I see you two are still sticking with the truce you made last night. That's good."

They both agreed.

"So if I can get some good information to look into, I think we can go see Spencer, and you can give your statement. He won't be able to keep you on circumstantial evidence."

Technically, all of that wasn't true, but things would be a lot worse for her if I let her stay hidden. And now my mom was involved. Loretta could get in trouble, too, just for being here.

"Aunt Maxi, we are going to need to establish your timeline." I took the pad of paper Mom had given me and a pen so I could keep notes. "Thank you." I smiled because it felt like old times, when I lived at home during college.

"What do you need to know?" She was agreeable. "I did make the cheese balls because Loretta—and don't take this the wrong way," she warned Loretta, "but you don't make the best appetizers."

"That's why I had Lana do it." I couldn't believe my ears or that Loretta actually told the truth about it, even if there was a pending murder charge.

"You did?" Aunt Maxi's mouth flew open.

"Yes. Lana said she'd keep it a secret." Loretta sighed. Her brows pinched as though she were regretting her decision to come clean.

I didn't dare tell Loretta that Birdie had already told me about Lana making the appetizers. It was something that didn't need to be mentioned.

"We all know she didn't poison herself, so it all comes down to what Lana did that day and what she ate." I clicked the top of the pen to make the point appear. "Loretta, can you tell me what happened that day?"

"Beverly Teagarden had called me the night before to let me know she'd picked up some of the boxes from the old Seifert place. She'd already agreed to sell me the Christmas set. That's when I showed up at the Bean Hive the next morning. Beverly hadn't gotten to the Wild and Whimsy like she said she would."

I wrote down her words exactly, though I already knew about it, since I'd talked to her and Lana that morning.

"After we left you, we went back down to the Wild and Whimsy, and Beverly still wasn't there."

"That's not like her," Aunt Maxi noted with furrowed brows.

"I know it's not, so instead of leaving, I figured she'd gotten stuck in the snow or something. There was no sense in driving home just to come right back out, so Lana and I went to the Buzz In and Out Diner for some breakfast." Loretta didn't do anything so unusual. "From there, we went to the Wild and Whimsy, where I picked up the china, minus the platter." She shot Aunt Maxi a look.

"What is up with this platter?" I just had to know why Aunt Maxi wanted it so badly.

"Both of us used to attend the Seiferts' Christmas parties," Loretta said. "Maxine knew I loved those dishes."

"I did, but I also knew Beverly and Dan bought the old Seifert barn with all their belongings in there, so when I heard about it, I thought to myself that I could buy the platter and put one of my cheese balls on there, and I figured that Loretta wouldn't notice the cheese ball if it was on the platter." Aunt Maxi was so sneaky to even think of such a thing. "I was going to let her have it after the progressive supper."

"That's mighty nice of you, Maxine." Loretta's jaw clenched. She was trying her best not to say something snide about why Aunt Maxi did it, so I just dropped the platter situation.

"Now that we have that established, after you got the dishes from the Wild and Whimsy, what did y'all do?" I needed all the details.

"We went back to my house and cleaned the dishes up really good before we started to plate the appetizers we'd made the day before." Her head shook back and forth, lips turned down. "After that, we took the appetizers to the Cocoon Hotel. While I arranged the furniture in the hospitality suite, I asked Lana to run back up to the Wild and Whimsy to grab me some antique doilies to go under the plates and really spruce things up, even though Camey already had that gorgeous Christmas tree in the corner."

"Did you see that fireplace mantel?" Aunt Maxi gushed.

"Mmmhhh, she sure can decorate," Loretta agreed.

"Okay, ladies. Can we please get back to the questions?" I asked.

They both readjusted themselves in the seats.

I continued, "Did Lana meet with anyone else?"

"I don't know. Not that she mentioned. She came back with items. While she was gone, I made placeholders with all the names of the cheese balls on them so when Camey went to put them out, she knew where to go." Loretta did like things just so. She did this at every event she hosted.

"Lana and I went to the Watershed, and I saw you there. That's when I went down to the Cocoon Hotel."

"I did see you and the Teagardens having what looked like a heated discussion." I recalled how Loretta's head was bobbing back and forth.

"I wouldn't call it heated. I was telling them how I really needed the platter, and they didn't tell me they'd sold it to Maxine. They just told me they sold it. You can imagine my surprise when I heard someone say they loved the chipped beef ball at the hotel. I knew I didn't make nothing with chipped beef in it.

That's when I saw the platter." There was a shift in her voice and the color of her face as she tried to keep her composure. "I know that you said you were going to give me the platter, but according to Roxy, that platter is as good as gone now that it's evidence."

"If I'd known Lana was doing the cooking, then I wouldn't've done it." Aunt Maxi's words were heated.

"We don't need to get into an argument." I put my hands out between the two women. "Where was Lana during this time?"

"I told her she didn't have to stay if she didn't want, so she opted to leave, only we know she didn't get too far," Loretta said in a shaky voice.

"How did you find Lana to hire?" I asked, moving on from the events of the day, since nothing was out of sorts with Loretta, making me wonder if she'd met someone after she left the hotel and that was when the poisoning occurred.

"Babette Cliff. She had done some hiring over the summer, since summer weddings in Honey Springs are becoming a destination," she said. "Babette and I were talking. I told her I needed some help around the house now that Birdie was living with me, and I knew Birdie couldn't do it because she's working for you and loving it."

"Babette gave you Lana's recommendation?" I asked.

"Babette gave me the top five applicants she didn't hire. She gave me their applications, and I called them, but Lana met with me, and I instantly liked her." Loretta looked off. She sniffled.

"What about the other applicants? Did anyone seem upset you didn't hire them?" I wondered if one of the other candidates didn't get the job and plotted out a way to get rid of Lana. It was a stretch, but people killed for far less substantial reasons than that.

"I didn't call them back and never heard again from them." Loretta shrugged it off like it was no big deal.

"Do you still have those applications?" It wouldn't hurt to look at them.

"I gave them back to Babette in case she wanted them." Loretta just confirmed what I'd thought earlier.

I needed to go see Babette.

Now I turned my attention to Aunt Maxi.

"After you left the Bean Hive"—I didn't need to remind her of how she'd acted that morning after finding out Loretta was taking Babette's job for the progressive supper—"that morning, what did you do?"

"I went down to the hotel and saw Loretta in the Buzz In and Out." That was when an eyewitness had told Spencer about Aunt Maxi confronting Loretta.

Spencer wouldn't tell me who the eyewitness was, and now that I knew it was at the diner, it could've been anyone.

"I made sure I went to the Cocoon and waited her out, but I also made sure I made an appearance at the Watershed so she'd see me and not think I switched the appetizers." Aunt Maxi's brows knitted.

"What did you do when they were putting out the appetizers before the progressive supper participants got there?" I needed every single little detail.

"I went into the hotel bar and had me a sweet iced tea. You know they have the best in town." Aunt Maxi licked her lips.

"It's that little bit of honey they boil in the water," Loretta chimed in.

"Did anyone see you there besides the bartender?" I knew we needed witnesses to everything.

"Yes!" Aunt Maxi smacked her hands together. "Newton Oakley!"

"Newton Oakley?" I asked to make sure. He was the eyes and ears of the Cocoon Hotel as well as the maintenance man.

"Yep." Aunt Maxi's lips twitched. "I might've told him what I was doing, and he might've been on the lookout for me when I did the switch."

"I thought he was hitting on me." Loretta glared. "He was trying to sweet-talk me, and this whole time he was helping you?"

Aunt Maxi nodded.

"I'm sorry. I didn't tell him to sweet-talk you, but I had to save the dinner from, well, you." Aunt Maxi should've just stopped talking because she was throwing one jab after the other, and the truce the two had agreed to didn't seem to hold water.

"Stop this." I stood up and looked at them. "You two need to stop this right now, or we will never find the real killer because let me tell you"—I pointed directly at Loretta—"you might not be a suspect, but you know they are looking for Aunt Maxi, and here you sit. No different than me, him, and her." I dragged my finger to point at myself, Mom, and Patrick.

"This is just awful." Loretta's nostrils flared before her eyes teared up. "We got to find that killer."

"The best thing we can do is get Aunt Maxi to the station so Spencer can question her. I'll go see if I can get those applications from Babette and try to find out what I can from Kevin." I had to get more details on Lana's life, too, but I had yet to figure that part out.

Maybe Kevin had contacted her family and I'd get some information from him about that.

"I also have to take Sassy and Pepper down to the Pawrade," Patrick reminded me.

"I forgot about that." I nodded. "Okay. Change in plans. Mom, can you take Aunt Maxi to the department? I'll call Kirk to meet you there."

"Kirk?" Aunt Maxi crossed her arms. "I'd rather go to prison for killing someone I didn't murder."

"I'm going to need you to trust him. Do not call him names or treat him like he did..." My voice trailed off when I noticed Patrick staring at me.

"What? It's okay." Patrick smiled. "You can treat him awful after all of this mess is cleared up." He bent down and kissed Aunt Maxi on the cheek. "I don't know what you said about him or what he said about you, but I love you, and I know Roxy loves you. She'd never do anything to steer you wrong."

"I'll go. But only because I love you." She pinched Patrick's cheek and got up to go.

CHAPTER FOURTEEN

On our way back home to pick up the dogs for the Pawrade, Patrick and I went over the notes I'd taken. We agreed Lana had to have met with someone to have been poisoned—but who?

The fur kiddos were looking out the family room window when we got there. As soon as they noticed us pull up in the truck, they ran to the door, and I could hear them barking.

"You stay here, and I'll get them," I told Patrick.

There was no sense in him getting out of the truck, since we were just going to get back in. We were already going to be late and, although it hardly mattered, I didn't anticipate us winning, since I'd gotten them some store-bought sweaters from A Walk In the Bark Animal Boutique, another cute shop on the boardwalk.

Sassy was wearing one that looked like an elf while Pepper was wearing a sweater that made him look like Santa Claus. Of course, his schnauzer beard was perfect.

"Do you two want to go bye-bye?" I asked the babies as they darted out of the cabin without bothering to greet me after they heard the magic words. *Bye-bye.*

I did a quick check of the cabin to make sure everything inside was okay.

Since I'd had the house fire a couple of years ago, I was still leery of the wood-burning stove, even though the fire was set deliberately.

"Everything all good?" Patrick had already gotten the dogs in the car and cleaned off their paws from the snow. They sat anxiously in between Patrick and me.

Pepper climbed into my lap once I had my seatbelt on and ready to go.

"Everything looked good," I said. Pepper shivered. "You're going to get all warm and fuzzy now." I put his little coat on him and decided to wait to put Sassy's coat costume on her until we got the truck stopped at Central Park. She was just too big for me to put it on her in such a confined space.

"What are you thinking about with Maxi?" Patrick asked.

"I'm hoping Mom did take her." While we were at the secret hiding space cabin, we agreed that Mom would take Aunt Maxi to the department. "I hate to do it, but I think Kirk needs to be her lawyer."

"Do you think she's going to let him?" Patrick was so good about Kirk being here.

I wasn't so sure I'd be so nice if it were the other way around.

"You know what?" I reached across Sassy and squeezed Patrick's arm. "You amaze me. I love you so much."

"I love you so much more." Patrick glanced quickly, taking his eyes briefly off the road to look at me. He smiled. His eyes held a softness only I knew when he looked at me. "I just want everyone at our table for Christmas."

My stomach did a topsy-turvy dive, almost making me nauseated at the thought of anyone not being there. I pictured Aunt Maxi's seat being empty but quickly put that in the back of my mind.

"What? You went silent." Patrick was so hyper-aware of my actions it was almost scary.

"The thought of Spencer even putting Aunt Maxi in jail really bothers me. But how did the methanol get into the coffeehouse?" I racked my brain for any and all reasons.

"I know you're not going to like this, but who has keys to the coffeehouse?" Patrick asked me a strange question.

"Me, you, Aunt Maxi, Bunny and Birdie," I said out loud, counting them off on my fingers.

"Who out of those would have any reason to harm Lana or possibly Loretta?" He confused me. "Obviously not me or you. Bunny and Maxine have their beef with Loretta, but if you break it down, they do like her. Then there's Birdie." My jaw clenched at his words. "I know. I know you adore her. You can't forget the fact she'd been accused of poisoning her teachers before she came here. She's got a temper from her past, and didn't you tell me something about Loretta saying she needed to go home for Christmas?"

I started opening my mouth to protest.

"Hear me out." He turned down Main Street.

The sidewalks were filled with tourists, locals, and dogs, all walking toward the park where the festival was always held.

"What if she thought it would only make Loretta a little ill? Sick to her stomach?" Patrick asked.

I gulped, wondering if that was what was going on with my stomach, since it'd been a little off.

Did I accidentally eat something with methanol?

"Not kill her, but she didn't get the dosage right, and Lana accidentally ate it." Patrick had put a little scare in me.

"Patrick, do you really think...?" I held Pepper close to me so my nerves would settle down from his warmth.

"I'm not saying anything for sure. I just know that she's gifted when it comes to chemistry. She's had a little bit of a past that could bring things into question. She has access to Loretta and Lana plus the keys to the Bean Hive, where she could potentially hide things." He parked the truck in a spot along the far side of the park.

My molars gnawed on the inside of my cheek as the possibility began to take form in my head.

"I don't know. She did say she didn't want to go home for Christmas." I hated to even begin to let this idea grow, but he was right on all accounts.

"And if Loretta got the tiniest bit sick, you know her parents wouldn't make Birdie leave Loretta here. They just might come here like Birdie wants." Patrick took Sassy's coat costume from the seat and put it on her. "Just talk to her and feel her out. That's all I'm saying."

I agreed, and we got out of the truck, filing in line with all the others on the sidewalk.

The gazebo was all festively lit up with colored Christmas lights. I was sad we'd missed the Christmas tree lighting ceremony this year, but from the looks of it, the tree was larger than ever before. No doubt that was Loretta's doing, since she was the president of the Beautification Committee.

Speaking of Loretta, I saw her and Birdie near the front of the Santa line, where they were handing out candy canes. I would be sure to stop by, not only to make sure everything was good between her and Aunt Maxi after I'd left them at the cabin but also to gauge Birdie's attitude toward her.

Darn Patrick had now given me the awful idea that Birdie could've accidentally killed Lana.

"I'll go get the kids signed up." Patrick referred to the pups. He kissed me before he and Sassy went to the registration table.

Pepper sniffed at everyone and everything as we made our way from vendor tent to vendor tent.

"Mom," I gasped when I noticed her and Aunt Maxi at the tent I'd rented for the Bean Hive. There were two display cases filled with treats from the coffeehouse. Four industrial coffee pots with the Christmas Special Blend and three little café tables for patrons to sit, chat, enjoy coffee and a treat as well as heat up next to the small bonfire. "What on earth?"

With everything going on, I'd not mentioned the space I'd rented for the festival and figured it was out of the question for this year.

"It was all Patrick's doing." Mom smiled.

"The reason he was not available to come get you at the jail was because he was here working on this before I threw a wrench in everything." Aunt Maxi referred to her hiding out in the cabin. "He knew you were busy at the coffeehouse, and Birdie had been making extra food at the coffeehouse at night so it could be a big surprise to you."

"Surprise!" A pair of arms hugged me from behind, but I recognized Birdie's voice. "Patrick and I wanted to do something nice for you, since you've always been there for me. I'd do anything for you and anything to be here for this."

Anything?

I turned around, my eyes wide and a smile on my face, wondering if I was staring into the eyes of a young killer.

"Thank you." I hugged her back. "And what about you?" I asked.

"I called Spencer and acted like he was crazy for not finding me. I told him I'd been running around all day getting things ready for this." Aunt Maxi leaned on the glass case. "He said he'd be down here to talk to me. I'm waiting on him." She shrugged. "If he wants to take me in, he can, but I called Kirk," she snarled. "Only because you suggested it."

She threw her chin up in a gesture indicating that I should look behind me.

Kirk and Jessica were walking up to the tent. The little puppy she'd adopted was on a leash and wore a doggy outfit with a huge lion's mane around her head.

"I have to tell you that I'm sorry I didn't introduce myself, and I admit I came to the coffeehouse to check you out." Jessica seemed to be nice. "I was all prepared to, but when I saw the puppy, my heart melted. Then you came in, and I just couldn't bring myself to introduce myself."

"Now you two have met." Kirk wrapped his arm around her. "I was really hoping it was going to be different, but this is how it happened."

It was interesting seeing Kirk with another woman who was his wife. They had an apparent love between them that Kirk and I had never shared. Something neither of us could give to the other and why our marriage didn't work out.

My reaction had surprised even me. Normally, my heart was cold to him. Now I watched how nice it was to see he'd finally gotten his happily ever after with Jessica.

"I'm sorry I didn't introduce myself when you were asking about my visit here." Jessica really did seem to be a nice person.

"It's fine." I returned the smile. "Now, what about a name?" I asked about the puppy.

"Biscuit." She reached down and picked her up. "Kirk hates the name, but I love it, and he responded to it." She snuggled him tight. "I could eat him up just like a warm biscuit."

The puppy wiggled and wormed in her arms, giving her big kisses on the nose.

Kirk had excused himself when Spencer got Aunt Maxi off to the side.

Instead of going over there and trying to listen in, I did let Kirk handle it because I'd been down this road once before with Aunt Maxi, and it truly was a conflict of interest. Not to mention it was hard for me to not be biased.

I had to notice Birdie standing near Aunt Maxi and trying to stay in a conversation with Alva, the waitress from the diner. Alva and Birdie were looking at Alva's phone. They were discussing something intently. Aunt Maxi's eyes were also fixed on the screen.

"Time for the Pawrade, Biscuit!" Jessica's glee showed all over her face. She darted off with Biscuit snuggled up to her neck.

"Are you ready?" Patrick asked me.

"Do you mind getting started without me?" I tried to avoid his stare when I handed him Pepper's leash, but I could feel the tension. "I'll meet you on the front side of the park."

"Yeah. Sure." He sighed before giving in to a kiss.

"Thank you," I whispered into his ear.

"Let's go, kids." He wrangled the leashes, leaving me with Aunt Maxi, Alva, and Birdie. Mom was with a customer, and Loretta was doing what she did best, retelling the story of Lana.

The crowd was dispersing to the far side of the park as they all went either to watch the Pawrade or to participate. I was so glad I wasn't judging the competition because all the animals were adorable.

"'Scuse me," Loretta said, asking me to move. "I've got to get to the judges' table." She patted my arm. Fake marble fur outlined her coat's collar and the cuffs of its sleeves. The jeweled buttons glistened as the snow hit them perfectly. She also wore a hat that was the same color as the coat on top and had the same fur trim along the bottom, making a furry crown around her head.

Perfect for the Pawrade judge, I thought as a smile curled up on my lips, though I would never tell her she kind of looked like my Sassy.

"Are you okay?" I asked just in case she'd heard something, and I wanted to know before she darted off.

"I called Elliot and told him it was probably best Birdie go home for Christmas." She reached in her coat pocket and took out her lipstick. "I told him it had to be presented that it was his idea. He, too, thought it would be best, since I'm a little stressed about Lana." She slid the top off the lipstick and twisted it up, applying a thick layer to her upper and lower lip. "She's been a pill ever since. Not listening to a word I'm saying. And I can't get her off that darn phone."

I looked back over at Aunt Maxi, Alva, and Birdie, all still looking at Alva's phone screen.

"I can't worry about that right now. I've got to go judge the Pawrade." She closed her lipstick and shuffled away.

"Be sure to come back after the Pawrade to warm up," I told the customers as they left the Bean Hive Coffeehouse vendor tent. "Can you believe Patrick did all of this?" I turned to ask Aunt Maxi.

"Mm-hhmm, but you've got to see this." She pointed at Alva's phone. "People will put and say anything on social media." She tsked.

Mom shrugged, her lips turned down. She opened a couple of the coolers filled with pastries, cookies, and treats. She went down the glass display case and refilled all the empty spaces so we would be ready when the Pawrade was over.

"I think Patrick is a keeper." Mom decided to answer me, since Aunt Maxi brushed me off.

"I'm so floored. He's been so amazing. And you too. Thank you." It felt so good to finally have a relationship with my mom after all those years of not seeing eye to eye.

Maybe I'd grown up, or maybe she was just better at adult children. Either way, my heart was filled with gratitude.

"Roxanne," Aunt Maxi called me over, gesturing wildly. "Get over here while everyone is gone."

"What's going on?" I didn't have time for social media, and Aunt Maxi certainly didn't need to entertain the idea of being on social media. I poured myself a cup of Christmas Blend coffee and walked over.

"Birdie is so smart." Aunt Maxi's bracelets jingled and jangled as she pointed and shook a finger at Birdie.

"I know that." I gulped and wondered about the whole idea Patrick had brought up, which I would look into later.

"Do you like the blend?" Birdie asked. "I made the special roast last night so it would be fresh. It was a chore trying to keep all of it a secret from you, but Patrick insisted."

I looked down into the cup. I couldn't stop seeing the skull and crossbones in my head, floating in the mug.

"Delicious." I set it down and looked at the phone Aunt Maxi was referring to. "What did Birdie find?"

"I found Lana's social media profile." Birdie took Alva's phone and showed me. "This is a guy she was dating. Apparently she broke up with him, and they had a fight."

"Really?" My eyes grew at the prospect of another suspect to investigate. "I'm listening."

"I've not fully gone back and clicked all the images, but there's definitely some issues, and it makes me wonder if she went down to the beach to meet him." Alma poked the screen and showed me a photo of Lana and this guy on the beach with the Cocoon Hotel behind them. "And it looks like the place where she died, right?" Alva asked.

"Why, sure it is. That boy killed her, and he ain't even on Spencer Shepard's radar." Aunt Maxi's lips contorted and snarled. "We've got to find him."

"We?" I shook my head. "You aren't doing anything. If anything needs to be done, then I can look into it—or Kirk can."

"Kirk smirk." Aunt Maxi frowned. "I don't trust him."

"You don't have to. I do." I held my hand out for the phone. "Do we have a name?"

"It gets better than that." Alva smiled, her brows rising. "I saw him and Lana in the diner a few weeks back. I didn't pay much attention to them, but when James told them to take their fight outside, it got some unwanted attention by customers."

"Wait. James. James Farley?" I wanted to make sure we were on the same page.

She nodded, and her eyes grew.

"Lana and this guy had an argument, and James made them leave the diner?"

"Don't hold me to it, but I do believe this is the guy." She touched her phone screen with the phone still in my hands.

"I need this guy's info." I gnawed on my bottom lip. My eyes drew up under my brows, and I looked at Birdie. "You have social media, right?"

I handed Alva's phone back to her.

"Yep." Birdie grinned. "I can get all the info for you." She took her phone out of her coat pocket.

She and Alva exchanged information back and forth about the guy so Birdie could find him.

"Now what?" Aunt Maxi asked.

"Now we get on social media and look this guy up. We also go see James

Farley to see what he remembers about the argument between Lana and this guy so we can take that information to Spencer." I sucked in a deep breath and noticed the Pawrade had started. They were halfway down the sidewalk opposite from where we were, near the place I told Patrick I'd meet him.

"This is good," Aunt Maxi agreed.

"Being a jilted lover is a big motive to have killed someone." My brows shot up. My head tilted, and my lips pinched.

CHAPTER FIFTEEN

S ometimes during the night my phone had chirped with a text. Normally those little beeps and bings didn't wake me up. Now that Aunt Maxi was in a bit of a pickle, every little noise had woken me up.

"Is everything okay?" The phone came to life when I picked it up off the bedside table.

Patrick turned over in the bed to check on me.

"Yeah. Better than okay. It's Spencer. He said the Bean Hive is clear and I can open in the morning."

"That's great, honey." Patrick wrapped an arm around Sassy, barely making it over to me, snuggling his girls for a minute before he and she went back to their snoring.

The disturbance had woken Pepper, who'd been sleeping at the foot of the bed. He made his way up alongside the bed. When giving him a couple of chest scratches didn't make him lie next to me, I knew he needed to go potty.

"Okay." It was all I had to say for him to jump off the bed and scuttle out of the room.

I didn't have to worry about being so quiet. Sassy and Patrick slept so hard that I could've turned on the lights while singing a chipper Christmas tune at the top of my lungs, and they'd never wake up.

Still, to be respectful, I peeled back the cover and slipped my feet into my fuzzy slippers. I grabbed my long robe from the chair next to the bedroom door and headed down the steps to let Pepper go outside. Then I put my phone in the robe pocket.

After his sweater was nice and snug around his little furry body, I told him, "I'll keep the door cracked."

While Pepper went potty, I walked over to the wood burner to check the fire. The embers were red and orange. A couple of pieces of wood sat next to the stove. I opened the little cast-iron door and threw them in.

Patrick had stocked plenty of wood on the porch between a couple of the rockers. I had nothing better to do, so I went out there, filled my arms with wood, and made a couple of trips to refill the bin inside.

Pepper joined me on the last load. He shook the snow off his coat and sat in front of the fire to warm his sweet little body.

"I guess I'm wide awake." I pulled the phone out of my robe pocket and noticed it was three a.m. "Why is Spencer texting me now?" I wondered.

The kettle was in the kitchen, and a good cup of cowboy coffee would wake me up, since I had no reason to hang around here for another hour. I was definitely going to go open the coffeehouse.

I peeked out the kitchen window while the water from the faucet filled the kettle. There was even more snow than when we'd gone to bed.

After the kettle filled, I walked over and put it on top of the stove.

"You look comfy," I told Pepper. He had curled up tight in the dog bed next to the fire. I went back to the kitchen to put some coffee grounds in a cup.

It didn't take long before the water was boiling, and I poured in my cup. The steam rolled out of the spout and continued to boil when I put the kettle back on. I set the cup on the coffee table and retrieved one of the afghan blankets from the basket next to the couch. Then I eased down on the sofa, settling in with my cup in one hand and my phone in the other.

I hated to do it, but I knew I had to.

I hit the apps store on my phone and downloaded the social media app on which Birdie and Alva had found this guy who'd been involved with Lana.

"I guess I've got to do this." I groaned, making my stomach hurt, since I'd been so against this whole social media thing. "It's for the good of Aunt Maxi and Lana."

It made me feel better to put it that way.

With all my information typed in and confirmation from an email they'd sent me, I was well on my way to getting into Cam Beard's social media profile.

"I guess we have to be friends for me to see your stuff." I hit the request button, and nothing happened. "Hhmmm." I tried to figure out why I couldn't see his stuff but quickly realized he had to accept me as his friend. "Oh no. He's going to see that I asked to be a friend." I gulped and quickly regretted the whole social media thing. I put the phone down.

Some tension built inside of me. This whole thing was new, and I didn't care for it.

I let go of a long, disappointed sigh and sipped on my coffee.

A notification lit up my phone.

"Cam Beard accepted your friend request," I read and hit the notification, which took me straight to his social media account.

Literally, I had to force myself to put the phone down and get ready for work. Not that it was hard to go into the laundry room, put on my uniform, and drive Pepper and myself to the boardwalk. But this social media had a hold that seemed to mesmerize me.

It was like Cam's relationship was a documentary right there on his profile, and his was linked to Lana's. I didn't bother asking to be her friend because she was dead.

I continued to flip through the photos of them on his account, using my fingers a few times to blow up the images. I needed to look at her face, read her body language. Nothing told me she was scared or worried for her life around him.

They were sweet photos.

"We've got to get to work." I finally forced myself to come out from underneath the warm blanket and put the phone down so I could get ready.

Pepper knew the drill, and he was waiting by the door for me when he saw me pulling my snow boots on my feet.

I'd given Pepper a little kibble in his bowl to occupy him while I went out to start the car, warm it up, and get the piles of snow off it.

While the car warmed and Pepper snacked, I got right back on social media and flipped through Cam's photos. I wanted to see if there were any work photos or anything else that would tell me where to find him.

Only I didn't have enough time to get through them all, since Pepper barked at the door, letting me know it was time for us to go.

I flipped on the radio and heard the weather report. The tree limbs along the edge of the road were filled with piles of snow. Sometimes when that happened to the trees, the snow would also be thick on the power lines, which could make the power and the internet go out.

That wouldn't be good for getting the coffeehouse open.

By the time I'd made it to the boardwalk, parked, and gathered Pepper, the radio hadn't broadcast an updated weather report, so I just took the chance that all was good at the coffeehouse.

Since Pepper had already done his morning business, I carried him to the Bean Hive and quickly got us inside.

I flipped on the lights and even turned up the furnace, which I knew I would have to do before I even got the fire going. It was one of those chill-to-the-bone mornings, and it was going to take a while before my joints got moving.

"Here you go." I put some kibble in Pepper's bowl to finish off his morning breakfast. While he ate, I went into the kitchen and noticed a few things out of place, which had to be from Spencer's search. Nothing too bad.

While I waited for the ovens to heat, I put everything back in place and made my way to the freezer to take out today's breakfast choice and the usuals.

Pepper was sitting at the front door of the coffeehouse, looking out at the door like he was surveying the large snowflakes.

One by one, I flipped on the industrial coffee pots that'd been set a few days before and yet brewed even though Spencer had shut me down. They gurgled to life.

"Good morning." Birdie popped through the door.

"Birdie, what are you doing here?" I asked, since I'd yet to call her or Bunny about Spencer letting me open the Bean Hive.

"I couldn't sleep, so I decided to come hang out here, but it looks like you're opening. Did Grandmawmaw tell you not to call me?" She looked like she was about to cry.

"I've not heard from Loretta." I hurried over to her and helped her out of her wet coat. "Spencer texted me and let me know I could open, so I thought I'd get in here early and see what they'd rummaged through before I called you or Bunny."

We walked over to the fireplace and worked together to get the fire started.

"What's going on?" I didn't want to let her know Loretta had told me she'd called Elliot, Birdie's dad, to come get her for Christmas.

This was their family business, not mine.

"They think I need to leave Honey Springs until this murder gets solved, but I told them I didn't need Grandmawmaw to keep me company. This is the last thing I planned to happen." She batted her eyes and sniffed.

"Last thing?" I asked, wondering if she'd just implicated herself in a plot to make Loretta a teeny-tiny bit sick with something like... methanol so she didn't have to go back home.

"Yeah. I hoped my family would come here, not me leave." She eased down on the couch, vigorously rubbing her cold hands together. "I feel like Honey Springs is my home. Who wants to be away from home for Christmas?"

I could relate so much to her feelings. At her age, I would come visit then have to leave when it was time for school to start.

"Things have a way of working themselves out." I was leery of giving her any advice.

"That's what you have to say?" She looked at me funny. "You are always giving me good advice, and this time you're telling me to just let it work out?"

"It's Christmas. Maybe your parents want you to come home to their home because they don't know how you feel about Honey Springs feeling like home." I walked over to the coffee pots and switched them out so I could start the ones for the Cocoon Hotel's hospitality room. "Take this time to tell them how you feel about it here."

"I guess I could do that." Birdie shrugged, making me think she really wasn't going to listen to me. "They never take my feelings into consideration. I would have to do something to get their attention first."

"I'm sure your parents miss you, and right now, I think they will listen. You've grown up so much over the past few months, and they will be able to see that." She started to fidget while I tried to encourage her to talk to her parents before she did anything rash. Or had she already done something that was just too unthinkable to consider?

No. I shoved aside the thought that she'd actually tried to make Loretta sick and accidentally killed Lana in the process.

"Why don't you take today to walk around the coffeehouse to make sure customers are happy," I suggested. I didn't want her around food.

You know, just in case.

"I want you to have a good day." I lied right to her face, her eyes wide open like she was trying to figure out what I was doing. "Which brings me to that." I pointed at the door when I saw Louise coming in with the old lady. "Louise said our furry friend needs some loving. There's no one who can give more snuggles, hugs, pats and treats than you."

Birdie hurried over to the cage and took it from Louise.

"I'm so glad you got here when you did," I told Louise. "I think Birdie needs some good cat therapy today."

"Charlotte is the best at giving all the therapy one needs." Louise referred to the older cat as Charlotte.

"She's got a little arthritis and is a little older, but other than that, she's purr-fect." Louise cracked a joke, making Birdie and me laugh.

"She's precious." I couldn't help myself. I went to go rub down the tortie feline. "You and Charlotte will greet all the customers today."

"That's paws-itively perfect." Birdie snickered and took Charlotte over to the couch, where Pepper waited to check her out.

"Everything okay?" Louise took me by the elbow as we walked back to the counter. "Birdie seems a little off."

"Yeah. I think with the murder, her parents want her to come home for Christmas, and she really doesn't want to." I poured Louise a cup of coffee. "Enjoy. Christmas Blend."

I glanced over Louise's shoulder and felt ashamed of myself for even thinking young Birdie could harm anyone, given the way she was taking care of Charlotte.

"What if I ask her to come to Pet Palace to volunteer a few days? Do you think that'd help her get out of here?" Louise caught me off guard.

"I'm sorry?" I asked and moved the brewed coffee for the hotel from the maker so I could start preparing the coffee for the coffee bar.

"Sometimes you can hear people in here talking about what's happening, and in this instance, it's the murder, which is really not for young ears." Louise looked over at Birdie. "Not that she's so young, but her parents could be worried she's hearing too much."

"I admit there's a lot of chatter in here." My gut gnawed. "I guess you could see if she wants to help out."

The bell over the door dinged, announcing the first customer of the day.

"Just think about it and let me know." Louise tapped the counter with her hand. "Have a great day with Charlotte," she called to Birdie on her way out.

Birdie barely lifted her head to acknowledge Louise's comment, though she did have a faint smile on her face.

The customers were filing in one by one as the sunrise peeked its head over Lake Honey Springs, which was almost frozen over. This was just in time for the upcoming opening of the winter ice skating rink, which had a long tradition even when I was a kid. The place wasn't an actual skating rink, but the locals made sure it was good and iced over before anyone decided to go out there on ice skates and roll around. It was a lot of fun to sit at the long window table in the front of the coffeehouse to watch a pick-up game of hockey.

"Have a good day," I called to a couple of customers on their way out. I sent Camey a text to let her know I was alone this morning. Though Birdie was physically there, she'd yet to move from the couch, which was what I wanted her to do.

Camey texted back that it was no problem and added that she'd send Walker up to grab the coffee and pastries.

I got their hospitality items gathered and took them up to the window bar, where I sucked in a few deep breaths. The window bar was actually my favorite spot in the Bean Hive, and today would show a gorgeous view of the lake with all the fresh snow lying on top.

"Good morning," I greeted another customer and left the Cocoon Hotel items on the window bar so Walker could grab them and go.

"What can I get started for you?" I asked the customer and waited for them to look down the display case.

With more and more customers filtering in and out, Birdie recognized the crowd and got up, leaving Charlotte on the cat tree up in the corner next to the Christmas tree.

"Louise mentioned something about you possibly going to volunteer at Pet

Palace, since you're great with the animals." I had all the orders lined up along the counter.

One after the other, we made them. Birdie was so good at being a barista, I wasn't sure how I would handle her leaving me for Pet Palace.

"Nah. I'm good here." Birdie glanced at me and smiled.

Birdie and I tackled the morning rush. There were a few inquiries about Charlotte, but it was going to be hard to place her, since most people were looking for puppies and kittens for Christmas presents.

"This weather is cramping my style." Bunny Bowowski shuffled through the door. She shrugged off her coat and shook the snow off it, pulled out one of the café table chairs closest to the door, and sat down to exchange her snow boots for her comfy tennis shoes. "I love snow, but this is getting ridiculous."

"I love it," Birdie said. "Meet Charlotte."

"She looks as old as me," Bunny snarled.

"She's spunky like you too." Birdie made Bunny jerk up a little taller.

"We old gals have to stick together." Bunny got up and headed over to the cat tree. "Ain't that right, Charlotte?"

It was sweet that Bunny loved on the tortie feline before she walked back to get the down low on the events of today and the recent past.

"Get to the good stuff." She wanted to know what was going on with the murder after I filled her in on Charlotte and how the morning had gone.

"I don't know a whole lot." I ran my fingers through my hair. "I do have a hair appointment at the Honey Comb Salon, so I'm hoping there's a bit of gossip there. Then I'm going to run down to see Kevin."

"The morgue?" Bunny wondered. "Why on earth would you go there?"

"I want to see what Kevin has to say about the poison." My eyes shifted to look at Birdie, but my face stayed still.

"What? Birdie?" Bunny leaned in.

My subtle movement hadn't gone unnoticed.

"Roxanne," she gasped in a whisper.

"What?" My chin jutted forward. "Is it that impossible?"

"I'd be ashamed." She reached around me and got a ceramic mug to pour herself a cup of coffee. "After everything that poor girl has done for you. You can't possibly hold it against her that she's related to Low-retta."

"Of course not. I can't help but wonder if she used her chemistry skills to make Loretta a tad bit ill so her parents wouldn't make her come home for Christmas." My jaw tensed, and my eyes grew big as I tried to silently tell Bunny to hush because Birdie was walking over.

"How's the coffee?" Birdie asked Bunny. "I roasted it perfect, didn't I?"

Coffee shot out of Bunny's mouth.

"Are you okay?" Birdie asked.

"I don't think I'm in the mood for coffee this afternoon." Bunny slowly poured the hot cup of coffee down the sink behind the counter.

CHAPTER SIXTEEN

Down at the Honey Comb Salon, more than hair always got twisted, if you know what I mean. If you didn't hear gossip over coffee chat, you sure could sit underneath the hair dryer and listen in.

That was exactly what I'd planned to do before I got on the social media.

"What is it you're doing?" Alice Dee asked as she dug her nails deep down into my hair and pulled it out to see exactly where she needed to put in some dye. "Are you on that Instagram?"

She looked over my shoulder. I could hear her chomping away on her gum.

"Hey there, Roxy." Jessica greeted me when she walked in. The puppy's head hung over the top of Jessica's purse.

"Is that a dog in your pocketbook?" Alice asked.

Jessica snorted and laughed.

"No, it's a dog carrier, but I would use it as a purse." She rubbed her hand along the front of it. "Biscuit loves it."

"Good golly, I've seen it all." Alice waved a comb in the air. "Honey, where you from?"

"This is Jessica, and she's a local now," I spoke up.

Jessica smiled at me.

"She is Kirk's wife. Biscuit is from the Pet Palace." I didn't continue to scroll through my phone. I felt the heat of stares.

"I love it here," Jessica whispered in an unsure tone. "I noticed you take walk-in nail clients." She pointed at the door, Biscuit's head bobbling as her forearm moved. "I'm in desperate need of a manicure."

"Sure, honey. You go on over there and pick out a color. We'll be right with you." Alice Dee Spicer gave me the side eye.

"She's nice. It's fine." I assured Alice Dee that I was appreciative of her loyalty, but it wasn't necessary. Then I took the stack of squared pieces of tinfoil from her.

"Anyways, I heard 'bout that poison killing Low-retta's hired hand." Alice Dee did exactly what I wanted—start right on in about the murder. "And it was from the platter."

"You mean the Seifert platter?" one of the ladies in another salon chair asked.

"Yep." Alice Dee took the sharp end of her comb, making strands with my hair before slapping some color paste on it. She poked at my shoulder.

I handed her a square of tinfoil.

"I told Beverly Teagarden she shouldn't try to sell that china. Especially the platter."

"And there you go. She sold it, and someone turned up dead," an employee of the Honey Comb said. She meandered over to look at Jessica's nails. "You want a gel nail or something else?"

"Gel." Jessica nodded and handed the color to the manicurist.

"You want this color, but it's for acrylic. So pick you out a gel color over there." She directed Jessica to another part of the bookcase lined with polishes used for the style of nail she wanted. "I'll be right back."

She left Jessica and Biscuit to go check on someone under the other dryer.

"My mama told me all about that platter, and when I heard the bank had released the stuff in the barn, I thought about that dish." She made Alice stop slapping the dye on my hair.

"I know. I couldn't believe it." Alice Dee shook her head and held her hand out for me to give her another piece of foil.

"What are you talking about?" I asked.

"That platter is death. That's why they stopped having those fancy Christmas parties." Alice began to tell a fascinating story. "Christmas death. Twice."

"Twice?" I wanted to make sure I heard her correctly over the hair dryers and chitchat between the other clients and hairdressers.

"Mm-hmmm," the manicurist hummed from behind my chair on her way back to see what gel color Jessica had picked out. "You go sit right there, honey."

Jessica went over to the table and sat down in the chair. She put Biscuit's carrier on the floor, took him out, and set him in her lap.

"He ain't gonna jump down, is he? Because we can't have any of that," Alice Dee said.

"He's really good. He'll stay right here." Jessica put her hands on the towel-covered wrist pillow when the manicurist tapped her fingers on it.

"What about the two deaths?" I wanted to get right back to the topic.

"It was Mrs. Seifert's mother then sister." Alice stared at my reflection in the mirror. "I'm guessing you've not heard about this?"

"No." I didn't dare move my head in fear her dye paint brush would slip and give me a skunk look.

"Honey, hush." She drew back. "Let me tell you it was a big thing around here then. Now we seem to get a lot of, *ahem*, crime. But back then, when someone died for no apparent reason, it was unheard of."

"Gosh. I couldn't imagine losing my mom or a sister in one holiday." I didn't have any siblings, but losing someone during the holidays had to be tough.

"It was a year apart, not in the same year," Alice clarified. "The first time the Christmas party turkey was served, Mrs. Seifert's mom cut it. She took the first bite out of it and keeled over."

I wasn't sure where she was going with this tale.

"Back then, when someone keeled over, it was just assumed it was a heart attack." Her voice grew mysterious. "Then the next year, Mrs. Seifert's sister, who lived with them—well, both the mom and sister lived at the Seifert mansion. Anyways, I'm getting off topic."

She stuck her hand out. I gave her a piece of tinfoil.

"Then the next year, the sister cut it," she started over. "Took a bite, keeled over right there."

"Was she older?" I asked.

"In her forties. That ain't a bit old, even for back then." Alice took the stack of tinfoil out of my hands. "You go on over to that dryer next to your friend Jessica."

I caught a wry smile on her face before she looked away.

"Did they figure out what happened to the sister?" I asked on my way over to the chair.

"Mr. Seifert was a magician, and he said he'd gotten the Christmas china somewhere out west, and it was rumored to be haunted, so he continued until his death to say it was the platter, since it was the only time Mrs. Seifert had ever used it." Alice pulled the helmet-style hair dryer over my hair and twisted the dial. "He had a creepy smile. Remember how thin and tall he was. Then he wore all that jewelry. Rings on all his fingers."

The ticking noise from the hair dryer timer counting down sounded loud to me.

"And nothing ever came of it?" I asked.

"Not a thing. They stopped doing the parties. Mrs. Seifert was rumored to go into a deep seclusion." Alice frowned. "Now you sit under there for twenty minutes. I'll get you a water and some magazines."

She took off before I was finished with my questions.

"So no one ever used the dishes again? Or looked into the deaths?" I had to be clear on this strange and intriguing story.

"That's why Loretta is so crazy about those dishes. She was at both of the parties with the deaths." Jessica put in her two cents, which she'd obviously heard from Kirk. "When she heard your Aunt Maxi had gotten it from the Teagardens, well, let's just say she told Kirk some colorful words."

"And now we have three deaths because of that platter," the manicurist said and filed away on Jessica's nails.

"Maybe I can get Kevin to test the platter," I said and took the ten-year-old magazines and glass of water from Alice Dee.

The idea was a long shot, but it was definitely something to explore.

"Talk about Christmas past. You can't get any more past to the future than that." The manicurist tried to give a parallel to *A Christmas Carol*.

"Someone sure is playing Scrooge." Alice Dee gathered up all the items she used on my hair and disappeared into the back of the salon with them.

CHAPTER SEVENTEEN

The snow was really coming down when I left the Honey Comb. The fluffy stuff had completely covered the boardwalk and the top of the lake, and the sky was grey. This told me the snow wasn't letting up anytime soon.

There was no reason to keep the coffeehouse open, so I made a beeline to the Bean Hive.

"It's coming down!" Bunny and Birdie were sitting at the window bar. Not a single customer was inside. "Birdie's been fussing with her parents, who are insisting she come home tonight now that there's a huge nor'easter coming through."

"I haven't heard the weather." I shifted my focus to Birdie. "I'm sorry. It seems like there's not much you can do but go home for Christmas."

"This is my home." She jumped off the stool and headed to the back of the shop.

"She's been a pill since you left." Bunny sighed and rolled her eyes. "She's saying all sorts of crazy things like she's going to run away. I've tried talking to her."

"She won't run away." I put an arm on Bunny. "Thank you for listening to her. Why don't you go grab your coat, and I'll take you home."

We walked to the back, where Birdie was on the phone, arguing with someone I assumed to be her dad. Bunny opened the glass display case doors and boxed up the leftover food. I poured out the coffee carafes.

"This is my home!" she screamed as she took the phone from her ear. "I just hung up on him."

"I'm closing the coffeehouse for the day, so why don't you go home and give Loretta one more good try." She met my suggestion with a wiggle of her head.

"I can stay and clean up." Birdie would do anything to stay and not leave.

"Nah. It's getting pretty slick out there, and the rest of this stuff can wait."

Birdie's face reddened with anger, but she didn't say anything else. She put her coat on and scratched Charlotte on her way out.

"Is that Alva's ring?" I noticed it on Birdie's pointer finger.

"Yeah, we did a little Christmas exchange, and I gave her a Bean Hive gift card, and she gave me the ring. She said she didn't have any money to buy a gift." Birdie looked at it. "I told her that I'd just wear it for a few days and give it back. It's present enough." She shrugged.

"I'm glad you found a friend. Now, I'm going to take Charlotte home with me. We gals have to stick together." Bunny was a softie at heart. This wouldn't be the first Pet Palace adoptee she took home. "We might even have an early Christmas snack because this snow makes me feel like it's Christmas."

"I'll get my stuff and be right back." I went to the back to make sure all the ovens and roasters were turned off.

Bunny was waiting by the door, all bundled up in her snow boots and coat with Charlotte tucked in her arms. She'd already gotten Pepper's coat on him and the leash attached to his collar.

"We old gals are ready to go." There was a twinkle in Bunny's eyes.

"All righty." I took the leash. Once we were all outside, I flipped off the lights and locked the door behind us.

"What did Kevin say?" Bunny asked on our way to the car.

I had tucked my arm in hers just in case she fell, but she was doing better than me.

Pepper was darting around, sticking his nose deep in the snow. He loved the white stuff.

"I didn't go see him yet. The snow has kinda put a damper on things." I was going to see what the roads were like and possibly stop by if they weren't as bad as I thought they were.

"I can go with you." Bunny leaned a little more on me when we walked down the steps, since Charlotte prevented her from holding on to the railing. "Me and Charlotte are curious. Two old biddies."

I laughed and thought it wasn't a bad idea in case I needed to snoop.

"You could keep Kevin busy while I look around." I smiled at her.

"I even brought some of your Christmas cookies with me, and I could give him some." She stood next to the door of my car, and I opened it and helped her in.

"You're so good." I loved how Pepper knew the drill. When someone was in the passenger seat, Pepper was more than happy to share and sit in the back. "Everyone ready?" I asked, looking over at Bunny to make sure she got her seat belt on. Then I looked in the rearview mirror at Pepper in the back seat with his doggy seat belt on.

Bunny made some chitchat to keep silence at bay the entire way to the morgue. I didn't hear a word of it, since my head was filled with things I wanted to learn from my little field trip there.

"I've never seen a body in the morgue." Bunny took off her scarf and made a little bed for Charlotte.

"You don't need to go in. Why don't you stay with the kids?" I wanted to give her an out, since her paling face had gotten visibly whiter on our way over.

"Are you sure?" she asked and took a box of my Christmas cookies out of her bag. "Here."

"I will tell him they are from you." I gave another glance over my shoulder at Pepper. "You stay and be a good boy."

"We will be just fine," Bunny told me and rubbed down Charlotte.

I got out of the car and headed into the building where Kevin had moved the morgue from the funeral home over the past year.

I'd not gone inside before, and I certainly didn't expect to see three stainless steel tables with three sheet-covered bodies on them once I found Kevin in the building.

My stomach got a little queasy at the sight.

"It gets everyone their first time." Kevin snickered when he saw I was about to give him a preview of what I'd eaten today. "Grab a pair of gloves and hold your hand over your nose."

To the right of the door ran a counter with some paper gowns in their own packaging, along with three boxes of gloves in sizes small, medium, and large.

I turned away, ripped open the package, and pulled the gown over my coat. I couldn't get the gloves on and plunge my nose deep into my hands fast enough. I got a medium pair of gloves, noticing they were too big. No need to replace them, since I didn't plan on being here any longer than needed or on feeling anything while I was here.

"What is that smell?" I asked, happy to see he'd covered the body he was working on.

"It could be a range of a lot of things, but since you aren't used to any of the amazing scents," he teased, "I'm guessing your reaction is going to be the same every time you stop in to visit. Which is what this is, right? A little visit?"

"I brought you some cookies." I found my coat pocket underneath the gown and pulled them out.

"You mean to tell me you made these just for me and brought them here?" He was waiting for me to tell him the truth about why I was there.

"You know why I'm here." I felt so sick watching him eat a cookie. "How can you eat in here?"

"It's no different than your job. You talk to people all day long, and I talk to people all day long, only your people talk back, and my people don't," he said through a mouthful of cookie. "Well, their bodies talk to me, and right now I bet you want to know about Lana."

He used his finger to brush off the crumbs on his bottom lip.

"Is there anything you can tell me?" I asked.

"Legally, no." He put the rest of the cookies on the metal tray table next to his scalpel.

I shivered.

"As your friend, I can tell you there was poison found in her stomach on part of the chipped beef. I'm not saying Maxine did anything, and I'm not saying she didn't. I am saying someone did." He sighed and frowned. "Poor girl. I really hate it when I get younger and younger people."

He pointed at the two other bodies, which told me the body we were currently standing near was Lana.

"Those two were old, which is a standard autopsy for their family. I get those, but young people is really hard." A call rang from his office, and his head jerked up. "I've got to get that. Hold on." He started to walk off, but then he said, "Now, friends, don't try to talk to Roxy."

He snickered, leaving me alone with them when he walked through the office door.

"Did you happen to test the platter all over?" I asked in a loud voice. "Or possibly there's still something in it from the past murders of the Seiferts?"

"You believe that old wives' tale?" He laughed so hard from his office. "No way."

I took a couple of steps back, and when my shoes hit the cabinets in the back of the room, I knew I couldn't get any farther away from them unless I climbed on top of the counters. I patted my hand around to see if anything was on them, thinking climbing was an option.

But when I felt some clothes, I turned around and noticed it was the same shirt and pants Lana had on when I'd seen her that day.

"Oh." I pulled my hands away, feeling icky. The pants leg fell off the counter's ledge and dangled. "I don't want to touch this." With my finger and thumb I reached out really far and picked up the edge of the pants to put back, but it felt heavy.

I shook it and realized something was in her pants pockets.

Kevin was so loud, I knew he was still on his phone call, so I started to shuffle through Lana's pants pockets to see why they felt leavy.

"Her phone." To say I was shocked at my find was an understatement and a big break. I needed to see who she talked to and at what time. Plus, I wanted to see if I could score Cam's number because his social media profile made it difficult to find out where this kid worked.

So many things were running through my head, things that I had to see on her phone to gain insight into what she'd been doing before she died.

The gloves I'd picked were too big. The fingertips hung down too long, and they didn't help me as I fumbled with the phone.

"Fingerprint." The steam ran out of me when I noticed that Lana had used the fingerprint-locked screen option to open the phone. "Fingerprint," I said to myself and slid my gaze over to the table. "Seriously, Roxanne?" I talked to myself. Then I answered, "You can do this."

I didn't let myself think too hard on my walk over to the table. I just needed a fingerprint. Lana's fingerprint. And the only way I knew I could get it, well, it was to peel back the sheet over top of her body, take her finger, and lay it on the button of the phone.

"Ewww." All the icky factors that you'd think would happen—the "oh my gosh I'm touching a dead girl's hand" and the idea of messing with a corpse—really did start to gnaw at me when I barely lifted the edge of the sheet and looked at her hand.

"What are you doing?" Bunny said, scaring the Christmas spirit right out of me.

"What are you doing?" I asked her.

"I've got to pee." She waddled up behind me. "Is that her?"

"Yes. And this is her phone. I need her fingerprint to open it." I showed Bunny the phone.

"Heck far." She tugged the sheet up on the side and pulled out Lana's hand. "Here you go."

"You are crazy." I nervously took the phone with my shaking hand, put it up underneath the finger, and let Bunny press her finger down. "Got it." I gasped when the phone sprang to life.

"Bunny? Roxy?" Kevin had come back into the room.

Bunny and I had been so focused on Lana's finger and phone we didn't hear him.

"Oh Lord," Bunny groaned, starting to pat Lana's hand, "we ask you to please bless this child and give her family peace."

I fell to my knees and put my hands in prayer position with my head slightly tucked so I could not only hide the phone but also thumb through her text messages and last phone calls.

Bunny was carrying on with a prayer.

"Shush," she told Kevin. "We are here for a prayer over this poor girl, and we are gonna do it. Do you understand me, Kevin?"

"Yes, ma'am," Kevin agreed. Though I couldn't see his face, I knew he was giving Bunny respect.

"Close your eyes," she instructed him. When he had them closed, she looked down at me. "Okay," she mouthed then continued to carry on.

I slid my phone out from underneath the gown and started to type in the phone's note sections the number of the last text, which matched the number of the last phone call.

The text message mentioned a date and a time but not a place. It was very cryptic, and I didn't have time to read all the messages, but I had the number, and it was a start.

Slowly I stood up and tiptoed backward over to the counter where I found Lana's clothes and put the phone in between the pants and shirt, not bothering to put it back in the pocket where I'd found it.

"All righty. We are done." Bunny lifted her chin.

Kevin looked back at me. "Why are you all the way over there?"

"It's all part of it, Kevin." Bunny shook her head. "Do we need anything else?"

"Yes. What time do you put Lana's time of death?" I slipped it in, not knowing if he would answer or not.

"That's not public knowledge." Kevin shifted on his feet and clasped his hands in front of him.

"Now, Kevin," Bunny said in her soft tone, "we have to know when so we can pray at that moment tonight."

"Fine." Kevin shuffled back to his office. "I can't remember off the top of my head."

"You are a genius," I told her through my gritted teeth and pumped my fist in the air. "But don't you think the whole church thing might be a little too much? I mean, what if we get struck dead right here?"

"Why? I can certainly pray for her. It's not a lie." Bunny made it all work out. Thanks to her, I had a number.

No name.

A number.

CHAPTER EIGHTEEN

Bunny's adrenaline must've made her bladder forget she had to go to the bathroom because the two of us jingled our way right out of there as quick as we could. We laughed the entire way to her house at how ridiculous it was for us to do what we just did.

"We are going to get put in jail." She snuggled Charlotte with one arm and retrieved her house keys with her other hand.

"Nah. If I find anything out with this number, I'll give it to Spencer. I really just want to find this Cam guy." I was sure the number was his. "Okay, well, I'll let you know about work tomorrow. As of right now, Pepper and I will go in if we can, and maybe you can come in later, but don't come out until I call."

In my mind, I was thinking it would just be a day for me. I wasn't sure where Birdie was going to be, in town or home.

"Thinking of the devil," I joked when I saw Loretta's name pop up on my phone. "It's Loretta. I'll talk to you later."

Bunny got out of the car with Charlotte, and I waited to make sure she got into her house before I gave my attention to the phone.

"I was just thinking about you and Birdie," I said, answering the phone.

"Is she with you?" Loretta sounded desperate and scared.

"No. What's going on?" I held the phone steady up to my ear.

"She said she was going to run off and hasn't come home. I was thinking she might've gone to the coffeehouse." Heavy breathing and a few sniffs came through the phone.

"Why don't I run by there, and I'll give you a call either way." I felt awful. I should've called Loretta when Birdie had mentioned doing something, but I figured it was teen girl talk.

"Either way," Loretta reiterated before she hung up the phone.

"Pepper, looks like we are going back to the Bean Hive." I turned around in Bunny's driveway and headed back toward town then straight to the boardwalk.

It was on the way home and not out of the way.

"Do you think she waited for us to leave before she went back?" I glanced in the rearview mirror at Pepper. He was fidgeting in his seat belt, trying to get to the front seat. "Maybe she went back to blow off steam and clean up."

That had to be it. She'd wanted to clean up, and she was good at it. Cleaning always helped me keep my mind occupied when I was upset or frustrated.

I pulled into the parking spot.

"Why don't you wait here?" I told Pepper and left my car running. "I won't be but a minute."

My plan was to see if Birdie was there, call Loretta, and take Birdie home or at least follow her home.

Before I got out of the car, I looked at my phone's notes and decided to give the number from Lana's call log, the last call she made, a ring-a-ling.

The phone rang a few times before heading to voice mail.

You knew the sound when someone sent you to voice mail. That was what it was.

I called again.

"Hi." I knew it was a long shot for a killer to call me back, but I gave it a good try. "My name is Roxanne Bloom Cane." I was still trying to get used to the new last name, though it was so new. "I am calling because you're the last person Lana called, and, well, I have some news for you. Please call me back."

If Cam got a nice message, and it didn't seem like I was calling to see if he killed her but to inform him she'd passed, then maybe he'd call me back.

"Just call me at this number. Thanks so much." I hung up the phone and put it in my coat pocket as I got out of the car.

The air was so cold, my fingers were numb before I'd even made it to the steps of the boardwalk. I tried to look around the parking lot to see if Birdie's car was there. When I didn't see it, I considered the great possibility she'd parked in the parking lot on the other side of the boardwalk.

I picked up my gait and thought about the clues to keep me from thinking about the freezing temperatures.

I was at a loss for words about who really killed Lana and just how the poison got into Aunt Maxi's appetizer.

I hated to admit it, but I was going to have to rely on anything Kirk came up with. He'd had skin in the lawyer game and still kept all the contacts we used when we were chasing leads for our old practice's clients, so it was only good practice to use his resources. I needed to tell him to break the platter and test it for possible poison. You never knew how things were made back then. Maybe no one poisoned Lana deliberately, and the problem was the old platter, just as it was when Mrs. Seifert's mom and sister died.

Time was running out, and Spencer was on pins and needles watching the days and hours click by just so he could make an arrest.

I looked down the boardwalk and noticed the stretch of it in front of the Bean Hive had a glow, just like it did when the lights were on in there.

I zipped up my jacket and decided to head down that way to make sure Birdie had turned off the lights. When I saw she hadn't, I took out my keys and unlocked the door.

"At least she locked the door behind her." I felt bad for not trying to help her process the plan her parents wanted for her.

Going home for Christmas was weighing on her mind even more than I realized.

I looked in the window to see if she was in there, but I didn't see her, which really meant nothing. She could be in the back, roasting beans or doing something with some crazy chemicals.

"Stop thinking that way," I told myself because it was ridiculous that Birdie could hurt anyone. I let myself in.

"Birdie?" I called and decided to head into the kitchen when I noticed her backpack was on the coffee bar.

On my way to the kitchen, I glanced behind the counter. A suitcase was sitting on the floor.

"Birdie?" I pushed through the door and didn't see anyone in there.

My eyes darted around the kitchen, where I noticed the mixer hadn't been washed, the ovens were still on, and a chill was coming from the freezer.

"What on earth?" I turned off the ovens on my way to check the freezer door. If the seal was broken, I would have to call Patrick to come fix it for the night until I could get someone from the company I'd bought it from to repair it.

It would be a catastrophe if I'd lost all the food in there.

"No wonder it's cold in here." Frustration nipped at me when I noticed the door was slightly ajar. When I went to shut it, something shuffled inside. I pulled it open. "Birdie?"

For a second, I stopped to process what I was seeing.

"What on earth?" I hurried in and ran to Birdie's side to pull down the handkerchief in her mouth.

"Alva. Alva." She huffed for air and shifted around to let me untie her. "She is the killer."

"Alva from the diner?" I was having a hard time deciphering what was going on.

"Get out of here." She jumped to her feet and scrambled to the freezer door.

"I don't know about this." Alva stood at the freezer door with a metal mixing spoon in her hand. "I'm thinking I'm in a little situation. I mean, I thought I had it figured out when I planted the methanol in hopes the dimwit sheriff would find it. He'd seen me at the barn so many times." She rolled her eyes. "It was one of those things where he'd run me off for trespassing after the Teagardens told him someone looked like they were living there."

"Were you?" I asked.

"No. Not really. I had the dishes laid out and would recall the stories my mom would tell about her time there as a child." She stared off for a brief second.

"So your mom was at the parties?" I offered a smile so she would think I understood why she would kill Lana, though we'd not even gotten that information yet.

"Her parents worked the parties when she was a child. They lived with the Seiferts, and it was the stories I lived for. All the lavish food, the magic tricks." She shot Birdie a look. "That ring."

"This ring?" Birdie tugged it off her finger and flung it at Alva. "I don't want it."

The ring hit the floor, making a secret lid pop open.

"The magician ring." I sighed. "I should've known. That's how you poisoned Lana."

"Yep. She came into the diner, and I knew Maxine was going to switch the cheese balls because, well, let's face it." She strolled back and forth like the story she was telling was no big deal. She continued to smack the back end of the hard metal spoon in the palm of her other hand. "When you fill up people's cups at a diner, they forget you're there and just talk openly to whoever they're with."

"And you overheard all the conversations about the progressive dinner as well as Loretta's cooking. But why Lana? What did she do?" I had so many unanswered questions, and as they formed in my head, I started to recall Alva being everywhere over the past couple of days.

"The job she took was supposed to be my ticket to stealing the china back. You see, over the summer, the rumors swirled among the diner customers about how the bank was going to put the Seifert barn up for auction. The Teagardens had made this elaborate plan over dessert one night at one of my booths. They had the money and knew they'd make a mint off of Loretta by selling her the dishes, my dishes." Alva had no legal rights to the Christmas china other than memories she held dear. "It was also around the time she needed help, and I overheard her and Babette talking about hiring someone. I approached Loretta about the job, and she'd already filled it, so I waited and waited. Listening and listening, working as many shifts as I could so I could hear when the Seifert barn was up for auction before I made my move."

She stopped, twirled around on her toes, and slid her gaze to me.

"It gave me many months to plan and calculate just how I was going to do it, until Maxine threw her weight around and got the platter." She held the spoon in one hand and looked at the platter Spencer had dropped off, since he didn't need it for the case anymore.

She ran her finger along the edge of the rim of the platter.

"The platter was my mom's favorite. It's the only piece I really wanted." She sighed. "She told me how it was thought to have been the magical piece in the collection, like Mr. Seifert had told them. He gave her the ring, and it was the only thing I had left from her, so I wanted the platter. I did approach the Teagardens about it a long time ago, and they gave me a price that was ridiculous."

"I understand you wanted the platter, but why did you kill Lana? Why did you blame it on Aunt Maxi?"

"It was easy to become friends with Lana and Birdie. You see, girls like us, the outsiders, we will become friends with anyone who will talk to us and overlook anything that might seem odd or out of place." She shot Birdie a look. "Sorry, kid. I wasn't planning on tying you up tonight or whatever else happens."

I knew she was referring to killing us.

"But I saw the sheriff bring that platter in earlier tonight when I came in, and I knew I had to get my hands on it. You see I'd already gotten rid of the murder weapon." She pointed the end of the spoon at the ring. She walked over, picked it up, and slipped it on her finger. She gently closed the secret lid. "You see…" She dragged one of the donuts sitting on the workstation.

Birdie must've been in the process of putting away the pastries when Alva showed up.

"Loretta ordered a hamburger for her and Lana to split." She grinned and looked down at the donut. She slid one of my knives from the butcher block holder and sliced the donut in half, flipping the secret compartment of the ring open, demonstrating just how easy it was to slip the poison on the donut if the ring had methanol inside.

A shadow from the kitchen's swinging door window caught my eye. Someone was looking into the kitchen, and I knew from the big melon head who it was.

"Just like that. Lana ate the burger, and off they went."

"Just because you wanted the platter bad enough to have killed Lana?" I said loudly so Kirk, who I knew was on the other side of the door, heard me.

"Yes. Don't you get it? You don't. You have everything you've ever wanted. A family. A coffeehouse. A life with your mom. A husband." She took a step back, just enough for Kirk to forcefully push the door open, hitting Alva on the back, flinging her forward. When she went to catch herself, she dropped the heavy metal spoon.

"Don't forget she's got an ex-husband!" Kirk yelled, grabbing Alva by the arm.

The spoon skidded across the floor, and I stopped it with my shoe.

"I'd never thought I'd say I am so happy to see you." My shoulders hunched as relief blanketed me.

CHAPTER NINETEEN

Christmas Day Supper at the Bean Hive Coffeehouse a Few Days Later

"Here, Maxine, you be the first to try my famous cheese ball you've been warning everyone about." Loretta cackled and held up a cracker overflowing with a mashed-up yellow-and-white gooey mound. "I had you in my head the entire time I made it."

"You're crazy, Low-retta." Aunt Maxi shoved Loretta's hand away from her face.

The Christmas table was filled with all of Patrick's friends and mine. And our enemies.

I glanced over and made eye contact with Kirk. He offered a smile in some sort of peace offering before he turned to Jessica. If it weren't for Kirk, Birdie and I just might not be sitting here.

She looked at him with loving eyes, something I never recalled doing. For Kirk and me, we bonded over law and all things legal and illegal. If I was really honest, we loved getting into arguments over cases and who was right versus who was wrong.

Though I'd never condone what he did to end our marriage and the morality of it, I did accept that he was seeking a level of comfort and love that I wasn't able to give him. If I was totally honest with myself, there was always a piece of my heart that belonged to Patrick since the day I left Honey Springs and him behind when I went off to college.

Still, I'd never left Kirk, even if our marriage wasn't based on the sort of true love that it appeared we both had now. No matter what was behind us, saving Birdie and me from the freezer a few days ago had made up for what he'd done in the past.

It turned out Alva had already committed a few crimes around Kentucky. Apparently, she'd come to Honey Springs to connect with her family's past and realized the past was long buried with the Seifert family. She just wanted so badly a piece of the tales her mother told her that she was willing to do anything, even kill Lana to get a job with Loretta so she could steal the platter, and Alva didn't care about the consequences if she got caught.

"It's not just any platter. It's *the* platter." I heard Loretta's voice coming from inside the table when I heard her explaining to Spencer after he'd given Aunt Maxi the platter back with a bow on top.

"Good golly, Loretta," Aunt Maxi said, her voice dripping. "See, this is why I didn't ask you to host any part of the progressive supper. Can't you just let everyone have a good time without telling some big tale?" Aunt Maxi lifted the platter over the big turkey that sat in the middle of the banquet table and handed it to Loretta.

"It's no tale, Maxine. Everyone here has heard about the platter." Loretta smiled, admiring the ornate dish she'd so longed to have.

"It looks like everyone got everything they wanted this year," Patrick leaned over and whispered in my ear.

"This platter has seen a lot." Loretta rubbed her hands over it and referred to the tale of Christmas past with the Seiferts and why they'd decided to stop their holiday party.

"Spencer, did you ever talk to Cam?" Kirk asked.

"How did you know about Cam?" I asked.

"Maxine told me about how Birdie and Alva found his profile on Facebook, and I reported it to the sheriff like we should." Kirk made a point to let me know he disapproved of my keeping the phone number I'd found on Lana's phone to myself.

"And I followed up on it, and he was pretty devastated about Lana's death, but he's in college and wasn't even in town when it happened." Spencer picked up the spoon in the broccoli casserole dish and put it on his plate. "I asked Alva about it during her interrogation, and she said she knew about him because Lana had confessed to her about her ex-boyfriend."

It was so sad that Lana had thought Alva was her friend when Alva clearly used her to pinpoint a murder.

"Ended up showing it to Birdie and Maxine so it would take the heat off her, and she'd get out of town before the truth came out about him." Spencer took a big bite out of the turkey leg.

"If you'll excuse me." I gulped when I felt like I was going to be sick.

"Are you okay?" Mom jumped up, and so did Aunt Maxi, following me into the bathroom.

"I was hoping my queasiness was over now that the killer has been caught." I hurried over to the toilet, where I bent down in case I lost my slice of pie.

My mom pulled my hair back while Aunt Maxi wet a paper towel to stick on the back of my neck.

"I hate that you're sick on Christmas. This is awful." My mom rubbed my back with her free hand.

"Terrible. Nothing worse than being sick on Christmas." Aunt Maxi sighed.

My mom laughed.

"What's so funny?" I asked, my voice echoing from the inside of the toilet bowl.

"We've been in this exact situation before, only I was pregnant. Remember, Maxi?" Mom's laughter stopped.

"Now what?" I asked, trying not to lose that delicious piece of apple pie.

"I remember holding your hair back after you ate my delicious piece of apple pie. And on Christmas." Aunt Maxi gasped. "Roxanne."

"Oh, Roxy baby," my mom cried.

"What?" I twisted my head.

Mom dropped her hand from my hair and covered her mouth.

"Dang, Mom." I lifted my head so my hair wouldn't hit the water.

"Roxy, I bet you're pregnant."

Mom's words made me lose that pie.

THE END

If you enjoyed reading this book as much as I enjoyed writing it then be sure to return to the Amazon page and leave a review.

Go to Tonyakappes.com for a full reading order of my novels and while there join my newsletter. You can also find links to Facebook, Instagram and Goodreads.

RECIPES FROM THE BEAN HIVE

Kentucky Cowboy Casserole
Maple Cinnamon Latte
Red Velvet Whoopie Pies

Kentucky Cowboy Casserole

Ingredients

- 1 lb. breakfast sausage
- 1/3 lb. chopped fresh mushrooms
- 1 medium onion, chopped
- 10 eggs
- 4 tablespoons sour cream
- 8 tablespoons salsa
- 2 cups grated cheddar cheese
- 2 cups Monterey Jack cheese
- 2 cups shredded Mexican Velveeta cheese

Directions

1. Sauté sausage, mushrooms, and onions in a large skillet until done. Drain and set aside.
2. Combine eggs and sour cream and season with salt and pepper.
3. Whip egg mixture one minute in blender and pour into a 9 × 13-inch baking dish.
4. Bake in a preheated 400° oven until softly set (6 to 8 minutes).
5. Spoon salsa evenly over top of eggs. Spread sausage mixture over top.
6. Sprinkle with combined cheeses and refrigerate until 30 minutes before serving time.
7. Then bake in a 325° oven for 30 minutes.

Maple Cinnamon Latte

A cozy fall drink made for lazy Sunday mornings.

Ingredients

- ¾ cup milk
- ½ cup coffee (brewed as strong as you like)
- 1 – 1 ½ tbsp maple syrup
- ¼ tsp cinnamon, plus more for garnish
- Cinnamon stick, for garnish (optional)

Directions

1. Pour milk into a medium-sized mason jar and screw on the lid.
2. Shake for 10-15 seconds until foam starts to form at the top.
3. Remove lid and microwave jar for about 45 seconds or until milk is hot to the touch and foamy.
4. Keep an eye on the milk as you microwave to keep it from bubbling.
5. Pour hot coffee into a mug and stir in the maple syrup and cinnamon.
6. Top with milk, spooning the foam onto the top.
7. Sprinkle with cinnamon and serve with a cinnamon stick, if desired.

Red Velvet Whoopie Pies

Ingredients

- ¾ cup butter, softened
- 1 cup sugar
- 2 large eggs, room temperature
- ½ cup sour cream
- 1 tablespoon red food coloring
- 1 ½ teaspoons white vinegar
- 1 teaspoon clear vanilla extract
- 2 ¼ cups all-purpose flour
- ¼ cup baking cocoa
- 2 teaspoons baking powder
- ½ teaspoon salt
- ¼ teaspoon baking soda
- 2 ounces semisweet chocolate, melted and cooled

Ingredients for filling

- 1 package (8 ounces) cream cheese, softened
- ½ cup butter, softened
- 2 ½ cups confectioners' sugar
- 2 teaspoons clear vanilla extract

Toppings:

- White baking chips, melted
- Finely chopped pecans

Directions

1. Preheat oven to 375°. In a large bowl, cream butter and sugar until light and fluffy.

2. Beat in eggs, sour cream, food coloring, vinegar, and vanilla. In another bowl, whisk flour, cocoa, baking powder, salt, and baking soda; gradually beat into creamed mixture.
3. Stir in cooled chocolate.
4. Drop dough by tablespoonfuls 2 inches apart onto parchment-lined baking sheets.
5. Bake 8-10 minutes or until edges are set.
6. Cool on pans 2 minutes. Remove to wire racks to cool completely.
7. For filling, in a large bowl, beat cream cheese and butter until fluffy.
8. Beat in confectioners' sugar and vanilla until smooth.
9. Spread filling on bottom of half of the cookies, and cover with remaining cookies.
10. Drizzle with melted baking chips; sprinkle with pecans.
11. Refrigerate until serving.

BARISTA BUMP-OFF

A KILLER COFFEE COZY MYSTERY BOOK 11

BARISTA BUMP-OFF

A Killer Coffee Mystery

Book Eleven

BY
TONYA KAPPES

"Pepper," I whispered-shouted. "Come here now," I demanded, only stopping him from barking for a moment.

He turned back and continued to bark and bark, the sound echoing off the lake into the dark that now completely lay overtop us. He stopped barking once I was next to him.

"Stop that." When I got to him, I didn't see anything on the pier. "Let's go back to the shop and wait for Daddy," I told him.

I took a step back to where I'd come from, and Pepper started barking all over again.

"What is it? A turtle?" I asked and leaned over the pier's railing to see what he was barking at in the lake below us. "I bet it's a fish. They are starting to come back around after their winter hibernation."

To show him, I pushed the flashlight button on my phone and held it over the railing to shine into the water.

I felt a little better knowing there wasn't anyone out there with us, unless you counted the floating body that appeared below.

CHAPTER ONE

"Settle down." Aunt Maxi stepped in front of the entrance of the Bean Hive Coffee Shop. "I'll go see what is going on," she assured me.

"I'm fine," I told her after we'd run to the front window of my coffeehouse to see what the shrill screams were about. "I'm a couple of months out from surgery."

Over the Christmas holiday, I had been a little nauseous. I had put it in the back of my head believing it to be a side effect of stress. Let's face it, who didn't have some sort of stress? Stress affected us differently, and I was no stranger to feeling sick to my stomach when I was extremely stressed.

"You wait right here." Aunt Maxi ran her hand over my black curly hair before she pushed it behind my shoulder. "Your pretty blue eyes still aren't sparkling like they normally do. That's how I know you're not up to one hundred percent."

"It was my appendix, not my heart." I sighed and tried to get out the words before she opened the door, passing a couple of high school kids on the way in. "Good afternoon," I greeted them and turned my attention back to the customers. "Let me know what I can get you."

They nodded and made their way over to the table Birdie Bebe had reserved for her weekly tutoring session for her fellow classmates and herself.

Birdie Bebe was Loretta Bebe's granddaughter. She'd been living with

Loretta for about a year now and really found Honey Springs, Kentucky, to be her home. I loved her. She'd really not only become a part of my family, but also a very valuable employee to me.

She was one of those kids who could see what needed to be done before she was even asked to do it. There were times when I didn't see something and she picked up on it before me.

Though she worked for me every afternoon after school, I'd started to take the afternoon shift when she asked if she could host her weekly tutoring session here. Of course I agreed to it because I wanted her to succeed in school but also because it gave me a chance to see all the customers who did come in later in the day when I wasn't there.

"Do y'all need anything?" I asked the group of students and their teacher, Hope Mowry.

"Is your oven set to four hundred?" Hope asked.

"I'm not sure, but you can go on in and check." I had gotten extra insurance for Birdie's tutoring sessions here at the coffeehouse because it was actually her home economics class.

In fact, it wasn't even a tutoring lesson. That was just what Birdie called it. The time the handful of students and Hope spent together was actually Hope giving them the opportunity to learn what they would learn next year in school in her class.

These students weren't graduating this year. The class itself was going away. The home economics department was the first to be cut from next year's curriculum.

These students loved it so much, Hope had agreed to cram as much as she could in during the spring semester if they could find a place. Naturally, Birdie knew I had several industrial ovens in the kitchen and a large workspace to go with it, and she asked me.

After I looked into what the insurance would be just in case someone got hurt, I'd decided it was in the budget to host the group once a week and sometimes on Sunday, now that spring had arrived.

"Thanks, Roxy." Hope smiled through the unspoken broken heart she had over the school board decision to cut the department.

She followed me back to the counter, where she disappeared through the swinging kitchen door.

"Do you see anything you like?" I asked a customer who'd been pacing back and forth between the two display counters. One had donuts in it while the other had cookies and pies.

"I'm so torn between the red-pepper donut here and fireside cookies." Her brows knitted.

The bell over the door dinged, and Aunt Maxi bolted through. Her eyes caught mine as she brushed her hand through her short pink hair before she ran it over her face.

"It's a dilemma I hear all the time." I plucked a plastic piece of parchment paper from the box with one hand and grabbed a to-go bag with the other. A talent I'd learned to do over the years, flicking the bag open. "Why don't we do a buy-one-get-one-free deal?"

"Really?" The customer smiled.

I nodded with a forced smile on my face.

"That's great. I'll take the fireside cookie. It looks like a s'more." She pointed to them after I slid the door of the display counter open and took out the sweet treats she'd asked for, slipping them into the bag.

"You can follow me down there," I told her and walked down the back of the counter to meet her at the register.

"What has this town come to?" Aunt Maxi walked around the counter. She didn't officially work for me, but she did own the building and a few others located here on the boardwalk, and she had graciously offered to help me when Birdie had her class here.

It was a big help too. Well, most of the time, when she wasn't using the time she was here as her social hour. She had no problem giving her friends free food and drinks while sitting for about an hour and taking in all the news and goings on around Honey Springs.

"There was a drive-by purse snatching." She had turned her head slightly to the right in the direction of the mayor. "I have no idea what is going to come of this town if we don't stop this crime!" Her voice grew audibly louder and louder with each word.

"Purse snatching?" I asked, making sure I'd heard her correctly.

"Purse snatching?" Hope had come back through the door.

"Yes. And on a moped!" Aunt Maxi had finally gotten the attention of the mayor. He cleared his throat and stood up. "There was duct tape holding the darn thing together too. I saw it with my own eyes." Aunt Maxi's words were running together.

For a second, I thought he was going to come back to the counter to address Aunt Maxi, but when the bell above the door dinged again, it was Sheriff Spencer Shepard.

His jaw was hard, and his green eyes had a serious look in them. His thick neck gave way to his deep chest beneath his brown sheriff's uniform shirt where he proudly wore the five-point-star sheriff's badge on the front pocket.

When he took off his sheriff's hat, like most men did when they entered an eating establishment, the waves of his sandy-blond hair lay flat against his head.

He scanned the coffeehouse and stalked over to the mayor.

"Do you think I need to take the kids out?" Hope asked as we all noticed the seriousness of the situation taking place between the sheriff and the mayor, both elected officials by the good citizens of Honey Springs.

"No. I think it's all safe in here." I tried not to alarm her since I did know a few things about the law.

By education, I was a lawyer. I'd left my law firm I'd shared with my ex-husband and moved to Honey Springs, where I had very fond memories of my time spent here with Aunt Maxi.

Wasn't that the case? When we were hurt, didn't we desperately seek times in our lives when we recalled we were the happiest?

That, for me, was Honey Springs and the long summer days and nights I'd spent on this very boardwalk as a teenager. Back then, there were just a few shops, including the Crooked Cat, the local bookstore that was still here.

Long story short, Aunt Maxi had this building unoccupied from a recent tenant, and it was easy to dream up my own coffee shop. She insisted on it, really, and I was so glad she did.

Years later I was married to Patrick Cane, the boy I'd chased all over Honey Springs in those teenage years, and we had two fur babies. Sassy was a black Standard Poodle who belonged to Patrick, and Pepper, a salt-and-pepper schnauzer, who had adopted me when I went to Pet Palace, Honey Springs's local SPCA.

"Stop gawking and close your mouth." I leaned around Aunt Maxi and stuck my face in front of hers. She was staring right at the mayor and Spencer as the two of them had a very heated conversation.

"If you don't get that budget passed, you won't have this cushy job." Spencer's words had a bite to them that didn't sit too well with the mayor.

"If you don't get these crimes under control, I'll see to it that my main platform this year will be to find our city a real sheriff who can keep the citizens of Honey Springs safe." The mayor was all too aware that the locals had been a little concerned with some of the crime that'd found its way into Honey Springs, leaving us with the task of making sure we kept our doors locked.

Something locals had rarely done in this part of Kentucky.

Honey Springs was a little lake tourist town that not only was secluded from big cities and surrounded by beautiful hills and Kentucky bluegrass, but located on Lake Honey Springs, where fishing, boating, and lazy days spent in a rental cabin was just part of daily life.

"Help! Help!" Loretta Bebe busted through the coffeehouse door all aflutter, almost coming out of her jeweled strappy sandals.

"Hey-lup!" She screamed in her very southern accent. Her head twirled around. She snapped her eyes at Sheriff Shepard Spencer. "I've been robbed! Right out in the parking lot! In daylight!"

She pointed directly at Spencer with her perfectly polished and manicured finger.

"You!" She gasped. The sparkle of the afternoon sun had filtered through the windows of the coffeehouse and landed perfectly on her shiny diamond ring. "Get out there and do your job. Find my purse or else!"

CHAPTER TWO

"Let me get you a cup of coffee." I'd patted Loretta after she'd thrown her hissy fit and rightfully so.

"I *cannot* even think about drinking anything. My person has been violated!" she cried out.

"Yes, it has," Aunt Maxi agreed, catching me off guard. "I can't believe the thieves sprayed you with self-tanner. Look at your eyes. You look like a raccoon."

Loretta was known to visit Lisa Stahl's tanning booth several times a week even though the fact was swept under the rug since Loretta claimed she was of Native American descent. We could look at Loretta and see she was lily white, not a trace of Native American in her, but if it made Loretta feel good, who was Aunt Maxi or anyone else to be Loretta's judge and jury?

"Why, Maxine Bloom. You're the worst!" Loretta screamed at the top of her lungs, clearing out what few customers I had left in the Bean Hive. "Why do you mock me in my time of need?" She picked at the end of her short, store-bought, black hair.

Birdie and I gave Aunt Maxi looks that told her she wasn't being nice. They'd had their differences in the past, and they weren't the best of friends, but in times of need—and this was one of those times—Aunt Maxi needed to be a little more sympathetic.

"I'm sorry, Low-retta." Aunt Maxi rubbed her hand in circles on Loretta's back, subtly making fun of how Loretta pronounced her own name without Loretta even noticing.

Aunt Maxi rolled her eyes, so I thought they were permanently going to stay that way after she'd paused to suck in a deep breath. Apparently, she was collecting herself and trying not to say anything negative to Loretta.

"You've been violated." Aunt Maxi went to the extreme positive end of what I was trying to convey with my facial expressions.

"Ye-us." Loretta's mouth took on an unpleasant twist. "That's exactly what has happened. I've been violated."

When the bell over the door dinged, we all jerked around in hopes it was Spencer with the good news that they'd recovered Loretta's bag.

"Sorry to disappoint." Louise Carlton stood at the door with an animal cage handle in her grip. "I guess you forgot I was coming. I can come back."

"Louise, I'm so sorry. Of course you can come in here." I waved her in. "There's been someone going around on a moped snatching purses along the boardwalk, and well, we were kinda hoping Spencer would walk through the door any minute with Loretta's purse."

"Dear me." Louise tsked. Her hair was a gorgeous shiny silver that was cut into a bob with blunt bangs across her forehead. She wore an armful of bracelets that jingled as she put the cage on the floor and hurried over to her friend. "Loretta, that's terrible. Are you okay? Is there anything I can do for you?"

Loretta drew an invisible pattern with her fingernail on the table.

"Just be my friend is all I ask," she said before she gave Aunt Maxi one good, scolding look. "It's all I've ever wanted."

"You don't ever have to ask that." Louise looked at Aunt Maxi. "Isn't that right, Maxine? We are all friends, and our motto at the Southern Women's Club is one of friendship and deep love."

"Motto my heinie. I'd hate to see how Low-retta would act if this was me." Aunt Maxi made a good point under her breath when she passed me to walk behind the counter, where she busied herself by cleaning up a little. "You gonna close early?"

"I guess." I shifted my gaze out the window overlooking the boardwalk.

There was very little foot traffic. The word about the purse snatching might've gotten out to the community, and people were too scared to come today.

"I can help clean up really fast while you get the intake animal." Birdie's group had gone a long time ago, leaving her here to console her grandmother. "Are you going to be okay, grandmawmaw?"

Loretta used the tissue I'd given her a while ago to dab at the edges of her eyes and gave a slow, slight nod.

"What do we have here?" I walked with Louise to see what animal she'd brought to the coffeehouse to be adopted.

Pepper had already gone over to put his nose into the cage, but for some reason, the animal didn't interest him like the others. He trotted back over to the fireplace where his bed was located and got in.

"We have a special one this time." Louise picked up the cage and held it at eye level. "Polly, meet Roxy. Roxy, meet Polly."

"Roxy. Roxy. Squawk." There was a bird inside. A big bird.

"Wow." Every week or two since I opened the Bean Hive, Louise has brought a shelter pet from the Pet Palace here to be adopted.

I was a firm believer that if shelter animals could be in an environment where they weren't in cages, they could be themselves. Not so stressed, so they could be adopted easily. I had to jump through a lot of hoops to even get the Health Department to approve the animals, but in the end it had all worked out and we've had a one-hundred-percent success rate.

"I don't think I've ever been around a bird before." I looked into the holes of the cage.

"You are going to love Polly." Louise looked at the cat tree Patrick had made for the animals. There was a stick that protruded out with a cat toy dangling from it. "She can perch right there. She doesn't fly, but she does hop around, so we can put her food on one of the ledges of the cat tree."

Louise handed me the bag of the usual things like the animal's paperwork, where all of the bird's history and shot records would be listed. *Did birds get shots?* I wondered then turned my attention back to Louise.

"Polly's food is in there. She drinks water. She's a talker, so I'm warning you that you won't ever be alone." She crouched down and opened the cage. She stuck her hand inside and then pulled it out slowly with Polly standing on her finger. "Be careful what you say because she will repeat it."

"Polly is a good girl. Good girl gets a treat," Polly chirped, bopping her head back and forth as she talked.

"I want her!" Birdie called from the back of the coffeehouse. "I want her bad."

"Can you even imagine if you did?" Aunt Maxi wiped down the front of the glass displays. "A bird with an accent like Loretta?"

I tried not to smile, but I couldn't help it. Neither could Louise.

"What did you say, Maxine?" Loretta asked.

"I said that I want Birdie to take these leftover treats because you're going to need to stay in tomorrow so you can get some rest." Aunt Maxi and Birdie looked at each other, snickering.

Loretta didn't let Birdie take Polly home, and that was okay. I still needed to figure out about the bird and learn a little more so I could tell potential owners, so after everyone left, including Aunt Maxi, I made myself a steaming cup of coffee and grabbed Polly's folder.

It was next to the register where I kept all the animals' files in case someone inquired about them when I wasn't there.

"You're fifteen years old?" I questioned the bird and looked down at the information. "My goodness, you can live to be sixty to eighty years old." And then my heart dropped when I noticed she'd been surrendered by her owner, who had gone to the local nursing home because she was getting older and couldn't care for Polly anymore. "We will find you the best family."

I closed up the file and put it back next to the register.

"Old. Old," Polly chirped. I smiled. It was different having an animal in here that didn't follow me around or that I had to take home. According to the file, I could leave Polly here, but I was under the impression birds liked living in a cage where they could be covered up.

"You be a good girl." I untied my apron and hung it on the coatrack next to the register.

I grabbed my coat and purse off the hook.

"Good girl. Polly good girl." Polly's head bobbled back and forth in a rapid movement before she extended her wings.

I stopped putting my coat on to watch her show off her many feathers of color, in awe at just how big she really was, and it was pretty darn neat.

"Pepper," I called to my furry sidekick. "Let's go."

"Pepper! Pepper!" Polly screamed at the top of her bird lungs.

Pepper ran over and growled, showing his teeth.

"Pepper," I scolded, unsure of what that was about, then decided not to say anything else because it was probably the first time he'd ever been near a bird, much less one that squawked his name.

"Be a good boy. Squawk!" Polly drew her wings back close to her side the closer I got to the front door.

"Yes. You are a good boy." I bent down and decided to pick Pepper up so I didn't leave the door open long enough for Polly to jump down and possibly get out.

I snuggled Pepper close to me and whispered in his ear so Polly didn't hear or repeat, "We are going to have to watch our p's and q's with this one."

Pepper twisted his little head to my face, licking my cheeks. I laughed and used my free hand to run it down the wall next to the door to switch off the lights.

Safely outside and with the door shut behind us, I put Pepper on the ground and dug into my purse to get the keys to lock the door.

Thoughts of the day swirled around in my head. It was dark out, and though it wasn't quite what we'd consider nighttime because it was spring and the time change hadn't happened to make the daylight longer, the idea of someone lurking in the shadows caused my heart to race.

"Don't be silly," I told myself, slipping the key into the door and turning it to lock. The sound of faint footsteps and the groan of loose nails from a board on the boardwalk caught my ear, then Pepper yelping from the pier got my attention. "Pepper?" I called into the darkness, taking a step back into the closed door of the coffeehouse so I was somewhat hidden.

I drew my purse close to my body.

The carriage lights along the boardwalk and pier were really just for looks. They didn't give any sort of spotlight but to the area right beneath them.

I gulped. My eyes shifted right, looking down toward the end of the boardwalk and the Wild and Whimsy antiques shop. I didn't see anything.

I slowly looked to my left toward the opposite end of the boardwalk, where the Crooked Cat was located, and didn't see anyone or anything.

It was footsteps and boards. Two distinct noises I knew all too well since opening the Bean Hive.

Pepper was barking.

My eyes moved to stare directly in front of me. The pier jutted out into Lake Honey Springs, and the only shop located on the pier was the Bait and Tackle, which I knew was closed. In fact, all the shops were closed.

Slowly, I contorted my arm and put my hand inside of my purse to find my phone. I was conflicted on who to call. Spencer or Patrick. The law or my husband.

If I called Spencer and had him come out here with nothing wrong, then I would look silly and scared. But not Patrick. He would definitely want me safe.

"Listen, I'm standing outside the coffeehouse, and I heard footsteps running away." I clearly heard them in the distance. "Maybe not running but they definitely hurried when Pepper and I were leaving the coffeehouse."

"Stay inside. I'll be right there." Patrick hung up the phone without hesitation.

Only one problem, he thought I was inside and I wasn't. I wouldn't go inside and leave Pepper outside.

Literally it only was a few minutes' car ride from our cabin down the road, so Patrick would be here in a minute, but Pepper was barking so loud my heart hurt thinking he might be in danger.

With my keys in between my fingers like I'd seen on television to use as a weapon, I took my first steps toward the pier.

With each step, I seemed to be holding my breath more and more, Pepper coming into my sight.

"Pepper," I whispered-shouted. "Come here now," I demanded, only stopping him from barking for a moment.

He turned back and continued to bark and bark, the sound echoing off the lake into the dark that now completely lay overtop us. He stopped barking once I was next to him.

"Stop that." When I got to him, I didn't see anything on the pier. "Let's go back to the shop and wait for Daddy," I told him.

I took a step back to where I'd come from, and Pepper started barking all over again.

"What is it? A turtle?" I asked and leaned over the pier's railing to see what he was barking at in the lake below us. "I bet it's a fish. They are starting to come back around after their winter hibernation."

To show him, I pushed the flashlight button on my phone and held it over the railing to shine into the water.

I felt a little better knowing there wasn't anyone out there with us, unless you counted the floating body that appeared below.

CHAPTER THREE

"Why didn't you call me?" Spencer asked, putting his hand on me to step away when Kevin Roberts, the county coroner, passed us on the boardwalk.

He'd parked on the wrong side of the boardwalk, which made him have to push the church cart across to get to where the body had finally floated to shore. The wheels on the gurney squeaked with each turn, creating a very eerie noise.

"I..." I wrapped my arms around myself to ward off the goose bumps trailing along my arms.

"I might've found out who did this. If you did hear footsteps, I might've seen someone running away on my way here," he said, directly looking at me.

"It's not like the boardwalk is shut down. People walk, jog, or just sit here and read all the time." I shrugged and tried not to look over my shoulder to see the woman lying facedown.

The only reason I knew it was a woman wasn't the long hair—many men around here had long hair. It was the dress plastered to her lifeless body.

"Do you know who it is?" I asked, wondering if it was a local or someone we knew.

"There isn't any identification on her, but the deputies are scouring the banks to see if we can find a purse, phone, anything." As he talked to me, the lights of the rescue boat were penetrating the water as the deputies and coast guard on duty were trying to see down into the water. "We are hoping we can find something. Maybe have to drag the lake."

When Spencer let go of a big sigh, I looked up at him.

"Do you think you can answer a few questions now, or do you want to wait until morning?" he asked.

"We can do it now in the coffeehouse. Patrick took Pepper in there when you got here. I'm sure he put on some coffee." I gave a wry smile knowing coffee wasn't going to solve who this woman was, but it sure was going to calm my nerves.

Wasn't it interesting how coffee did bring people together? By the scene tonight, it was a testament that it didn't matter what type of situation, coffee always brought people to the table, where there would be conversation.

Tonight's conversation just so happened to be about the dead body Pepper and I'd found floating in Lake Honey Springs just about forty-five minutes ago.

"Who is it? Who is it?" Polly squawked when Spencer and I walked into the Bean Hive Coffeehouse.

"Who is that?" Spencer's brows rose, and he slowly shook his head in disbelief. "You're adopting out talking birds?"

"Watch what you say," I warned, knowing she was probably repeating something Aunt Maxi had said since she, too, was in the coffeehouse. "Polly repeats everything."

"Maxine." Spencer had taken his hat off and placed it on one of the many café tables that dotted the inside of the coffeehouse. "I see you had your scanner on."

"I reckon I did. I got right down here when I heard it was Roxanne who called in the body." Aunt Maxi used my full name, which told me she meant business.

"Do you mind giving us a few minutes while I talk to her?" He asked when Aunt Maxi decided to take a seat at the same table he'd put his hat on, sipping on her coffee.

"I'll just be right over there if you need me." She said to me but kept her eye on Spencer.

It wasn't like she went far. She sat her coffee on the counter and decided to go ahead and change the menu.

"Let me get you a coffee," I told Spencer and walked behind the counter where Patrick had, in fact, made a fresh pot of coffee.

"Are you okay?" Patrick asked and put his hand on my shoulder, giving it a little squeeze in a massage kind of way. His big brown eyes and tender smile told me he was right there where I needed him. His jaw was tight, which told me another thing altogether.

He was worried.

"I'm fine." I tried not to let him see the stress on my face, though he could probably feel it in my muscles. "I'll answer the questions as best as I can, and then we can go home."

I busied my shaking hands by pouring me and Spencer a cup of coffee, but not without first giving Aunt Maxi the stink eye.

She tried not to glance out of the corner of her eye at me while she tugged on the pulley that lowered the three hanging chalkboard menus. I still gave her a hard look to let her know her snooping didn't go unnoticed.

"Here you go." I sat the coffee mug down in front of Spencer. He helped himself to the bourbon barrel lids turned into lazy Susans with all the condiments he needed to doctor up his coffee. "I don't know what more I can tell you other than the day didn't seem out of place, but then there were the purse snatchings." I blew on my coffee before I took a sip. "Do you think the lady was a victim?"

"Not sure. Not even sure if the footsteps you heard came from the pier. And I'm not so sure she didn't just float downriver." He used a spoon to slowly stir the sugar and cream into the mug. Steam rolled up and round his nose as he took a drink.

The happy sigh that came from him told me he'd just taken a sip of some good-to-him coffee. As the owner and the roaster of the blend he was drinking, it made me somewhat happy, though the circumstances of why he was drinking it did damper the feeling.

"I'm having missing person cases looked into from not only here but at least sixty miles down and upstream. You just never know." At least he had already started his investigation, just an hour after when I found her.

I took comfort in that.

"You didn't hear or see anything before you left for the night?" he asked to make sure. He was reading what I'd told him earlier from his little notebook.

"No. I cleaned up so I could be ready for tomorrow." My heart skipped a beat. "I'm so glad I was here and not Birdie."

"Birdie Bebe?" He gave me a funny look.

"Yeah. She generally closes for me except on the days her classmates are here." I gnawed at the inside of my jaw, thinking I should hire someone to work with her. "I'm starting to think Loretta was right about crime."

"I've been going to the mayor for the better part of two years in hopes he'd get the budget increased, but he's not even considering it for this year's election." He shook his head as the disappointment appeared. "I told him crime was up, and every week I personally take the crime reports to his office. He said the tourism industry is where all the extra dollars need to go." Spencer took his finger and ran it around the rim of the mug. "There won't be any tourists in Honey Springs if we become known for all this crime and no law enforcement or at least not enough law enforcement to keep eyes and ears on the street."

"Maybe this is a body that floated from another part of Lake Honey Springs." It wasn't like Lake Honey Springs only covered Honey Springs.

It didn't. There were several other Kentucky counties that bordered the huge lake, but it just seemed odd for this time of the year. Plus I'd not heard lately of anyone missing. The state Amber Alerts and the news were pretty good at getting the word out and being on the lookout.

"Tell me one more time about Pepper." He sat back and looked at me intently.

"Let me show you." I stood up, and he followed. Both of us took our coffee. "I said goodnight to Polly and held Pepper." I nodded to Pepper.

He'd gotten up on the couch in front of the fireplace and found a comfy spot in his bed. Not a care in the world that he'd found the floating body.

We opened the door and stepped out.

"I turned off the lights." I pretended to go through the motions. "I locked the door. I did put Pepper down before I locked the door. He usually sticks with me but does smell around." I shrugged. "When I turned around, he was already down the pier and barking. That's when I heard footsteps in the distance." My eyes widened. "And creaky boards."

"As in the boardwalk boards?" he asked.

"Yes. And I even thought to myself it was odd because I knew the Beautification Committee had recently renailed down any after the winter months because they do come loose during the bitter temperatures and snow."

"That means we can find the boards along here and see where the footsteps came from." Spencer and I were thinking along the same lines.

"That's right. Possibly get a camera hit." There were a couple of cameras along the boardwalk, but I really wasn't sure if they were properly working. There wasn't ever a concern the boardwalk would be dangerous.

"I can get a look at those in the morning." He made a quick note, leaning into the small light coming from the closest carriage light. "Then what?"

"Like I said, I heard Pepper barking, and that's when I called Patrick. I didn't want to make a false alarm with you, so it was easy to just go back into the coffeehouse to wait for him," I said, and when I heard the squeaky wheels of Kevin's gurney at the far end of the boardwalk, I looked.

The moon had made its appearance by this time, giving off more light to the boardwalk. A dark outline of Kevin's shadow, along with the gurney's shadow, grew bigger as he got closer.

I tried not to look.

"I yelled for Pepper several times and hid in the doorway here." I gestured behind us. "When Pepper didn't come, I knew I had to go get him. I didn't want anyone to hurt him."

Spencer didn't even question my thinking process when it came to Pepper. Everyone in Honey Springs knew I was crazy about my little dog, and I dared them to question what depths I'd go to keep him safe.

Pepper had saved me when I was in one of the darkest periods of my life. I had dedicated myself to keeping him safe.

"That's when I went out on the pier to get him. There was nothing there, and I told him to come on, but he continued to look over the railing into the water. I took my phone's flashlight and shone it down." I took a big deep breath to steady the trembling in my voice. "That's when I saw the body."

"That's also about the time Patrick got here?" he asked.

"Yes. Patrick actually heard me scream, and he came running to get me and Pepper. I stood about two feet from the railing after I'd picked up Pepper and pointed. He looked over and saw the body, then he took me in his arms and led me back to the coffeehouse, where he called you."

Kevin approached. Spencer put his hand out for me to hold on.

"Can you tell how she died?" Spencer asked Kevin.

"Stab wound to the back. I'm thinking she was standing on the pier, since the water is pretty still. Someone stabbed her from behind." Kevin talked, and Spencer pulled the sheet back.

An audible gasp came from behind me.

Aunt Maxi was standing in the doorway of the coffeehouse with her hand over her mouth.

"Do you recognize her?" Spencer asked Aunt Maxi.

"Yes. She's one of my renters in my cabin on Queen Bee Lane." Aunt Maxi's voice shook with fear.

CHAPTER FOUR

There were so many cabins in Honey Springs. Most of the seasonal owners never stepped foot in the Bean Hive Coffeehouse or even on the boardwalk. They either came for a quick weekend getaway during the year or used a local realtor, like my mom, Penny, to help rent the cabins to tourists, who did come into the Bean Hive.

"Don't you remember her?" Aunt Maxi asked. "She's been in here a few times." She looked at me with her head tilted and her mouth gaped open.

My nose scrunched up, and I squinted my eyes, trying to think back. Nothing. I shook my head.

"Five foot three. Petite little thing. She had real red hair." Aunt Maxi pointed to her fake color which changed with the wind. "Still don't place her?"

About that time Loretta and Birdie Bebe hurried through the coffeehouse door even though we were closed for the evening.

"Get out of my way, Sheriff." Loretta batted Spencer away. "Another crime?"

"Outta my way. Scwack!" Polly bounced and pulled back when Loretta glared at her.

"Crime? Murder." Aunt Maxi added to Loretta's excitement. "And one of my tenants too."

Birdie made her way over to Aunt Maxi. The two of them whispered from behind the counter.

I could only imagine what Aunt Maxi was saying. I was sure it was something about the victim.

"Murder?" Loretta's head whipped around. I couldn't see her face, but by Spencer's expression, Loretta was giving him holy hell. "Just what are you going to do about it?"

"I'm going to let the system do its job." He looked at me from over Loretta's shoulder. "You can come down in the morning and sign off on your statement."

"Statement?" Loretta's head swiveled my way. "You found her?"

"Murder! Murder!" Polly screamed.

"Shut up!" Loretta was fit to be tied. "Patrick"—she turned to my husband—"how many more dead bodies is Roxanne going to find before you've had enough of this type of crime going on in and around Honey Springs?"

"Loretta." Patrick wore a thin-lipped smile. "Those other crimes were specific and not just some random serial murderer or crime."

"It still doesn't make it any better." She wrung her hands.

"Maxine," Spencer spoke up. "You can come down with all the information I need from you so we can get in contact with next of kin."

"Sure. No problem." Aunt Maxi gave him a quick look but went back to talking to Birdie.

The bell over the door signaled Spencer leaving, and that's when I noticed Birdie and Aunt Maxi giving each other a look.

"What is that about?" I asked.

"Well." Birdie hesitated.

"What is it, Birdie?" Loretta raised a penciled-on brow. "Speak up, child."

I knew when Loretta talked to Birdie like a child and not the teenager she was, Birdie didn't like it.

"Did you know her?" I put two and two together after seeing her and Aunt Maxi whispering behind the counter. "Aunt Maxi did say the woman was in here a time or two. I don't remember her. Maybe she was here on your shift?"

"She was. Her name is Stella Johnson. She's a very nice lady, and she's been here a few months," Birdie recalled.

"Six to be exact." Aunt Maxi sighed.

"Six months?" Patrick clarified.

"Mm-hmm," Aunt Maxi ho-hummed. "That's right. One, two, three, four, five, and six." She held up her fingers as she counted. "She started out by signing for a month. Then extended it to two months. The week after she extended it to two months, she called back and asked if it could be six instead." Aunt Maxi frowned. "I'd only seen her once. When she first drove into town. Penny had set up the visit. She didn't want the usual code to the door to rent like most of the renters do. She actually wanted the owner, me,"—she pointed to herself—"to come and show her the place."

"Mom had you go to the cabin to meet Stella?" I asked.

It was odd that my mom had Aunt Maxi go since Mom was the real estate agent Aunt Maxi had used to list all of the rentals. And it was Mom who would meet the potential client if they wanted to see the place, leaving Aunt Maxi out of it.

"Yes." Aunt Maxi fiddled around with some of the mugs on the counter, moving them, then moving them back where they had been.

"She won the lottery," Birdie blurted out. "Like a lot of money."

"Now that you say that, it made sense she came right down to Penny's office and paid all the extra months up front." That caught my attention since Stella had been murdered.

"I never win on them scratch-offs." The wrinkles in Loretta's forehead had somewhat relaxed.

"It wasn't a scratch-off." Birdie's lip tugged in like she was holding another big secret. "I told her I wouldn't tell and I didn't."

"Tell what?" Loretta's worry wrinkles came back. "When someone tells you to keep a secret, you know that ain't good."

"I don't believe that." I knew Loretta always thought someone was out to get her or keep secrets from her. She hated being an outsider on anything. I was sure that's why she had her hand in every single club and organization and now had a vested interest in our criminal justice system. "But I do believe if she won a good amount of money, someone could have motive to have killed her."

"Ten million dollars." The color left Birdie's face.

I coughed.

"I'm sorry. I don't think I heard you correctly." Loretta put a hand on her chest. "Did you say ten million dollars?"

"You heard me just fine." Birdie's cheeks looked a little flushed now. "She won ten million dollars and decided to claim it anonymously. She wasn't sure what she was going to do with it, but she took it in one lump sum. The morning she claimed it, she rented a car, drove to the bank, and withdrew some."

"How much did she have on her?" Loretta asked.

"I have no idea. But does it matter? She's dead." Birdie's eyes teared up. "I really liked her. She always was willing to try my new concoctions before I presented them to Roxy."

Birdie was always coming up with creative ways to make iced coffees, lattes, and designs that appealed to the kids her age. They always came in after school to grab some sort of caffeinated drink and treat while they gossiped about the day. Birdie loved working the after-school shift because she viewed it as a social hour.

She'd told me a few times how if she didn't have the job, Loretta would've made her come straight home, but this way she was able to be with friends and make money.

"She tried one tonight." Birdie frowned.

"She was in here tonight?" I asked.

"Mm-hmm." Birdie shook her head and blinked a few times as if she were trying to hold back on her emotions.

"It matters because of these sudden purse snatchings. What if someone knew there was a rich person here in Honey Springs, and now they've decided to snatch all the purses..." Loretta's words lingered. "What if they killed her for her purse?" Loretta's eyes grew, and her fake lashes batted quickly.

"It's a good possibility." I shrugged, gnawing on the inside of my bottom lip. I was still trying to wrap my head around the ten-million-dollar thing, not put the purse-snatching possibility on top of that.

"I think it's a very real reason to have been killed. Someone knew she had the money, and she must've been in contact with someone from her life. They found her." Patrick was so cute. He was spitting out all sorts of reasons why Stella was murdered.

A first for him since he always told me to stop meddling in people's business. It was hard not to since the coffeehouse was the exact place people would meet up with each other to tell their business. I couldn't help if I overheard them. I'd certainly not overheard anyone saying anything about a person in town who'd won ten million dollars in the lottery.

That would've been big-time gossip around here.

"No. No." Birdie refused to believe what we were saying.

"No! No!" Polly went back and forth on the stick, moving from claw to claw. "No. No. Good bird. Pepper! Good bird!"

"Louise gave this bird to you because she was sick of listening to it all day long." Aunt Maxi put her hands on her hips. "I've about had enough too."

"Let's get back to what you were saying, Birdie." I smiled at her. "Do you feel up to answering any questions?"

"Sure, if it's going to help find whoever did this." She gulped back the tears and used the sleeve of her sweatshirt to wipe her eyes. "I'm telling you she didn't tell a soul about her winnings. She told me that. She said it wasn't unusual for her to go out west and backpack. It was her thing. She said on a whim she went into a convenience store and got a water along with some sort of granola snack. While she was standing in line, everyone in front of her was buying a lottery ticket for the big drawing. She had two dollars in change, and the cashier asked if she wanted a lottery ticket. She said she was about to respond no when the cashier handed her the ticket."

"Are you saying she didn't want the ticket and the cashier gave it to her?" I had to clarify because if this was the case and the cashier knew it, then I couldn't help but wonder if the cashier had found Stella here.

"Yeah. Stella said the cashier handed her the ticket, and Stella told her she didn't want it, and she wanted her cash. But she took it after the cashier was going to have to get a manager to redo the transaction and something with the lottery." Birdie smiled. "That's how she got the winning ticket. One winner. Her. Ten million."

"My goodness." Loretta eased down in the closest chair in shock.

"She didn't tell no one?" Aunt Maxi asked with disbelief because we all knew if Aunt Maxi won something as goofy as a hair tie raffle down at the Honey Comb Hair.

"She said she didn't want to be one of those lottery-gone-wrong people like they have on that cable show," Birdie said.

"Wow." I eased down in the chair next to Loretta, actually pretty stunned.

That didn't stop my amateur-detective mind though.

"I blame the law." Loretta tapped her fingernail on the table. "It doesn't matter how much money you have or don't have, you should be safe. If they'd had deputies patrolling this boardwalk at night like they should, this could've been prevented. Or at least gotten whoever did this in custody."

"And to think they are still out there." Aunt Maxi lowered her eyes.

"They have my purse! With my address in it. If they know I've got money, they'll kill me." Loretta's concern had turned even more fatal.

Aunt Maxi snorted back a comment, and I was glad she did because by the way she was bursting at the seams trying to keep her mouth shut, I was sure it was some sort of ill comment to or about Loretta.

I puckered my lips. My eyes grew big, and I gave Aunt Maxi the look.

"Did she ever mention anything about her past?" I asked Birdie.

"Nothing about any names or jobs or even where she's from." Birdie turned to Aunt Maxi. "You said she rented from you. Do you have the paperwork like Sheriff Shepard mentioned?"

"Penny should." Aunt Maxi looked up at the clock on the wall. "I'm sure she's in bed, like we all need to be."

"You're right. We aren't going to get anything accomplished with it almost going on eleven." Loretta stood up, steadied herself using the table, and found her footing. "Birdie, get your things. We are going home, and you have school in the morning."

Birdie did what Loretta had told her to do.

"I'll see you tomorrow afternoon." Birdie's lips gave in to a sad smile.

"You don't have to work. I can do it." I didn't want her to be sad at work. She'd obviously had more of a relationship with Stella than she was mentioning. Why else would Stella confide in Birdie about her winning the lottery?

Unless Stella wanted to unload on a stranger. That probably did feel good to Stella.

"That's okay. I'd rather work." Birdie slipped her arms into her light coat, zipping it halfway up. "Keeps my mind busy."

I gave her and Loretta hugs on their way out the door. Patrick picked up the dirty coffee cups and headed into the kitchen.

"Busy! Busy!" Polly stretched her wings out.

"What are you thinking?" Aunt Maxi had walked up behind me and put her hands on my shoulder.

"I'm wondering what else Stella told Birdie that just might lead us to more suspects." My voice was quiet, but my thoughts were loud.

Something told me this was not a random murder.

CHAPTER FIVE

Since my cabin was pretty close to the lake, I didn't have to drive my car to the boardwalk and the Bean Hive on beautiful spring mornings. I would ride my bike with Pepper tucked in the large wire basket in a blanket.

Patrick was insistent that we ride home with him since there was a killer on the loose. His words, not mine.

Pepper went straight to the bike and whimpered a little when Patrick picked it up and put it in the back of the truck.

"I know, buddy." I picked Pepper up to get him out from underneath Patrick's feet. "It's been a long winter."

Both Pepper and I enjoyed the bike ride so much. Though we were in the midst of spring, the mornings were still dark when we left. Really it was always dark when we left, but as the spring would carry on, the nights would be lighter longer. Currently it was just as dark as the morning.

"You two have plenty of time to ride the bike," Patrick said and scratched Pepper's ear as he opened the passenger door for us. "Tonight, I want you to be safe." I opened my mouth. He beat me to the punch. "Just tonight."

Most of the citizens of Honey Springs rode bicycles when the weather allowed. It was such a small southern town that it was much easier to ride a bike than to park a car.

Pepper found his way back to the extended cab and watched out the window.

"I know you're thinking about Stella. What is the next move?" he asked, pulling out of the parking lot and hanging a left toward the cabin.

"I think we need to see the paperwork she filled out to rent Aunt Maxi's place. Which reminds me." My mind finished my sentence, but pulling out my phone to call my mom was what I did.

Though Aunt Maxi had suggested Mom was in bed, I thought I'd take my chances.

"Hello, dear," Mom answered, not a drop of sleepiness in her voice. "I'm out to eat with a client. Can I call you back?"

"A client? At this hour?" I asked. It was odd she'd not texted to let me know when she told me everything she was doing every morning when she popped into the Bean Hive to get her to-go coffee.

"Yes, Roxanne." Mom's whisper told me she was telling me part of the truth.

"Okay, well, be careful," I said nonchalantly. "There's a killer on the loose."

Mom let out an audible gasp, followed up by a choking sound.

"Mom? Are you okay?" I felt bad I'd said it the way I did, but I did want her to be safe.

"I'm fine," she choked and repeated herself a couple of times mixed in with a little shuffling in the background. "Excuse me," I overheard her say with the sound of her heels clicking on tile floor.

I held the phone closer to my ear to hear a little better.

"Mom, are you on a date?" I asked, not able to even recall the last time I'd seen her go on a date. I mean, she did after my dad died and did her own thing after I went off to college, but never since she'd lived in Honey Springs.

At least none I'd heard about.

"Roxanne, I said I was with a client," she snapped back.

"First off, I've never seen you go to eat with a client. Also, I don't recall seeing you in heels when you show houses. Plus you called me 'Roxanne,' which tells me that I've hit a hot button in my questioning you."

"You're being ridiculous now. You've investigated one too many crimes, making a molehill into a mountain." She was talking in circles, trying to confuse me.

Did she forget I was a lawyer and asking all the questions I did had just become part of my DNA? I let it drop.

"I just want you to be safe. Pepper found a body." I'd wanted to finish the story before we got to the cabin, but Mom kept interrupting.

"Pepper? Body? Again?" The again part was directed right at me. "Your silence is the answer that tells me I'm right."

"And heels tell me something." I pinched my lips together, knowing I just crossed the line. "I'm sorry."

I immediately apologized, knowing I wasn't too old for a mama scolding, and she was an adult who, if my hunch was right, no matter how much she denied it, could date or do whatever she pleased.

"You don't need to pay no mind to what I'm doing. How is it that Pepper and you found a dead body?" she asked. A car driving past was in her background, so she must've walked outside.

Patrick had pulled up to the cabin and parked. He went ahead inside to get Sassy while I sat down in one of the rocking chairs on the front porch as Pepper did his business. I got a round of rocking in, but it wasn't too long before Sassy came darting out the door, running over to me to get some good scratching before she went and joined Pepper.

I took the opportunity to tell Mom about the body.

"Her name is Stella Johnson," I told her.

"Why is that name so familiar?" Mom asked.

"She's the one who rented Aunt Maxi's cabin out on Queen Bee Lane." I jogged her memory.

"Oh no. Yes! I do remember that name. She didn't come in. She did everything over the internet with me. That darn internet." Mom groaned. "You said she was murdered? Doesn't surprise me with the round of crime we've been having."

We talked a little about the purse snatching.

"You think they stabbed her just for her purse?" Mom asked.

Sassy and Pepper danced at the door. I got up from the rocking chair and opened the door to let them in.

The chill in the night, or at least I would blame it on that, was the cause of the goose bumps traveling up my body. I grabbed one of the afghans from the basket next to the rocking chair and pulled it over my legs when I sat back down to finish the conversation.

Slowly the toe of my shoe moved the chair back and forth.

"They'd have reason to." I cleared my throat. "She was a big lottery winner. Like millions. She confided in Birdie." I told Mom everything we'd known and how she didn't tell anyone she won the money.

"That would explain the odd money issues she had. She also continued to ask me about the bank here in Honey Springs." Intently I listened for any clues I could follow up on while Mom told me about her interactions with Stella. "I gave her Evan's number down at the Honey Springs National Bank."

She was talking about Evan Rich, the local bank president, who would definitely give me some information. His daughter Emily had worked for me when she was in high school before she discovered she wanted to be a pastry chef and headed off to a fancy school in France where she earned a much-deserved culinary degree with her emphasis in baking.

"Do you think she stored her millions there?" Mom asked.

"I'm not sure, but that can't be safe for the bank." I had a niggling suspicion I should probably give Spencer this information, though I knew he wanted to try and get a deputy down on the boardwalk to keep an eye out for those purse snatchers.

"I'm also trying to figure out if the purse snatchers knew her, and she could've been a victim of a snatching that went wrong because they didn't find a purse on her. It was Aunt Maxi who had ID'd her." A rustling across the road in the wooded area between the road and Lake Honey Springs put a little fright in my soul.

I quickly folded the blanket and laid it across the ladder-back of the rocking chair before I headed inside to the cozy cabin we called home.

When I moved to Honey Springs, Aunt Maxi had begged me to live in town with her, and it would've been nice to have her soothe my torn-in-two heart. Though it would've been easy to fall into that, I wasn't one to wallow in my sadness, so I had asked her if I could rent one of her cabins.

This one was the only one in town that was available, and she didn't own it. It wasn't in the best of shape. Luckily, I knew a great contractor, which was how Patrick and I started our new relationship. Thank goodness for old knobs and tube wiring that needed to be replaced.

The price tag on the old cabin had been cheap, and cheap was my price. Thankfully Aunt Maxi had a lot of furniture in storage, and I was extremely happy she'd given me the run of what I needed and wanted.

The two rocking chairs on the front porch were made by my grandfather, were a perfect addition to the cabin, and were my favorite part of the cabin.

The inside was one big room with a combination kitchen and dining room. The bathroom and laundry room were located on the far-back right. There was a set of stairs that led up to one big room that was considered the bedroom. The natural light from the skylights and the large window in the bedroom really made the room inviting. After I'd added the white iron bed suite from Aunt Maxi's storage unit and a few quilts she had stored, the bedroom was cozy and perfect for me and now my little family.

Patrick did have a much larger house—in fact it was Aunt Maxi's at one time—and had wanted us to live there. It wasn't that easy for me, and the cabin suited our needs just fine.

Thank goodness Patrick was understanding. He loved the cabin just as much as I did.

"What can I do?" Mom asked.

"I wanted to see if I could come by the office tomorrow and take a look at the paperwork Stella had filled out online?" I asked and sat down on the couch where Pepper was waiting for me.

Sassy and Patrick had gone upstairs to get ready for bed.

"Hold on, honey." The phone went silent for about a minute before she came back on. "That was the sheriff. He wants to come see me in the morning."

"I figured he wanted to get any information you have on Stella." I wasn't going to push her to get me the information at this point because it would be interfering with Shepard's case.

"I'm going to meet him there first thing." I could hear something in Mom's voice like she wasn't paying too much attention to me but was thinking.

"I'll let you get back to your client." I tried not to put too much of an emphasis on the word client.

"I'll call you after Spencer stops by," she told me before we said our goodbyes.

I put the phone on the coffee table. I pulled the quilt off the back of the sofa and put it over my curled-up legs.

"I know it's none of our business," I said to Pepper and ran my hand down his soft fur. "But I just can't help it. There's so much that intrigues me."

Pepper looked up and blinked his eyes. His bushy brows were so cute. He laid his head back down on the couch.

"The lawyer in me can't help but wonder if she was just a victim of a purse snatching gone wrong. Possibly had money in her bag they took or tried to take." From what I had gathered from Spencer at the coffeehouse, they'd yet to find any sort of belongings of Stella's.

If she was a random victim of purse snatching like Loretta and fought them, they stabbed her because she fought back or because she saw them.

If she was a target of this crime, was the killer smart enough to do some purse snatching beforehand so it looked like a random purse snatching gone wrong?

There were so many questions I had, and as a lawyer, those questions continued to itch and itch like a bad case of poison ivy. Those were hard to ignore and not scratch.

"Maybe we can just go look around tomorrow," I suggested to Pepper and curled the blanket up under my chin.

I glanced at my phone.

"Or now." There was no way I was going to go to sleep. It was one of those instances where I couldn't quiet my mind.

There were so many things I could do, like google lottery winners. From what I'd seen in the past with these big winners, most loved the attention and wanted to be seen. Not in Stella's case. From what Birdie told me, Stella didn't tell anyone.

There were two things that stood out about Stella keeping this huge thing a secret.

She was private, and she knew it wouldn't be good to tell. But she had to have come from somewhere. Someone had to have realized she'd been gone for months.

Was there a missing person's case? When was the last lottery winner who claimed the prize anonymously?

These were two questions I could google.

"Missing woman," I said out loud and typed on my phone internet search without a filter.

I scanned down the phone screen and looked at the websites listing all the ways to search before I got to the images.

"Maybe?" I asked Pepper and clicked the tab for images. "Red hair, red hair," I repeated and scrolled through the photos until I came upon one that had red hair. "Hmm."

I clicked the image and pinched it with my fingers to magnify the photo. When Kevin had pulled back the cover over top of her and Spencer had stopped him, I didn't get a real good look at her, so I wasn't sure if it was her. The name didn't match.

I clicked on the photo, and it took me to a town in the northern part of Kentucky. With all of that information, I cleared the search and typed in the search bar "anonymous lottery winner in northern Kentucky."

"My goodness, Pepper." I clicked on the first article with the headline that read Big Lottery Winner Is Local.

"According to this article, someone won the lottery last summer. The single winner didn't come forward until late fall." I quickly counted back the number of months. "It would be about the time she rented from Aunt Maxi."

I hit the back button of the internet to take me back to the young missing woman with red hair.

"Okay, so if we see where this woman is from and it matches an area of the winning lottery ticket, then we just might have our girl." The name Roselyn Bohlen popped up with not only more photos and articles on her being missing but her social media.

Instaphoto was a social media app where it was mainly just photos. It wasn't like the other social media platforms, and I really liked this one. In fact, Birdie had made one for the Bean Hive Coffeehouse. She was putting photos of her latte creations on there as well as photos of the weekly menu items. There were a lot of customer photos on there, and she'd even started a weekly customer appreciation where they got a free coffee.

Roselyn Bohlen was on there and public, which meant I could see her photos. It looked like the last time she'd posted was around the time she went missing, which was about the time she showed up in Honey Springs.

I scrolled through the photos and zeroed in on the last one she'd posted.

The photo was taken pointed down to her shoes and focused on something next to her leg. The background was blurry, but there was something I recognized that only I would probably notice.

A big bushy brow.

Pepper's big bushy brow.

"So you know Roselyn Bohlen?" I asked Pepper, who didn't move. "This is how it went down. She won the lottery. Didn't tell anyone. Drove into Honey Springs and didn't leave, as she'd probably only intended to drive through. Stopped at the Bean Hive Coffeehouse. Met you. Took a photo and that was that." I continued to scroll through the photos. "She made herself a new identity and a new life."

There were so many photos of this young woman at a coffeehouse, and that's when I knew I had the right person for sure.

No wonder she had found a home at the Bean Hive Coffeehouse.

Roselyn Bohlen was a barista in her previous life.

CHAPTER SIX

The cool morning air whipped across my face as the pavement glided under the wheels of my bike. We were just days away from when the early chill would warm up and the four thirty a.m. bike ride would be so nice and pleasant.

Pepper didn't care. He was nestled in the front basket with his nose in the air, taking in all the early-morning smells from all the critters that liked to roam around these parts in the dark.

The day was going to be gorgeous. The millions of glowing stars in the sky lighting up the curvy, old country road to the boardwalk told me there wasn't a cloud in the sky.

Good thing too. I had a lot of snooping around to do since I'd pretty much narrowed down exactly why this Stella had tried so hard to keep her real identity as Roselyn a secret.

On my list of things locally was to stop by my mom's real estate office located downtown, go see Evan at the bank, and see if I could get Aunt Maxi to let me in the cabin she'd rented to our victim.

I'd spent the better part of the night awake and wondering just which scenario I'd played out in my head was the real reason Roselyn was killed. A purse snatching gone wrong? Or made to look like a purse snatching to rob her?

The thought made my skin crawl with chills.

I wasn't a detective, but being a lawyer and knowing how the law worked, I knew the more time that went by, the harder it was to collect good clues.

The bike made the final curve where off in the distance the cute carriage lights from the boardwalk glowed. Cane Construction had put them in during the renovation of the boardwalk, and they were beautiful. Patrick really did nice work.

Most mornings he and Sassy were fast asleep when I went to work, but this morning he was up and ready to take me to work. Though I had my own car, he was being protective. As the conversation progressed, I used my litigation skills to get him to agree that my life needed to go on and that making everything normal, such as me riding my bike to work, was the best all-around solution for the community.

Speaking of community, my mouth watered at the thought of eating one of the freshly made scones and a cup of coffee while the ovens heated up and the other coffees brewed.

My legs pedaled faster just thinking about the coffee. I needed a good cup of strong coffee to settle my nerves.

Thump, thump. The tires crossed over the wooden boards of the boardwalk, echoing off the trees and the lake, breaking the silence. The dark silence.

Pepper had sat up like he always did once we hit the boardwalk. I was much more vigilant of my surroundings, when most mornings I'd let the wonderful wind hit my face for a refreshing start to the day.

It wasn't one of those mornings.

In my head, I'd already played my strategic moves to get into the coffeehouse as fast as I could. That started at home with Pepper going potty there and not me taking our time for him to take a nice sniff walk along the boardwalk.

I popped off the bike and stuck it in the bike rack outside of the coffeehouse. I had my key at the ready as I picked up Pepper, and then I shoved the key into the door, quickly opening it then shutting it behind me.

"Morning!" Polly squawked, sending me into an airborne karate chop.

"Polly," I gasped. "I forgot all about you."

Pepper didn't like Polly. When I put him down on the floor, he tucked his little nubby tail and ran to the back of the coffeehouse.

"Polly good girl. Polly good girl." Polly bounced up and down.

"You sure are." I snickered and flipped the light on to illuminate the inside of the coffeehouse.

What little bit of nerves I had left had been shot to pieces after Polly scared me. Instead of taking a minute to enjoy a cup of coffee and a bit of scone, it was easy to busy myself with starting the morning ritual.

On my way back through the coffeehouse, I couldn't help but still have that deep down feeling of how much I loved the exposed brick walls and wooden beams. It made the place so cozy, and though we'd grown over the past couple of years where we added the roastery, it was still a perfect job for me.

I'd spent so much time and energy learning DIY projects when I'd remodeled the place, there was just a feeling of love for all the hard work and an appreciation for how much this place was part of me.

I walked past the café tables to go behind the counter and flipped on all the industrial coffeepots to brew, and I couldn't help but think of Roselyn when I arranged all the condiments in the middle so they'd be ready for customers.

It wasn't unheard of for people to keep it a secret they'd won the lottery, but to actually leave their life and even change their name was something I'd consider odd.

Strange.

The swinging door separating the kitchen—where Pepper or any other animal was prohibited—and the actual dining area of the coffeehouse almost hit me in the keister.

"Whoa." I jumped forward so I wouldn't get smacked. "I need to get my head in the game," I muttered to myself, knowing there were a lot of things I needed to do before we opened at six a.m.

On my way to the walk-in freezer, I turned the ovens to preheat and flipped on my personal coffeepot to let it brew while I retrieved the menu items for the week.

There were always one or two choices for a lunch item and a few desserts to fill the weekly menus. Initially I was going to make it coffee-only since that's where my passion was, but quickly I realized customers loved to chat, eat, and drink. With those customers in mind, I kept a very limited menu.

During the winter months, the coffeehouse was closed on Sundays, so after church I would make a day of it in the kitchen. It was fun to create various recipes and make the popular items that could be frozen for a few months and keep their fresh taste so I could simply reheat or bake them as the spring and summer months arrived. I didn't have time to bake on Sundays then since we opened after church during those times.

"Ding! Ding!" Polly was so loud, I could hear her while I was in the freezer.

"What on earth is that, Roxanne?" Bunny Bowoski made it into the kitchen faster than she did on the other mornings.

"Good morning." I knew she'd get a kick out of the bird. "That's Polly. And I warn you to watch what you say unless you want someone to know it."

"This has gotten ridiculous." She pulled the bobby pins from the edges of the pillbox hat that sat on top of her gray, chin-length hair. She put the hat that matched the colors of her shawl on the island workstation. "I am all for having dogs and even cats here to help out Louise, but a bird?" She waved her hand in front of her. "They are stinky."

"I was hoping to see if I could get someone to take Polly home and maybe just put up a featured animal photo of her, but we've been a little busy around here." I knew she'd yet to hear about Roselyn Bohlen.

"Busy?" Her head popped up, her eyes lighting up with interest.

Bunny helped me peel off the plastic wrap and tinfoil and place the items on the necessary baking pans before we popped them into the oven.

"And you said her name was Stella Johnson, but really it's Roselyn?" Bunny picked up the kitchen timer off the counter and twisted it to go off in twenty minutes.

"Yes. I think so." I washed my hands and retrieved my phone from my apron pocket to show her what I'd discovered from the little bit I'd already snooped.

Bunny took a seat on one of the barstools butted up to the workstation.

"My word," Bunny gasped. "I have seen her in here in the afternoon. Birdie talked to Stella."

"You recognize this woman?" I used my fingers to blow up the profile photo of Roselyn so she could get a good look.

Not that I didn't trust her, but she was elderly and insisted I needed her help when I didn't have any employees and couldn't even afford one, so she kinda hired herself. But truly I believed she enjoyed the company and loved the gossip.

"I told you I did." She leaned into the phone. "That's her. The young woman

193

who came in here a few times when I was leaving." The barstool underneath her groaned when she sat back. "You said she was stabbed?"

"That's what Kevin said, and I'm not sure if it was a purse snatching." The coffeepot had beeped off a few minutes ago, but I just now had the time to get me and Bunny a cup. I slid one in front of her and took a seat across from her, minding the timer so nothing would get burnt.

Many times I'd get to talking and forget about something in the oven. We didn't need that this morning.

My eyes followed Bunny's. They focused on the shelf underneath the work-station.

I leaned back and noticed she was looking at the wipe-off board.

"You thinking what I'm thinking?" she asked with a grin.

I shrugged.

"It ain't gonna hurt." She shrugged back. "What else do we have to do? I can't think of nothing better than keeping Honey Springs safe."

Without getting up, I reached down to grab one of the whiteboards along with the dry-erase marker.

"Victim," I said and wrote at the top. "After all, too much crime and our economy will tank," I told her, knowing it was just an excuse I needed to tell myself to throw us right into the investigation to catch a thief and a killer.

CHAPTER SEVEN

Bunny and I had listed everything I'd found out from the time Roselyn died until the moment the Bean Hive Coffeehouse opened.

It was a busy morning. Bunny and I found we were unable to look each other's way, much less talk about what'd taken place on the pier.

I barely had enough time to get the industrial coffeepots down to the Cocoon Inn where Camey Montgomery offered free coffee to her guests. I also used that time to take Pepper with me so he could potty before I brought him back into the coffeehouse to eat. After his belly was full, he snuggled up in his little bed next to the fireplace—though there wasn't a fire—and slept the morning away.

Spencer and his deputies had been out near the spot where Pepper had found the body all morning. I did glance a few times out the Bean Hive windows to see if the yellow police tape was still up.

It was.

"Any news?" Aunt Maxi asked after she made her way up to the display case where everything I'd made for the day had been picked over.

She made her way down the L-shaped glass countertop.

"You're out of everything." She shook her head. "I swear, murdering is good for business."

I gave her the stink eye to be quieter in case a customer heard her.

"That's why I'm changing the boards you did last night," I said and went down the line of hanging menus.

The first chalkboard menu hung over the pie counter and listed the pies and cookies with their prices. The second menu hung over the tortes and quiches. The third menu before the L-shaped counter curved listed the breakfast casseroles and drinks. Over top the other counter, the chalkboard listed lunch options, including soups, and catering information.

"I reckon I can help if Bunny is going to sit on her laurels," Aunt Maxi said out of the side of her mouth but loud enough for Bunny to hear.

"It's the least you can do with the steep rent you make your own niece pay." Bunny wasn't going to let Aunt Maxi get away without sending a jab back.

"Not today," I whispered on my way past her. "You take the coffee bar, and I'll do the tea."

On each side of the counter was a drink stand. One was a coffee bar with six industrial thermoses with different blends of my specialty coffees as well as one filled with a decaffeinated blend, even though I clearly never understood the concept of that. But Aunt Maxi made sure I understood some people only drink the unleaded stuff. The coffee bar had everything you needed to take a coffee with you. Even an honor system where you could pay and go.

The drink bar on the opposite end of the counter was a tea bar. Hot tea, cold tea. There was a nice selection of gourmet teas and loose-leaf teas along with cold teas. I'd even gotten a few antique teapots from Wild and Whimsy antiques shop, which happened to be the first shop on the boardwalk. If a customer came in and wanted a pot of hot tea, I could fix it for them or they could fix their own to their taste.

A few café tables dotted the inside along with two long window tables with stools butted up to them on each side of the front door, which was my favorite spot to sit and relax.

"Can I get you something else?" I asked the customer and held up the coffee carafe to refill their mug.

"No thank you." The customer smiled. "What's going on there?" The customer pointed to the crime scene.

"Maybe one of the boards needs to be nailed down. Boating season is around the corner, and the Beautification Committee is always making sure we are ready." I didn't see a reason to tell the customer the truth.

It must've satisfied him. He got up and left. I took his mug back to the counter. Bunny was behind the register taking some orders, while Aunt Maxi had put their differences aside and helped fill them.

"Look at you two." I smiled with pride and left it at that.

"I came in here to tell you something about the you know what." Aunt Maxi gestured for me to go back into the kitchen.

Bunny told us to go on, and she'd get the coffee changed over as well as refill some of the items in the display case. Aunt Maxi plucked her hobo bag from one of the arms of the coat-tree and swung it over her shoulder on our way into the kitchen.

"I called Penny this morning to see what she had on Stella." Aunt Maxi noticed the wipe-off board on the workstation. "Who's Roselyn?" Aunt Maxi pointed to the name I'd written down underneath Stella's name.

"That's Stella's real name, I think." My brows knitted. "I've not had time to really dig into it, but I'm hoping this afternoon I'll be able to investigate a little more."

"We will get back to that. Before I forget what I was telling you, your mom said Spencer had already come to get the files. There's not much. Stella didn't leave any sort of information but a contact number." Aunt Maxi dug down into her bag and pulled out a piece of tissue paper with a number written on it. "Don't judge. I couldn't find any paper."

"I'm not judging." I reached down into the pocket of my apron and pulled my phone out to plug in the number. "Hello?" I asked when someone clicked the other line. "Yes. I'm looking for someone who knows Roselyn."

"Or Stella!" Aunt Maxi hollered.

The phone went dead.

"So that's odd." I pulled the phone from my ear and looked at it, clearly seeing the person had hung up on me. Immediately I redialed the number. "Straight to a recording that says no voicemail has been set up."

The kitchen door swung open.

"Spencer." I reached across the workstation and grabbed the top of the wipe-off board, sliding it next to the stool and resting it on the ground. "I was just telling Aunt Maxi she needed to give you this phone number Stella had given her."

"Stella? I thought you said..." Aunt Maxi's curious tone was cautious.

"It could be her phone number or couldn't be." I tried to cover up whatever Aunt Maxi was going to say so he didn't think we were snooping. "I mean, I guess we could call it."

Spencer had shifty eyes. Very shifty eyes. They darted from Aunt Maxi to me.

"What's going on here?" He wagged a finger between us.

"I'm gonna leave now," Aunt Maxi said. "I'll meet you at the cabin," she told Spencer and left the kitchen.

I looked away.

"Roxanne." The stern tone in Spencer's voice told me I better come clean. "You're a lawyer, and you know the rules. If you know something that will help me get this case solved or possible information that will lead to an arrest, you have to tell me."

Have to? He was right. I did know the law, and everything I had was honestly circumstantial evidence that was searching the internet even though I knew a lot of cases these days were solved by looking up people's internet footprint.

"Fine." I tugged the whiteboard back up to the workstation and began pointing to the board while telling him about what I'd found just on the internet alone. "I believe Stella, the victim, is the missing woman, Roselyn, and that she is an anonymous winner of the big ten-million lottery."

Spencer's eyes narrowed, his face contorted, and his head tilted.

"I think." I picked up my phone and tapped around until I found the article about the missing woman before I showed it to Spencer to let him read. "As you can see, I googled missing persons and came up with the photo, which got me a name, then I searched it on all the social medias."

Spencer's head didn't move as his eyes shifted up to look at me from underneath his brows.

"When did you do all of this?" he asked.

"Last night when I couldn't sleep." I turned around and got him a mug. "Do you want a cup of coffee?" I asked before a ruckus happened in the front of the coffeehouse.

"Help!" The shrill scream made me and Spencer jump to our feet.

"Help! Help!" Polly squealed too. "My purse was stolen! Stolen!"

Spencer had beat me to the punch. He'd already gotten in front of whoever it was yelling and sobbing in the entrance of the Bean Hive Coffeehouse.

The customers had already gathered around Spencer and the victim, leaving me little room to maneuver my way in and out of the crowd.

"I'm sorry. Excuse me," I told them and squeezed in between the clusters and kept my eyes on Spencer's head since he stood taller than the crowd.

When I made it to the middle, I shoved past the last customer and couldn't believe my eyes.

"Roxanne! I was getting on my bike and someone... my purse!" Aunt Maxi's face was red. Her eyes twitched as though they were on fire. "I'm gonna get that purse snatcher if you don't." She reached up and grabbed ahold of Spencer's uniform and got a fistful of fabric.

CHAPTER EIGHT

Aunt Maxi had had about enough by the time we'd gotten her out of the sheriff's department, where she gave her statement after becoming the next victim of the purse snatcher.

I'd gone with her in Spencer's sheriff's truck since neither of us had a car today. While she was in the department, I called Patrick and gave him a quick update on what had happened so he'd not hear it around town.

In true Patrick fashion and without letting me know that he knew now that Aunt Maxi had become a victim there was no way I wasn't going to put my nose in it, he told me he was going to run by the coffeehouse and get Pepper so Bunny didn't have to fool with him today.

Patrick knew me so well. This purse snatching thing was too close to home for me now.

"I'm telling you, they didn't say a word." Aunt Maxi had me take her to the real estate office instead of me taking her straight to her house. "I fought like a cat."

"I'm sure you did. But why would you do that?" I had to ask knowing Roselyn had been killed.

I drove past Central Park, the park located in downtown Honey Springs and across from the real estate office, and did a U-turn at the next light so I could snag a parking spot.

"I wanted to get the mask off of his face." The disgust spewed from her mouth. She unbuckled her seat belt. "It had my lipstick that I love. You know the one that's been discontinued?"

Her shoulders slumped, and she sighed.

"Why do makeup companies do that?" Her mind was moving in so many different directions that it made it hard to keep up with her. "They get you all roped into one perfect lipstick shade then they stop making it."

"His?" I asked, bringing her back to the purse snatching. "You said his face."

I wondered if this was the first big clue.

"Yes. He was strong and had big black gloves on." She bent down to look at the floorboard right before she smacked her hand on her forehead. "I was looking for my bag. See, it's a part of me." She let go of an exhausting sigh.

"Are you sure you don't want me to take you home?" There was no reason why she wanted to come to the real estate office. "Take it easy the rest of the day?"

"That barista." Her head turned to look at me.

"Roselyn?" I asked to confirm we were on the same page.

"Whatever her name is." Aunt Maxi threw a wrist. "He said, 'Give me your purse, or you'll turn out like her.'"

She popped open the door and got out. I jumped out and hurried around the car.

"What? You can't just leave that little bit of information hanging out there. Did you tell Spencer? Because this is the first time I've even heard you mention this." It was true that victims of crimes or even traumatic experiences often remembered small bits of information hours or even months later.

Somehow the brain protected us from bad memories, which was probably a good thing.

"I kept that little bit to myself. Because I want to find him and make him pay." Not only did her words come out in an angry tone, but her footsteps were also heavy with a voice of their own. She twisted the handle of the door and walked into the real estate office.

The receptionist looked up when the bell over the door rang.

Since Mom took over the real estate office, she'd not bothered to update the interior. Though it was tastefully decorated with a sitting area with a fancy area rug, the drink station along the wall could stand to use a little upgrade.

The old coffee pot let out an odor of burnt coffee as soon as you stepped into the lobby, which to me didn't go well with the cinnamon candle burning on the receptionist's desk.

"Your mom will be right with you." The receptionist smiled. "She's on a private call."

"Private, huh?" With all the hullabaloo of the initial investigation of Roselyn's murder I was doing on my own and Aunt Maxi getting robbed, the receptionist jarred my memory of Mom's late client dinner last night.

The receptionist started to say something, but the button on the old phone sitting on her desk went off, sending her into the flurry of activity she did when someone was there to see Mom.

It was all relativity formal and odd, but Mom called it cozy and southern. I didn't tell her how to run her business, and she didn't tell me how to run the Bean Hive.

"Mrs. Bloom," the receptionist said when she hit the call button that went straight into Mom's office, which just so happened to be on the other side of the wall. "Ms. Bloom and Maxine are here to see you."

"This is nuts." Aunt Maxi walked past the receptionist's desk and bolted right into Mom's office.

"Maxine!" My mom's bewilderment was heard through the thin wall. "You can't just barge into an office."

"My tail end I can't when I own the building and pretty much pay your salary with all the rentals I give you to lease for me. Besides, I can do what I want in this critical time of me being robbed." Aunt Maxi made it clear she wasn't going anywhere.

When I walked in behind her, she'd already planted herself on the love seat Mom kept in her office, which looked more like a family room than an office.

"Robbed?" Mom's eyes popped open.

"Hey, Mom." I made sure I walked over to her and gave her a proper greeting with a hug.

"Just like the rest of them." Aunt Maxi smacked her hands together. "Well, most of them, except Roselyn. That's why I'm here." Aunt Maxi edged up on the end of the seat. "I need the extra keys to the cabin you rented Stella Roselyn."

Aunt Maxi combined the names to cover her bases.

"I don't have time to dillydally. I need my bag, and I'm going to go look around Stella Roselyn's rental for my own answers before I meet Spencer there." Aunt Maxi had made an appointment earlier for Spencer to get keys for the rental.

Now that she, too, had been a victim of the purse snatcher, I wasn't sure what had come of their arrangement to get into the cabin, but Aunt Maxi sure did have one thing on her mind.

Getting there first.

"I told Spencer earlier we needed a warrant when he stopped by here to get the information packet, which I gave him seeing as Stella, um, Roselyn didn't really fill anything out." Mom pulled a file from the standing organizer on her desk and laid it open in front of her. "The only thing she put on here was a phone number."

Aunt Maxi got up, and I walked over to the desk to see the number.

"The same number she gave me." Aunt Maxi shrugged.

"Maybe Spencer can find something out." I let that trail die because I knew I would call the number again and see if someone answered later. I could do that all by myself and not with Aunt Maxi and Mom there to interrupt when or if I did get someone to talk to me on the other line.

"I don't think it's a good idea for you to go into the cabin." Mom looked at me with big eyes. The kinda look that told me without saying she wanted me to back her up with all the lawyer talk.

"Why not?" I asked.

"Yeah. Why not?" Aunt Maxi straightened her shoulders and put her fists on her hips. She looked at me. "Tell her, Roxanne." She threw her chin up a smidgen. "Go on."

"There's not been a warrant served, so Spencer hasn't taped it off. Though we don't want to disturb any evidence, as the owner, Aunt Maxi—and I'm sure it's in the contract the renter signed…" I talked as things popped into my head in the order they appeared and for clarification purposes. "Aunt Maxi needs to check on something."

"Like the bathroom sink leak." Aunt Maxi pointed at me. "I told Quentin Russell to get over there and fix it. I even gave him Stella Roselyn's phone number. He had all sorts of nasty things to say about her not letting him in, so I reckon they figured it out. I haven't heard hide nor hair from him since I told him to just get in there and get it done."

"Wait." I couldn't believe I was just hearing this now. "You mean to tell me you had Quentin go in the cabin, and they didn't have such a great chemistry?"

"Yes. Why?" Suddenly her jaw dropped, rendering her speechless after she'd taken a second to realize she might've just given us our first suspect.

CHAPTER NINE

"What exactly do we know about Quentin Russell?" I asked Aunt Maxi on our way out of Mom's office with the extra cabin key in our possession.

I stopped to give her time to answer before we got back into the car and drove to the cabin Roselyn had rented from her.

It would be one thing if we were going in not knowing the things we did and Aunt Maxi possibly being a victim of the same person who killed Roselyn, which all pointed to purse snatching. It's a whole different ball game if we go in there knowing what we know and disrupt anything before Spencer gets his warrant.

There was no doubt in my mind the judge would give Spencer the warrant. It was a matter of time. And that's what I needed.

Time.

"We can talk about this in the car." Aunt Maxi took a step forward.

"I think we need to talk about it now. Get a game plan so we don't do anything that will land us behind bars," I said and took an inventory of our surroundings.

"I hate when the lawyer side comes out in you. It's not a good side." Aunt Maxi never wanted me to be a lawyer.

No wonder. She liked to live on the spicier side of life and not know the rules so she could play dumb when the rules didn't play to her favor. In this case, there wasn't any sort of law that would be on our side if we went into what could possibly hold the answers to why Roselyn was killed, unless it was just a case of a purse snatching gone wrong.

The sidewalk around Central Park was filling up with people who were walking their dogs, sightseeing, or power walking. The gorgeous spring day had brought out a lot of people. Even the big white gazebo was full of people.

There was a young couple sitting perfectly on the sidewalk with the spring daffodils that had popped out of the soil. The marigold, daisies, lilies, and wildflowers were also standing at attention as if they dared the daffodils to outdo them.

"I don't know much about him. I know he needed a job. He was sleeping on a park bench, and I gave him a job." I listened to Aunt Maxi tell me about Quentin, her new handyman, and couldn't stop myself from smiling when I heard a woman pointing a camera at the happy couple telling them to smile.

Young love.

"He needed a place to sleep, so I gave Jean Hill a call. I know she's been needing someone to come out to her place and work around out there." Aunt Maxi, of course, didn't get any credentials.

"I know you do these things out of the kindness of your heart and past experiences, but times are different." I hated to give her a lecture, but she needed to know things had changed. "People aren't as honest as they used to be."

It was a fact. Something I didn't like, but it was, and now that it was getting warmer, there were a lot of people who came to Honey Springs that we didn't know a lot about. We might think they were campers out in the tent or something when in reality they didn't have a home. It was sad.

"He had credentials." Aunt Maxi's forehead wrinkled. "Kirk said he used him."

"Kirk? As in my ex?" My cheeks puffed out as my lungs deflated like balloons.

"I didn't want to say anything, but I didn't have anything at the time for Quentin to do, so Kirk and what's her name..." Aunt Maxi looked as though she was searching for the name.

"Jessica," I reminded her.

"Her." Aunt Maxi started walking to the car. I'd held her off as long as I could. "Bought the old cabin off your mom, and they needed a lot of work done on that place. You and I both know Kirk isn't good with his hands."

"Oh, he was good with his hands, just not on me." I made Aunt Maxi spit out laughter that bounced off the roof of the car and echoed over into Central Park. "Get in."

I couldn't stop my eyes from rolling as I recognized there was no way of getting around it. I was going to have to go talk to Kirk and Jessica, something I'd tried to avoid since they took up residency here.

Kirk and I had buried the hatchet, living amicably in Honey Springs. He'd gone back and forth from Honey Springs to his law firm, but Jessica seemed to love it here so much she'd stayed.

From what I understood—not because anyone had told me because no one wanted to discuss Kirk in my presence, but it was hard not to hear gossip when you owned a coffeehouse where the gossip poured out of people's mouths as much as I poured hot coffee into their cups that kept them there to talk—Jessica had a job at the Bee Happy Resort, which was really a fancy spa.

It would make sense because Kirk and Jessica were Crissy Lane's financial backers when she first opened the spa located on the island across the lake.

Why couldn't this be easy? I wondered to myself.

"Okay. Get in." I pointed the key fob at the car and clicked the locks open.

"I can tell you're mad," Aunt Maxi said to me after I got into the car. "Quentin was out in the cold, and I just couldn't stand it. I'd never seen the mad side of him until the day he told me he went over to the cabin and knocked on the door like I told him to do. When Stella Roselyn didn't answer, I told him to go on in and announce himself."

I started the car and looked over my left shoulder to make sure I wasn't going to pull out into oncoming traffic.

The courthouse was the tallest building and was located in the middle of Main Street. It was also the busiest building with all the government offices. I noticed Kirk's fancy sedan parked right up in the front.

I threw the car in drive and did a U-turn.

"Where are you going?" Aunt Maxi held onto the door. "The cabin is that way." She gestured toward Lake Honey Springs.

"I know, but Kirk is that way." I needed to get some solid truth on who this Quentin Russell was and Kirk's take on him.

Kirk was a lot of things, and a few that weren't very becoming of him, but he always told it like it was and didn't sugarcoat anything. Most times I didn't like what he had to say, but in this instance, I wanted to know.

"I knew you were going to be mad." Aunt Maxi's lips pulled together. "What is it you're going to do? Run into the courtroom if Kirk is in court and interrupt?"

"No." I shook my head. "I'm going to put a note on his car so when he gets out, he will call me."

The medical building where the dentist, optometrist, podiatrist, and good old-fashioned medical doctors were was just a block over from the courthouse, and beyond that was Honey Springs National Bank.

It also crossed my mind to head on down to the bank to see Evan Rich about Roselyn's account, but time was precious since we needed to get to the cabin before Spencer.

I did one last U-turn in the medical building parking lot before I illegally pulled behind Kirk's car.

"Can you get the pad of paper from the glove box?" I asked Aunt Maxi.

She didn't make a peep as I wrote Kirk a note with a little information about why I needed to talk to him about Quentin Russell.

Aunt Maxi sat in the passenger seat while I jumped out and snugged the note under his windshield wiper so any sort of sudden spring breeze didn't take it on its travels.

"Satisfied?" Aunt Maxi's question held a sarcastic tone.

"Very." I shoved the car in drive and took off toward the cabin Aunt Maxi had rented Roselyn Bohlen.

CHAPTER TEN

There were so many old hunting cabins in and around Honey Springs. They were run-down and needed a lot of work. As Honey Springs continued to become a destination for tourists due to Lake Honey Springs, the need for places for those visitors to stay increased.

The Cocoon Inn was about the only place to actually stay, and even then there were limited rooms.

When I moved to Honey Springs, a lot of those old cabins were being bought for the sole purpose of fixing them up and using them as rentals. Aunt Maxi was in a position to purchase a few, and with the help of Patrick, she'd made a decent little side hustle being a landlord to a few of the tourists who ended up staying for more than just a vacation.

The one Roselyn had rented for the six months was really a cute cabin nestled in the hillside. If you didn't know it was there, you'd never see it from the road.

"I'm going to need to talk to Quentin," I told her after her lengthy reasoning of why she didn't think Quentin could do such a thing.

"Have you not listened to anything I've said since we've been in the car?" She huffed and folded her arms.

The long grass and wildflowers grew up along the edges of the windy drive-way. It was enchanting, as though we were driving up to a fairy garden. Aunt

Maxi knew how to put those romantic touches that gave off all the feels. The old fence that should've been torn down had strands of white twinkle lights tossed about it, giving a feeling of peace and calm.

She'd even had a small wooden sign stuck in the ground halfway up the drive that read: Shhh... Unwinding.

"I have listened to you, and the only thing I keep hearing is what a nice guy he is, when I am sure he is. But the facts are the facts." I parked in front of the cabin and looked out the windshield where the firepit still had the unused wood stacked up against it with the ax still stuck into the cutting stump.

Something rustling just beyond the tree line caught my attention. Just as I squinted to see what it was, the tail of a doe shot up, giving me a glimpse of the white stripe before it darted deep in the forest.

Just to the right of the cabin was an old covered well and an outhouse that held stories of long ago. Aunt Maxi had dabbled with the idea of tearing those things down, but after Bunny had told her it was history, Aunt Maxi took pride in owning a piece of the past, so she left all the remnants of the old ways of life.

I was glad she did.

"You're telling me Quentin and the victim had a few words. It's worth exploring." I turned the engine off and looked at Aunt Maxi. "I'm not saying you have to say anything to Spencer right now, but I do think you need to call him and tell him you're here so he can't find out on his own and charge you with tampering with evidence." I unbuckled so I could get out of the car. "I want Quentin's phone number."

I reached into the back seat of the car where I still had my winter kit in case the car ever broke down. The kit included more things for Pepper and Sassy than me. The thought of running down with the fur babies in the car weighed more heavily on me than taking care of myself.

But I did have an extra coat and few pairs of gloves.

"Here." I handed her a pair of gloves. "Be sure to put these on so when we go into the cabin and touch something, we won't disturb fingerprints."

I left Aunt Maxi in the car after I noticed she had her cell phone. Luckily that wasn't in her hobo bag when it got stolen.

I walked around the cabin to check things out and keep an eye out for any sort of footprints near the window as if someone were looking in or just in general. The only thing I noticed were wildlife footprints and some hooved prints.

Still in my head I couldn't help but think someone knew Roselyn had won the ten million dollars and possibly stalked her. Even found out she was here.

The person on the other end of the line had to have known her.

I pulled my cell phone out and noticed there wasn't any service.

"I called, so we better hurry up." Aunt Maxi caught me off guard. I jumped. "Something frighten you?"

"My thoughts. They always frighten me." I shook off the scared feeling and took a deep breath. "You got the key?"

"Right here." She held up the single key.

"I will follow you in, but do not disturb anything." I followed her back around to the front of the cabin. There wasn't a large porch like mine. It was a simple wood square with a triangular roof covered in dead leaves left over from the winter.

Immediately I looked at the gutters to make sure they were cleared. I was always keeping an eye out for the foliage that took tolls on the houses and cabins around here. Though it was a gorgeous place to live, nature could do some damage if you didn't keep up on things.

By the way the gutters appeared, it did seem as though Quentin had kept the outside nice and tidy with everything working in tip-top order.

"Take your shoes off," I told her once she opened the old wooden door.

Slivers of sunlight glinted through the grimy glass windows on the side of the cabin.

"She certainly didn't clean the windows." I frowned since most times people rented such a place so they could see their surroundings. "This makes me think she was hiding out from something or someone."

"I think it's a safe bet at this point to think she was hiding from someone." Aunt Maxi slipped her shoes off. "Nothing in here looks any different than when I rented it."

I walked around the one large room Aunt Maxi had fixed up really cute for a television room. There was a stack of *This Old Cabin* magazines on the coffee table. I was a sucker for a front cover with a decorated porch on the front of it.

Aunt Maxi used things like magazines and locally made items to decorate her rentals. I picked up the magazine and noticed the dusty outline where they'd not been moved.

"She didn't use this room at all." I made the observation to an empty room since Aunt Maxi had left me alone in there.

I put the magazine back and found her in the kitchen where she was shuffling through a few pieces of what looked like mail.

"She rented a PO box." Aunt Maxi held up the mail. "In Taylorville."

"Really?" I took the envelope and looked at the return address. "That's kinda a far piece to drive."

Though the small town was a neighboring town, it was the windy roads and time it took to get there that surprised me when Roselyn could've used a local PO box from our post office.

"If you think about it," Aunt Maxi said as she thumbed through the rest of the papers, "it would've been on her way from her hometown."

I smiled at Aunt Maxi using her sleuthing skills to deduce Roselyn's route.

"Yeah. She would've driven through Taylorville to get to Honey Springs." I pictured Roselyn driving. "What time of the day did she call you?"

"It wasn't day. It was night." Aunt Maxi had found a notepad and was reading the first page.

"At night? So if she'd opened the PO box then drove here, got tired, and then called you…" It didn't make a whole lot of sense, and I knew it, but talking it out always helped me when I was a lawyer, which made me use it to reason out Roselyn's steps. "How did she know to call you?"

"Sign. I had Quentin put a sign out by the road." She shrugged and pointed to the paper. "She's listed a few places here and marked through them."

"What do you mean a few places?" I asked.

"Things like the bank, the Bean Hive, though it does have a question mark through it." I looked over her shoulder to see what she was talking about.

"She was a barista before. I wonder if she was going to ask for a job?" I questioned.

"Ten million dollars?" Aunt Maxi wasn't buying it. "Why would she want a job that pays minimum wage?"

"To have some sort of social life. Even just talking to a young teenager like Birdie, it got her out of here." I put the piece of mail still in my hands on the table when I heard the door open.

"Hello? Roxy, don't tell me you're in here." Spencer's disappointed voice fluttered through the cabin. I could tell by the way his footsteps sounded that he already knew the answer to his question.

He walked into the kitchen with a couple of deputies. He gave a head whip, signaling them to sweep through the cabin.

"We came in from the cold. We've not touched a thing." I tried to ignore the fact that Aunt Maxi wasn't trying to even cover up the fact she was still thumbing through the notepad.

"You weren't planning on touching things." Spencer's eyes shifted to our gloved hands.

"It's cold out." I put my hands behind my back.

"It's sixty degrees and spring," he shot back.

"I'm old, and old people get cold." Aunt Maxi played along before she said, "And this gal was hiding from someone. She even stopped in Taylorsville to set up a PO box."

"Actually she set it up online. We got her phone records and pinged her phone. There were no calls made from this location."

"I couldn't even get cell service from my phone when I was walking around. I'm guessing you had cell service to have called Spencer." I glanced at Aunt Maxi.

"She didn't call me." Both of us looked at Aunt Maxi.

"Who did you call when I left you in the car alone?" I asked.

"No one." Her eye twitched. She was lying. "I checked my voicemail."

I let it go because there had to be a reason. I sure hoped it was a good one because if she was caught, Spencer had no issues with locking her up.

"It appears as though she made a list of places she'd gone or was going." I had to jerk the edge of the notepad a couple of times before Aunt Maxi let go of her death grip. "She even had the Bean Hive on here with a question mark. I'd never talked to her, but we know Birdie did, so maybe this afternoon I'll ask Birdie some specifics about their interactions."

"I think that would be a good idea. She'd probably open up to you more than she would me." Spencer flipped through the notepad before he called the deputy over to put it in an evidence bag.

The deputies worked around us bagging things that didn't seem very important, but I wasn't a detective. They bagged things from the dishwasher, the laundry room, and the master bedroom.

"You two stay put," Spencer ordered us.

"Isn't that cute?" Aunt Maxi nudged me.

"What?" I whispered when I noticed the deputy look over after Aunt Maxi questioned me.

"How he thinks he can tell us what to do." Aunt Maxi slipped me a piece of paper. "Before you came into the kitchen, I ripped that off the notebook."

"Aunt Maxi," I gasped through my gritted teeth and slowly closed my eyes, wondering if I should look or just hand it over to Spencer.

There was a reason she was keeping information from him, and I had to get to the bottom of it.

Against my better judgement, and more out of curiosity, I slowly unfolded the piece of notebook paper and noticed a name. "Nikki Dane," along with a phone number. The phone number we'd been calling.

"I'm telling you Quentin did not do this." She squeezed my arm.

I gave a subtle gesture with my head for her to follow me outside. Both of us nodded and smiled to the deputies when we passed them.

"Where are you two going?" Spencer had peeked his head out from the bedroom when we walked down the hall from the kitchen to the television room.

"I've got to get back to the Bean Hive." I didn't lie. I did. I wanted to talk to Birdie, but I didn't mention that I also wanted to stop by the Honey Springs National Bank on my way.

"I'll be in," he said as though he were telling me he had more things to ask me.

"I'll be sure to have you a tuxedo mocha ready." I grinned, trying to hide my wonder and detection of his warning to me that he'd be in to see me.

"He's got a hunch we are hiding something," Aunt Maxi said on the way to the car.

"We are. You are," I corrected myself and put my hand on the door handle of the car while speaking to her over the roof. "Why on earth are you trying to convince me or insist Quentin couldn't be a suspect? Because in any sort of homicide they always look at the person who was in conflict with the victim. Quentin and Roselyn had words, according to you."

"Oh, ladies!" Spencer stood in the doorframe. "The weapon was a screwdriver. Does Quentin, your handyman, use a screwdriver?"

Aunt Maxi glared then turned to me. The blood rushed from her face. Aunt Maxi kept pretty tight-lipped when I peppered her with question after question about Quentin.

"Don't you think we need to look into this Nikki Dane?" Aunt Maxi was so protective of Quentin, and I wasn't sure why.

"I think you are protecting Quentin, and I can't figure out why for the life of me." I gripped the wheel.

"He's innocent. I'm telling you he's innocent," Aunt Maxi insisted. "Right now we need to leave it at that."

"So you aren't going to tell me why you think he's innocent?" I knew I was going to get nowhere with her. She was the type of person that when she made up her mind, there was no one going to change it.

"That's right. For now, I think we need to look into the purse snatchers and this Nikki Dane." She pulled her lips together and stared out the window.

"I guess I'll go to the bank tomorrow." I really had wanted to go today, but the day was getting away from us. I wanted to talk to Birdie to see what she had to say. "Why don't I drop you off at home and have Patrick drop off your bike later today."

I knew she'd left her bike at the boardwalk in the bike rack in front of the Bean Hive because it was where she'd gotten her purse snatched.

"No. I need to jump back on the horse, so to speak." She meant she wasn't going to let the robbery define her and not let her go about her business.

This was the one personality trait I loved most about her. She was able to put any sort of difficulties behind her and move forward. My dad and mom had told me many times when I was growing up how I'd gotten that same trait from Aunt Maxi. I had actually taken pride all those years with being told that. It wasn't until I'd gotten divorced and run back to Aunt Maxi here in Honey Springs that I'd questioned myself.

After Aunt Maxi had given me a good talking to about life, she also gave me a big piece of advice: Never question yourself. And don't let others make you question yourself.

Remembering this piece of information had actually come in very handy in this moment. Aunt Maxi told me with conviction she didn't believe Quentin killed Roselyn even though we knew he'd had a disagreement with her and the murder weapon was a screwdriver. I was questioning her, and I was happy to see she didn't question herself and her belief Quentin didn't commit this crime.

"As long as you are good." I had to make one final statement in order to feel better.

"I'm good." She looked a little more relieved, and the color had come back to her face.

I parked the car on the side of the boardwalk near the Crooked Cat, and we walked in silence to the Bean Hive, where I kissed her goodbye.

"Where have you been?" Loretta Bebe stood in the middle of the packed coffeehouse with a paintbrush in her hand. It was dripping blue paint. "I can't have my campaign manager not be here when I need her."

"Campaign manager?" I darted over to the coffee bar and grabbed a few napkins to sop up the wet paint off the floor.

"Yes. If the mayor isn't going to stop this crime invading our city, then I'm going to." She put down the paintbrush and picked up a poster board that read: *If you want something done, elect a woman! Me! Loretta Bebe!*

CHAPTER ELEVEN

I wasn't sure how the Bean Hive Coffeehouse had become Loretta Bebe's campaign office, but she'd gotten everyone and their brother to help, including Birdie and her study group friends along with Hope , their teacher.

"Birdie has told me several times what a good mentor you've been to her." Hope shook the hot-pink glitter generously over Loretta's name, which I'd just written in glue.

Loretta had appointed me to write her name because she said I had pretty handwriting on the chalkboard menus. I wanted to protest since I needed to go to the bank and go to see Jean Hill so I could find Quentin and question him before I did the unthinkable... go to Bee Happy Resort and find Jessica, Kirk's wife, since I had yet to hear from him.

"It's odd, you know." I shrugged and moved to the next piece of poster board to scribble Loretta's slogan in the white glue. "I wasn't sure if I could help Birdie when she got here. She was very angry at her parents for moving her to Honey Springs. In fact, she's amazing, and she was acting out to be seen and heard. She's a pretty smart kid once she does get her voice." I looked up and smiled at seeing Birdie helping the customers. "I'm so glad Loretta has accepted Birdie for her. Not the daughter she never was able to mold and shape into a Southern debutante like herself."

"How is she?" Hope asked and opened a new bottle of glitter. "You know, since the attack? Birdie said she's been taking it pretty hard."

"Look at her. It's made her determined to get this crime under control," I said. Both of us stopped for a minute to see what Loretta was telling one of the locals.

She was rambling on about her agenda and how she was going to get more deputies hired for Sheriff Spencer. I'd also heard her say it wasn't his fault the mayor wouldn't give money in the budget to hire. This told me she must've talked to Spencer, and since it was an election year, they might've had each other's backs.

"Good. There's so much going on." The corners of Hope 's lips turned down.

"Are you okay?" There was a pit in my stomach telling me she was sad.

"I'll be fine." She put on a fake smile for me that didn't need to be there. My face fell flat at her response. "I'm fine." She tried to shuck me off.

"You don't look fine." I didn't want to interrogate her, but I wanted her to know she had an available ear. "I'm a pretty good listener." I nodded at Birdie. "Ask your student."

"You mean soon-to-be former student." Her words shook me to my core.

"What?" The pit in my stomach had switched to Birdie as my thoughts whirled, wondering if Birdie had done something wrong. "Please don't tell me she got kicked out of class."

"No." She shook her head. "The curriculum got kicked out of school. Apparently home economics isn't as important as it used to be. No one wants to bake, sew, learn how to do a budget anymore. Including the school."

"Are you saying they've not budgeted properly to teach students?" I questioned.

"I'm saying students aren't signing up for the electives like they used to and going to more languages or college-required classes. Home economics is not one of those." She covered her hurt with a smile. "The board voted over the winter break during their budget meeting for the upcoming school year to move the money they are paying me to go to the language curriculum and sporting activities. Mainly football." She rolled her eyes.

"I'm so sorry, Hope ." I knew my sincerest apologies couldn't really help her, but I could offer her a job. "I know I can't pay you what you would be making as a teacher, but if you find yourself needing a job, I'm always looking for nice people."

"Thank you, but I am no barista. I couldn't pour a cup of coffee without spilling it all over the counter." She laughed when she noticed I giggled. "That's very kind of you. I'd expect nothing less since Birdie talks so fondly of you."

"Well, the invitation is still open." I left it at that and finished writing Loretta's name and logo on the boards, leaving the rest to the volunteers, and I used the term loosely due to the fact I was positive no one really did spare their time and were only here on Loretta's orders.

The afternoon was smooth, and I'd yet to hear any more from Spencer, so I wasn't sure where the case stood with Roselyn. I'd given him all I could but knew I needed to at least make one of the three stops.

There was little time to get to the bank before it closed. With that in mind, I decided I would go on out to see Jean and hope Quentin would be out there getting ready for his night, though it was a few hours until nightfall.

"Are you leaving?" Hope asked. She must've noticed how I'd taken my apron off and exchanged it for my light jacket.

Spring in Kentucky was a funny season. The mornings and late afternoons were chilly enough to require a light jacket, while midday was so warm a T-shirt was required.

"I am." I smiled and took my purse, snugging it up underneath my armpit. The fear of getting my purse snatched once I walked out the door had become a little deeper rooted than I'd thought.

"Since this semester will be my last at the school, I wondered if I could take Polly to my classroom. I think she'd be a great addition to the students on how to care for a pet. They truly need to know how owning a pet greatly affects the family, not only regarding their time, but also financially." Hope had come up with a brilliant idea.

"I don't see why not. Birdie!" I called for her over my shoulder. I pointed between them. "Can you call Louise for me and get it set up for Hope to take Polly"—I giggled at the rhyme— "to school?"

"Of course! I'll even help her with Polly tonight." Birdie's phone was never too far from her fingertips. I was pleased to see her grab the file next to the register and look up Louise's number as I headed out of the door.

With Pepper already home, I didn't take my usual time pedaling back to the cabin to get my car so I could go see Jean Hill. Really I was going to see Quentin Russell. Hill's Orchard was the opposite of my cabin and near Pet Palace. I'd not been out that way in a long time.

After the third hairpin curve, there was a fork in the road. A fond memory of Jean's husband, Fred, surfaced. He had given me directions to the farm a few weeks before he died.

"At the fork in the road remember, the tine is the right time." It made no sense whatsoever but made perfect sense at the same time. "Tine" meaning fork in the road, and "right" was the direction.

I smiled at the memory and veered right, and when I got to the old, weathered barnwood sign that said Hill's Orchard in bright-red letters, I turned in.

Jean had taken really good care of the land she and Fred had cultivated into the only orchard around.

The apple trees were on the right, and the grapevines were on the left as far as the eye could see.

The first time I'd come out here, I'd bought a lot of preserves from Fred and Jean to incorporate into my recipes at the Bean Hive. I tried to use as many of the town's locally grown and owned shops as I could. As one small business owner, I supported the next in order to give back to the community.

I made sure each time I made something with the Hill's Orchard ingredients to tell the customer and display a few of Jean's jars.

My mind and my car came to an abrupt stop when I saw Mom's car parked next to the small market building where Jean sold her packaged goods.

"Hello?" I called when I got out of the car. "Jean? Mom?"

No one came, so I headed toward the building, and before I opened the door, I looked through the glass.

Mom and some man were inside with Jean. The three of them were laughing at something before they took a sip of what appeared to be wine.

"Did I interrupt something?" I swung the door open.

"Roxanne." Mom nervously laughed. I knew that laugh. She did that laugh when she didn't want me to know something. I heard that laugh last night on the phone when I interrupted her client dinner.

Jean took an uneasy pose of straightening herself. Her eyes darted to the man.

"Hi there." I hurried over with my arm extended. "I'm Roxanne. My friends and family"—I gave Mom a look since she'd called me formally—"call me Roxy. At least they used to."

"Where are my manners?" Jean pinched a smile. "How are you, dear?"

"I'm good. I'm looking for someone who lives here by the name of Quentin." I got interrupted by the man.

"I'm Quentin." He sure didn't look homeless or uncapable of getting a job. "I've heard a lot about you from Penny."

My eyes darted at my mom before I turned my head to face her.

"Really?" I spoke to him but directed my attention to her. "Funny. I've not heard about you at all. At least not from her."

CHAPTER TWELVE

"**W**hat is wrong with you? Where are your manners?" Mom had dragged me out of Jean's shop and into the field. "You are being disrespectful, and this is exactly the reason I have kept Quentin from you. You will never get over your father passing, and you would never ever forgive me if I were to date again." She stomped. "I'm lonely!" Her voice carried. "You have Patrick. Heck"—she threw her hands up—"you have Maxine, and I have no one. I get the leftover scraps of time you have. Leftovers isn't good anymore. I'm moving on with my life, and right now I'm tired of covering up who I am with and that's Quentin."

I could feel my face contort with every word she was saying. My body had gone through all sorts of emotions leaving me shaking in my shoes.

"You don't even know this man. He doesn't have a job." My mouth dropped open.

"He does. With Kirk at the Bee Happy Resort. He's a great handyman. You just won't even think of giving him a chance because of your dad." Mom used my dad as a weapon, but she was right.

No one was ever going to be good enough to replace my dad. Especially not a murderer.

"Do you know that a screwdriver was found in Lake Honey Springs? It has the blood of Roselyn Bohlen or, as you know her, Stella Johnson on it." I swear I wasn't trying to spit as I talked, but little spurts came out. It was like I'd lost my mind. "And that he had a fight with her just hours before she was murdered?"

"He didn't murder anyone." Mom's calm voice sent chills up my spine.

"How do you know?" I folded my arms, jutted out my right hip, and tapped the toe of my shoe a few times.

"Because Quentin has been with me for the past two weeks, but you wouldn't know that because I get your scraps of time, and when I've tried to tell you, something comes up." Her words nearly bowled me over. "He was with me the entire time Kevin Roberts had put her time of death and even before that."

It didn't take my law degree to also realize she was with him last night at dinner.

"Spencer already came out this afternoon and questioned him. They also looked all over Jean's farm for any evidence. And my house. Quentin is no longer a suspect." Mom had the answer I'd come to seek.

The squeaky door of the building caused both of us to look back.

"Everything all right out here?" Quentin stood about six foot five. He was rather a large man with a thick mustache. He put his hand over his eyes to shield off what little bit of sun was left to the day.

The sun was setting, leaving the sky threaded with red and orange. The beautiful sunsets were always welcomed into my soul, but with the news I'd just received about my mom keeping her love interest from me, the feeling of joy wasn't there.

"We are fine. Right, honey?" Mom asked in her good old sweeping-it-under-the-rug tone.

"Actually you're fine. I'm not. I am concerned about what you see in my mom." I shrugged and moseyed my way back over to the building. Mom was fast on my heels.

"Now, Roxanne. This is none of your business." She might've been right, but I was making it my business.

"Then he should be able to answer my questions as a daughter of the woman he's..." I waffled my hands for him to finish the sentence.

"I think it's safe to say that my feelings for Penny run deeper than friendship, if that's what you're trying to get one of us to say." He held the door open. "Why don't you come back in so we can all discuss it?"

"Deeper than friends? And you live together now?" I couldn't tell if I was more upset that mom was dating someone or if the person I for sure thought killed Roselyn had an alibi. Either way, I wasn't going to give him a pass this easy. "Deeper isn't deep enough."

"Roxanne," my mother gasped.

"It's a fair assumption, dear." My insides started to seethe from how he said *dear*.

"I won't let her disrespect anyone. Even at her age." Mom sucked in a deep breath and passed by me to link her arm with Quentin's.

"I'm sorry if I am coming off as disrespectful, but I was coming here in order to help Aunt Maxi's handyman, only to be blindsided that it's you who my mom is not only dating but living with." This, too, was so odd for me.

"We are not living together." Mom made that quick clarification. "We do spend a lot of time together, and some of those times are well up into the night."

"I gave Quentin a job here at the orchard," Jean Hill said. "He is a very hard-working man who had fallen on hard times over the last year. I'm surprised you've not seen him around."

There were so many farmhands with hats on when I came by the orchard to get my weekly baking supplies that it was hard to tell one from the other. To be truthful, I only wanted to see Jean when I came to visit. I adored her and Fred.

"He keeps me company. I don't live alone or scared someone will come here and rob me. Plus he's handy with a gun in case there's a fox coming round to the hen house."

All of these were good things for Jean. But Mom?

"It's true. He asked me about Penny when she came out here to get something for you. I told him she was single, and it took him a while to ask her out." By the look on Jean's face, I could tell she really liked him.

As did Aunt Maxi.

"Did Aunt Maxi know that you two were together the night Roselyn was killed?" I asked.

"She sure did, and she told me it was up to me to tell you." Mom and Quentin looked like two teenagers with their arms entwined and holding hands. "I knew by how you acted on the phone last night that you knew something was going on, and I was going to tell you about it, but you haven't been available."

"What about your argument with Roselyn?" I asked.

"You don't have to answer this." Mom shot her words at me but patted on his arm with her free hand.

"It's fine, Penny. I have nothing to hide. I told the sheriff the same thing." He pulled away from Mom and gestured for me to sit down.

I took a seat and declined a glass of Jean's homemade wine. Now, if she'd had coffee, I'd have been all over that.

"I've been doing work for your aunt now for the better part of the year. She did introduce me to your ex Kirk, and he said he was looking for a full-time maintenance man for the spa." He gave Mom a sweet smile. "I didn't want to ruin any sort of connection I might have with Penny, so I did ask her before we started dating if you would care if I worked for him."

"That's when I knew he kinda liked me, but I didn't date him until he asked," Mom butted in.

"I'll get to that." He held up a hand to her. "I told Kirk I wanted to think about it because I had been keeping an eye out for Penny and knew of the history he had with her."

It was interesting how he knew Mom and Kirk weren't the biggest of fans of each other, but I continued to listen.

"Right after Christmas, Kirk said they were going to need someone full-time and that I had until the end of spring to decide because summer is their biggest season. That's when they'd need someone there full-time." He picked up the glass and took a drink of the wine. "I asked Penny out, and we spent New Year's Eve together."

"And we weren't doing anything because you just had surgery." She was right. I'd gotten sick on Christmas Day, meaning I was in recovery during the beginning of the new year.

"We had a lot of fun. I couldn't let her go, and I'm glad you found us. Now I can ask you to your face like I've been wanting to do because I love Penny and I would never want to hurt someone she loves so much. That's you." His confession about his feelings to my mom were very sweet, and it kinda melted my leery heart.

"Are you asking me if I care if you go work for Kirk?" I wanted to make sure I was following along. He nodded. "As messed up as this is, I guess we will be one big happy family."

Boy was I about to eat those words. I just didn't know it yet. By the way Mom was reacting to what I'd said, it was like she'd received the best present of her life.

"But." I held up a finger.

"I knew it!" Mom yelled. "There's always a 'but' with you, Roxanne. You can never leave well enough alone."

"I'm sorry if you've forgotten there is a woman dead. *But*"—clearly I had to emphasize the word—"I am looking into it. If Quentin has any information about Roselyn then I would like to hear it. Even the smallest bit of information, like what was in her trash?" My head jerked to Quentin. "Did you see her trash?"

"You know…" A puzzled look lay on his face. His eyes rolled up as if he were searching his brain for a memory. "I didn't realize it until just now, but she never had trash. I had gone over there a handful of times for Maxine to make sure there was enough firewood, that the leaves were out of the gutters back in the fall, that the driveway was cleared when it snowed, that salt was thrown down. It wasn't until this week that I needed to go into the cabin."

"Aunt Maxi said Roselyn acted funny about it."

"Funny is an understatement. She insisted I come back, and when I told her I was there to do it then because I had to go to work at the spa, she huffed and gathered her things from the kitchen table." He didn't seem too alarmed by her actions.

I was.

"What things? Did you see them?" I asked.

"No. She went down into the cellar, and I did my job. I wasn't there long." He eased down on the stool and crossed his arms, his legs extended out in front of him with his boots crossed at his ankles.

"The cabin has a cellar?" I didn't see any sort of cellar door.

"Really it's an old ice chest the hunters used back in the day to store their kills while they hunted so it would keep them fresh until they were ready to leave." He scratched his chin. "It's about twenty feet as the crow flies from the cabin."

"There's electricity in there?" I questioned.

"I don't know. I just saw her open it up and walk down in there. I didn't even mention it to Maxine."

"Do you think we need to go there?" Mom took a vested interest.

"We?" Quentin shook his head. "I don't want you anywhere near a murder case. I think I need to tell Spencer."

"It's late." The darkness lay outside of the building's windows, and I knew if I was going to spend the full afternoon tomorrow going to the bank and possibly going to the cellar if the sheriff's department had cleared it, I was going to need to get a good night's sleep.

"I will tell Aunt Maxi." I got up and apologized to Jean for my behavior earlier.

"Honey, don't you worry about it. I can understand how hard it is at any age when a parent goes back into the dating pool." She was so sweet. "I have some pickled beets fresh today in the house. I'll go grab you a jar."

"Patrick will love that." I gave her a hug and told her I'd meet her outside. "Quentin, I'm sorry I was such a pill. I'm not really like that, so I guess I've surprised myself at how protective I am of my mom."

"I actually liked seeing that side of you." Mom hugged me, giving me one good squeeze.

"No problem. I'm happy you showed up. Now we don't have to hide." He tapped Mom on the back. "I told you."

"He did tell me to tell you." Mom draped her arms around his shoulders. "I just never want to disappoint you anymore like I did when you were growing up."

"Mom." I was going to tell her that she never ever could disappoint me even though I knew she had a hard time forgiving herself for how she reacted when Dad had brought me to Honey Springs for the summer.

"Don't." She put a finger up to my lips. "We don't need to discuss it."

The screen door of Jean's porch slammed shut.

"I better get out of here so Jean doesn't have to come find me." I gave one quicker hug to Mom and a wave of my hand to Quentin.

I wasn't at the hugging stage for him just yet.

CHAPTER THIRTEEN

"What do you know about cellars?" I asked Patrick over the jar of beets. "Quentin said he saw Roselyn go in the cellar on the property of the old hunting cabin."

"There's a cellar?" Patrick didn't even know, and he had done the electrical upgrades to the cabin after Aunt Maxi had bought it as a rental. He forked a beet and put the entire thing in his mouth.

"Yeah." I stood over the gas stove in our house with the tongs in my hand, flipping over the fried chicken. Pepper and Sassy sat at my feet, both wide-eyed in hopes something was about to drop. "He said she'd gathered up some things and that's where she went. Do you think she's hidden the money there?"

Patrick shook his head and smiled.

"You've got one active imagination." He forked another beet and held it up to my mouth. "I don't like beets, but I like Jean's."

"Honestly, Patrick, do you think she's hidden something in there?" I couldn't shake off the idea it would be a wonderful place to hide something. "I'm guessing Aunt Maxi doesn't know the cellar is there."

"If it will make you feel better, after you get the Bean Hive open and Bunny is there, I'll pick you up, and then we can go eat lunch together." He put the fork down and walked over behind me. He wrapped his arms around my waist and rested his chin on my shoulder. "That fried chicken looks so good."

"There's nothing I love more than feeding you." I thought about Kirk for that moment and recalled how he didn't eat anything I baked, fried, or cooked. All of it was too fattening for him.

Even though I had accepted the fact Quentin was now my mom's new boyfriend and he was with her the night of the murder, it still tickled my curiosity to talk to Kirk about the whole situation.

Kirk was one of those guys who loved to know things others didn't. Sorta hold-it-over-your-head type of guy, and knowing Mom and Aunt Maxi were keeping something from me would be right up his alley.

"Why don't we do lunch at Bee Happy Resort?" I asked.

Patrick's chin popped off my shoulder as his arms unraveled. He folded them and moved to the side of the stove, leaning his hip against the counter.

"What's going on in that head of yours?" he asked.

"I know you're going to think I'm crazy," I started to say.

"Me? Nah. If you've got something in your head, I know you've got a reason. Spill it," he said and reached up to the open shelf to grab a plate so I could take the fried chicken out of the cast iron.

"I only want to make sure Quentin's story is correct about him working for Kirk." That was really it.

"Do you have a reason to not believe him? I mean, the guy knows you can ask and find out." Patrick grabbed the bowl of green beans and the bowl of mashed potatoes while I took the plate of chicken.

We moved to our small two-person table and set all the food down. Both of us took a seat. Sassy and Pepper had moved from the stove to underneath the table, still keeping the hope alive that we'd drop something from our forks.

They knew better. We didn't feed them table scraps. Sometimes I did make them some chicken and rice only because the veterinarian had told me a little bit every once in a while was good for their coats.

"Fine. I can see I won't be talking you out of this, so we can go eat at the spa." Patrick picked up his knife and cut his chicken into pieces. "Though I do think it's overpriced."

"Of course it is. It's Kirk." I ate a spoonful of mashed potatoes. "How was your day?"

It was nice to have a sit-down supper with Patrick and the fur babies. A few times, my mind wandered thinking about Mom and Quentin. It was somewhat comforting to know she wasn't spending her extra time alone.

"Where did you go?" Patrick asked.

We had moved to the couch to settle in for a night of binge watching our favorite detective show. He liked it more than me, and I used it as time to snuggle up with him and the dogs while I read my book.

"I was thinking about Mom. I didn't realize until tonight looking at you across the table how lonely she must've felt eating alone for all these years after Dad died." I felt ashamed of how I'd acted earlier. "I only want her to be happy."

"I think she knows that, or you wouldn't've been so protective of her this afternoon." He pulled the quilt off the back of the couch and pulled it over my legs. Though it really wasn't cold in the cabin, I just loved having something on my legs, and he was so in tuned with me.

"Just like this." I patted the quilt. "You automatically know I want my quilt on my legs even though I'm not cold. I want that for Mom."

"Maybe Quentin is the one. I think you should just be happy she's enjoying herself and not be so consumed with it." He kissed my head and pointed the remote to the television. "Let's enjoy the rest of the night."

It was a sure sign he was done talking about it.

I held my book up to my face, and I saw the words, but my mind was doing something totally different.

There were so many questions I had for Roselyn and such little time in the day. I stroked Pepper's back and made a mental list of exactly what I wanted to accomplish on my little snooping-around tour of Honey Springs.

Nikki Dane had to be someone Roselyn trusted. If they were still in contact after Roselyn had won the money, Nikki had to know something. Was she the killer?

I'd failed to ask Quentin about the screwdriver. Was he missing one? If so, was the weapon his screwdriver? If so, how did the killer get it? How did Nikki get it? If Nikki was involved.

There was one person who would know these answers outside of Sheriff Spencer Shepard.

Kevin Roberts, the Honey Springs Coroner.

CHAPTER FOURTEEN

Patrick had woken me up off the couch at some point during the night and gotten me to bed. The four a.m. alarm jolted me awake. Immediately I put my feet on the ground while thinking of the list of to-dos on my plate.

There was no time to dillydally either.

"You're going to stay home today," I told Pepper as I pulled my hoodie over top of my head. "I have a lot to do today, and I don't want to have Bunny feel responsible for you."

When Pepper realized I wasn't getting the bag I took for him every day, he went over to his bed in front of the wood-burning stove, only there wasn't a fire, and he lay down. His chin rested on the edge of the bed, and his eyes were focused on me as if he were waiting for me to pick up his bag so he could dart to the door.

Patrick was still asleep, and I didn't want to wake him or Sassy, so I scribbled a note for him about my decision not to take Pepper today, leaving it on the counter with his to-go mug on top of it. That way I knew he'd see it.

I grabbed my keys off the hook next to the door. Pepper's chin shot up. His little ears were alert, but when I started to pull the door shut, he laid his chin back down on the edge of the bed.

It tugged at my heart to not take him. Leaving him at home was a rare occasion, but it was best.

I had driven my car to work instead of biking because I needed to go to the bank and back out to the hunting cabin, which made it much quicker to drive.

The morning at the Bean Hive started off like every other morning. I'd gotten there first and started all the brewing along with the menu items. I'd run the industrial pots down to the Cocoon Inn so their guests could enjoy some delicious coffee.

I left Bunny at the coffeehouse since traffic had been slower than any other time I'd ever recalled. There was no doubt the crimes on the boardwalk had made tourists and citizens leery to come down and do some shopping.

This was very concerning to me as a business owner.

Bunny was just fine without me. She more than likely preferred it, so she could sit down and talk to the customers, if we got any more today. They loved her. It was like coming to have a cup of coffee with your granny.

The Honey Springs National Bank was a typical bank. The old concrete floor played a huge role in the ability of your voice to echo and bounce off the walls. When I came in the door, I headed straight over to the two large glass offices on the right, giving the employees at the teller line a wave.

"Roxy." Evan Rich sat behind his desk. He offered a friendly smile. "Is that what I think it is?" he asked about the Bean Hive coffee cup and to-go bag in my hands.

"A bribe?" I laughed and put it on his desk.

"Uh-oh." He ran his hand over his bald head and leaned back, dropping his hand over his mouth. "It's hard to resist any of your food. I did hear traffic around town had pretty much come to a halt. Even the customers at the bank are to a trickle."

He gestured for me to sit.

"What's up?" he asked.

"You can still have the treats even if you don't tell me what I want to know." I set the treats in front of him and sat down in the chair. I crossed my legs.

"This is about the body found at the pier?" he asked.

"Roselyn Bohlen." I could tell by his slight reaction of his head lifting that he knew the name. "I did really well in body language reading."

He laughed. "Sometimes I forget you were a lawyer." He peeked inside of the bag. "Poppyseed lemon biscuit?" He licked his lips.

"Yep. It's spring, so I brought it back and knew it was your favorite." It technically wasn't a biscuit but a biscotti, but I wasn't one to correct anyone's pronunciation of anything.

"Black coffee?" He tried to see in the small hole of the lid.

"Of course." It was fun to know what people loved so when I did get to visit someone I was able to take them a little treat. Rarely did I go somewhere empty-handed.

There were a few treats in the car for the Bee Happy Resort folks. Even though they had their own pastry chef who used the most natural ingredients, they did love a good sugary and somewhat-bad-for-you-if-you-ate-too-many treat.

"What's this all about?" Evan dug his hand into the bag. "Because you know I can't tell you any private information about any of our customers." He picked up his coffee and put it to his mouth.

"I'm not asking you to really. I am going to say that by the way your body reacted when I said 'Roselyn Bohlen' you knew the name. If you were to google search her, you'd find she's a missing woman. Just disappeared and her family is awfully worried."

He stopped tipping the cup to his lips. His eyes popped open.

"By the way you just reacted to that news, you and I both know she was alive and well until…" I let the fact of her murder sink in without even saying it before I went on with what I knew. "I also know she came in here to do some business. I'm assuming there's a safety deposit box here, and I just want to know if there's someone else on the box. Maybe someone by the name of Nikki Dane?"

Evan folded his hands around the coffee cup and rested his forearms on the top of his desk.

"If the sheriff came in here with a warrant, then you'd have to disclose the information anyways. If I told the sheriff, then I'd get my answer." I pulled my phone out of the pocket of my hoodie.

"Now that I have information regarding the demise of a customer, I would, out of courtesy to that customer's wishes, contact the other person on the safety deposit box." He in no uncertain terms confirmed there was another person listed on Roselyn's box.

"And you would have the contact information of this person?" I asked, feeling like we were playing a childhood game of charades.

"Let's face it. You and I both know what is going on here." Evan got tired of the dance between us. "I can't say any more than that, or I could get fired."

"I've got the number of Nikki Dane. I can call her myself." I noticed Evan had put on his straight poker face. "I'm glad you keep your secrets. It makes me trust you even more than before. How's Emily?"

Just the mere mention of his daughter's name made him go into a long story about her and how she was doing, making her name in the culinary world.

"Thanks for asking." His shoulders dropped. "Roxy," he called after me when I took a step out of his office. "You're on the right track. I hope they find her killer. She was a nice young woman. I'd hate to see someone had taken her key, because anyone can come here and gain access with the right key."

"I didn't know her, but from what I hear she was a nice woman." The bit about the key got my attention. "I just wish I knew if she was murdered for the money in a purse snatching gone bad or murdered because someone knew she'd won the lottery." I drummed my fingers on the doorjamb. "Was anyone in here the day she opened the account? Anyone that could've possibly overheard she had that kind of money?"

"I don't recall. I guess I can roll back the tape, but I was pretty shocked at the amount said customer wanted to deposit. We never keep that much cash on hand, so I did have to call in the federal reserve to make a special stop."

I left on that account and decided to swing by the coroner's office before I made my way back to the boardwalk, where I'd have to take the ferry across Lake Honey Springs to meet Patrick for lunch at the spa.

My phone started to ring just as I left the bank.

"Hey, Spencer." I didn't waste any time with pleasantries. Let's face it, if it weren't for this murder, he would not have been calling me. "What's up?"

"I wanted to touch base with Quentin." He was going to waste his breath, so I stopped him.

"Yeah. I know. He was with my mom." My voice was flat, and I got into the car. "I did a little digging around myself and found that out when my digging led me straight to them."

"You okay with all that?" It might seem like an odd question to some people, but even coming from the sheriff, it wasn't.

Honey Springs was so small, outside of the law, everyone knew everyone else's business, and that included the history my mom had with Aunt Maxi in years past that I thought had been buried since it was so long ago.

When mom showed up in Honey Springs, the past stories reared their ugly heads, and the old stories about my dad, Mom, and Aunt Maxi resurfaced. It was Aunt Maxi who had to put on a face like the hatchet had been buried a long time ago and made everyone in town drop the rumors.

Like Aunt Maxi told me when I was worried what locals would think and hold against my business, it's not your business what others think of you.

She was right. And it all worked itself out.

It just went to show that secrets or people's pasts didn't stay buried under the rug—as we Southerners would prefer.

"I'm fine. As long as Mom's happy and he's good to her." I left the sentence dangling so he could form his own opinion of what their relationship was. "I guess he's marked off the list."

"That's why I'm calling." The tone of his voice told me he was a little perplexed. "I talked to Kevin today when I went by to get the official report. The screwdriver isn't from Quentin, so he is cleared. There's no prints or nothing. Plus there was a piece of the handle that had been scraped off like there was something written on it. Quentin keeps the tools he uses spotless, and Kirk told me Quentin takes time every night after he works at the spa to clean the tools before he puts them away."

"It sure does look like you checked out everything." Though I did find the handle bit a little interesting, as if someone had a marking on it that would identify them.

"Loretta Bebe and Maxine said they didn't recall any sort of weapon when they got purse snatched. Just a moped drive-by. Grabbed the purse and off they went," he said.

"Do you think these are two separate crimes?" I asked.

"It's beginning to look that way."

"You still didn't find a purse?" I asked.

"No. And the number you gave me, it goes straight to nothing. It's a burner phone. You know, the kind you can buy with minutes on it and dump it." That was something I didn't want to hear.

"And you're sure Quentin is innocent?" I had to ask and get any other crazy notions out of my head.

"I'm pretty positive." He sighed. "I'm going to go back to the leads we have for the purse snatching. It looks like it's a purse snatching gone bad."

"You're thinking it's all a coincidence?" The same old feeling of dread settled in my stomach as I wondered if this was going to be one of those cases where the law got it wrong. "Girl missing because she won the lottery but ends up dead after she was a random victim of a purse snatching?"

"When you put it that way, it doesn't sound like it was a coincidence, but the facts are the facts. And until we find either the purses or the robbers, I won't know." There was a pause before he said, "I'm going to hold a press conference and contact the sheriff where she's from and let them know we've ID'd our Jane Doe, and it's their missing person."

"It might generate some leads or gossip if people find out it's her. That way if—and it's a big if—she was targeted, not a victim of a purse snatching, then this case could turn into more than random." I couldn't see why he wouldn't go public with it.

"It'll open up some more doors, like being able to talk to family and friends. I'm going to drive up there myself, so if you need me, you'll have to call." He acted as if I ran down to the department to see him all the time.

"Okay. I was actually going to go see Kevin this morning, but I don't have to do that no more." Nikki Dane popped into my head. "Why don't you find out if you can go see Nikki Dane?" I suggested. "She's listed as another person on the security box at the bank."

"I can get a warrant to open it, but it would be so much easier if she'd cooperate. I've got her on my list. I'm planning on getting her location from the sheriff. I'll let you know what I find out. I was going to tell you something, but now I've forgotten," Spencer said. "I guess it was a lie." Both of us laughed before we hung up the phone.

There was absolutely no reason to go see Kevin. With the engine running, I needed to rethink my strategy. It was too early to meet Patrick for lunch, but not too early to go check out the old cellar at the cabin, which prompted me to call Spencer back.

"Hey, I wanted to know if you found anything at the cabin?" I asked before I laid the groundwork for him to kinda give me permission to snoop if I did turn anything up.

"Nothing. That's what I was going to tell you. I'm sure you'll check in with

Maxine before I do. You can let her know she can have access back. It's been cleared, and we got all of the victim's items out and in evidence."

It really bothered me when they would use the word victim and not the name. These were people. People who had a life and loved ones. Maybe Roselyn didn't have a lot of people who loved her, I had no idea, but I was pretty darn sure if she'd listed Nikki Dane as a person on the lockbox, then Nikki cared for her.

There was enough time to head out of town to the hunting cabin and just take a look at the cellar for myself.

When I pulled up, glancing around, the naked eye wouldn't've caught too much, but I knew there was no way Spencer or any of his deputies would leave the door wide open.

I backed out of the driveaway just in case someone was in there. I'd been face-to-face with a killer before, and I certainly didn't have that on my list of to-dos today.

"It's about time you called to check on me," Aunt Maxi teased. Her voice sounded upbeat.

"I'm sure I'd have heard from you if you weren't okay. Actually I'm calling because Spencer cleared the cabin and I decided to come back out here to check out the old cellar. I'm here, and the door is wide open. You're not in there are you?" Her car wasn't there, and it was too far for her to ride her bike, but it wouldn't be unusual for her to have someone like Quentin drop her off. "Or is Quentin here?"

There were many possibilities other than the ones I had running through my head.

"Nope. I've not heard from Spencer, and Quentin is at the spa this morning working. I told him once the cabin was clear, I'd have him go and give it a good cleaning so we could start renting it again. This time, I'm going back to weekly rentals. I don't need a headache like this one," Aunt Maxi said. "Maybe the sheriff accidentally left it open."

"Yeah. Let me call him, and I'll get back with you." I hung up with her and called Spencer.

"Now what?" Spencer joked on the other end of the phone.

"Did you or your men leave the cabin door open?" I asked. "I'm here, and the door is wide open."

"No. I was the one who cleared it last night. In fact, I pulled the door closed and locked it from the outside."

A sense of dread washed over me.

"Don't go in. I'll be right there."

From the other end of the phone, I could hear tires squealing before the phone went dead.

There was no way I was going to go into the cabin. If Spencer had locked it last night, that meant there'd been plenty of time for someone to break in, especially if they had a key.

I ended up pulling down the country road looking in the direction from which anyone from town would be driving here, namely Spencer, but when a car skidded around the curve and the bright-orange hair sticking straight up glowed, I knew it was Aunt Maxi. Obviously with a new hair color since yesterday.

Our eyes met when her car zoomed past me, and she didn't let up off the gas.

I threw the car in gear and whipped it around to follow her. With a good try, I put the pedal to the metal and still didn't catch up to her.

She'd already parked and had darted into the cabin without one bit of hesitation.

"Aunt Maxi!" I started yelling before I could even get fully out of my car. "Stop!" Even though I didn't see her because she was already inside, I still wanted her to stop.

Just like her, I ran in the cabin. *Like I was going to be able to do something if there was someone in there.*

When I stepped through the door, the previously untouched family room had definitely been touched. The sofa was overturned with the cushions strewn all over the place. The coffee table had been shoved out of the way, the magazines were on the floor, and the rug was curled up.

"They are looking for something." Aunt Maxi found me in the family room. "The entire cabin looks like this."

CHAPTER FIFTEEN

"This screams to me that her murder wasn't just a random purse snatching." I needed Spencer to hear me. Really hear what I was saying.

Spencer had made it a few minutes after Aunt Maxi and I had discovered the entire cabin in shambles. Every piece of furniture had been overturned—mattress off the bed, kitchen drawers, and anything else that could pull out, dumped. It was an utter mess.

Spencer stood outside with us while his deputies were dusting for fingerprints and looking around outside for any signs of footprints.

"Another crime?" Loretta Bebe must've been one of the cars that'd driven up when we didn't bother to turn around to see who had stopped.

The flurry of activity taking place did seem like the investigation had just stepped up.

"Low-retta!" Aunt Maxi put her hand up. "I don't have time for this. You get in your fancy car and get out of here."

Loretta had flipped her phone around.

"This is exactly what I'm talking about. Not only has the crime been violent down on our beloved boardwalk, but the crime has also filtered into our homes." She talked into the phone with the screen facing her. "This has to stop. As mayor of Honey Springs, I will not only bring justice to those who are criminals, but do you see this?" She flipped the phone around. "These are our only

239

deputies. They are here at this crime. Who is patrolling the boardwalk? Let's find out."

"What are you doing?" Aunt Maxi shoved Loretta's phone out of her face.

"Sheriff, if all of your deputies are here, who is making sure the rest of Honey Springs is safe?" Loretta put her phone up in his face. "I'm on social media live," she whispered to me. "Birdie showed me."

"Loretta, not now." Spencer gave her a flat look.

"If not now, tell the people on our Keep Honey Springs Safe social media page *when*." She emphasized "when." "We have over thirty people tuning in."

"Thirty?" Aunt Maxi snorted.

"It's nothing to sneeze at when our town is in peril." Loretta drew her hand to her chest, giving off a huge expression of concern. Mainly for her audience. "Now there's forty people on here waiting for you to tell us who is keeping our town safe."

"I can assure you, Mrs. Bebe, we are taking the necessary actions to keep the citizens and our tourists safe. We aren't even sure what has taken place here today." Spencer had changed his tune and attitude as he looked into the phone.

"Well, that's a lie if I ever heard one, Spencer Shepard," Aunt Maxi scoffed. "You oughta be ashamed of yourself."

"Do you care to elaborate?" Loretta pointed the phone back at Aunt Maxi. "The people are sending up little hearts." Loretta's eyes sparkled like the diamond on her finger.

"Yes. Yes, I would." Aunt Maxi straightened up her shoulders, and she glared right into the phone. "I don't know who has broken into my cabin and destroyed it, but you mark my words, if the sheriff of this town doesn't get his act together and find out who is behind it and the boardwalk purse snatcher, we will elect someone who will." Aunt Maxi gave a hard chin nod before she turned to Loretta. "Ain't that right, Low-retta?"

"The only way to make sure the elected sheriff is held accountable is to create a budget that will allow us to keep our town safe by hiring more and more deputies." Loretta began her campaign promises with Aunt Maxi looking over her shoulder into the phone.

Spencer took a deep breath, and with his cheeks puffed out, he made a long sigh. He had his hands full, and he knew to just let the two older women keep on yapping.

In reality, their little live on social media was getting some traction, and when we made it back to the Bean Hive Coffeehouse, it was packed with citizens.

The place erupted in cheers after Loretta walked in after me. Immediately she pulled out her phone and went live again on the social media page she'd created. Or the one Birdie had helped her create.

Bunny had the social media account pulled up on her electronic tablet for everyone to watch and rewatch the live between Aunt Maxi and Loretta.

"The time is now. If we don't do something about this crime, we will all become victims just like me and Maxine Bloom!" Loretta fist pumped the air.

"That's why Loretta has chosen me to be her running mate!" Aunt Maxi screamed, also doing some fist pumps.

"Wait? What?" Loretta jerked around and looked at Aunt Maxi.

"Yes! You heard that right. I'm running with Loretta Bebe for vice mayor!" I wasn't sure, but I think Aunt Maxi had just made up her own title.

"There's no such thing." Loretta tried to keep her composure. "You have to be a city commissioner and the top one to be the vice mayor, and that election isn't for a while." Loretta smiled, and a worry line formed between her Botoxed eyes.

"As the newly elected mayor, Loretta Bebe is creating an office for vice mayor." Aunt Maxi had gone on to making stuff up. Then she started to chant, "Maxine and Loretta for change!"

"You mean Loretta and Maxine." Loretta's eyes snapped, and her lips drew into a thin line at the realization that Aunt Maxi was starting to take the limelight. "Thank you so much for coming to the Bean Hive. My campaign manager will be distributing pins with Vote for Team Loretta, so be sure to stop by here tomorrow and get your free pin and one for a friend from Roxanne Bloom Cane!"

Loretta swiveled around and gestured to me.

"I... um..." I stammered before I rolled my eyes as the citizens cheered.

"Looks like you're gonna need some extra caffeine." Bunny nudged me and put a hot mug of freshly brewed coffee in my hands. "Honey help you."

"I guess it can't be all bad." I brought the mug up to my lips and wondered just how I could use this new title as Loretta's campaign manager to get a look at some files. "I just might have an idea."

"Yeah, what's that?" Bunny jerked her head toward the swinging kitchen door for me to follow her.

As soon as we walked in the kitchen away from the crowd, I joined her at the workstation where she'd picked up the wipe-off board where we'd started our little investigation.

"Maybe I can get Spencer to endorse Loretta, but he'd have to agree to campaign for her. As much as I hate to say it, Loretta does have a lot of pull in this town." It was a fact. Loretta was on every possible committee, women's group, and Bible study. She knew everyone in town. She just might win the title of mayor on recognition alone.

Something not only the current mayor should be concerned with but also the current sheriff. Loretta was making some big promises to the citizens on a subject they found very important. Not only was the crime keeping some tourists away, but some businesses were leery of opening.

"We need to find Nikki Dane," I said just as Aunt Maxi came through the swinging door with a young woman. "I'm sorry. You can't be back here due to the ordinance." I gave Aunt Maxi a hard look.

"Roxanne, this here is Nikki Dane." Aunt Maxi practically pushed the girl through the door.

CHAPTER SIXTEEN

There were a lot of questions I needed to ask Nikki, but most of all there was a tickle in the back of my head that wondered if it was really a coincidence she showed up on the day the cabin was broken into.

My curiosity clicked up a notch. I slid the whiteboard off the workstation table and onto the floor so she wouldn't see all the stuff Bunny and I had jotted down.

"When I started receiving phone calls from these other numbers, I knew something had gone wrong with Roselyn. I came here to find out what." Nikki had taken the cup of coffee I'd offered as she answered my question.

Just the first of many I needed answered before I called Spencer.

"Did you know she was murdered?" I asked.

"I figured." She tried to keep her composure. Her lips quivered and her nostrils flared, but there was no stopping the tears flooding her eyes before they dripped down her cheek.

"Oh, honey." Aunt Maxi grabbed a dish towel, the closest thing to us, and handed it to Nikki. "I'm sorry. It's always hard to lose someone. Especially a good friend. The cabin she rented was mine."

Nikki rubbed the tears with the towel as soon as they fell. She continued to nod and swallow.

"She'd given me the address to where she'd decided to lie low for a while.

Honestly she was on her way to sunny Florida. I was shocked when she told me she'd found a cute little town in Kentucky." Nikki sighed, a faint smile curling on the edges of her lips. "Roselyn had never ventured out of our town, so she was very surprised when she got lost going down the Bluegrass Parkway after she got off to get gas, leading her straight into Honey Springs."

"This all paints a very rosy picture of your friend. How long had you known Roselyn?" I wanted to make her feel at home. At ease like I used to be in the courtroom when I interrogated a witness.

"All of our lives. We were in Girl Scouts together. Our parents couldn't afford to pay for cheerleading, and you could get assistance with Girl Scouts. My mom was a great seamstress, so she would sew all of our badges onto our sashes." She looked into her coffee mug as if the memory were playing in the dark roast. "I just can't believe she's dead." Her voice fell away.

"I'm guessing she trusted you since she only kept in contact with you, making everyone else in your community think she was missing." I was going to start laying the groundwork so I could ask the harder questions.

"We were best friends." The tears quickly dried when she snapped her gaze to me before she lowered her eyes. "Of course she trusted me."

"We know she won the lottery," I said as I watched her jaw clench ever so slightly as she tried to play it cool. "Did you know about that?"

"I did. And that's why she left home." She sucked in both cheeks as if she were gnawing on the insides with her molars. "We live in a very poor community. And she has a daughter that was taken from her when we were sixteen. She didn't want to give her up for adoption, but her parents made her."

Bunny, Aunt Maxi, and I had shifted uncomfortably in our seats.

"'Scuse me!" Loretta Bebe popped her head around the swinging kitchen door. "What are y'all doing? We need coffee for our volunteers, and all three of y'all are in here sitting down on your laurels."

"I'll go," Bunny told me when I started to get up. She wagged a finger between me and Aunt Maxi. "You two get this thing sorted out."

Loretta popped the door open wide so she could let Bunny through.

"Go on, dear." Aunt Maxi patted Nikki's arm.

"Where was I?" she asked.

"The baby," Aunt Maxi coaxed.

"Yes. When she won the lottery, she about died." Nikki scoffed. "Interesting how she did, huh?" She shook off the notion. "She was determined to find her daughter. It's been six years now. She said she was going to take the huge lump sum. Get in the car and drive to Florida to find her daughter."

"Why Florida?" I asked.

"After she had her daughter, they let her just take a look at her before they rushed the baby out. She overheard them saying to her parents that the baby was going to have a great life playing on the beach where the adoptive parents lived. She didn't hear the town, but she swears she heard Florida." The edges of her eyes dipped. "Roselyn took the lump sum and held onto it in cash in her car. It took her a month or so to get in touch with a lawyer in Florida who specializes in these sorts of cases. He was so backed up that she couldn't get in with him for like eight months."

"That's why she decided to extend the lease on the cabin." I nodded toward Aunt Maxi. "She loved it here and figured why not stay until she had to leave."

"That's right. She did love it here." Nikki looked around the kitchen before she settled her eyes on me. "This coffeehouse was a sanctuary for her. We are servers at our little diner, and she took pride in coming up with all sorts of coffee concoctions. She didn't go to barista school, but we still called her a barista." She smiled at the memory. "She said that when she came to check out the town, she had to stop at the cute boardwalk and walked in here. When she told me about you, I thought you were a teenager, not a woman."

"She wasn't talking about me." I laughed. "I have an afternoon employee who is a teenager. Her name is Birdie, and she was very fond of Roselyn. Birdie knew her as Stella, as did the rest of the community."

"Stella was what she always wanted to name her daughter, and she didn't want anyone to find her so she tried to use cash as much as she could." She dug down into her purse. "She did send me this."

She pulled out an unopened envelope stamped and addressed to her.

"It's the safety deposit box key. She wanted me to have it so if anything happened to her while she was here, then well, I could get to the money." Her shoulders dropped, and she glared at me. "What?"

My poker face was obviously not as good as I thought.

"You think I killed her. You think that I want the money." She grabbed her purse and put the strap on her shoulder. "I didn't."

"I have to be honest with you." I got up from my stool and picked the white-board off the floor. Her eyes scanned it.

"What are you? Some sort of weirdo who likes to snoop around in real crimes where people's lives are at stake?" Her chest heaved up and down. Her eyes filled with tears. "That is my friend. A very good friend, and well, she would do anything for me. You are making her seem like she's done something wrong. Or that I have. I haven't."

"We are sorry to upset you, but you don't really understand what Roxy has done for our town." Aunt Maxi was good at calming Nikki down while she quickly told her about how I was a lawyer and used my skills to help law enforcement see some of the crimes that'd taken place in Honey Springs from a different angle. "We are trying to figure out if this purse snatching crime spree was just a purse snatching in her case since she ended up dead. That's all."

"I have to say that winning that much money in the lottery and going AWOL from your family and friends makes us wonder if someone knew she was here and killed her." I couldn't just be silent anymore. "To be honest with you, it does seem weird the only person who knew she was here shows up on the day the cabin Roselyn rented was ransacked. Did she have the money in there or the safety deposit box? I don't know, but I do know one thing. You told me you are from a very poor area of Kentucky. That probably means you had no better means than Roselyn, so why wouldn't you be worthy of the money? Why would she go to Florida to pay some lawyer all this money when you've stuck by her all this time? Why wouldn't she just give you a few million? Even one million is good for a friendship, right?"

I belted her with all these questions. Her face contorted with emotions. For a minute, I felt like I was back in the courtroom.

"That's the least she could do, especially if you were keeping her plan a secret. Did you two get into an argument over the phone? Now that she'd dead, you can waltz right on in that bank and take out whatever is in that safety deposit box because you knew she'd trust you, and you knew you had the key."

"You're crazy! Crazy!" She yelled at me. "I loved her! I would do anything for her! I kept her secret. I knew she was living here. I showed you the key." She still had it fisted in her hand as she waved it in the air. "I came here because she loved it here, and I had no idea she was dead."

"It looks like I've walked in on something." Spencer stood at the swinging door. None of us had noticed he'd even come in.

"How long have you been standing there?" I asked.

"Long enough to know what's going on here." He gave Nikki a hard stare. "I'd like for you to come down to the station with me."

"For what?" She looked at me then back to Spencer.

"It seems like you knew our victim very well, and I'd like to ask you some questions on the record for myself." He gestured to the door. "I'm more than happy to give you a ride to the station."

"Not without my lawyer present." Nikki crossed her arms. "Roxy, now you have to prove I'm innocent, and that means you have to believe me."

With the turn of events, going over to the Bee Happy Resort to question Kirk and Jessica about any dealings with Quentin, as well as meeting Patrick for lunch, was put on the back burner. Besides, Quentin had already been released as a suspect, and honestly I just wanted their opinion of him since he did seem to have stolen my mom's heart without her even noticing.

I had taken Nikki down to the station, and Bunny stayed at the coffeehouse later than usual since it was my night to stay late while Birdie and her study group met with their teacher, Hope.

The only thing that was going to satisfy Sheriff Spencer Shepard was to see inside of the safety deposit box once and for all.

With a quick phone call to Evan Rich, since we knew the bank would be closing at six p.m., we had barely enough time to get there.

"You have the key?" Evan started to go through the protocol.

Nikki took the key and handed it to him for him to inspect. He gave Spencer a nod to confirm.

"I'm going to need to see your identification as well." He left us alone for a second to get the log notebook where they kept all the signatures that were required to sign in.

Nikki presented Evan with her identification.

Evan smiled, saying very few words, and had Nikki sign the log.

"It looks like this box was opened a few days ago right before closing." Evan pointed to the line that clearly had "Stella Johnson" written in the small box with a date and time.

It was dated the night she died and literally just hours before someone stabbed her.

Spencer's shoulders fell as though he'd figured out a piece of this puzzle, but he tried not to give it away. I'm sure no one other than myself noticed.

Evan led us into the small room where the walls were lined with the little metal containers one after the other.

"This is it." Evan tapped his master key on the front of the one Roselyn had rented.

Evan inserted his key then stepped away, letting Nikki insert her key. Once they were both clicked in place, he pulled the safety deposit box out and placed it on the table in the middle of the room.

"I'll be outside if you need me." He excused himself.

"Here goes nothing." Nikki put her hands on the top of the box so she could open the hinged top.

The air in the room got tight and tense as we all held our breath to see the contents as she peeled up the steel lid.

"I guess you were right about here goes nothing," I said when there was literally nothing in the box.

All of us, even Nikki, seemed to have lost all steam.

CHAPTER SEVENTEEN

Birdie was sitting with the group and Hope when I walked into the Bean Hive.

"I'm so glad you're here," I told Hope. "How is Polly doing?"

"She's great. The kids love her, and Louise did bring someone by to check her out, but I don't think they wanted her after she made a couple of comments about losing weight." She grimaced. "I have been researching on how to deprogram a bird's learned language."

I couldn't help but laugh.

"Louise said that since Polly is older, she has no idea what her vocabulary is, so I'm always keeping an ear open." Hope's laughter fluttered up into her eyes. "I really enjoy her though."

"Maybe I'll pop in tomorrow and get a photo of her to put up here." I shrugged. "All the Pet Palace animals of the week here have been adopted out. I sure don't want to break that streak."

"Stop in anytime. My classroom is always open. Until I leave, that is." The smile faded as the grim reality of her job came to her.

"You've always got a job here," I reminded her.

"I appreciate that." She nodded and went back to the students.

When Hope started to wrap up the tutoring session, I knew it was my time to get the coffeehouse ready to close, which meant that I needed to get all the things ready for opening in the morning.

It was so nice to be able to come to work in the mornings with the industrial coffeepots already brewing on the timer, all the condiments restocked from the day before, the floors swept and mopped, all the dishes and mugs cleaned as well as put away, the counters wiped down, and all the next day's specials labeled where they would go in the glass display.

Since Pepper wasn't with me, it was easy to get all the things done and locked up before I headed out with the students and Hope.

I'd made sure to have everything done so that when they left I could go with them and not have to walk the boardwalk alone. Though I honestly was starting to have doubts that the purse snatchings, which hadn't happened in the last twenty-four hours, and Roselyn's death were tied, there was something to be said for being vigilant.

"Hi," I greeted Pepper and Sassy. They must've heard me drive up because I could hear them barking and whining before I stepped foot on the front porch.

I dropped my purse on the floor so I could give my attention to them then stood up, after each one got a good and satisfying scratch, to give Patrick a kiss.

"Something smells good." I took a big inhale and peeled my arms out of my lightweight jacket as Patrick helped me.

"Meat loaf." Patrick hung my coat up. "It's almost done."

I followed him into the kitchen area and couldn't help myself. I had to look in the oven. My mouth watered. Patrick's meat loaf was delish. He used a couple different types of beef to make it, and he swears it's the fat content of each married together that makes the beef loaf moist.

"How was your day?" I asked and made my way around him in the kitchen to grab a couple of plates, forks, cloth napkins, and glasses to set the table. Patrick had already put the bowl of brussels sprouts and sweet potatoes on the table.

"It was good. I had bids for a couple new possible contracts for some remodels." He opened the oven, and with an oven mitt on his hand, he pulled out the meat loaf. He used the spatula to serve a nice piece of meat loaf on each of our plates. "How about you? Did you make any headway with Roselyn?"

"You won't even believe it." I told him how the cabin had been broken into with the details since I'd already talked to him in brief moments throughout the day. "What you haven't heard is how Nikki Dane just so happened to show up."

He stopped, put his knife down, and looked at me.

"Right. Coincidence?" I asked. "I thought the same thing. Long story, Spencer had us go to the bank and open the safety deposit box. It was empty."

"The money wasn't in there?" he asked because we had all assumed Roselyn had put the money in the bank, the safest place.

"Nothing was in there. She claims she came to town to see what was going on because we all had started to call the phone Roselyn had given her to keep in touch on her way to Florida." I nodded when Patrick's eyes grew big. "Yep. Supposedly Roselyn was on her way to Florida to meet with a lawyer because she'd had a daughter six or so years ago when her parents made her give up the baby for adoption."

"Why Florida?" he asked and got himself another helping of sweet potatoes.

"That's where Roselyn overheard some of the hospital staff tell her parents the baby was going." It broke my heart to think of Roselyn's heartache over losing her baby like that.

"What's going on in that head?" Patrick asked me.

"I just feel bad for her and her journey all this time. Can you even imagine her mental state over these last years, and the first thing she thinks of was trying to find the baby once she saved enough money? Then she wins the lottery?" I sucked in a deep breath. "Where is the money?"

"I'm guessing you're going to find out." He smiled.

"Seeing how Nikki appointed me her lawyer, she's kinda given me free rein to travel to their hometown to snoop around." I shrugged.

"Does Spencer think Nikki killed Roselyn?" he wondered.

"He didn't charge her, but he did tell her not to leave town until he got some more questions answered as well as some evidence back from the cabin's break-in." I had no idea what the evidence was because he'd not disclosed that yet to me, which he would have to do since I was Nikki's lawyer if they were going to charge her.

"What you're saying is that you're going on a road trip?" he questioned.

"Yes. I'm hoping to do that tomorrow after Aunt Maxi wakes up so she can go with me. In the morning, Bunny is going to open and I'm going to go to school to take some photos of Polly." I continued to eat while we talked about the crimes.

"At this point, are they thinking the purse snatching and murder aren't related?" He asked the million-dollar question.

"If you're asking me my thoughts, I have no idea. There's so many ways this can go, but I don't think we will know until one of the crimes is solved and we see if that leads to the other or not." It wasn't a real answer, but it was the best answer I could give. "There's one thing that really did make my stomach clench, and I wasn't expecting it."

I put my fork down and prepared the reaction I was going to have when I let out the feelings I'd been keeping inside all day.

"This sounds a little serious." Patrick followed me and put his utensils down. He reached over the table and put his hands on mine. "You know you can tell me anything, right?"

I took a deep breath in order to get it out.

I smiled to help keep me positive.

"You're scaring me a little." Patrick's hands slid off mine, and he stood up, making his way over to me, bending down in front of me. He took my hands again. "What's wrong?"

"When Nikki told me about Roselyn's baby, it took me right back to Christmas Day when I got sick to my stomach." I swallowed back tears. "Aunt Maxi and Mom told me how they thought I was pregnant. As we both know, I wasn't." Without going into much detail about the surgery and how I had to maneuver those feelings of healing so I could get better, I continued, "I actually got a wee bit excited to think we might have our own little baby. Our child. Obviously I wasn't pregnant, but today these feelings of loss hit my heart, and I had no idea they were there."

"Baby," Patrick whispered, lifting his hand to my face. He curled his fingers around my neck and used his thumb to wipe off the tear dripping down my cheek. "I'm sorry. I had no idea you had these feelings."

"I didn't either or at least didn't let myself have those feelings." It wasn't fair to just dump things on Patrick like this because we hadn't talked about expanding our family yet. At some point, I had guessed we'd have a family, but when it was presented to me in the bathroom at the Bean Hive during our annual Christmas Day supper with friends and family, I didn't think I'd actually be excited at the possibility. "I'm sorry I didn't share these feelings with you. I honestly had no idea I had these deep down until Roselyn's story came out as to why she was passing through Honey Springs."

"And if I know you, you want her mission to keep going." Patrick knew me so well. "I only ask you to stay safe. Do not put yourself in danger."

"I won't. I've got Aunt Maxi to keep up with." I laughed, forcing the sadness back to the depths of my soul where I needed it to stay. "But I do want you to know that I do want us to have a family."

"And we will. When you think it's time, I am here for that." He pulled me out of the chair and cuddled me in his arms as we sat on the floor of our small kitchen.

Sassy and Pepper weren't about to leave us alone. Both of them jumped on us, trying to lick our faces while both of us grieved as we let the disappointment of the false hope of pregnancy blanket us.

CHAPTER EIGHTEEN

There was something about being able to sleep in, a rare occasion for me. Even on the days Bunny Bowoski opened the Bean Hive, I still got up at my normal time and did things around the house like laundry, dust, vacuum— anything the house needed.

Not today. Today I let the early morning hours swim past me and snuggled with Patrick since he never got out of bed until seven a.m.

"I could get used to this." We sat on the couch with hot mugs of coffee in our hands. "Slow coffee in the morning with my wife."

"Cheers." I snuggled back on his chest. Pepper had found his spot behind the crease in my knees, and Sassy was lying on the floor behind Patrick's feet. "But I have to go get photos of Polly before class starts." I took the last sip.

"No. Don't go." Patrick tried to hold me down when I attempted to get up. "Let's just take off all day and stay here."

"You have those contracts to get, and I have to get Polly adopted. No way am I going to let a bird break my one-hundred-percent adoption streak." Patrick let go, knowing I had some fighting words.

"You don't like to lose," he teased.

"You're right." I gave him a kiss on the tip of his nose before I jumped up the steps and got ready for the day.

Pepper had followed me up and continued to keep up with every step I made while I got more of a professional, lawyerly outfit than my usual coffee-house uniform of khakis and the Bean Hive logo shirt.

"I've got to leave you home again today," I told him and buttoned up the white collared shirt since I'd opted to wear a black power pantsuit. "And I promise I will bring you some special treats since I am going to be making some of your favorites this afternoon."

The word "treat" was all Pepper needed to hear to be sent into an all-out tail wagging dance around the room. But when I mentioned banana butter, Pepper lost his mind.

He jumped and barked.

"Did you say banana butter?" Patrick called up from the steps.

"I did. I'm making all sorts of promises up here." I snickered. "If we do have a child, we are in trouble."

I grabbed my lipstick from the bathroom drawer and looked in the mirror to brush some across my lips.

"You mean when we have a child." His words made me smile. When I saw my reflection in the mirror, I couldn't help but think that one day I was going to have a baby in this cabin with Patrick.

I shrugged off the notion as I bent down and scratched Pepper's ears before I grabbed the suit coat lying on the bed and headed downstairs to kiss Patrick goodbye.

It's funny how one thing can change your entire day around. Yesterday I was dreading driving to Roselyn's hometown to snoop around in an effort to find out who could possibly have hunted her down after she'd tried so hard not to be found.

Mainly I wanted to see her parents. The question was why would Roselyn need to keep her actions a secret? She was an adult with a lot of money, unless she would think someone would have other plans for the money. Nikki did mention the town was poor, and if that was me, I would feel like I'd need to help my family before I put my needs first.

The urge to find her baby trumped her family. Or was I going to find a completely strange family dynamic when I got there?

The questions and thoughts swirled around in my head and kept me occupied until I pulled up in front of Honey Springs High School.

The designated parking spots for visitors were already spoken for, so I had to go around the building and park in the overflow parking lot. The bike racks were overflowing with the students' bikes, one piled on top of the other.

The parents trained their children early to ride their bikes since we loved that particular mode of transportation.

Then there were the wealthy kids, which made me think of how Loretta had probably raised her son. The golf carts lined up next to the bikes and a few mopeds.

Mopeds?

I didn't see many mopeds around town since they weren't street legal or allowed to ride on the boardwalk.

Then it hit me. Aunt Maxi had vaguely mentioned a moped after she'd been the victim of the purse snatching.

"Yes. And on a moped!" I remembered her saying. *"There was duct tape holding the darn thing together too. I saw it with my own eyes."*

Duct tape. The one tried-and-true distinction she remembered from that incident.

I clicked my key fob to lock the doors of my car and hurried over to the bikes, golf carts, and mopeds. There were four mopeds that were spotless. But the fifth one had duct tape holding on the back fin over the tire.

I shook my head and pulled out my phone, sliding it open with my finger so I could scroll to the camera, where I snapped a quick photo from the back since I figured that's what Aunt Maxi had seen.

I texted her after I sent the photo to see if this was the moped she believed she'd seen driving off with her purse.

"That's it!" Her shrill voice pierced my ear after she'd decided to call and not text back. "Where on earth did you find it? Who does it belong to? And did they have my purse?"

"Whoa." I knew I was going to have to go inside and see if the students even registered things like mopeds to drive to school. I knew they had to purchase parking passes because Birdie had to pay for her own with money out of her paycheck from the Bean Hive.

Loretta believed if Birdie got used to paying for little things she would realize things weren't just handed to you in life, and you had to work in order to pay for things you wanted.

"Actually I'm at the high school and going in to take photos of Polly. When I pulled around to the overflow parking lot, I noticed the mopeds. Let me get inside and see what I can find out."

"You mean to tell me teenagers are behind this purse snatching?" She acted as if it was the most impossible thing ever.

"I guess we will find out." I looked around and noticed the door didn't have a handle to get inside, which meant I had to walk around the building in order to go in. "Let me call you back when I find out more."

"You find those little snot-nosed brats, and if they drive mopeds that means they have money. Do you think it's one of them Sear boys? They drive mopeds when they aren't supposed to on the road. I told the committee they need to start fining those boys." Aunt Maxi rattled off a few other names, and I let her ramble if that meant she wasn't going to show up.

She fussed and hollered in the phone the entire time I found my way inside, where I had to be buzzed in.

"Hi, I'm Roxanne Bloom, and I'm here to take photos of Polly for Ms. Mowry's class." I had bent down and spoken clearly into the microphone before I looked up at the small, round camera tilted down at the door and waved.

The door buzzed then clicked.

"Let me call you back, " I said to Aunt Maxi then clicked off the call and slipped the phone back into my pocket as I walked through the door straight into the office. "Good morning."

"Hope put you on the visitor's list. I need to see an ID, then we will get you a visitor's pass." The lady put a clipboard on top of the counter and set an ink pen on top.

I reached inside of my purse and took out my wallet, retrieving my ID and handing it to her. While she did the necessary checking, I wrote down my name, the date, the time, and the reason why I was visiting the school.

There was some comfort that the school had taken this level of security. It made me smile thinking one day I just might have my own child here.

"Let me call one of the office aids to take you down there." She handed me my ID back and went to pick up the phone.

"If you don't mind, can I talk to the principal or whoever might be in charge?" My question warranted a very curious expression. I knew recently the principal had changed, and I had yet to meet the new one.

"Sure." She looked at me from under hooded brows and picked up the phone. She hit a couple of buttons then spoke softly, "There's a woman here to see whoever is in charge. I have no idea, but she's the owner of that bird down in the home economics room."

She glanced up at me then grabbed the clipboard.

"Roxanne Bloom," she said into the phone. She curled her head around and whispered, "I don't know. I didn't ask her." Followed by a couple of "mm-hmms" and then a "bye."

She turned back around with a planted smile on her face.

"Principal Waters will see you now." She gestured for me to walk down a side hall. "He's the last door on the right."

There was no need for me to find the office because the short, portly man in a suit that looked more along the lines of a small child playing dress-up in his father's coat and pants waved at me.

The closer I got, the more I could tell he was definitely an older man with his hair combed over to the left to hide a growing bald spot.

"Ms. Bloom." I didn't bother correcting him when really my name was Bloom-Cain, though I'd yet to change my driver's license. I figured I'd do that when the current one expired. "How can I help you?" he asked once we walked into his office.

He pulled a chair out for me to sit.

He rested his backside on the desk in front of me with his hands gripping the side of the desk.

"I was wondering if you could tell me who drives the mopeds to school. Namely the one with the duct tape on it." I took my phone out of my pocket and pulled up the photos to show him.

"Is there a problem?" he asked.

"I'm not sure if you heard of the purse snatching on the boardwalk on the outskirts of town," I said.

He let go of the desk and folded his arms across his chest.

This was a definite pause on his part to keep me talking. It was a wonderful technique we lawyers liked to use when talking to possible witnesses, suspects, heck, even the perpetrator to make them feel a little uncomfortable so they'd break the eerie silence and eventually spit something out we could use on the particular case they were in there for.

I lifted my brows at him in order to get a response.

"Mm-hmm." He tilted his head. "I read it in the paper. Why?"

"Unfortunately, one of the victims was my aunt, and it took place in front of my coffeehouse. The Bean Hive Coffeehouse. I'm not sure if you've heard of it." I glanced at his desk where I noticed he had a can of soda, which told me he wasn't a morning coffee person.

Plus I'd never seen him, which also told me he'd not been drinking my coffee, unlike the last principal, who I did know because I had teenagers who worked for me.

"I am well aware of our students coming to get their little jolt of caffeine there after school, and I believe Ms. Mowry has been meeting with a group of students there a couple of times a week. Polly." He smiled, and I was glad he had his finger on the pulse not only of his student body, but of the town. "What does all this have to do with the mopeds?"

"You see, my aunt is very observant, and this was a drive-by purse snatching on a moped. My aunt got a good look at the moped, and this one happens to be the one the two people were on who drove past and ripped her purse off her shoulder."

"This one? Out of all the mopeds in Honey Springs, you're sure it's this one?" He tapped my phone.

"Good possibility." I didn't know anything for certain. "There was duct tape holding the back fender on over the tire just like this one. I sent her the photo."

My phone buzzed.

"Sir, the sheriff is here to see you, and a woman with orange hair is demanding to come in with him." The woman from the front sounded a smidgen frazzled.

"That's my Aunt Maxi, and she probably called Sheriff Shepard." I winced.

Principal Waters gave me a flat stare when he handed me the phone back. He reached behind himself and hit the phone.

"You can send them back." He pushed off the desk and met them at the door.

"There you are. Did you get the names of the hoodlums? I bet you it's them Sear boys." She pointed a finger at Mr. Waters. "You get them boys down here to this office right now. I know their granny, and she will die when she has to face me in Sunday School."

"Maxine." Spencer stepped in between her and the principal. "Let's just see what Principal Waters has to say."

"I'm sorry. She's a bit feisty." I apologized for her.

"Feisty? I was assaulted!" she hollered. I could see she was winding up for a good-sized hissy fit that needed to be tamped down and fast.

"Aunt Maxi, we cannot have you acting like this in a school. You sound like you're ten years old. And nothing is going to happen until you calm down. They certainly won't bring down whoever owns the moped with you acting as such." As I tried to talk her down, the fear of her reality was really in her eyes. "I understand this has caused you a lot of pain. It has caused a lot of suffering to many of the people in town."

"Not to mention people are scared to come to the boardwalk to go shopping or eat or just sit and read a book on the pier." She jutted a finger at Mr. Waters. "So I'm telling you that you need to call them Sear boys down here right this minute."

"Ma'am, the Sear boys drive a golf cart to school, but I do know who owns the moped in question." He looked at Spencer. "If I could have a minute alone with the sheriff."

It wasn't like an invitation for us to give him permission. Nope. Principal Waters had walked to the door and opened it, politely showing us the way out.

"Let the law handle it." I pulled on the sleeve of her oversized sweatshirt so she'd follow me back out to the office, where we took a seat.

It wasn't too long after that the principal and the sheriff emerged. The principal had whispered something to the secretary, and she got on the intercom asking the teacher who had answered to send a student to her locker. I didn't recognize the name.

"Locker?" Aunt Maxi jumped around.

"Stay here." Spencer left no room for negotiation in his tone as he followed the principal out of the office and into the depths of the school.

Aunt Maxi fidgeted around in her seat, crossing one leg over the other, swinging her foot. She put her nails in her mouth then stood up, pacing back and forth.

"I reckon you can just leave your car here so after I get a few shots of Polly we can head on over to Roselyn's town." I made some chat so there wasn't this deafening silence in anticipation of what the sheriff was looking into.

"If this doesn't pan out as the killer." Aunt Maxi nodded and jumped around when the principal, Spencer, and a young lady walked into the office. "There's my purse!"

Aunt Maxi ran over and grabbed the hobo bag she had snatched that morning.

"You little hoodlum." Aunt Maxi pointed at the girl. "Who is your mama and them?"

"Maxine, step aside and let me do my job." Spencer motioned for the young girl to walk down the hall to the principal's office. He held up another purse. "Is this Loretta's?"

"It's gawdy enough to be." Aunt Maxi was right about all the fake jewels stuck all over the outside of the bag. "I bet it is. Did you look inside?"

"Not yet. Do you mind checking the inside of your bag to make sure all the contents are there? Money? Checks? Keys?" he asked.

Aunt Maxi dumped all the contents of the hobo bag on the counter and patted through it.

"I don't keep money in my bag, but everything looks like it's here." She sighed.

"Do you think you're going to press charges?" he asked her.

"Did she kill Roselyn?" Aunt Maxi asked.

"I'm going to be taking it one crime at a time. This one has to do with you."

The secretary cleared her throat, stopping Spencer from talking.

"I'm sorry. Gillian is a sweet girl. She's had a hard life. She lives down in the mudflat, and well, I know she has had a hard time getting a job. She does do some odd jobs around town to get some money to contribute to her family." My heart broke as the secretary told me about this young girl's home life.

"Mudflat, huh?" Aunt Maxi's brows knitted. "I guess I won't press charges. If she killed someone, she's in enough trouble."

"So you aren't going to press charges?" Spencer clarified.

"No." Aunt Maxi started to scoop up her things and put them back into the bag. "Everything is here."

While Aunt Maxi continued to put all the junk, which was what it looked like, in her bag, I asked Spencer if I could talk to him outside.

"What's going on with the young lady?" I asked.

"Mr. Waters is calling her parents." He shook his head.

"Did you find any other purses?" I asked.

"Just Maxine's and Loretta's. If you're asking me about Roselyn's, Gillian told me she didn't go to the boardwalk at night because it was when she had to be home to babysit her siblings." He and I both knew this would be an easy alibi to confirm. "I'm still going to take her home and let her parents know what she did. I know it was to get some money for her siblings and her, but this is certainly not the way to make money."

"Yay." I pinched my lips.

"Are you sure you didn't hear any sort of moped the night you found Roselyn on the pier?" He'd asked me this once before.

"I didn't. I heard footsteps." I could still recall how the thumping echoed around the hollow part of Lake Honey Springs. "Now I have to believe Roselyn was killed because someone found her in Honey Springs."

"I did get in touch with Roselyn's parents. They came early this morning to identify the body." He didn't need to give me details. The look on his face told me all I needed to know.

"Is there any way you'd let me talk to Gillian?" I asked. When he hesitated, I added, "I feel bad for her. I'd hate to think any child has to resort to stealing in order to help her family out."

"I'd rather you didn't at this time. Principal Waters is having her call her parents now, so I'd like to play this by the book." Spencer wasn't going to budge even if I tried to lawyer him.

"No problem." I knew I had other ways to get in front of the girl. Birdie just might be that way.

"I'll be in touch." He excused himself and passed Aunt Maxi on the way back into the school on her way out.

"Well?" Aunt Maxi had her bag gripped in her hand.

"He won't let me talk to her, but he doesn't seem to think she killed Roselyn. Regardless, there's nothing more we can do here." I turned and headed toward the parking lot. "I think we can get more answers later this afternoon, so we should go on to see Roselyn's parents. Spencer did say they drove here this morning and claimed her body."

CHAPTER NINETEEN

"You've been awfully quiet." Aunt Maxi had done enough talking for the both of us on our two-hour drive west to Roselyn's hometown.

"Just thinking, I guess." I looked at the GPS on the phone. "Just a few more minutes until we get into town. I got Roselyn's family address from Nikki, so I think we just need to go straight there."

"Speaking of Nikki." Aunt Maxi knew I'd gotten the address from her. "What is going on with that?"

"Spencer isn't letting her leave town, so I ended up getting Mom to take her in since Mom has an extra bedroom. That way Nikki can go to work with her and Mom can keep an eye out."

"Huh." Aunt Maxi scoffed. "You ain't fooling me. You are having Nikki keep an eye on Penny and Quentin." Aunt Maxi twisted around to look at me.

"I am not. I needed Nikki to stay somewhere where she couldn't run off. I'm still not sure she didn't do it now that we are pretty sure Gillian didn't." I threw a hand up in the air. "Look around." I gestured to the run-down area. "She knew about the money, and who knows." I shrugged. "What if Nikki asked Roselyn to give her some money to keep her secret, her whereabouts? Roselyn said no, and Nikki knew where she was and she killed her. Maybe Nikki does have the money and just played along with us."

"What if Nikki and Roselyn had a fight? Roselyn took the money out of the safety deposit box. Nikki knew it, and she ransacked the cabin looking for it. And you're right. She did play along when you and Spencer took her to the bank." Aunt Maxi added a little to our speculation. "Look around. A little bit of money would go a long way here. Just think what millions could do."

The town looked abandoned. The buildings along the main streets had several For Rent or For Sale signs in the windows. The wood electrical poles had flyers stapled on them with a missing person. The photo was of Roselyn.

"It looks like they were looking for her," I said, staring out the window when we got caught by the red traffic light.

"Poor thing. Look at this place. It needs a good dose of something." Aunt Maxi tsked out the window. "I remember when Honey Springs was going down this path, and though I hate to admit it, Loretta Bebe did start the Women's Club, then the Garden Committee, and not to forget the Beautification Committee."

I never thought I'd see the day Aunt Maxi gave Loretta Bebe credit for anything other than a hard time.

"I guess we all have our purposes in life." I drummed my finger on the wheel, waiting impatiently for the light to change. "I want to talk to Birdie about Gillian and if she knows her."

"Is that what you've been thinkin' on this whole way here? That youngin'?" Aunt Maxi asked.

"I guess I have. I feel bad for her. From what I understood the secretary to say, the girl has to help out with some sort of odd jobs to get some money for the family. I hate to hear of anyone stealing for such a reason. I have money in the budget to hire another part-time teenager. If Birdie agrees." I was a sucker for a person in a tight spot.

I continued to drive once the light turned and made the next left.

Even as a lawyer, I did a lot of pro bono cases. Those made Kirk nuts and were probably another reason to add to the cause of our marriage collapsing.

The GPS dinged we were at our destination. There were cars all lined up along the street and people sitting on the front porch smoking and talking. It was definitely a gathering. In this case, I knew it was for Roselyn and what her parents had found out about her, making it the perfect time to blend in and see for ourselves what anyone knew.

"Are you ready?" I asked Aunt Maxi.

"We are going to blend in just fine." She picked up the purse she'd been using since the purse snatching and opened it, dumping its contents into the hobo bag she'd just gotten back. She put it over her shoulder and across her body.

"I don't think you're going to blend in too good." My eyes shifted from the hobo bag to her orange hair.

She got out of the car and waited for me to walk up the walkway to the front porch. She was right. We headed up the steps without anyone really paying a bit of attention to us. There was a lot of chatter that I didn't bother listening to yet.

I held the screen door for the person walking out of the house. I gestured for Aunt Maxi to go ahead of me.

She was always much better in these types of social interactions than I was, so I let her take the lead.

"The kitchen?" she asked a lady once we were inside. The woman pointed the way. "Mothers always gather in the kitchen," she said out of the side of her mouth on our way where the woman had pointed.

The entire kitchen was filled with women. They were uncovering all sorts of casserole dishes and putting them along the countertop, the kitchen table, and what looked like a small rollaway island.

The smell of coffee caught my attention, and I looked around to see there was a coffeepot next to the stove along with a bottle of two percent milk and a bag of sugar.

The necessity to make anyone right at home at such a horrible time.

"I'm so sorry to hear about Roselyn," I heard Aunt Maxi telling someone. When I looked back, she was bent over an older woman with gray hair, deep purple bags under her eyes, and a tissue gripped in her hand.

She nodded and dabbed her eyes.

"I don't know why she would go off like that. She had a good job. She had family and friends who love her." Roselyn's mom put her head in her hands and sobbed.

"Scooch." Aunt Maxi sorta pushed the woman next to Roselyn's mom out of the way and sat down. She put her arm around Roselyn's mom's shoulder. "And Roselyn was a good friend to Nikki."

"Where is she?" She sniffed. "The authorities need to be looking for her."

265

"Did they not get along?" Aunt Maxi asked. "I mean the two seemed like good friends."

"Just because they have matching purses doesn't mean they are good friends." Roselyn's mama's words had me recall the purse Nikki had with her.

It was a very distinctive black cloth purse with silver discs sewn on like little mirrors. Not my style but it was very cute.

"Nikki was always jealous of Roselyn." The woman next to me nudged me, handing me a plate of crackers with an aerosol can of cheese spray, taking me away from hearing what else Roselyn's mom was telling Aunt Maxi.

It was fine. Aunt Maxi would be able to let me know if there was something said that would help with the investigation.

"Do you know how to make some curlicues like you see on television with this cheese? All fancy-like?" the woman asked.

"Sure." I snapped the lid off the can. "Why would Nikki be jealous of her?"

"The baby. Roselyn's baby. It was no secret really how Nikki had a crush on the father of Roselyn's baby. Men." The woman tsked. "The two girls didn't talk for months after Roselyn started showing. It was only after the baby was born and Roselyn went back to her life that Nikki started to come around again." The woman rolled her eyes. "Some friend."

"Maybe one of them won the lottery from the store here." I slipped in that little bit of information. "And took off." I threw it out there to see if anyone in town had heard Roselyn's news or if Nikki had told anyone.

From what I could tell, the gossip around here was just as hot as the gossip in the coffeehouse.

"Nah." The lady snorted and looked at me. Her face stilled. "Really? You think?"

"I guess stranger things have happened." I gulped trying to keep my wits about me.

"Honey, if someone around here won that money and not someone passing through, we'd all have heard by now." She put more crackers on the platter for me to spray out more cheese.

"Why, after all of these years, would Nikki still be jealous of Roselyn?" I went back to the possibility Nikki just might be the killer.

"Everyone in town knew Nikki was always jealous of Roselyn. Nikki did everything Roselyn did. Roselyn got a job at the diner, so Nikki got a job.

Roselyn got her hair cut short once, and Nikki showed up the next day with her hair short. Roselyn left town, and now Nikki has left town." She picked up one of the crackers I'd just swirled with cheese. "Nikki called into work the other night sick. The next day Roselyn shows up dead in another part of the state, and we've not seen Nikki since." Her brows lifted. "You think that ain't some funny business then I don't know what is."

She picked up another of the crackers.

"You sure do know how to make them fancy curls. Like you've done this before. Now which side of the family are you kin to? Nikki's mama's side or daddy's?" She put the entire cracker in her mouth.

"Excuse me." I did a quick walk past Aunt Maxi, pinching her shirt. "Come on," I told her and headed out the way we came.

"Nikki isn't the most loyal friend she claims she was to Roselyn," I told Aunt Maxi on our way down the few steps of the front porch.

On our way to the car, I gave Aunt Maxi the details of what the woman had said about Nikki and Roselyn's friendship.

"What seemed so interesting was the fact Nikki had called into work sick the night before, and that lady was right. There was something fishy, and Nikki sure didn't tell me that little bit of information." I put the keys in the ignition, turned the engine, and pulled out of the space heading our car straight back to Honey Springs.

There was a reason I went into law. It was to get to the truth of things. There was a reason I got out of law. Not just because Kirk had cheated on me and he was my law partner, but sometimes taking on other people's truth got me a little nervous.

The more I thought about Nikki keeping these details from me, the more anxious I became, and I knew I wouldn't be able to not check in on Nikki since I left her with my mom. So I called my mom.

"Hey, Mom," I greeted her after she answered. "Can I talk to Nikki?" I asked her over the car's hands-free audio system.

"It appears Nikki Dane didn't tell the truth. Imagine that." Aunt Maxi also put her two cents in. "I knew something was wrong with that girl."

"Honey, I dropped her off at the boardwalk this morning after she got up. She said she'd wait for you there." Mom told me something I didn't want to hear.

"I told you to keep an eye on her. I'll call you back." I told my phone's voice commands to call Spencer.

It went to voicemail.

"Hey, Spencer, it's me. I went to see Roselyn's mom's family, and it does appear Nikki has been jealous of Roselyn all these years. I really want to make sure you check out her alibi. I know I'm supposed to be her lawyer, but you know me. I'm too honest for my own good. Call me when you get a chance. I'm driving back now and have plenty of time in the car to think on this."

I tossed my phone to Aunt Maxi.

"Can you please call Bunny and see if Nikki is there?" I asked.

Aunt Maxi asked Bunny all sorts of questions after we found out Nikki was still at the coffeehouse. They'd come up with some sort of scheme to keep Nikki there until we made it back to the coffeehouse.

The drive back didn't seem to take as long as the drive there. It didn't help that I was going a little faster than I should've been, though not too much over the speed limit.

"I bet you've come up with some doozies in that head of yours because you've not said a word this entire time." Aunt Maxi did break my concentration.

"The cellar." I slid my eyes to Aunt Maxi. "I bet you money Roselyn put the money in the cellar at our cabin."

"Quentin did say he saw her go down in there while he was there," Aunt Maxi recalled. "I haven't looked down in the cellar for a while. I just let the weeds grow up over it. I know Quentin keeps clearing it."

"I even made it a point to stop by and go look in there, but that's when we found out the cabin had been broken into." It had totally slipped my mind.

"We have time to stop. We will be driving right past there on the way back to the Bean Hive. Or actually we need to go to school to get your car." I had almost forgotten we'd left it there after she'd come with Spencer after I'd showed her the moped photo.

"You can drop me off when you leave to go home. Isn't Birdie working tonight? Or is it her study friends night?" Aunt Maxi asked.

"Birdie closes. We can go by the cabin and take a look in the cellar. If there's nothing there, then we can go to the Bean Hive before we go by the school." It sounded like a good plan, but as we all knew, plans more than likely didn't go the way we played them in our heads.

Certainly not how I'd planned the last few days.

Spencer had called just as we drove over the city limit line. I told him about what I'd found out about Nikki and my hunches on the cellar.

"Think about it. Roselyn did keep in contact with Nikki. When Nikki told her she was on her way, Roselyn knew Nikki just might stop at nothing to become her, be like her, and she knew she gave Nikki the key to the safety deposit box where she'd kept the cash she wanted to keep on hand." The theory in my head didn't sound as good when it came out my mouth.

We knew she had Evan deposit a lot of the winnings because he did mention how he had to call the reserve to come pick up the money because he never kept that much in the bank.

I continued with my train of thought.

"Roselyn brought the money to the cabin, and she got really upset when Quentin got there because of her own doing. Not because he was there to do the job but because he was there when she had all that cash on hand. That's when she decided to pack it up and take it to the cellar. There's no way Nikki knew about the cellar." Aunt Maxi gave me a few head nods in agreement while I talked to Spencer.

"Why did she go to the boardwalk?" Spencer asked a question that only Roselyn could answer.

But I could theorize about it.

"What if she knew Nikki was coming to town? The safest place to meet her is the coffeehouse. But they never made it there. They met on the boardwalk and walked to the pier before they were going to come inside, only they had an argument out there." The only way to find out was to get to the cellar, see if the money was in there, and ask Nikki even more questions.

"I'm almost at the cabin." Spencer had the same train of thought as me.

"I'm pulling in." I clicked off the phone and pulled into the driveway. Aunt Maxi unbuckled and popped open the door. "Where are you going?"

"I'm going to see if the money is in the cellar," Aunt Maxi stated as a breeze passed through the door, landing chills on my arms.

"We need to wait for Spencer!" I yelled after her as I jumped out to stop her. "And don't touch the door! Fingerprints!"

Spencer's sheriff's truck pulled up. He rolled down the window with his eyes set on Aunt Maxi trotting off to the side of the house.

"I'm guessing she's going to go look?" He gave her a sharp glare. "Maxine! Don't touch! I'm coming!"

She stopped at what appeared to be the cellar and lifted her hands up in surrender.

"I ain't going down." She did a little shimmy-shake. "Kinda gives me the creeps."

Spencer and I walked over. The three of us looked down at the strange door before Spencer bent down and tugged on the round steel handle.

The door lifted right open. The sunlight exposed what it was, a set of six or so steps that ended in a small room with what looked like wooden shelves that weren't in great shape, but back in the day I bet they served their purpose.

Spencer unclipped his flashlight from his utility belt and darted it around before he looked at me.

"I'm going in," he said and took the first step before he had to bend down in order to fit inside once he was at the bottom.

"Do you see anything?" I asked.

"Suitcase." He appeared at the bottom of the steps with the small piece of luggage in the opposite hand from the one with the flashlight.

"Is that the money?" Aunt Maxi anticipated him, grabbing me by the arm. "I've never really been too involved when you're solving a case, so this is pretty exciting."

"The tag does say Roselyn Bohlen on it, so I'm guessing something she wanted to hide is in here." He picked it up and slowly came back up the steps, handing me the bag so he could completely get out.

"Can we open it?" Aunt Maxi had bent down and had her finger on the zipper.

"Let me do it just in case this does become evidence." He laid the suitcase on its back and slowly unzipped it before he peeled back the top. "Just as I thought."

There were at least seven rows of stacked twenty-dollar bills along with some little-girl toys.

"It looks like Nikki was telling the truth about Stella." I called Roselyn's little girl by the name she wanted her to have. "But did Nikki want a cut before Roselyn made it to Florida?"

"Roxanne, it looks like I'm going to go to the Bean Hive and take her in for questioning. This time, I'm going to use my authority to hold her in the jail." Spencer zipped the suitcase back up.

I pushed my finger on the bottom of Aunt Maxi's chin to close her mouth for her since she appeared to be stunned from what she'd seen.

"I'll be down to see how she wants to proceed." I knew at this point, with Nikki not telling me the truth about where she was the night of Roselyn's murder, that things weren't looking good.

Even as her so-called lawyer, I wasn't sure if I could get past this minor detail. These all seemed small, but it was the littlest of clues that solved the biggest of cases.

CHAPTER TWENTY

Aunt Maxi had really geared herself up for some big hoopla that might take place when Spencer walked in to take Nikki Dane down to the station for what we felt was the questioning that would reveal more details of what really happened to her best friend, Roselyn Bohlen.

It was as if Nikki knew we were coming. As soon as the three of us walked in, she gathered her purse and stood up, going with Spencer rather quietly.

"That was a big windup," Aunt Maxi said flatly.

"She did look like she knew why he was there." I still couldn't get all of that money out of my head. In order to do that, I busied myself around the coffee-house, giving myself a few minutes before I needed to take Aunt Maxi to her car.

She was already busy spreading the gossip about the small amount of time we'd spent in Roselyn's hometown.

"How are you?" I asked Birdie after I'd found her in the kitchen getting more items out of the freezer so she could refill the display case. "Are you doing okay?"

"Grandmawmaw is mad at me for leaving my notebook at school. She said I'm grounded except when I come to work. This is a time I'd complain to Stella, um, Roselyn."

"I'm sorry." While she was in here and for me to keep her talking, I decided to make the banana butter dog cream. "Can you grab those few bananas for me?" I asked and went over to the refrigerator to get the yogurt.

"What are you making?" she asked. She put the bananas on the workstation and watched me get a bowl from the shelf underneath.

"Dog ice cream. Pepper and Sassy love it," I told her and watched as she did exactly what I expected her to do.

She peeled each banana and put them in the bowl.

"You can smash those while I get the peanut butter." I found it so much easier to have conversations over coffee with adults, but I'd learned if you had food or were making food, it was easier to keep my teenage staff engaged in a few words. "Speaking of work. Do you think you could use some help?" I asked in hopes she'd be able to give me some insight on Gillian.

"It would really be great, but it's no biggie. I can do it by myself." Birdie was pretty reliable, and that's one thing I truly loved about her. "You'd think now that she has her purse back, she'd be too happy to even think about grounding me." Birdie rolled her eyes and used the back of the tines to really get in there and mush those bananas together.

I added the yogurt for her mix-in.

"Do you know Gillian Harvey?" I asked and fiddled with the top of the jar of peanut butter.

"Yeah. I heard she stole the purses. I feel bad for her." Birdie was definitely an empath. She took on other's emotions, and by her tone, I could tell she could somewhat feel what Gillian must be going through.

"She admitted to taking your grandmawmaw's and Aunt Maxi's purses to help feed her family, but neither of them had enough money to amount to a hill of beans." I scooped out a few tablespoons of peanut butter, tossing those in the bowl.

"She's really nice. She keeps to herself a lot. She was cleaning the school's bathrooms for the janitor at lunch, but then kids started to make fun of her." Birdie rolled the edge of the fork around the bowl to make sure she got all the ingredients mixed up.

"What about the dog bone ice tray?" I headed over to one of the storage shelves with all the tins, trays, and other things we used to bake things in. "And the kitty cat faces. Or the bird one?" I held it up for her approval. "I still need to get photos of Polly."

"She's hilarious." Birdie laughed and helped me fill up the three ice trays I'd decided to use. "While we were in class today, she was trying to get on everyone's project."

I laughed just thinking about it.

"What are you making?" I asked.

"We are making birdhouses for our moms for Mother's Day presents. Ms. Mowry doesn't know if we will still have enough supplies when it comes to that late into the school year, so she's planning ahead. I am going to miss her next year."

"That's a shame. Maybe your grandmother can put that on one of her campaign signs. More money for school funding." I took the edges of the ice trays and gave each one a little shake so the liquid homemade ice cream would even out on the top. "Look at me trying to save Ms. Mowry and Gillian by giving them jobs."

"That's why we get along with each other so well." Birdie wrapped her arms around me and gave me a hug. "We want what's best for everyone. You were even willing to go the distance for Nikki. She turned out to be a killer." Birdie shrugged and walked off to the freezer with the trays.

"Hmm. Yeah. I guess so." I slumped a little at her observation before Aunt Maxi popped into the kitchen.

"Can we go? I want to get home in time for my television shows." She stood at the swinging door with it propped open with her shoe. "Good night, Birdie."

"Night." Birdie shut the freezer door and walked over to the sink to wash her hands. "I'm fine. You can go, and I'll see you tomorrow."

"Are you sure?" I asked her and couldn't help but wonder exactly what it would've been like if I were pregnant, had a daughter, and had this sort of relationship with her.

It certainly wasn't one I'd had with my mom.

I smiled after Birdie waved me off.

"What's that smile about?" Aunt Maxi asked as we walked down the boardwalk to get into the car.

"Oh, nothing." I wanted to keep that little feeling inside to myself.

CHAPTER TWENTY-ONE

"Hey, kiddo." Aunt Maxi stopped on the way to her car after I waited to make sure it started. "You know I love you here and really encouraged you to open the Bean Hive, but after the past couple of days really being with you and watching you do all the lawyering stuff, I have to say you're pretty good at that too."

"It sounds like you think I've made a mistake coming back here and opening the coffeehouse." I rolled up the window and turned off the engine before I got out. "This is my passion. I just like the little investigations here and there to whet my appetite. And don't forget, I keep up my skills in case I need them."

"I felt like I needed to tell you because it was the first time I really watched you take all these clues and put them together to help solve the crime." She waved her hand for me to let her finish when I started to say something. "I know you've done it before, but this time I was with you along the way. I don't want you to wake up and suddenly realize you miss something you're really good at."

"What I'm good at is different than what I'm passionate about. My heart is with you, with Patrick, with Mom, with Honey Springs, and with the Bean Hive." I smiled. "One day that will include a baby of my own who I can take to the Bean Hive or just stay home if I have a hankerin'. If I was a lawyer, I wouldn't have such luxuries."

"Are you trying to tell me that I just might be getting me a little niece or nephew?" Aunt Maxi bounced on the toes of her shoes before she couldn't stand it any longer and ran over to me, wrapping her arms around me.

"Not yet, but with any luck, I hope so soon." I squeezed her back. "In the meantime, you head home. I'm going to run into the school and see if I can get the janitor to let me go get some photos of Polly."

"Then you get home to Patrick." Aunt Maxi's shoulders squeezed up to her ears, her face squished together with glee at the prospect of a baby.

"Go!" I pointed to her car and waited for her to pull out before I headed up to the front of the school where the parking lot was just as packed as it was this morning before Aunt Maxi and I had set off on our adventure to visit Roselyn's hometown.

The parents and children coming in and out of the school with sports bags reminded me there were spring sports happening. Another thing I hoped to one day look forward to. It was hard to ignore images of Patrick on the sidelines of the Honey Springs High School gym rooting for our child as I passed by and took a quick peek into the gymnasium.

The giggling young cheerleaders outside of the gym were clapping to the beat of their chants as though they were practicing for the halftime show of the basketball game taking place inside.

My phone buzzed.

I pulled it out of my pocket.

"Patrick, I was just thinking about you." I tried to stop smiling but couldn't. I hurried past the gym and around the bend, passing the library to take the steps up to the second floor where Hope's class was located.

"I'm always thinking about you." His southern voice was so warm and comfortable, he still made my insides gooey. "Now, when are you coming home? Me and the kids miss you."

"Kids." The word came out faint. "Pepper and Sassy."

"And me." He had no idea what scenario I was playing in my head.

"And you, but you don't wag your tail when I get home," I teased and noticed through the window of the door that the light in the home ec room was on.

"Supper's almost ready. I made salmon croquettes. Aunt Maxi's recipe too."

The saying was about the way to a man's heart being cooking, but it just so happened to be the way to *my* heart.

"That sounds so good. I'm at the school to grab some photos of Polly to hang at the coffeehouse tomorrow." I tapped on the window when I saw Hope in there. She waved me in. "I'll only be a minute. I love you."

"I love you too."

"Hey there. Did I catch you at a bad time?" I asked after I peeked my head through the door. I slipped my phone back into my pocket.

"Hey there, squawk!" Polly was perched next to the window. She was standing on one leg with her wing extended.

"She can do better yoga than me," I joked. "Not that you would know, but I have taken a yoga class or two at the Bee Happy Resort."

"It looks like I'm going to have plenty of time to check that out soon." Hope pinched a grin as she taped up a cardboard box. "The board had a meeting last night, and they put the nail in the coffin. I thought I might have a chance, but I didn't."

"I'm sorry. The offer still stands if you'd like to work at the coffeehouse." I walked over and clicked my tongue at Polly. "Do you want me to take Polly back to the coffeehouse so you don't have to worry about her?"

"No. She's good company until she gets adopted." Hope pulled out a desk drawer and put some of the items in the box.

"Then if you don't mind"—I pulled my phone out of my pocket—"I'm going to take some photos of her so we don't miss out on some potential families at the coffeehouse."

"Sure. Have at it." Hope packed a few more things while I snapped a few photos. "I'm going to go to the teachers' lounge and grab a snack. Do you want anything?"

"Nah. I've got to get home. Patrick." I had no idea why I felt like I needed to tell my life story whenever I talked. "I'm good."

"Okay. I'll see you at the coffeehouse soon." She exited the classroom, leaving me alone.

I looked around the room, and on the windowsill were at least five birdhouses dripping with paint. They had creatively used old license plates for the little tented roofs. They had four screws to hold them on the wood structure.

The nail in the front was stuck right under the hole where the bird would enter.

"Very creative." I walked over and looked at one with flowers painted on it and recognized Birdie's signature. I ran my finger over the screws. "Of course the nails are screwed in perfectly."

"Where's the screwdriver? Squawk. No money in her purse. Squawk."

"Oh, Polly. You're so fun. Someone is going to…" I aimed my phone at her to get a photo. I looked at the screen of the phone. At her. I dropped the phone and walked over to her. "What did you say about a screwdriver?"

"Screwdriver. Where is it? Squawk! No money! Money!"

"Did you hear Gillian talk about money?" I asked Polly like she was actually understanding me, but she wasn't. She just repeated things over and over. Things she'd heard.

"Think about it, Roxy." I talked to myself and looked around. The back of the room had a pegboard on the wall with a select few house tools hanging on the hooks. The screwdrivers got my attention. One in particular. One that was missing. At least there was an empty hook that looked like it was missing one.

The one that looked similar to them all just so happened to be in the evidence room down at the Honey Spring Sheriff Department. All of these had the school's name written in black Sharpie on the handle.

I pulled my phone out of my pocket and snapped a photo of the pegboard.

Does the screwdriver you found at the scene match these? And was there anything written on the handle in black Sharpie? I texted Spencer and hit Send.

"She's a child." I talked to myself to get that curious side of me scratched out of thinking Gillian could possibly kill.

It wouldn't be outside the realm of possibility if I took a second to think about it. She's a young girl who was trying to help provide for her family. They needed money. She was in class with Birdie. Did Birdie mention to Gillian how Roselyn had won the money?

I tried to recall if Gillian was in the study group at the coffeehouse, but I couldn't get my mind to stop racing to even think clearly.

I laughed.

"We are in a school. Children misplace things all the time. Calm yourself and just look for the other screwdriver that one of the kids didn't put away in the right spot." My heart had slowed down along with the crazy thoughts.

One after the other, I began to open some of the cabinet drawers to look for the tool.

"Did you get your photos?" Hope had come back in. "What are you doing?"

"I noticed you had a missing screwdriver up there, and I was looking for it." I shrugged with a wry smile on my face with one of the doors half open.

"You can use one that's hanging up," she offered. "Why do you need a screwdriver? Are you having Polly hold it or something?"

"No." I shook my head and decided to come clean. "You know that murder on the pier?"

"I heard something about it, but I thought Gillian Harvey confessed to the purse snatching. I hated to hear it. She really is a good person. Just in a tight spot." Hope heaved a sigh.

"The murder and the purse snatching are believed to be two separate crimes." I turned back to shut the cabinet door and leave well enough alone until I heard back from Spencer.

There was a flicker of something in the cabinet that caught the light of the room. Instinctively, I opened the cabinet all the way instead of closing it like I was going to.

"Oh no," I groaned when I noticed the black cloth purse with the round silver embellishments that resembled mirrors sewn all over it.

"What is it?" Hope hurried back to the room to see what I'd found. "Where did that come from?"

"I think we both know." I shook my head and went for my phone to call Spencer to tell him how Gillian had stashed Roselyn's purse in the classroom.

She was smart. Not hiding the purse from the person you killed with the other purses.

"You couldn't leave well enough alone." The sound of metal sliding out of one of the hooks on the pegboard caught my attention.

"Yeah. I'm so glad I opened the—" I turned around and noticed Hope had one of the screwdrivers in her hand, her arm lifted in the air.

"You don't understand. She won ten million dollars. I just needed a few hundred to pay the bills. She used me since she's been here the past few months. I was a friend to her." Hope had started to confess why and how she killed Roselyn Bohlen. "I'll never forget the first night she came into the Bean

279

Hive. Me and Birdie were talking. Stella—whatever, Roselyn—came in and ordered a fancy drink. She didn't look none too fancy to me."

I took a side step to get myself out of the corner in the back of the room because the way she was looking at me and talking to me made me think she was crazy enough to use the screwdriver in her hand on me.

"Where do you think you're going?" she asked me, moving directly in front of me. "Do you not see this?"

I flinched as she jutted the raised arm at me. She lowered her arm and pointed the screwdriver at the door.

"They are the ones who are taking my income away." She had a dark look in her eyes as if she had no idea what she was doing.

"I think so too." I agreed and would just about do anything to get to the door.

My phone beeped a text.

"Give me your phone." She put her hand out.

"We don't have time to do this if you want to go free. I sent a photo of the screwdrivers on the pegboard with one missing to the sheriff. I'm sure that's him responding to me, and he will be here any minute." My goodness, I had no idea if Spencer was coming or even noticed the screwdrivers had the school's name on it, but she didn't know that.

"Fine, we will go." She stepped forward and jabbed the screwdriver in my side to get me to walk toward the door at the front of the room.

Slowly I walked and let the idea of what was going on in my head work its way into the puzzle of Roselyn's death. I knew Hope could jab me in the side with the screwdriver and I would survive, possibly even be able to fight her off, but I was hoping to give Spencer a moment to get here.

"The school is filled with parents, students, and staff right now." I wanted to put a little self-doubt about her actions in her head.

I winced as she dug the screwdriver deeper in my side with each step.

The pain jolted free the memories of Hope in the coffeehouse with Birdie. Birdie really liked Hope , and I was sure she used her as a confidant, which meant Birdie probably told her about Roselyn and her winning the lottery.

From what little bit Hope had said, she must've been at the coffeehouse more than the times she was there with the study group.

"We are going to play it like we are two old friends, just like I did with Roselyn. I called her up to meet me at the coffeehouse for a coffee after I was leaving here. I had one of the birdhouse supplies with me because I thought I would make one at the coffeehouse as a demo."

"So this wasn't a premeditated murder?" I asked. "I'm a lawyer. I can get you out of this."

Her eyes lowered as if she were trying to read me. Not that I would get her out of it, but I would say just about anything to get me out of this situation.

"When I approached Roselyn outside next to the pier, I pretended to be really upset about my job. Of course I didn't want Birdie to see me so upset." She talked in a dramatic voice as if she were so proud of her actions.

She was such a narcissist that she stopped in front of the door and dropped the screwdriver from my side so she could use her hands to finish the morbid story.

"I asked Roselyn if she didn't mind taking a walk down the pier so I could collect myself before I saw any of my students. That's when I asked her for some money, and she refused to even think of it. She gave me some pitiful story about how she needed the money for her little girl. I told her I would pay her back, and she started to tell me how I was just like all the others. Something about how she had trusted her best friend and how now even she wanted a piece of the pie."

Without Hope saying it, I knew she was talking about Nikki Dane.

It all fell into place. Nikki must've asked Roselyn for some money after she'd kept Roselyn's secret, and that's why Roselyn had taken out whatever cash she'd put in the safety deposit box and stored it in the cellar. She knew Nikki well enough to know she would show up.

"I'm so glad you're here." The door swung inward, knocking Hope into me. Instinctively I shoved her to the side. "I need to get Birdie's homework she left here." Loretta's voice trailed off as her eyes took in the situation.

"I've never been so happy to see you in my life!" I screamed and slammed my foot down on Hope's arm. "She killed Roselyn Bohlen. And I hope Spencer gets here soon."

"Goodness. We are going to need some more help down at that sheriff's department." Loretta Bebe stood over top of Hope with her drawn-on brows arched halfway up her forehead. "I can't be mayor and a sheriff's deputy."

Oh Lordy. Bless Honey Springs' heart. Loretta Bebe was on a mission to fight this crime all on her own.

Sirens whined in the distance, and soon the blue-and-red lights glowed through the classroom's windows.

"Before all of the hullabaloo about to happen here, I need to tell you to bring some sugar cookies with sprinkles and some brownies, along with some of that new coffee blend Birdie told me you've been roasting for city council meeting at the Bee Happy Resort tomorrow morning." Loretta barely got finished barking her orders before Spencer and a couple of his deputies rushed into the home economics classroom with their guns drawn.

CHAPTER TWENTY-TWO

"You sure were wrong about Nikki," Aunt Maxi said. We were on the ferry to get across Lake Honey Springs so we could go to the anticipated city council meeting. She scooted over on the bench closer to me to make room for more citizens who were also headed to the meeting.

I laughed. "So much for being good at something," I told Aunt Maxi since she had bragged on my amazing sleuthing skills just last night before I'd met my date with the devil... um, Hope . I patted the boxes in my hand. "At least I know I am good at baking and coffee roasting."

After Spencer had taken Hope Mowry into custody for killing Roselyn Bohlen, taken my statement, and let Nikki go, I had gone home to spend what was left of the evening with Patrick and the fur babies.

We had a very intimate conversation about starting to have children of our own and ended up having a very romantic night.

"These brownies smell so good." I pulled the boxes closer and wondered if there was a little bundle of joy inside me. The thought of it filled me with a joy that not even Hope or what had happened last night was going to ruin.

"You seem awfully happy for someone who almost died." Aunt Maxi had always been so good at reading me, and this time I wasn't going to let my emotions show.

If I was pregnant, I wanted it to be between me and Patrick first. Not me and Aunt Maxi, which was good as putting it in the local paper.

"I am happy to be here for life. And coffee." I nodded to the thermos of my specialty roast coffee sitting on the floor of the ferry between her legs. "Plus the money, the ten million, well Roselyn's family is going to honor her wishes to give some of it to her daughter in her legacy. They did take some to pay off their debts and to be able to live on for the rest of their life, but they set up a legacy fund in Roselyn's name for unwed mothers."

"I love when something so good comes out of something so awful." Aunt Maxi wiped away a happy tear. "She was a very nice girl."

"Yes, she was, and she only wanted to do the right thing for her daughter." I sighed, thinking happy thoughts.

The ferry came to a stop, and I was going to thank Big Bib for the smooth ferry ride across the lake, but he was too busy talking to Katherine Nero, the owner of the bee farm located on this same island along with the Bee Happy Resort.

There would be plenty of time to catch up with them later today on our way back to the mainland since this was our only way back across the lake.

"I reckon we're gonna have to see Kirk and whatshername." Aunt Maxi's words ran together in disgust.

"Jessica, and she's really nice." I didn't tell Aunt Maxi yet how Jessica had gone to the coffeehouse last night and seen Polly there since she couldn't stay at the school any longer.

Jessica ended up adopting Polly because she said the spa needed a greeter. Polly was perfect for the job, and Birdie did all the paperwork by herself.

The Bee Happy Resort was located on the opposite side of the island. There were clear paths that led you right there.

Wooden signs dotted the pathway, displaying various messages like Serene, Quiet Your Mind, Bliss, Pure Indulgence, Calm, Cozy, and Relaxation. Even though I knew Crissy had strategically placed the signs there, they did make a feeling of ease wash over me.

I let go of the boxes with one hand and gently placed my other hand on my stomach. The what-ifs of having a baby just wouldn't leave my thoughts. My baby would be the first baby in Honey Springs in a long time, and I could actually picture me and the baby, and Patrick, riding in the ferry, coming over to the bee farm and collecting honey for the coffeehouse.

"Where are you at today?" Aunt Maxi stopped right in front of the three-tiered mosaic building where the resort was located.

The resort was amazing and nestled completely in the woods with thick brush, trees, and critters. The clay roofs popped above the budding spring trees and over the open living areas of the spa.

The chatter filtered around us when we finally made it inside.

"There you are!" Loretta Bebe rushed over and grabbed up the boxes. "You're late. This is how you thank me for saving your life, Roxanne Bloom?"

She waved Birdie over to take the coffee carafes from Aunt Maxi before the two of them hurried off toward the big room where the signs pointed to the city council meeting.

"I see Low-retta is back to her old ways," Aunt Maxi muttered.

"She's nervous. Today she's going to ask to be put on the ballot as a candidate for mayor." It was a big day for Loretta, and I was going to support her even though I never told her I'd be her campaign manager like she'd told everyone I had.

"Hello, squawk!" Polly had found a home on a perch as soon as you walked in. "Welcome to the Bee Happy Resort!"

Aunt Maxi slid her chin my way.

"I haven't had time to tell you that Polly has found a home here too." I smiled, thinking Jessica wasn't all that bad. Bad taste in men, maybe. "That's two animals adopted by her."

I looked past Polly and saw Jessica holding Biscuit, the little dog she'd adopted over Christmas from Pet Palace.

Jessica smiled and waved really big when she saw us.

"Be nice," I told Aunt Maxi between my teeth then smiled and waved.

"She's got to stop dressing that dog up like a baby." Aunt Maxi snorted.

"Baby! Squawk!" Polly screamed so loud that everyone in the building turned to look at her. "Kirk! Squawk! We are having a baby!"

My jaw dropped.

My eyes slid to Jessica.

She gave me a little shrug before she was crowded with people congratulating her.

THE END

If you enjoyed reading this book as much as I enjoyed writing it then be sure to return to the Amazon page and leave a review.

Go to Tonyakappes.com for a full reading order of my novels and while there join my newsletter. You can also find links to Facebook, Instagram and Goodreads.

RECIPES FROM THE BEAN HIVE

Poppy-seed Lemon Biscuit
Frothy and Frozen Caramel Latte
Banana Butter Puppy Cream

Poppy-seed Lemon Biscuit

Ingredients

- 2 cups all-purpose flour
- ¾ cup white sugar
- ½ cup finely ground almonds
- ½ teaspoon baking powder
- ½ teaspoon baking soda
- 1 tablespoon lemon zest
- 3 tablespoons poppy seeds
- 1 egg
- 2 egg whites
- 1 teaspoon lemon extract

Directions

1. Preheat oven to 350 degrees F (175 degrees C). Line a baking sheet with parchment paper.
2. Combine the flour, sugar, ground almonds, baking powder, and baking soda.
3. Combine the lemon peel, poppy seeds, egg, egg whites, and lemon extract. Add the dry mixture and mix well. Form the dough into 2 logs.
4. Place logs onto the prepared baking sheet. Bake at 350 degrees F (175 degrees C) for 30 minutes. Let cool slightly and cut diagonally into 1/2-inch slices. Bake slices another 8 to 10 minutes until dry. Cool completely and store in an airtight container.

Frothy and Frozen Caramel Latte

The Bean Hive doesn't just have the best hot coffee around. Roxy also serves up delish cold coffee too. The students at Honey Springs High School love this frothy espresso drink. It gives them just the right combination of not-too-much energy and not-too-much sugar so when they are studying at the coffeehouse, they are getting the work done.

Sometimes they like a little extra caramel sauce and whip on top.

Ingredients

- Blender
- 3 fluid ounces brewed espresso
- 1 tablespoon caramel sauce
- 2 tablespoons white sugar
- ¾ cup milk
- 1 ½ cups ice cubes
- 2 tablespoons whipped cream

Directions

1. Take your brewed coffee/espresso and pour it into the blender.
2. Add the caramel sauce and sugar to the blender and mix on high.
3. Pour the milk and the ice into the blender.
4. Keep blending until the mixture is smooth and frothy to your liking.
5. Pour into a glass.
6. Add extra toppings as you see fit!

Banana Butter Puppy Cream

Ingredients

- 3 ripe bananas
- 32 ounces of plain yogurt
- 1 cup of peanut butter

Directions

1. Mash the peeled bananas in a bowl.
2. Add the yogurt to the bowl and mix thoroughly with the bananas.
3. Add the peanut butter to the mix.
4. Pour the mix into freezer ice molds. I like to get the cute silicon dog bone molds just because they make the cutest treats ever and customers at the Bean Hive love to get these for their pups. But you can use simple ice trays.
5. Put in the freezer for at least two hours.

This treat will not only keep your pups cool, but it'll make them very happy!

Barista Bump-off Book Club Discussion Questions

In the beginning of this book, Roxy is hosting a tutoring group for Birdie's Home Economics Class. Hope, their teacher, is working with them because her budget has been cut, and the class will not continue next year. Home economics was one of my favorite classes. I especially loved cooking.

#1-What was one of your favorite elective subjects? Is it still available to students today?

Hearing commotion outside, Aunt Maxi goes to investigate returning with the announcement of a drive-by purse snatching, loud enough for mayor to hear. Next Sheriff Spencer arrives looking for the mayor. A heated discussion takes place between the two with budget cuts coming up once again, followed by Loretta Bebe yelling that SHE had been robbed. Looking at the sheriff, she told him to "get out there and do his job!"

#2-First Maxi comes in announcing the purse snatching, that leads to the sheriff accusing the mayor. Loretta Bebe comes in yelling about her purse snatching and yelling at the sheriff. Wow! Chaos in the coffeehouse! First thoughts on the events that were happening?

Roxy hosts shelter pets from the town's animal shelter, the Pet Palace. This time rather a
    furry dog or cat, Louise brings a parrot, Polly. A very large and loud parrot. After looking
    over Polly's file, Roxy finds out she is fifteen years old, can live to be 60 – 80 years old and, she was surrendered by her owner! Pepper is definitely not a fan of Polly!

#3-Have you ever adopted a rescue? Have you ever owned a parrot or other bird? Show us your furry or feathered family members.

As Roxy is leaving the Bean Hive, she hears footsteps and someone running away. Although her nerves are on edge, she hears Pepper barking loudly and becomes afraid he might be in danger. Trying to figure out what Pepper is barking at; Roxy turns on her phone's flashlight. Rather than a turtle or fish, she discovers a dead body. The body turns out to be one of Aunt Maxi's renters, who was stabbed in the back.

#4-What were your thoughts at this point? Did the purse snatching escalate to murder?

It turned out that the woman's name was Stella Johnson. Aunt Maxi reveled that although Roxy's mom, Penny, had set up the rental, Stella only wanted to meet with the owner. While discussing the murder, they discover that Birdie knew her as one of their customers, and also knew more about her than anyone. Stella, had won the lottery and claimed it anonymously. Roxy decides her next move is to contact her mom to see Stella's paperwork. Since it was too late to go anywhere, and her mom was with a "client" which Roxy doubts, she decided to search the internet to see what she could find.

#5-Have you ever checked to see just how much information can be found on someone? I have. There is a crazy amount of info out there floating around on the web.

As Roxy was researching Stella's, (who she now knew to be Roselyn) background, she found out several things. Past experience as a barista, articles that someone local had won the lottery, and also her public social media account. Roxy realized the last post on social media was right before she was murdered. There are several questions to consider at this point.

#6-Was Stella hiding from someone in general, and did they steal her purse in hopes of getting the money?

Did you find it strange that she left her old life behind and created a new identity? What were your thoughts at this point?

The next victim in the drive-by purse snatching is Aunt Maxi. This time Aunt Maxi was trying to fight back when the purse snatcher told her to, "give me the purse or you will end up like her." Aunt Maxie referred to the purse snatcher as "him."

#7-Now, I was wondering if the purse snatching was related to the murder or a way to throw the sheriff off. What about you? Were you convinced they were related at this point?

A new suspect comes into play when Aunt Maxie admits she sent her handy man, Quinten Russel, over to the rental to fix the leak in the bathroom sink. Stella/Roselyn wouldn't let him in. The argument was heated and he never went in to fix the leak. Aunt Maxie didn't have much information on Quentin, other than he was homeless and needed a job. She hired him based on credentials Kirk, Roxy's ex, gave him. As the owner of the cabin, Aunt

Maxi had a key and was authorized to enter. Sheriff Shepard and his deputies showed up at the cabin while Roxy and Aunt Maxi were there going through Roselyn's things. Aunt Maxi finds a name to go with a cell phone number and Spencer finds a screwdriver that could possibly be the murder weapon.

#8-Aunt Maxie swears up and down that Quinten is innocent and to follow the phone number. Which direction would you head to investigate?

Nikki Dane, a friend of Roselyn's showed up in town talking about their relationship, best of friends, and Roselyn had given Nikki a key to safe deposit box. Yet, when it was opened, there was nothing inside of it. Did this rule Nikki out? Roxy wanted to be sure and headed to Roselyn's hometown. Once she and Aunt Maxie were there, a completely different picture of Nikki emerged.

#9-Was Nikki the killer? She didn't seem like a true friend to Roselyn. Did you think she was hiding something? Trying to get away with the money? Thoughts?

Roxy went to the high school to check on Polly and get pictures to post to help promote the

adoption. She hadn't gotten far when she discovered the moped Aunt Maxi described. Rather than heading to the classroom, she made a detour the principal's office to ask a few questions after she had called Maxi, who then called the sheriff. When the purse snatching was happening, and Aunt Maxi, described the moped. I didn't even think it could be a high school student. I considered it might have been a person down on their luck.

#10-Which directions did your thoughts go when the moped was found at the high school?

THE ENDING!!!!! This killer was not on my radar at all. I was completely caught off guard! Don't let us know the ending, that would be a spoiler for those that haven't finished the book, but did you know who the killer was?

#11-Yes, or no?

CAPPUCCINO CRIMINAL

A KILLER COFFEE BOOK 12

CAPPUCCINO CRIMINAL

A Killer Coffee Mystery

Book Twelve

BY
TONYA KAPPES

PREVIEW

As I rode, I couldn't help but think about last night's emergency council meeting again. The room had been packed with passionate citizens, and the tension had been palpable. I recalled the way Danielle, the environmentalist, stood up and argued against the proposed country-club development. She had discovered a natural spring on the land, and many of us agreed that it shouldn't be disturbed. She even had a gorgeous slideshow with photos.

I was relieved when the council voted down the project, but I knew some of our neighbors were still furious. The look on the developer's face was unforgettable. Especially when he looked at Leandar Taylor, the local real estate agent who'd sold him the land.

As I approached the contested land, I spotted the unmistakable flash of red-and-blue lights in the darkness near the lake.

My heart skipped a beat, and I slowed my bike, curiosity getting the better of me.

What could be happening at this hour? I wondered, my thoughts racing.

I pulled off the road and got off my bike. I walked cautiously toward the commotion, the gravel crunching under my feet. The sounds of the woods around me seemed to grow louder— the wind rustling through the trees and the distant hoot of an owl. My heart pounded in my chest as I drew closer to the scene.

"Stop right there!" I heard Sheriff Spencer Shepard call out with his gun drawn in front of him and pointing directly at me.

"It's me. Roxy!" I yelled and sort of slumped down, just in case he fired.

"Roxy, what are you doing here?" Sheriff Spencer Shepard called out, his brow furrowed with concern.

"I was just on my way to open the Bean Hive when I saw the lights," I explained, my voice barely above a whisper. "What's going on, Spencer?"

The sheriff hesitated then spoke in a somber tone. "Someone was out for an early-morning jog and found a body."

A chill ran down my spine, and my stomach tightened.

A body? In our peaceful town?

I couldn't wrap my head around it. I glanced around, searching for answers, when the moon slipped out from behind a cloud. Its silvery light illuminated the scene like a spotlight, revealing the lifeless form of Leandar Taylor.

CHAPTER ONE

I knew the smell anywhere.

It wasn't the aroma of the freshly brewed coffee that filled the air at the Bean Hive, my coffee shop, and it wasn't the smell of the warm and inviting pastries filling the glass display counters. Nor was it the scent of the strong and rich aromas from the espresso coming from the hissing espresso machine.

"Good morning, Loretta." It was Loretta Bebe's perfume wafting through the coffee shop as soon as she walked in, adding an extra layer to the sensory experience.

She must have literally bathed in the stuff because as soon as she flung the door open, the stench of her perfume saturated every corner of the small coffee shop.

"I have no idea how you do it, Roxy." She had already made it to the counter before I'd turned around to actually put eyes on her. "You know it's me before you even look at me."

"You have a vibe." I smiled and watched her pluck the gloves off her hands, finger by finger, before she neatly laid them over the top of and between the handles of her pocketbook.

I would never hurt Loretta's feelings in a million years. She'd probably not care, but still. The community had welcomed me with open arms a few years ago when I decided to leave my job as a lawyer to fulfill my dreams of opening my very own coffee shop. Granted, I was getting a divorce, but all of that was behind me.

Until it wasn't, and my ex, Kirk, and his wife, Jessica, brought their new baby in here to grab their daily afternoon cold brews.

Yeah.

"A vibe?" she asked, nervously raking her fingernails across the edges of her short black hair. "I bet it's the Cherokee in me."

"Yep, I betcha that's it, Low-retta." The sarcasm was thick as it came out of Bunny Bowowski's mouth as she did a drive-by behind me with a couple of customer orders on her tray. Her soft gray hair was parted to the side and cut at chin length. She didn't bother wearing the shirt with the coffee shop's logo I'd purchased for the employees to wear.

Bunny and her best friend, Mae Belle Donovan, had started a knitting club that met at the coffee shop every Sunday afternoon during the winter. Instead of the Bean Hive shirt, Bunny always wore a shawl she knitted, clasping it with a fancy pin.

Honey Springs was a tourist town on Lake Honey Springs in Kentucky, and the tourists didn't really come during the snowy winters, which allowed me to have different operating hours for each season. It only made sense to close the shop on Sunday, making it a perfect spot for Bunny and her group. I wasn't sure what they'd do about the new spring hours when we opened for a few hours after church. I didn't ask. Bunny always had a plan.

"I wasn't talkin' to you, Bunny." Loretta snarled. The white line where the tanning bed couldn't reach showed when she crinkled her nose. "I don't know why you keep her around. She's not good for business."

"Bunny?" I asked Loretta. I turned my back on her so I could make her usual black coffee and disguise the smile on my face, knowing Bunny was getting Loretta's goat. "Everyone loves her." I pointed my chin into the coffee shop for Loretta to turn and look at the customer Bunny had in stitches about something she was saying.

"She's harmless." I put the coffee down next to the register and looked at my elderly employee.

Bunny Bowowski waddled over to the next table, and by the way the customer waved their hand in the air, I knew Bunny was asking them if she could get them anything else.

"You're a saint for putting up with her," Loretta said. The line of bracelets jingled and jangled as she fiddled with the zipper of her wallet to retrieve money.

I smiled. If you only knew that was what people say to me about you, I thought to myself.

"That's the girl from the environmental office," Loretta said about the customer in the corner. "I can't believe what they are thinking about doing down there past the Cocoon Inn."

"You said the key words." I took the money Loretta had tucked in between her fingers, admiring how her long red nails shone. I stuck the cash in the register. "'Thinking about.'" I straightened out the information card for the pet of the week Louise Carlton had left on the counter before I grabbed the carafe of freshly brewed coffee to go and fill up customers' cups.

It was free refills, and the fuller their mugs were, the more they ate, and that's where I made the most money.

Pet of the week was a feature I offered to the Pet Palace, the local SPCA, where I kept one of the animals in the coffee shop for the week to help out with their adoptions. There were many hoops we had to jump through with the local health department when I opened the Bean Hive, but it was well worth the hassle when an animal was adopted.

It was kinda like one of those cat cafés but with more than just cats. This week, Louise had brought in the cutest speckled puppy. I knew it wouldn't take long before someone adopted him.

Currently, he was snuggled up against Pepper, my gray schnauzer, who was a staple around here. Me and Patrick, my husband, also had a black standard poodle, Sassy. Sassy loved to go to Cane Constructions with Patrick. Really, I think she liked riding around to the various sites in his big truck with her head out the window.

"We have to talk!" The voice was loud enough to catch my attention and take me out of my conversation with Loretta. Not only did I look, but everyone must've also heard because the chatter inside the Bean Hive had ceased.

With the handle of the coffee carafe in my hand, I twisted around to see what all the ruckus was about.

It was Leandar Taylor, a local Realtor.

At five feet, ten inches, he had a lean and athletic build in his charcoal-gray tailored suit. The coat was open, and his crisp white dress shirt was tight enough to show he must work out with weights. He wore a leather belt, and when he pointed at Danielle, the cuff of his suit coat inched up enough to expose the designer watch on his wrist.

My mom had mentioned Leandar before and commented on his polished image.

I'd never met the man, and today wasn't a great example of a first meeting.

"I'm sorry, but I'm having my breakfast," Danielle said to him, but her eyes were shifting left to right to see if anyone was looking.

Now everyone *was* staring.

Danielle was a woman of striking appearance. She had chestnut-brown hair that tumbled down her back in loose waves. Her eyes were a piercing shade of emerald green and blinked back what I thought was a look of grave concern on her face.

"I don't care. We have to talk and talk now." He shoved his big finger in her face and tapped the toe of his fancy black snakeskin boots with toe brass. "You won't get away with these lies. I've already got a call in to your boss, and I know your history. When he calls me back, you bet I'm going to pull that card."

"Please leave me alone," she whispered. Red blotches started to crawl up her neck. "I'm more than happy to meet with you at the site or somewhere else later this evening."

She pulled out what appeared to be a day planner from the bag on the floor.

"I don't want no stinking appointment. Right here and right now."

Leandar's demands were enough for me to put the carafe down and go over to tell him to leave or tell them to take whatever was going on between them outside on the pier. I hurried around the counter and grabbed a hot drink Bunny had just made for a customer.

"I'll leave you alone and won't tell your boss about you if you do what is right." Leandar planted the palms of his hands flat against the table and got up in Danielle's face. "You only have yourself to blame for what is coming your way."

"Excuse me. Leandar, right?" I interrupted him and looked at the hot drink. I couldn't help but notice those fancy brass fittings on the toe of his boots had his initials engraved on them.

"Here's a delicious cappuccino for you." I read the label before I shoved it into his face. "Please enjoy it outside."

"I didn't order a cappuccino, and the name says 'Frank.'" He read off the name we'd written on it.

"It's on the house." I gestured for him to leave.

His lips curled in, and his nostrils flared like a bull's before it rushed a matador. His eyes bore into mine.

"I'd like you to leave my coffee shop now." I pinched out a smile. "And I'll be sure to tell my mama, Penny Bloom, you said hello."

Mentioning my mama was something I rarely did to scare off people. She wasn't at all scary, but I'd heard her talk about Leandar. He and my mama were in the same industry.

Real estate agents.

It was a competitive business, and there weren't very many in Honey Springs. But they had their own little network, and Leandar knew if word got around he was making a scene, it wouldn't go well with the others in their little circle.

So I used Mama to get his attention in this situation.

And I would be sure to tell her he stopped in.

His eyes moved past my shoulder, and he gave one more good, hard, and scary stare at Danielle. Poor lady, her hives had almost covered her entire neck area and were now creeping up to her jaw.

"I'll see you later." He held up Frank's cappuccino. "Thanks for the coffee. Tell Penny we need to get together soon."

"Oh, I'll tell her," I muttered behind my gritted-teeth smile. "To stay far away from you," I finished saying after he shut the door behind him. I turned around to face Danielle. "I'm so sorry. Are you okay?" I asked, pulling out the empty seat at the small café table to sit.

"I've lost my appetite." She pushed the plated strawberry scone away from her. "I'm sorry he made such a scene."

"It's okay. I'm sorry he did that to you." I pointed to her hands and forearms where more hives had popped up.

"I get hives when people confront me." She snorted and placed her hands in her lap. "Nothing a little prednisone can't fix." She pulled a bottle out of the workbag sitting on the floor.

"Wow." I laughed. "People confront you often?"

"In this line of business, they do." Danielle had been coming into the Bean Hive for a couple of weeks every morning.

She'd introduced herself but never told me why she was in town.

"So you're in Honey Springs for business?" I asked.

"Yes. Initially, I was hired by Blackwood Associates to come and evaluate a potential piece of property down past the local inn for a new country-club development," she confirmed. "But then there were some findings coming back that I'd sent off some samples of, and honestly, I'm hoping Blackwood Associates will rethink the location if they still want to use Honey Springs."

There were rumors of a big country club coming to Honey Springs, and I'd heard rumblings about it during one of our chamber of commerce meetings. Golf didn't interest me, so I didn't listen very closely to the debate, but when there was a country club being built, I would definitely try to get in front of the owners or shareholders to get my coffee in there.

After all, now that we had the space with the roastery next door, I was making all sorts of my own concoctions. I could easily make a blend just for a country club.

"What are you looking for when these companies hire you?" I asked, very curious now.

"It depends, but mainly things like environmental impacts of the proposed development. This assessment would involve studying the local ecosystem, habitats, and species, as well as understanding how construction and operation of the country club might affect the environment." From what it sounded like, she was saying Blackwood Associates really did care about the areas where they planned to build, which seemed rather nice.

"I think that's wonderful." I had to talk a little louder because the Bean Hive was filled with the morning customers chatting and enjoying their drinks. "I'm all about keeping Honey Springs a tourist destination where visitors come to enjoy the nature and beauty."

Honey Springs was a wonderful place not only for couples to come to stay in one of the cozy cabins the town had to offer for romantic getaways but also for families to enjoy Lake Honey Springs.

The Bean Hive was located on the boardwalk along with several other little locally owned mom-and-pop shops.

I glanced over at the counter. Bunny had restocked the variety of pastries, muffins, and biscuits, and my baristas were busy taking orders and making drinks. It wasn't until after the roastery was up and running that I'd had to hire two new full-time employees. I still kept the afternoon shift for the local high schoolers who worked for me.

The sounds of the espresso machines hissing and the spoons clinking against ceramic mugs were comforting to me, were enough for me to realize life had gone back to normal in the coffeehouse.

"I'm sure Leandar heard about some of my initial findings because he's standing to gain over half a million in commission from the sale of the land alone, not even including what they will give him for the condominiums they are going to build." As Danielle told me about the plans Blackwood Associates had made for the lakefront property, the more I wished I'd paid attention during the chamber meetings.

"You said something about findings that might make the community change their minds." She nodded, and I continued, "What do you do then?"

I didn't ask about what she found. If Bunny was here, she'd get the information, no problem. But I didn't want to seem too nosy yet.

"I'll be visiting the site to engage with local stakeholders, such as community members, local organizations, and government officials. They could be providing information about the potential environmental impacts, discussing mitigation measures, or soliciting feedback on the proposed development. Blackwood Associates are very involved with the communities where they build." She stood up and gathered her things.

Standing at five foot eight, Danielle appeared to be athletic, from what I would bet had been from years spent exploring the great outdoors.

Her sun-kissed skin bore the marks of a life spent in the elements, with a smattering of freckles across her nose and cheeks. Her style was practical and functional. She was often seen wearing cargo pants, sturdy boots, and light-weight jackets that allowed her to navigate the rugged terrain with ease.

"If you'll excuse me." She pushed in the chair, and I stood up. "I need to make some calls. I'm afraid my reports for your lake town have now turned to advocating for the protection of the lake and its surrounding environment around the development."

"Oh. That doesn't sound good," I blurted out.

"If you want to save Honey Springs, I suggest you come to the emergency meeting I'm going to ask your mayor to hold tonight." She shook her head, leaving me standing there feeling gut punched.

"I told you, she's up to somethin' 'round here." I hadn't heard Loretta walk up behind me. Her accent had taken a fifty-degree dive.

I knew that accent, and it was never followed up by anything good.

"Excuse me." A gentleman with glasses came up to me. "I'm Frank. Did you just give my cappuccino away?"

CHAPTER TWO

"Emergency meeting." Aunt Maxi vigorously rubbed her hands together. "I can't imagine what the mayor has to say that couldn't wait until next month's real meeting."

Aunt Maxi had come into the Bean Hive later that afternoon after word got around town about the emergency meeting.

"Danielle Quillen, the environmentalist hired by Blackwood Associates, has been coming in here every morning. She's been assessing the land where they want to develop the proposed country club," I said.

The afternoon staff were students from Honey Springs High School. I'd been blessed to be able to work with the economics teacher there and let them use the kitchen in the back of the coffee shop as well as teach them a few things about running a business. They'd even been able to open and run their own school coffee shop using the funds, and, of course, my deep discount on coffee, to help raise money for the home-economics department for updated supplies. It didn't just involve coffee supplies—I'm talking anything they needed for their projects.

Most of the students I'd met had really taken to the coffee side, and when they applied for the job, I had hired three of them. It freed up so much of my time.

It wasn't like they were actually roasting the beans or making the pastries.

After a certain time in the afternoon, we only offered coffees and what was left in the display cases.

While Aunt Maxi and I waited for the emergency council meeting to start, she came into the kitchen with me and helped me clean up all the dirty dishes accumulated throughout the day and get some of tomorrow's pastries and food items out of the freezer so they could thaw overnight.

"She mentioned how she'd found something on the property or in the report that would pretty much change the fate of the club." I shrugged as I walked over to the walk-in freezer where I pulled out a tray of frozen quiches I'd made ahead of time.

"Oh dear." Aunt Maxi's brows knotted. The lines around her eyes were getting much deeper.

Aunt Maxi was inching up to seventy years old, and though it wasn't elderly, she was starting to slow down more and more each year. I loved her so much.

Honey Springs was never my physical home. Aunt Maxi, Maxine Bloom, was my home. When Kirk and I had gotten divorced, I didn't move to where Penny, my mom, lived. It was here in Honey Springs where I ran to seek comfort.

It was in Aunt Maxi's arms where I found the home I'd always needed. Honey Springs had always felt cozy to me. My father, before he died, brought me here every summer to visit Aunt Maxi. Sometimes he'd leave me here for weeks, months even. And that's how I met Patrick Cane.

He was my first-ever boyfriend, but because of a little misunderstanding between two lovesick teenagers, life happened, and I moved on. I went to college then eventually law school, where I met Kirk.

When my heart was broken, it was to Honey Springs I ran. Aunt Maxi just so happened to own a few buildings on the boardwalk, and the council had invested a lot of money to revitalize the touristy spot. Aunt Maxi had the grand idea I should take the empty building and make something of it.

It was a no-brainer to turn the building into a much-needed coffee shop, and it was already equipped with the kitchen due to the fact it had been a diner before. Here we stood today.

The Bean Hive, now a Honey Springs staple.

"She didn't tell you what it was?" Aunt Maxi eased down on one of the stools butted up to the workstation island in the middle of the large kitchen and helped herself to a piece of the coffee cake I'd just taken out of the oven.

She reached across the island and dragged the butter dish over to her, knifing a large chunk to smother the piece of coffee cake before she took a big bite out of it.

"She didn't. In fact, she said they would address it at the meeting. But you've not heard the best part." I looked at the clock because we had just enough time to have a cup of coffee. And like I loved to say around here, the gossip was just as hot as the coffee.

"Leandar Taylor came in here demanding to talk to her." My words made Aunt Maxi's brows go from a knot to a large arch.

"Do tell me all of it." Aunt Maxi held the coffee up in both hands and leaned on the island, her forearms holding her up.

That was one thing I loved about owning the Bean Hive. The connections.

There was just some sort of human connection that made us want to gather with others to talk and share stories in an innate way of bonding and fostering a sense of belonging as we sipped on coffee. Though no one wanted to claim we were gossiping, we totally were, but it created strong relationships and built trust among us.

I thought that was what the Bean Hive had become to the community over the years. Not only a place to come grab a hot cup of coffee but also an atmosphere that fostered a warm, cozy atmosphere that helped people relax and unwind.

The act of sitting around a table with friends and a hot beverage was comforting and calming, allowing people to escape from daily stresses and responsibilities.

Aunt Maxi sitting there right now did that for me. It was stressful for me to tell Leandar to leave. Like I mentioned, he was one of just a couple Realtors in the area, and he knew a lot of people.

"I'm not sure what he was yelling at her about. Danielle kept her cool and said that he'd find out about it at the emergency meeting." I took a sip of the coffee. "He was so mad. I told him to leave."

"You did?" Aunt Maxi shook her head. "When was this?"

"I don't know. I don't recall the time. It was this morning because Danielle was eating breakfast. She told him to let her eat her breakfast." I didn't know the exact wording, but it was enough to tell Aunt Maxi. "Something like that." I handed her a napkin.

"No wonder he was mad at the estate sale walk-through." Aunt Maxi's shoulders bounced when she laughed.

"Estate sale?" I wondered why she'd not invited me. I loved to use old pieces of china and mismatched items in the shop.

I glanced over at the cow creamers I'd gotten from Wild and Whimsy Antiques, a shop a few buildings down the boardwalk.

"Did they have any creamers?" They were so charming, just an added touch to the cute coffee shop when they were filled with cream and sitting on the table for the customer to doctor up their coffees the way they liked.

"It wasn't an actual sale." Aunt Maxi used the napkin to wipe the crumbs from her mouth that'd stuck to her bright-orange lipstick. "The Featherstones have the farm out on Gutter Road."

I'd never been there, but I knew it was a large piece of farmland.

"They've gotten so many offers from different horse-breeding farms up near Keeneland because the soil tested so good for limestone." Aunt Maxi knew all the ins and outs on the history of the property and their families.

Limestone was huge around here since we had the lake, but it also made for great vitamins and minerals for the racehorses. One of Kentucky's largest money-making industries was horse racing.

So to hear her say someone wanted the large farm for their horses didn't surprise me. There were many farms around here where people not only kept their racehorses but also trained them locally.

"I can't believe they are selling." I pushed back off the island and took her plate and our cups to clean since it was almost time for us to go to the meeting.

"I couldn't believe it either. I thought for sure Raffery Featherstone was going to keep that place forever. He's the sixth-generation owner, but that's what happens when your kids go off and leave home, not ever wanting to come back to the family business."

"I guess so." I gnawed on my lip, thinking about Raffery's kids. Who on earth wouldn't want a farm and estate like theirs to be handed down to them? Man. What a waste. I kept those thoughts to myself.

If I opened my mouth about leaving a legacy or mentioning children, Aunt Maxi would start harping on me and my biological clock.

316

For now, Patrick and I were good with our four-legged fur babies.

"Anyways." Aunt Maxi had gotten up and walked over to the coat-tree inside the kitchen's back door to get her big hobo bag. It landed with a thump when she put it on the island. "Leandar was there to try to get the sale. You know, be the Realtor. Penny was there too."

She dug down into her bag.

"What on earth were you doing there?" I asked, untying my apron and placing it on one of the free pegs on the coat-tree.

"I was thinking on making an offer to buy it without a Realtor, but the place is too darn nice to get a good deal. But when they do put it up for auction, you're gonna die when you get a look at the fine bone china." She knew I was a sucker for good dishes for the coffee shop.

"Don't tease me," I begged and pointed to her when I saw her take out her big can of hairspray. "Don't spray that in—" I let go of a long sigh.

I wasn't able to get out the words quick enough before she pressed her finger down on the nozzle with one hand and used her other hand to rack her short, this-season-blond-colored hair to high heaven to stay in place.

"Oopsy." She grimaced. "Just another little spray." With her finger pressed down on the nozzle of the can, she did one more sweep around her head, just for good measure, before she moved on to reapplying her lipstick.

"I guess Leandar didn't really care too much about what Danielle had done, or he would've still been mad at the Featherstones." I grabbed Pepper's leash off the coatrack and motioned for Aunt Maxi to follow me out the swinging kitchen door into the coffee shop.

The health department made it very clear about no animals being allowed into the kitchen. It was one rule I did live by because I didn't want to be shut down.

I gave the coffee shop a good once-over to make sure there wasn't anything left undone for me to do to get ready for a smooth morning tomorrow. I liked to have as many things completed and ready as possible, so when I did open early in the morning at four thirty, I had little or nothing to do.

With the afternoon employees already working on the closing checklist and the puppy from the Pet Palace well taken care of, Aunt Maxi and I were off to see exactly why the mayor had called this emergency meeting.

The meetings were always at the event center on the boardwalk, All About the Details. It was due to the fact the courthouse was located in downtown Honey Springs, and though it was literally about a ten-minute walk—three minutes on a bicycle, the most preferred mode of transportation—a lot of citizens came to the meetings. There weren't any rooms in the old courthouse to hold that many people.

By law, the meetings had to be open to the public, and it just made sense to have them at the big event center on the boardwalk.

"Save me a seat," I told Aunt Maxi as I prepared to take Pepper to the grass off the far end of the boardwalk to let him do his business so I could sit through the entire meeting without him interrupting to go potty.

She disappeared inside All About the Details while Pepper and I hightailed it past Buzz-In-And-Out Diner, Honey Comb Salon, and Wild and Whimsy Antiques, stopping briefly when something in the antique's store display window caught my eye.

Pepper pulled, extending his leash to full capacity, not allowing me time to get a good look at the cute antique cake stands that would look good sitting on top of the glass display cases in the coffee shop.

I made a mental note to ask Dan or Beverly Teagarden, the owners, about the cake stands.

Pepper practically dragged me down the boardwalk steps where the grassy area and the beach area of Lake Honey Springs met. He ventured along the grass toward the water's edge, and before I knew it, we were at the water.

I stood at the edge of Lake Honey Springs, feeling the soft grass beneath my sneakers as Pepper sniffed around for the perfect spot to do his business. My gaze shifted to the marina on my left, a picturesque scene filled with boats bobbing gently in the sparkling water.

To my right, the gorgeous Cocoon Inn stood proudly, its exterior welcoming visitors from near and far. The double-decker porches with the rocking chairs looked all occupied.

I sighed, taking in the idyllic scene that was about to be disrupted by the chaos of the emergency council meeting. My thoughts kept going back to the meeting. There was something not settling right in my bones, and that was never a good thing.

The boardwalk buzzed with activity, people meandering in and out of the quaint, cozy shops that lined the waterfront. Laughter and conversation filled the air, mingling with the distant sound of seagulls crying overhead. I tried to appreciate the moment, but my thoughts were consumed by the meeting and the mysterious findings in Danielle's report.

Danielle's cryptic words hung over me like a dark cloud.

"The community will change its mind about letting the company build."

But she hadn't given me any more information, leaving me to anxiously await the emergency meeting called by the mayor.

A cool spring breeze rustled through the leaves overhead, and it made me wish I'd brought the jacket from the Bean Hive with me. The sun was deceiving on these spring days. During the day, it was warm and almost hot, but in the evenings, as it was setting, the breeze off the lake made it so much cooler.

The scent of blossoming flowers filled my nostrils, and I closed my eyes for a moment, trying to calm my racing thoughts. The sounds of Lake Honey Springs—the gentle lapping of water against the shore, the rustling of leaves, and the chirping of birds—usually brought me comfort. But today, they only added to my unease.

Pepper, seemingly oblivious to my inner turmoil, bounded back to me, his tail wagging energetically. I reached down to pat his head, his soft fur offering a brief moment of solace amidst my concerns. He looked up at me with his big brown eyes, as if to say, "Everything will be okay." I took a deep breath, trying to hold on to that comforting thought.

"Roxy!" I heard someone call behind me and away from the lake. "Roxanne!"

I turned around to see Camey Montgomery, the owner of the Cocoon Inn, standing still on the concrete sidewalk that ran between the inn and the boardwalk.

"Are you going to the meeting?" she hollered to me as Pepper and I walked closer.

"I am. Are you?" I called out to her, but by the time she responded, we were already standing next to her and she was bent down, patting Pepper.

"Yes. We can walk together." She stood up and greeted me with a hug. "It has to be about the development."

"I know it is." I nodded to confirm. We walked side by side, only stopping briefly when Pepper would catch a scent. "The environmentalist Blackwood Associates hired has been coming into the coffee shop. She mentioned today the mayor had read her findings and she asked him to call this emergency meeting."

I didn't bother telling her about Leandar Taylor because telling her would be gossiping, and there was no need for that since once Danielle was done with her job, she'd be leaving Honey Springs and we'd probably never see her again.

"Do you know something?" I asked Camey, curious to why she'd mentioned it the way she did.

"There's been people there all day long. I can see it from the honeymoon-suite balcony." Camey ran the inn like a five-star hotel. Though she had employees, Camey had her hand in all the areas and little details that made the inn so homey to all her guests. "I was sweeping up there, getting it ready for a newlywed couple coming in this weekend for the start of their honeymoon, when I saw people standing way past the lake and in the weeds of the area. I wasn't sure what they were looking at, but Quentin told me his cousin worked in the public works, and they were called there to look at something."

"Public-works employee? Really?" I questioned, wondering what on earth they had to do with the land.

"It's state property, and if they found anything on there that would need to be preserved, there's no way the state will let them build." Camey should know.

The historic white mansion, built in 1841, had been in Camey's family for years. Camey had hired Cane Construction to help rebuild the old structure into an amazing hotel that was situated right on Lake Honey Springs and kept its cozy character. The two-story white brick building with porches across both stories was something to behold, especially when you were standing on the beachfront in front of the property, looking back.

Gorgeous.

"I guess we'll find out soon." I nodded toward the door going into All About the Details when the mayor shuffled in ahead of us.

I took one more look out at Lake Honey Springs. Sunset was one of my favorite times of day. It was beginning to set, casting golden rays across the water and bathing the bustling boardwalk in a warm glow. As the shadows grew longer, so did my sense of foreboding.

What could be so important that the mayor would call an emergency meeting? The future of our beloved Lake Honey Springs hung in the balance, and all I could do was wait, hope, and prepare for the storm that was coming.

CHAPTER THREE

Alice Dee Spicer wildly waved her arms in the air as soon as she caught my eye from the back of the filled room. I'd not seen the room this filled since Patrick and I had come to the chamber of commerce Christmas party.

Alice was the president of the Beautification Committee, which made her an automatic member of the town council. She was sitting in front with all the other town officials, facing the crowd from behind a large banquet table.

She pointed, gesturing at a place for Camey and me to sit.

"Up here." I nudged Camey. She was looking around for a spot before I gestured to Helen.

"Lordy." Camey nervously patted around her scarlet hair before raking her fingers down her thick bangs. "Alice just wants us to sit there so she can stare at my hair."

"Your hair?" I snorted and picked up Pepper so I didn't have to worry about him sniffing everyone's shoes when we passed. "Your hair looks great."

Alice was the owner of Honey Comb, the local beauty salon.

"Alice doesn't think so. I canceled my hair appointment the other afternoon because Amelia had a spring play at school. It was during the middle of the day, the day before their spring break started." Camey spoke out of the side of her mouth as we maneuvered our way down the right side of the aisle around the crowd. "She told me how my bangs needed to be cut and thinned out and refused to cancel my appointment."

"Refused?" I glanced around my shoulder to look at her but kept walking up the aisle.

"Yes. She hung up on me." She snorted and rolled her eyes. "Hi, Helen."

Camey gave Alice a little wave before we noticed there was only one seat. Apparently, Alice had only gestured for me.

"You take it." I waved a hand. "I will sit on the floor with Pepper."

"No," Camey insisted. "She obviously meant it for you." Camey glared at Alice, but she had already turned to talk to someone else.

"Here." Big Bib was sitting in the row behind us and offered Camey his seat. He was sitting next to Aunt Maxi, who was already situated in the chair with her big hobo bag nestled in her lap. Her hands were clasped on top. "I might have to leave soon, so you take it."

"No." Camey shook her head.

"Then someone else will." The big, burly, but softhearted boat mechanic and owner of the marina was dressed in his usual overalls that looked like he'd just poured an entire container of oil down them.

"Thank you," Camey said.

"I tried to save you a seat." Aunt Maxi had eased up on the edge of her seat and whispered. "What took you so long?"

"Pepper." I ran my hand down my sweet pup, who was more than happy to be sitting on my lap. "He had to do his business."

"Sweet baby." Aunt Maxi reached around me and patted his head. "Why is Penny up there?"

She pointed out how Mom and Leandar Taylor sat on the stage, as well as Danielle Quillen and another gentleman and woman I didn't know.

As I scanned the room, my eyes landed on a man I didn't recognize. He was tall, standing at around six-one, with a lean, athletic build that demanded attention. His wavy, jet-black hair fell just below his ears, accentuating his chiseled jawline and partially hiding his deep blue eyes.

His slight tanned skin hinted at his love for outdoor adventures, and I couldn't help but notice the faint lines around his eyes, suggesting that he was no stranger to laughter and smiling.

He had a day or two's worth of stubble, which only added to his rugged charm.

He was dressed in a casual style that suited him. He wore a tailored shirt with the sleeves rolled up, revealing his toned forearms, and paired it with well-fitting jeans. His leather boots completed the ensemble, giving him an air of effortless sophistication.

I found it impossible not to be drawn to the man's charismatic presence and could tell the others near him felt the same.

"If I could all have your attention, we'd like to start the meeting," the mayor said through the microphone at the podium, silencing the room. "As you know, Blackwood Associates has been in town over the past six to nine months, give or take. They have been interested in building a new community that includes a country club, a swim club, and a neighborhood surrounding it, past Cocoon Inn."

The mayor pointed out to a plan on a hardboard propped up on a tripod. It looked like a blue print of a plot of land.

There was a bit of shuffling coming from Leandar Taylor. That was enough movement to have caught my eye.

"Blackwood Associates has hired Danielle Quillen, a well-known environmentalist, to survey the land, take samples, and make sure the land is environmentally sound or viable for such a project." The mayor really didn't seem like he understood all the words, so he passed it off to Danielle. "She can best explain it."

Danielle got up from her seat and smiled as she passed the mayor on her way up to the podium.

"Thank you," she said into the microphone and nodded over her shoulder to the mayor. "Like the mayor said, this is Caspian Blackwood," she said.

While everyone gave notice to Caspian, I watched Danielle set down and flip open the folder I'd seen many times on top of her table at the Bean Hive.

"When I took the job and came to Honey Springs, I found a delightful group of citizens that were welcoming and who love their town. In fact, no one was unhappy that a large developer wanted to come in and take up all this lakefront. They simply told me they wanted to make sure the land around the development wouldn't be compromised."

She took a moment to pause, and if I could read her body language, I felt like she was trying to compose what she was going to say and make sure it came out properly.

"With the help of local Realtor, Leandar Taylor—" As soon as she said his name, Caspian groaned, rolled his neck, and looked opposite of Leandar, making it seem as though the mere mention of Leandar's name made him ill. Danielle continued, "He was able to provide us with a plot and helped get the property in question staked off."

She had a clicker in her hand that I'd noticed, and when she pushed it, a slide of photos popped up on the screen offstage.

There were photos of the entire process she'd done to get an accurate report.

There was a shot taken from the lake's edge of the sun sinking low in the sky. The glass-like surface of the water contrasted with the trees in the background from the small island in the middle of Lake Honey Springs.

"It was beautiful to stand there and look at this wonderful piece of land your entire town has preserved over the years." She lifted up items as she talked about them. "Armed with my notebook, my camera, and a collection of scientific equipment, I began my investigation."

As she talked, the buzz of the clicker as she pushed the button was the only sound in the entire building. The slides went along with her story.

It was a story that captured everyone's attention.

Even Pepper's.

She went on to tell us how she'd meticulously examined the soil, tested the water quality, and identified the local flora and fauna. As she wandered through the site, she said she couldn't shake the feeling that there was something unique about this place, something she couldn't quite put her finger on.

"As I ventured deeper into the forest surrounding the lake, the air grew cooler, and the once lively sounds of the woodland creatures began to quiet. I stumbled upon a small hidden clearing carpeted in lush green moss and surrounded by tall ancient trees. At the center of the clearing, a crystal-clear spring bubbled up from the earth, its waters shimmering in the fading light." When she showed the photos she'd taken, the entire audience gasped.

She looked out into the crowd, and it showed on her face that she was taken aback because none of us knew that was there.

"I can see you are as shocked to see this as I was. I felt an overwhelming sense of awe when I realized that this spring was the source of the lake's pristine water." The significance of her discovery was not lost on her; she knew that the construction of a country club could threaten the delicate balance of this rare ecosystem.

"I have worked tirelessly with Leandar and Blackwood Associates, along with their investors, to convince them to rethink their plans and use their money for the good of Honey Springs to transform this area into a nature preserve." Danielle turned and pointed to Alice Dee Spicer. "I've included Alice Dee Spicer into the talks since she is the president of your Beautification Committee."

"I think we need to have a second opinion." Leandar stood up and protested.

"Sit down," Raffery Featherstone hollered out from the back. "Haven't you ruined enough of this already?"

That got everyone's attention.

"What did he ruin?" I overheard Aunt Maxi ask Camey. "Is that what he said?"

"If I could just say something." The voice drew us all back to look at the stage where Caspian had gotten up from his seat and walked over to the microphone. "This is why we hired Danielle."

Caspian was not without charm. He had a disarming smile that seemed to melt away any resistance he encountered, and he had a charisma that I could tell allowed him to secure deals that others would have thought impossible.

Even though he appeared to be a skilled negotiator, able to use his charm and wit to persuade even the most skeptical partners to see the potential in his projects, I wasn't buying his act.

Like I said, I've seen his kind before.

"I, too, find myself at odds with Danielle Quillen. Yes, we clashed over the fate of the land, but eventually she saw that I had to confront the consequences of these actions and reevaluate the priorities for why we wanted to bring this amazing country club to Honey Springs. The people." He drew his arms out in front of him. "We want to bring more and more people to Honey Springs to create even more of a small tourist town. It will bring so many new jobs to you, and that's growth. Leandar Taylor was the Realtor we had believed had full knowledge of the spring. We didn't know it was there."

Caspian was starting to create a case for him and his company. Another tactic I'd seen done in a court of law when cases such as these had already begun to build and there was no one there to stop them until someone with even the slightest bit of environmental knowledge found out it was hurting the earth.

"That's why we are going to continue looking for property in the area with the help of Penny Bloom." Caspian was about to lay out their plan.

"Save our land! Save our land!" Camey stood up, punching her fisted hand in the air to start the chant. "Save our land!"

It only took three chants for her to start the entire room yelling it and pointing to Caspian. The loudest in the room was Raffery Featherstone. He was louder than anyone in the room, probably because he was walking up the center aisle, his eyes focused on Leandar Taylor and pointing at Caspian Blackwood.

Raffery reached the tripod with the building plans on it and ripped them in half, throwing them up in the air.

The entire room erupted.

Even Pepper barked, but I knew it was my cue to get out of there.

There was nothing good going to come of what the emergency meeting was about. The only thing I felt was sadness for Patrick. He'd hoped Cane Construction was going to be able to bid on the job.

He'd had big plans for that money.

CHAPTER FOUR

The next morning, I sat on the front porch of the little cabin where Patrick and I lived, sipping a hot cup of steaming coffee and waiting for Sassy and Pepper to go potty before I needed to go to work.

They seemed to have found a new scent. The two of them stepped over each other to get a better sniff. I reached into the basket next to the rocking chair and took out a thin blanket to put over my lap as I waited. Thoughts of yesterday's emergency meeting had rolled around in my head all night, leaving me with little to no sleep.

I'd even turned on my book light at around one in the morning to read a few chapters of the cozy mystery I was reading, due to the fact I wanted to quiet my brain. When that didn't work, I just laid there, trying to think of something other than the piece of property with the spring that was literally between our cabin and the boardwalk.

Patrick and I had taken the dogs across the street and down to the lake so many times over the past few years. I found it odd we'd not stumbled upon it.

"Sassy." I sighed when I noticed her silhouette in the light from the moon, rolling around in something. "Your daddy isn't going to be happy about that."

I could hear Patrick now, fussing about having to give her a bath because she's stinking up our little home to high heaven.

When I first moved to Honey Springs, I knew the little cabin was exactly what I needed. It was small and inviting—even though it needed a lot of work—but charming and cozy. A great place to heal my heart and soul.

With the old knob-and-tube wiring long gone, I'd turned the cabin into a wonderful home. It was small. There was one big room with a combination kitchen and dining room.

The bathroom and laundry room were located on the far-back right. There was a set of stairs that led up to one big room that was considered the bedroom.

The natural light from the skylights and the large window in the bedroom really made the room inviting. After I'd added the white iron bed suite from Aunt Maxi's storage unit and a few quilts she'd had stored, the bedroom was cozy and perfect for us.

As much as I wanted to stay and snuggle in that morning, I had to get going or the coffee wouldn't be ready for opening at six thirty a.m.

It wasn't like I was going to have too much to do. As soon as I got the dogs inside, I went back to the laundry room where I kept my standard uniform work clothes, slipped something on, and prepared for the short five-minute bike ride to the boardwalk.

I had also prepared myself for all the gossip that would be flying around the Bean Hive. There was nothing like a good council meeting, death, wedding, or baby being born that brought the locals in to see what everyone else knew.

That was why I had taken a few more quiches, donuts, and various other pastries from the freezer before I left the coffee shop to go to the meeting.

Sassy wandered back up the steps to get back in bed with Patrick. It would be a few more hours before they'd get up and go to the office. Pepper stayed downstairs with me, looking at me with his big eyes as if he were telling me he was ready to go to work.

"Not today," I told him. His small tail fell. "It's going to be really busy, and it wouldn't be fair for you to have to listen to all that gossip. I don't even want to hear it. I love you too much to put that on you."

He followed me out of the laundry room and into the small kitchen, where I took a scoop of his food from one of the bottom cabinets in the small galley-style kitchen and poured it into his bowl.

Sadly, he walked into the family room where he laid down in his little bed in front of the potbelly stove. He loved to lie there during the winter months when it was roaring with a fire inside.

He rested his chin on the edge of his bed, looking at me with little hope that I'd agree to take him. He knew when I fed him there, he wasn't going to the shop.

"I love you, Pepper. You be a good boy." I plucked the keys from the hook next to the door, and I grabbed my bag from the coatrack.

A car wasn't necessary to get around town. I had a small car, but mainly it stayed parked during the warmer seasons, and I biked everywhere unless Patrick and I were going somewhere together.

There was a small wire basket attached to the front of the bike where Pepper fit perfectly when he came to work. Today, I threw my bag in there, flipped on the flashing light on the front, and headed out into the dark early morning.

The cool morning air bit at my cheeks as I pedaled along the familiar path to the Bean Hive coffee shop. The quiet hum of the bicycle chain and the rhythmic crunch of my tires on the gravel road formed a soothing soundtrack to my predawn ride. It was four thirty, and the world was still slumbering. My small lake town felt like a dream, with the dark woods on one side of the road and the peaceful lake on the other.

As I rode, I couldn't help but think about last night's emergency council meeting again. The room had been packed with passionate citizens, and the tension had been palpable. I recalled the way Danielle, the environmentalist, stood up and argued against the proposed country-club development. She had discovered a natural spring on the land, and many of us agreed that it shouldn't be disturbed. She even had a gorgeous slideshow with photos.

I was relieved when the council had voted down the project, but I knew that some of our neighbors were still furious. The look on the developer's face was unforgettable. Especially when he looked at Leandar Taylor, the local real estate agent who'd sold them the land.

As I approached the contested land, I spotted the unmistakable flash of red-and-blue lights in the darkness near the lake.

My heart skipped a beat, and I slowed my bike, curiosity getting the better of me.

"What could be happening at this hour?" I wondered, my thoughts racing.

I pulled off the road and got off my bike. I walked cautiously toward the commotion, the gravel crunching under my feet. The sounds of the woods around me seemed to grow louder—the wind rustling through the trees and the distant hoot of an owl. My heart pounded in my chest as I drew closer to the scene.

"Stop right there!" I heard Sheriff Spencer Shepard call out with his gun drawn in front of him and pointing directly at me.

"It's me. Roxy!" I yelled and sort of slumped down, just in case he fired.

"Roxy, what are you doing here?" Sheriff Spencer Shephard called out, his brow furrowed with concern.

"I was just on my way to open the Bean Hive when I saw the lights," I explained, my voice barely above a whisper. "What's going on, Spencer?"

The sheriff hesitated, then spoke in a somber tone. "Someone was out for an early-morning jog and found a body."

A chill ran down my spine, and my stomach tightened when the moon slipped out from behind a cloud, its silvery light illuminated the scene like a spotlight, revealing the lifeless form of Leandar Taylor.

My breath caught in my throat, and my eyes widened in shock. I knew Leandar but never imagined I'd see him like this. My emotions were a tangled mess of confusion, sadness, and fear.

Sheriff Spencer noticed my distress and placed a reassuring hand on my shoulder.

"I know this is tough, Roxy. But I'll need your help. If you saw or heard anything unusual, it might be important."

I nodded, swallowing hard. "Of course, Spencer. I'll do whatever I can. But are you saying this is foul play?"

Kevin Roberts, the local coroner, was already on the scene. I couldn't tell what he was doing because Spencer had held me back a little, plus it was still dark. The sun wouldn't come up for another couple of hours.

"If you want to call blunt-force trauma to the head 'homicide,' then yes." Spencer nodded.

As I stared at Leandar's body, the reality of the situation began to sink in.

Our cozy town had just become the setting for a chilling mystery, and I knew I couldn't rest until I helped uncover the truth.

CHAPTER FIVE

"It wasn't like he was telling me to go out and find clues." I told Bunny about what happened on my way into work and how Spencer had told me to keep my eyes and ears open. "He knows once news breaks this morning about Leandar, everyone will be talking."

"Why on earth would he need you?" Bunny shook her head and waddled around the coffee shop with the tray of cow coffee creamers. She was placing one on each café table and making sure all the little table condiment containers were filled so they were ready for when we flipped the sign on the door to Open.

I went down the line of the industrial coffee makers and flipped them on before I made my way over to the coffee bar, where we kept an honors system for customers who didn't want to wait in line to buy a simple black, hot coffee. The six thermoses I kept at all times at the coffee bar were ready to be put in place. I grabbed three and headed toward the end of the counter.

On my way over to the bar, I looked out the front windows. Since the Bean Hive was located in the middle of the boardwalk, right across from the pier, we had a gorgeous view of the lake.

The lake was holding a dark secret that only it knew, for now.

I shook the thought out of my head and placed the three industrial thermoses with different blends of my specialty coffees on the bar, one filled with a decaffeinated blend even though I never understood the concept of that.

But Aunt Maxi made sure I understood some people only drank the unleaded stuff. The coffee bar had everything you needed to take a coffee with you. Quickly, I walked back behind the counter to grab the other three.

Just as I placed them, my heart stopped and I jumped at the sound of the hard knock coming from someone at the front window.

"Let me in!" Aunt Maxi knocked again but harder.

"I oughta have known she'd be here this early. I'm gonna have to take me an aspirin." Bunny acted as though the sight of Aunt Maxi had given her a sudden headache.

On my way over to the door, I had a habit of glancing around to see if the coffee shop needed any repairs. It was something I'd done daily since I had redone the entire inside by myself after watching DIY YouTube videos.

The white shiplap I'd put on the walls could probably stand a fresh coat of paint, but currently there were bigger things to worry about.

Leandar Taylor.

And I was one hundred percent positive it was why Aunt Maxi was here this early.

Bunny had started to pull down the chalkboard menus that hung from the ceiling over the L-shaped glass countertop so she could write the daily specials on them.

"The first menu is the same," I called as I unlocked the door for Aunt Maxi. "All the pies and cookies are the same. And the tortes and quiches are too," I told her and decided to flip the sign because I knew people would be getting here much earlier this morning.

Sadly, it was how it worked.

"What needs to be changed?" Bunny glanced at the third chalkboard listing the lunch options, including soups and catering information.

"We have broccoli-cheddar soup today." I sighed and gave Aunt Maxi a hug. "Did you hear?"

"Did I hear?" She jerked back. "The whole town has heard. You know, Gloria has already enacted the church's telephone chain."

Gloria Dei would know. She worked at the sheriff's department.

"Leave it to y'all to gossip," Bunny couldn't resist the jab. "Poor man is dead, and you're runnin' y'all's mouth about it."

"Bunny, I don't know who you think you are. Mae Belle Donovan already sold you out. She said you called her as soon as the telephone chain reached you. And she wasn't even who you were supposed to call." Aunt Maxi and Bunny Bowowski had what some would call a love-hate relationship friendship, but I knew I could wrangle them in on helping me get some ideas on who I needed to be listening for, since Spencer had asked me to do so.

"Okay, you two, we aren't going to help Spencer out this way." I caught Aunt Maxi's ear on my way over to the tea bar on the opposite side of the counter from the coffee bar, which was where Aunt Maxi had gone to make herself a cup of coffee.

The tea bar had a nice selection of gourmet teas and loose-leaf teas along with cold teas. I'd even gotten a few antique teapots from Wild and Whimsy Antiques, which happened to be the first shop on the boardwalk. If a customer came in and wanted a pot of hot tea, I could fix it for them, or they could fix their own to their taste.

"You mean to tell me Spencer wants to endanger my only niece?" Aunt Maxi's drawn-on brows rose.

"I love you, but it doesn't take snooping around to know it was Caspian Blackwood." Bunny had no problem saying out loud what I was thinking.

The distinct aroma of freshly brewed coffee, mixed with the scent of warm pastries, filled the air, wafting through the cozy space as I busied myself with the morning preparations.

As Bunny meticulously placed the pastries in the glass display case, her eyes twinkled with curiosity.

"You know, Roxy," Bunny began, "I've been thinking about Leandar's murder, and I can't help but suspect that Caspian Blackwood is involved. He's always been a shady character, and with the development being halted, he certainly had a motive."

This was one of those situations where I'd let the two of them mull over what each one of them had in their heads before I would mix their two ideas together and come up with a plan.

The three of us weren't exactly new to being nosy. We'd put ourselves in a couple of crime investigations over the years and, well, let's just say we've been able to come up with a good system on how to get things out of people. Spencer knew it, too, and that's why he'd asked me to keep my ear to the ground.

The soft clinking of cups and saucers could be heard as I arranged them on the counter.

Aunt Maxi nodded in agreement, her silver bracelets jingling as she arranged the tea selection. "As much as it pains me, I have to agree with Bunny. Caspian has the most to gain from Leandar's death, especially if it means the development can move forward. Just think of all that money Blackwood Associates has put into this development, and if Leandar would've just done his job before all this got started, he'd probably still be alive."

I mulled over their words, the gears in my mind turning. I hurried through the swinging door between the kitchen and the coffee shop to grab one of the whiteboards I used to write the specials on when I was in the kitchen.

"You both make a good point," I conceded as I headed back through the door.

I reached for a towel and wipe-off board. "We need to create a murder board to organize our thoughts and explore all possible suspects."

As I began to jot down names and motives, the scent of rich coffee beans enveloped us, providing a sense of comfort despite the grim task at hand. Problem was, I only had one suspect: Caspian Blackwood.

Aunt Maxi piped up, "We can't rule out Danielle Quillen, the environmentalist, either. She may have had good intentions in stopping the development, but who knows what lengths she would go to in order to protect that natural spring?"

Bunny chimed in, "And what about the potential investors of the development? We don't know who they are, but they must have had a vested interest in the project. They could have easily turned on Leandar if they felt their investment was at risk."

I nodded, adding their names and suggestions to the murder board. "We can't jump to conclusions. We need to keep an open mind and consider all possibilities."

As we continued discussing the case, the first customers of the day began to trickle into the Bean Hive. The lively chatter of our fellow townspeople filled the air, blending with the enticing aroma of coffee and freshly baked goods. We knew we had a long day ahead of us, but the prospect of solving Leandar's murder and restoring peace to our cozy town fueled our determination.

There was one person I knew I needed to see first. The person who was generally first in line as soon as I opened every morning but who wasn't here today.

Danielle Quillen.

"Do you know where Danielle is staying?" I asked Bunny a few hours later when the breakfast rush died down.

Aunt Maxi had left the shop to do whatever it was Aunt Maxi did during the day.

Bunny always held conversation with Danielle every morning since Danielle had been in town.

"I don't know. I'm guessing she's been paid by Blackwood Associates." Bunny pointed to the last quiche. "Can I take that with me to Floyd?"

"Of course. Take whatever you want." I didn't mind, and my thoughts were preoccupied with how I was going to get information on where to find Danielle.

I'd spent the morning watching the door at the coffee shop as customers entered, waiting for Danielle to come in like she'd done every single day for the last few weeks. Not today.

Suspicious?

I was.

You won't get away with these lies. I've already got a call into your boss, and I know your history. Leander's words were unsettling to me as I recalled them.

What lies?

If anyone besides Blackwood Associates had motive, it would be Danielle. Especially if the victim was about to uncover lies that were bad enough for her to lose her job.

"Then I'm off," Bunny said, taking me out of my thoughts. "Are you sure you don't mind if I go early?"

The bell over the door dinged, and in walked Crissy Lane. You couldn't miss that sun-washed blond hair from a mile away.

"I guess you don't mind." Bunny waved and stopped briefly to chat with Crissy.

Even if I did mind, Bunny wasn't going to stay. She'd already gotten her shawl all buttoned, her pocketbook in the crook of her arm, and her pillbox hat bobby-pinned in her hair.

"Go. Tell Floyd I said happy anniversary," I hollered to her after she and Crissy said goodbye.

"You remembered." Bunny had been telling me nonstop since the beginning of the year how this was her and Floyd's two-year dating anniversary.

They were cute. She cooked for him, and he was good companionship for her. Though she vowed she'd never get married again, I still had my doubts.

"Of course I remembered. Enjoy your date." I gestured for her to get on out of there and waved her off.

"I'll have me the usual." Crissy Lane's Southern accent was truly charming. Her long fake lashes batted above her freckled cheeks. "But give me an extra shot of espresso. I'm so tired. I got a call last night about raccoons in the dumpsters at the spa."

"Be Happy Spa is on an island." My brows knotted. "How did the raccoons get over there?"

"I reckon they swam over." She shook her head. "Now I've got to go over there and pick up trash. So the extra shot of caffeine will do me some good."

I had about one hour until the afternoon staff would get there. It was that weird transition time during the day when the coffee shop was at its slowest time.

There was only one customer, sitting at the bar along the front window and facing Lake Honey Springs as she worked on her computer. It was a great time to clean all the tables and make sure the condiments were filled and the coffee was fresh for the afternoon customers that were mainly schoolchildren who liked to come in after school and visit with their friends before they went home at night.

Then the coffee shop turned over in customers and became the after-dinner coffee drinkers who had supper along the boardwalk and stopped by for an after-dinner coffee while they sat on the boardwalk to stare out over Lake Honey Springs.

I should've been doing all the cleaning, but the one true chore that had to be done was the coffee. My mind wasn't into cleaning and refilling. The puppy was asleep in the puppy bed and the one customer was occupied, so I took a moment to run back to the kitchen and grab a bag of the coffee beans I'd roasted a week ago and the whiteboard that Aunt Maxi, Bunny, and I had written on earlier that morning.

There wasn't any news, only rumblings this morning in the coffee shop when practically the entire town had come in to gossip, but as the day went on, I was sure there'd be some sort of gossip, secrets let out.

I was banking on getting whatever secret Leandar had on Danielle to come out of hiding, but there was nothing. Or at least I'd not heard anything.

The customer was gone when I pushed back through the kitchen door, but I wasn't alone.

Loretta Bebe was standing at the counter, drumming her long hot-pink fingernails on top of the glass display.

"I was beginning to wonder if someone was here," she said in her slow Southern drawl, eyeballing me. "I guess I was right about the country club."

Loretta beamed with joy.

"I'm guessing that Raffery Featherstone did Leandar Taylor in." She looked at the whiteboard. "What is that?"

"It's nothing." I laid it facing down on the counter. "What is it you were saying about Raffery?"

"Don't tell me you've not thought about who killed Leandar, Roxy." Loretta batted her fake lashes at me. I swear, if she blinked them faster, she'd create a tornado, those things were so long and thick. "Raffery was selling his farm so he could use the money to invest in the golf course."

A smile crossed her lips.

"My, my." She laid her hand on her chest. Every single finger had some sort of ring with a large stone on it. "I know something you don't? I was guessing Penny had already filled you in on the whole situation."

"She has not, but you are right about one thing." This was one of those times when I knew Loretta Bebe just might be the gossip I'd been waiting for. "Why don't I heat you up the last piece of butter-pecan bread I made this morning to go with the freshly brewed cup of coffee I just made before you walked in, and we can compare notes."

I had to phrase it in such a way that Loretta would feel like she was getting something out of this too.

"I'll be right over there." She twisted around and pointed to the couch that sat in front of the coffee shop's fireplace, though it wasn't turned on. "We might be visiting for a minute, and I want to be comfortable."

"I'll be right there." I knew partnering with Loretta was going to cost me dearly if Aunt Maxi found out.

Aunt Maxi and Loretta were always at odds. Aunt Maxi had little to no tolerance for liars. According to Aunt Maxi, Loretta Bebe's tall tales about being part Cherokee tore Aunt Maxi up when we all know Loretta would sneak over to Lisa Stalh's garage for a good ol' fake-n-bake in that tanning bed.

To each their own, and right now, I needed to know what Loretta knew about Raffery Featherstone.

After starting all the industrial coffeepots brewing for the arrival of the afternoon customers and plating Loretta's piece of bread with a pat of butter, just like she liked it, I headed over to the couch.

"Here you go." I set the small tray on the coffee table in front of her, along with the cow creamer. She always commented on how cute it was with the little cowbell dangling around its neck, filled with the Italian sweet cream she liked. "Italian sweet cream."

"Low-fat, I hope." She rubbed her belly and winked.

"Yes, that," I lied, but she knew it as I winked back. "I also wanted to show you this," I told her as my voice carried to her while I grabbed the whiteboard off the counter. "I sure can't slip nothing by you, Loretta."

There was nothing like buttering up someone's already inflated ego.

"I could see right through you when I pranced right on in here a while ago." She nodded proudly.

I sat down on the edge of the hearth across from her and flipped the board around.

"A murder board," she gasped. "I've seen these on that British streaming station." She pinched off a corner of the bread and used it as a knife to spread the melted pat of butter around.

Evenly.

"I see you have Caspian and Danielle on there, which came right to my mind after I heard what happened, but do they really care the deal went south?" she asked, and I was all ears to listen. "Danielle will just go to the next job."

She had no idea, nor was it written on the board, about Leandar threatening to reveal Danielle's big secret.

"The Blackwood group has so many other dealings in different states that this is just a drop of money in the bucket for them." All the information rolled off her tongue, making me wonder how on earth she knew all of this already about them. "But the Featherstone family." She tsked. "That's a whole different kinda motive."

"How so?" I asked.

"I'm not gossiping, you know, but it was brought to my attention a few weeks ago at bunco. Jean Hill had told me Raffery Featherstone had put a stop on purchasing hay for the farm from her because he was selling," she said and then paused to pick up the cow creamer, slowly pouring the liquid into the coffee. "So she sold his hay plus any extra to other farmers. You know Jean Hill has some good hay." Loretta nodded.

Jean Hill was the owner of the local dairy farm. She had all sorts of things she sold that included items such as dairy, vegetables, flowers, and anything else she could grow. Her quality never suffered. She had the best homegrown vegetables I'd ever eaten. I made sure I used anything grown locally in all the dishes I made to sell at the Bean Hive.

"Wow. I guess Raffery was invested in moving." I took the moment to interject like I was shocked, too, not letting her know Aunt Maxi had already alerted me to the big estate sale they were going to have, which made me ask the next question. "What on earth are they going to do with all those treasures?"

In particular, I was wondering if Loretta had heard about the bone china.

She picked up the spoon I'd put on top of the napkin and slowly stirred.

"They did have an estate sale planned, and they've got a legal contract with Leandar for the sale of the house, but if he's"—she took the spoon and dragged it across her neck—"it would be null and void, I guess. The estate sale is tomorrow, right?"

"I think so." I had to remember to ask Aunt Maxi for sure. When she told me earlier today about the estate sale, it didn't seem to matter as much as it did now. "Where were the Featherstones going to live?" I asked her, thinking Leandar's murder had nothing to do with the country club.

I was wrong.

"The country club. Raffery was an investor. He had to sell the farm in order to invest." The more Loretta talked, the more I had to use the poker face I'd worn so many times in court when the prosecutor would throw me a curveball.

This was a curveball.

A game changer.

"He was going to have the best view of the lake, the million-dollar home with tiny square footage. From what I heard from Jean, he won't be able to get enough hay to keep the horses on the farm alive." Loretta nibbled on the bread. "It's too late in the season to get some at a reasonable price. I'm not sure if he can afford what he's going to need. So he's going to have to sell."

"What are you talking about?" I had lost whatever she thought I understood. "Break this down for me."

"Roxy, have you not been sleeping?" She swung her right leg over her left and clasped her hands together before she cradled her right knee. "Because you ain't following along at all."

"I'm sorry. I didn't get a lot of sleep last night, and then this morning when I saw the body..." I had to keep giving her little bits of information for her to want to give *me* information.

"You saw Leandar's body?" Her jaw dropped. She picked up the empty mug. "I'm gonna need a refill, so I can sip while you tell me all about it."

Loretta got up and helped herself to the coffee bar. She didn't slip any money in the convenience jar, but that was okay. Maybe the gift of her knowledge of the day's gossip would pay for the coffee.

"You mean to tell me he asked you to keep your ears peeled?" she asked after I told her about seeing Leandar and Spencer asking me to help.

She sat back down.

"He did, and my thoughts were on Caspian because Leandar's negligence is what got him here, but I never figured on other dealings Leandar had. I mean, it could be anyone he had a real estate agreement with or someone else." There was more to Leandar Taylor than met the eye.

The more I thought about it, the more I realized his fingers and hands were in a lot of people's pockets.

"You know Leandar," Loretta continued, thinking that I did know him. I didn't. I moved here as an adult, running a business. Most people here forgot I didn't grow up here, but I'd positioned myself for them to think I had. "He loves the almighty dollar, and we know that ain't good."

She let go of a deep and long sigh before she brought the cup to her lips, tipping it slightly to blow on the hot liquid before she took a sip.

"If anything, Raffery had so much more to lose. Did you see him rip up the plans last night after Danielle gave her presentation?" Loretta put the outburst in the forefront of my mind.

I'd been so fixated on the development, I'd not really taken into account that the entire group of citizens screaming how we needed to keep our land safe was probably directed more at Leandar than the development.

"Now that Leandar is dead, Raffery won't lose out on his millions. The only thing he's going to have to do, according to Jean, is find hay somewhere else to feed all those racing horses he was going to sell with the property." Loretta gave another little hint for an additional motive for Raffery to have killed Leandar. "But like I said, the hay will cost him a pretty penny, and I'm not sure he can afford it."

"He just might need to sell a racehorse or two," I held up two fingers and said, feeling like it was a pretty logical thing to do. But who was I to be logical?

I'd already made him a suspect and had an entire theory on why he was the killer. None of it was exactly logical, but it was enough to make me want to talk to him.

I updated the murder board after Loretta left, making a visit to Danielle and Raffery my first priority.

Underneath my newest suspect, Raffery Featherstone, I wrote down his motive to have killed Leandar Taylor.

"Raffery was going to sell his millions to invest in the new country club." I talked as I wrote the bullet points on the whiteboard. "It was a safe bet to say it would've been a great investment. We could use a golf course here."

I stepped back and looked at what I'd written. I took a sip of coffee and continued to think back to everything Loretta had said.

"With the development going under and the reaction Raffery had..." The look on Raffery's face came to my mind. The more I'd thought about his reaction to what Danielle had laid out, I wondered if she'd even told Caspian about it. "Did she drop the ball on him too?"

Both Caspian and Raffery had the look of a murderer on their faces. But Caspian was a businessman, and he'd probably been in this situation a time or two.

I quickly started to write Caspian's motive to murder Leandar.

"He had spent millions already on architecture plans. How much did

Danielle charge him? And what about the investors? Who are they?" I tapped the end of the dry-erase marker on the board as I tried to figure out how I could get my hands on any documents.

The puppy had made his way over to the stool without me even hearing him until he stood next to the feet of the stool, whining.

"Hey, buddy. Do you need to go potty before we go?" I looked down at the cute puppy and popped off the stool.

The bell over the door dinged, and my afternoon employees stumbled in, giggling.

"Hey, Roxy!" the two greeted me. "Hey, Jessie!" They squealed and rushed over to grab the puppy.

Shanda and Shelley Riddle were twins who'd started working for me at the beginning of the year. They were in their junior year of high school, which made me believe they'd at least be here for the next couple of years before they went off to college.

"I'll take him out," Shanda said and darted out the door with the puppy.

"Jessie?" I asked, not knowing they'd named the dog.

"Yes. I think there might be someone who wants to adopt him. We have a regular who comes in at night to grab a decaf, and she said she's thinking about adopting him. She calls him Jessie." Shelley shrugged and headed on back to put her backpack away so she could start her work shift.

"What are you working on?" Shelley called out to me.

"Nothing." I grabbed the whiteboard and carried it with the backside facing out so she didn't see the words "murder" and "victim." "Just some recipes."

"For murder?" she asked and snickered. "Is that about that guy they found at the lake?"

"It's nothing for you to worry about," I said and pushed through the door of the kitchen so I could grab my things and head home.

I had so many questions I could look up on the internet, like who was investing into the country-club development. Plus, my mom hadn't called me back. I wanted to call her and ask her about all of these real estate dealings.

She would be able to steer me in the right direction.

"Hey!" I heard Shelley yell out, and it made me dart back through the swinging door. "That's Jessie's mom."

She pointed to the television we kept on the back wall with the sound down for those customers who liked to come watch the news in the morning while sipping on a coffee.

It was Danielle Quillen.

"Turn it up." I gestured for Shelley to grab the remote from underneath the counter.

We are looking for Ms. Quillen. We only want to talk to her. She worked with Leandar Taylor on the development where we found his body. We also have his phone, and she was the last person he called. We just want to talk to her.

Spencer Shepard was giving a quick television update with Danielle's face plastered all over the television.

"Do me a favor." I turned to Shelley and ripped my bag off the coatrack, forgetting about the stuff in the kitchen. "If she does come in tonight, call me. If not, make sure the puppy, er, Jessie is okay for the night."

My phone rang.

I waved goodbye to Shelley and hit the green button to answer my phone when I saw it was Mom.

CHAPTER SIX

"Hey, Mom. I guess you heard the news about Leandar," I said right off and unchained my bike from the bike rack in front of the shop.

"Yes. I was meaning to call you all day, but with the latest news, some of his clients have come to me after hearing. You know, the house-buying business doesn't stop for death." Mom really never had a good way with words.

She wasn't from the south or Kentucky, which already put her on Aunt Maxi's bad side. Mom didn't help herself, either.

My mom wasn't the typical mom when I was growing up, and Aunt Maxi was more of a mother figure, so it was natural for me to show up here years ago instead of going to find my mom who, at that time, was galivanting all over the world, God knows where.

It was the history between Aunt Maxi and Mom that was a difficult hurdle to jump through when Mom showed up in Honey Springs. When she decided to stay and call it home, it was just a little unnerving for me.

Mom didn't like it when my dad brought me here, and she certainly wasn't a fan when my dad would leave me here for the rest of the summer. Thankfully, he didn't listen to her, and I was able to stay, but still, the animosity was something she and Aunt Maxi had to work through.

I loved them both, but Mom was different. I had to give her credit. She had done what she set out to do, and that was create a new life with me in it as well as become a Realtor. She'd done well for herself. Aunt Maxi saw Mom was trying, and they'd come to a truce. If I had to make a comment about their relationship, I'd say they were more than friendly, and I'd like to think they'd call on one another if they were in a pickle.

"Did you happen to get a phone call from Danielle Quillen?" I asked and rolled the lock up to put in my bag before sticking it in the basket.

"Why would she call me?" Mom asked.

I held the bike steady with one hand, one foot on the pedal and my heinie resting on the seat while I finished the conversation.

"Because she was probably staying in one of Leandar's rentals." I made the assumption from deductive reasoning. If Blackwood Associates used him, it would seem natural that all the people they subcontracted out or employees would also use him.

"That's not true. He wanted an arm and a leg for a cabin that didn't even have a view of nothing but the old junkyard on the far side of town." Mom had a large clientele of owners who had not only bought old cabins from her, but after they'd redone them, they used Mom as their rental agent. "She came into the office, and I showed her the cabin over on the island with the perfect view of the property they were building on."

"You mean one of Kayla and Andrew's cabins?" I asked.

"Yes. She loves it, from what I understand. She'd extended her stay just a few days ago to two more months." Mom didn't make sense.

"You mean a month ago or at least a week or two ago, right?" I questioned the timing. If Danielle had gotten all her samples completed and now the project had all but come to an abrupt halt, especially now that it was a crime scene, why would she stay?

"No, honey. I said a couple of days ago," Mom confirmed. The distinctive sound of a filing cabinet clicking open and the small balls rolling along the rails was a sound I heard Mom make all the time when she was looking for a rental agreement or client file. It was followed by shuffling of papers. "Yep. It's right here. It was two days ago. And about the same time."

I pulled my phone away from my ear. It was almost four o'clock in the afternoon, which meant if I went to the marina, I could catch the four o'clock boat ride over to the bee farm and go see if Danielle was still at the cabin.

"Can you tell me which cabin?" I asked and decided to get off the bike, resting it up against the outside of the coffee shop so I could head inside to get some of the leftover donuts.

It was clear I was going to have to encounter some folks that weren't above donut bribes.

"Now, you know I can't do that. It's a privacy thing, but I did tell you it was directly across from the development." Mom sighed with satisfaction. "Why are you asking? You don't think she had anything to do with Leandar's murder, do you? I mean, there's so many other people I think would have motive. It wasn't like he was on the up-and-up with his shady real estate dealings."

The Riddle girls' brows knotted when they saw me come back in as they wondered what I was doing. They didn't ask as I hurried behind the counter and grabbed a few to-go bags and dumped donuts in them, putting them in my bag.

"What do you mean?" I asked and rushed back outside.

I put my bag back in the wire rack and started to walk the bike down the boardwalk. I had to make sure I caught the boat in time and heard what Mom had to say.

"Listen, honey. I have to go. I'm going to be late for the cruise the Feather-stones paid for before the news of the development going south. I have to go home and get cleaned up." Mom was full of wonderful information.

"Cruise? You mean a dinner cruise at the Watershed?" I asked since it was the only local restaurant that offered such a thing.

"Roxanne Bloom." She only said my name when there was cause for concern. "Are you feeling okay?"

"I have a lot of questions about Leandar's death, and I can't help but wonder if Danielle or Raffery didn't have something to do with it." I rambled on. The low-pitched *thud* of the tires as they moved along the wooden planks of the boardwalk made it hard for me to concentrate.

"You mean to tell me Danielle and Raffery are a couple and they killed Leandar?" Mom had created a whole love triangle.

And this was how rumors started.

"No. Not at all." I had to stop the rumor train before it left the station. "You have to promise not to say a word," I told her and looked off toward the marina where I could see people getting on Big Bib's boat to hitch a ride over to the island.

"I promise." Mom didn't sound too convincing, but she did sound curious.

"I mean pinky promise. Like cross-your-heart-and-you'll-die if you don't keep it." I maneuvered the bike around some tourists down the ramp that led right to the marina. "That kind of promise."

"I promise, but I'm not sure I'm going to like it." Mom agreed enough for me to tell her about me seeing Leandar's body and how his skull had been bashed in, and I was sure he didn't do it himself. "Oh dear. Both Danielle and Leandar would have motives, plus Caspian Blackwood."

"Yes. And that's why I need to talk to Danielle. I also need to get in front of Raffery, which is why I wanted to know if you can take me as a guest to your cruise dinner they are hosting." I was a big ask for Mom to do this for me. "I know it's business for you, but there won't be business in the real estate market if it gets out there was a murder in town. No one wants to invest in crime-ridden communities."

The one thing I could count on with my mom was the power of the almighty dollar. It wasn't a good quality she had in her, but she looked at every transaction as a business deal. Leandar's murder was no different.

And I was using it as a way to get information. Yes.

"I was offered two tickets," she muttered as though she wasn't convinced I should go. She paused.

"Listen, I'm already at the marina to go find Danielle," I told her and handed my bike to Big Bib so he could put it somewhere for me until I got back from the island. "Thank you," I mouthed to him.

He winked.

"I'm stepping foot on the boat right now." This was when she knew I wasn't going to take "no" lightly, and I would do whatever I had to do to get on the cruise. "You know I will get on the cruise one way or the other, so you might'swell take me and save us both the embarrassment."

"Fine, but you can't go around asking if they murdered Leandar. I'm trying to get them to switch all of their property dealings to me, now that..." She didn't have to finish the sentence for me to know she was referring to Leandar's death.

"I'll meet you at the Watershed at... What time?" I asked and stepped down into the boat. I had limited time to talk. Soon I'd be surrounded by tourists and the hum of the motor of the boat as it crossed the lake, leaving me to talk loud, and I didn't want to risk anyone hearing me talk about murder.

"Be there at seven and wear a cocktail dress." Her words posed a problem, and before I could protest, she hung up.

I felt a mix of excitement and apprehension. The sun was beginning to dip lower in the sky, casting warm golden hues across Lake Honey Springs as we prepared to head toward the island. The late spring air was filled with the scent of blooming flowers and fresh grass while birdsong accompanied the gentle hum of the boat's engine.

"Ugh," I blurted out loud enough to catch Big Bib's attention as I tugged my bag in my lap.

"What was that about?" he asked, grinning underneath that heavy beard of his.

"Mom." I rolled my eyes. "I'm going to go as her guest on the dinner cruise tonight, and she told me I have to wear a cocktail dress. I don't have any. There's no need with slinging coffee and pastries all day."

He took his spot at the helm of the wheel boat, revving up the motor. I leaned on my hip and tugged my bag off my shoulder.

"Speaking of donuts," I said and put my hand down into my bag to pull out one of the to-go Bean Hive bags. "I thought you could use a couple after-supper dessert donuts."

His big beard couldn't hide the large grin on his face.

"You're butterin' me up, Roxanne Bloom." He gladly took the bag. "After supper, nothin'. I'm gonna eat these right now while you tell me what it is you want to know."

"You see a lot of people coming and going on this boat. Have you seen Danielle lately?" I asked in a casual tone.

Big Bib scratched his beard thoughtfully, his eyes never leaving the water ahead. "Well, Roxy," he said, "I did see her a couple of days ago. She seemed mighty upset, said she needed some time alone at her cabin on the island."

His hand gripped the handle, and he pushed it forward, accelerating the boat as it cut through the water, creating a gentle spray that misted my face. I looked around at the other passengers, who were chattering excitedly and snapping photos of the picturesque landscape. They were oblivious to the storm brewing beneath the surface of our seemingly peaceful community.

I bit my lip, mulling over this information. "Did she mention anything about Leandar or their argument at the Bean Hive?"

He shook his head. "No, but she did say she had some important information that she needed to sort through. Something that could change everything for this town. But that was before the town council, and we both know what happened there."

"Yeah. I'm going to go see if I can talk to her. See if she's okay. She'd been coming into the Bean Hive every day. Never missing once. She didn't show up today. Did you happen to give her a ride today?" I asked.

"No, but that doesn't mean someone else didn't." He shrugged.

"Like who?" I asked.

"I don't know. Look around." He nodded as the boat cut across the lake, missing other boats traveling downstream. "It's the beginning of boating season. I'm not the only ride someone can hitch back and forth. All the boat slips at the marina are all taken for the rest of the year. That means there's going to be a lot more boaters."

He pointed out to the dock we were headed for, and there were at least four boats tied up.

"Right there. Four boats. All of which are probably going to the resort." Bib had a point. "Speaking of which, you could ask Jessica for a dress."

"You're joking, right?" I asked, snorting to myself. But he didn't seem to laugh. "You're not."

"I'm just saying that woman has so many shopping bags when she comes from town, they are going to have to build a new resort just for her clothes." Bib laughed at his own joke.

Me, not so much.

My ex, Kirk, and his wife, Jessica, had been the secret investors for Crissy Lane's Be Happy Resort. It was a fancy spa and resort with all sorts of strange drinks like matcha or something that sounded icky. Plus all these crazy yoga classes that didn't sound like any kind of yoga or meditation I knew of.

When Crissy came back from California at some retreat, she got this harebrained idea to open something similar right smack-dab in Kentucky. Of course, we thought Crissy had lost her ever-lovin' mind, but who knew it would be so wildly popular and always packed after it was open?

It was quite a bit of a shock to find out my ex and his new wife had funded the place. To add insult to injury, they'd even moved to Honey Springs, now calling it home with their dog, who Jessica adopted from the Pet Palace. Biscuit. Cute feller. And now they had a newborn baby.

I didn't hold any grudges against either of them. They did contribute to society, but Kirk was a local lawyer, and I tried to stay as far away from them as possible.

Honey Springs wasn't that big, but it was big enough for me not to see them on a regular basis.

As we neared the island, I felt a knot forming in my stomach. Was Danielle truly capable of murder? What secrets was she hiding? And what would I find when I confronted her?

The sun's golden rays began to fade, replaced by the soft pink hues of dusk. The scent of the lake and the sounds of nature surrounded us, but my thoughts were consumed by the mystery that lay ahead. I braced myself for the confrontation, determined to uncover the truth and protect the town I loved.

"So you don't recall Danielle ever saying anything about Leandar?" I asked Big Bib one more time after all the tourists had gotten off the boat.

"No, but I did hear Caspian Blackwood say if the nitwit Realtor didn't pull through with the deal, then it would be his last deal." Big Bib's observation wasn't one pointing to Caspian as the killer, but it was a situation I would ask Caspian about when I got in front of him.

There was a little itch of curiosity about who he'd been talking to.

"What time is the last ride back?" I asked Big Bib after I stepped off the boat onto the wooden dock, feeling the late-afternoon breeze brush against my face.

The air was filled with the sweet scent of honey and the sound of buzzing bees from the honey farm behind me.

"I'll be back here in about an hour." His eyes lowered. "Do I need to come looking for you if you don't show up?" He shook his head. "I'm always wondering about you."

"You just might." I smiled, referring to his offer to come look for me. "Can I get you anything from the bee farm?"

"I don't think he needs anything." Kayla Noro had crept up behind me. "We just gave him two big honey pots yesterday."

"Hey!" I was happy to see Kayla. It was a long winter, and I'd yet to get over there that spring.

Though the island was literally a Big Bib pontoon boat ride away from land, it did seem like it was a trip. Like most things, Kayla and Andrew had their hands full with taking care of all the bees and hives in order to keep them healthy for the popular tourist farm.

"I'm so glad to see you." Kayla tucked her elbow in the crook of my arm.

We walked off the dock and headed up the cute little path toward the bee farm.

"I have loved getting to visit with Maxine. She's never gonna change." Kayla shook her head. "The older she gets, the worse she gets."

"You're not telling me anything. But I'm glad she's been able to get over here to get my supply of honey." I sighed, thinking how grateful I was for Aunt Maxi's involvement in the Bean Hive.

She really was someone who thought I could do anything.

"I'm glad you came here and not there." Kayla's eyes shifted toward the Be Happy Spa that was located on the opposite end of the island.

It was a piece of property Kayla and Andrew sold off to Crissy and her investors after the bee farm had taken a hit. Seasonal weather sometimes took a toll on the bees' health, and the Noros didn't have enough funds to keep the hives open, keep the bees healthy, and make a living unless they sold some land.

"No, but I am glad it's all going good over there. Crissy sure does love all that woo-woo stuff. I'm here to try to find one of the rental cabins." That was another business deal the Noros had done during their time of need.

They'd not sold off land, but they'd built a couple of cabins so they could rent them for income. I'd never seen them, but I knew they rented them, and Mama told me Danielle was currently renting one of them from the Noros.

"Oh." Kayla pulled her arm from mine.

"Yeah. Danielle Quillen." As I said her name, Kayla's facial expression changed considerably. "I can see you've heard about Leandar."

"It's awful, and immediately I thought about the last time I saw him." Her lips tugged in as though she wasn't sure she wanted to let out whatever it was she was itching to tell me.

"If you know something, please tell me." I blinked at her before I told her, "Spencer asked me to keep my ear to the ground, and you know what that means."

"Yeah. I hate to spread rumors or gossip." She shook her head, still unsure if she wanted to tell me what she knew.

"It wasn't too long ago that I helped you and Andrew." I didn't want to throw it in her face. "Since I'm still a lawyer, I might be able to help Danielle."

"I wondered if she was a suspect in Leandar's murder after I heard about the emergency meeting at All About the Details." When Kayla sucked in a deep breath, her shoulders lifted to her ears and suddenly dropped as her mouth opened. "He came to the island looking for her. He seemed quite upset and muttered something about her past. He was determined to find her and said he wouldn't leave until he did."

"Did he find her?" I asked.

"No. I told him she wasn't here and how she'd taken the ferry." She used "ferry" loosely when we were actually talking about Big Bib's pontoon. It was the only official ride over to the island.

"Did he go look for her?" I wanted to know.

"Not on the island. I told him she always took the first ferry off the island and usually stopped by the Bean Hive." She pointed to me. "He jumped back on the ferry, but he was determined to find her." Kayla frowned.

"When was this?" I asked.

"Yesterday morning," she said, placing him at the Bean Hive about the time I'd overheard him threaten Danielle.

"Do you think I need to tell Spencer?" she asked.

"I probably would. He's asking for anyone with any information to come forward, and there's nothing too small. All clues add up," I said. "Like you said, Danielle does come to the coffeehouse every morning, but she didn't show up today."

Kayla's face elongated as her eyes bolted open and her jaw dropped.

"That's why I'm here. I have a few questions for her and can possibly be able to help her." It was my way of reminding Kayla I was still a lawyer and used it to my advantage. "Can you tell me what cabin she's staying in?"

"You'll find her cabin just beyond the old oak tree over there," she said, pointing toward a massive tree in the distance. "There are a couple, but the one she rented..." She paused then said, "Extended her rental recently." She followed her comment by saying, "If she killed someone, then she's probably taken off. Right?"

"Not necessarily." My lips tugged apart in a grimace. "Either they run or they hang around to see what people know."

"Oh." Kayla tugged her bottom lip under her front teeth. She closed her eyes and shook her head. "I can't even imagine her doing something like this."

"Me either. That's why I want to talk to her before Spencer tries to arrest her or take her in for questioning."

"I didn't see her this morning. Not that I look, but she usually has Big Bib pick her up just as the sun is popping up and my bees need to be checked while I'm drinking my homemade cup of coffee from the Bean Hive special roast." She made me smile.

I pointed off in the direction of the big tree.

"Yep. Hers is the one on the beach," Kayla said. "Stop by before you head back over. I'll give you some fresh honey I collected today. It's so sweet."

"I will, but before I go find her, did you happen to see Caspian Blackwood, the development owner, here?" I asked since Big Bib had told me he'd over-heard Caspian on the phone.

"No. He's never been here." She shook her head with confidence. "He could've killed Leandar. Can you imagine all the money he's out? I know when Crissy and Kirk—" She pulled her lips together. "Sorry," she apologized.

"Don't be. It's fine. I've moved on, if you've not heard," I teased, holding up my ring finger, since she was one of the first people to congratulate me during our annual Neewolah Festival, where Patrick and I tied the knot without telling anyone.

"Good," she sighed. "Kirk did pay for all the environmental things we had to do in order for them to build the spa, and let me tell you, I got a gander at the figures on a piece of paper when we were we meeting with him, and they were staggering. So I'm sure Blackwood Associates is out a pretty penny."

"Danielle Quillen might've been hiding some secret Leandar knew about and she didn't want him to reveal, but was it enough to kill him to shut him up?" I asked myself because I wasn't sure.

"What? A secret?" Kayla looked shocked. "What kind of secret?"

"That is the million-dollar question and why I'm going to go find Danielle to ask," I said. "Now that you mention the money that it took for just the environmental inspection of the spa, Caspian Blackwood had invested a lot—if not millions—on making this country-club development community come to life, and all the money he's spent so far is money that doesn't come with a return policy."

"No, siree, it's not returned," Kayla repeated. "And money is a big stick in the gut, and when you lose a lot of it, it can make you crazy."

"Crazy enough to kill?" I asked.

Kayla slowly nodded her head and said, "Enough if it's a lot of money and currently the only project you're banking on to bring you to early retirement."

"Early retirement?" I was beginning to think Kayla knew more than she was telling me.

"I wasn't going to say anything because, well, Kirk." Kayla frowned and gave me an empathetic look. "You said winters are long, and...", she hesitated.

"You and Kirk and Jessica have gotten to be friends," I finished for her.

"Yes. And Jessica is lovely. She's so sweet, and Kirk is so smart about business. He and Andrew clicked. It's been nice. Not lonely, and it gives me and Andrew more than just each other to talk to." Kayla was making a good argument for why they were friends.

"Truth be told, I liked Jessica the day she came into the coffeehouse, not telling me who she was and immediately adopting Biscuit. If she wasn't tied to Kirk, I would say we'd be friends too." My words landed on Kayla like a breath of fresh air.

"Thank you." She put her hands together up to her third eye. "We will always be better friends."

"You don't have to go that far." I assured her. "Are you telling me Kirk mentioned something about Caspian?"

"Yes. Of course, when he heard about the development, he said he wondered why he'd not thought of it first and was mad. Then he told us how he went to Blackwood Associates to talk to Caspian. Later, Jessica told me Kirk went there to see if he could become one of the investors." I was all ears about their little get-togethers. "That's when Caspian told Kirk he'd put all his money into this one development because he was planning on moving here to retire. All of his money. Like every single penny."

"Did Kirk invest?" I asked.

"Yes." Kayla nodded. "A lot, according to Jessica. After what happened at the meeting yesterday, I called her, and she said she couldn't talk. Things weren't good at home."

"Wow." I wasn't expecting to have this big bombshell laid out on me. I only had limited time to talk to Danielle and get back on the ferry ride home, but while I was there, I wanted to pop into the spa and maybe have a little chat with my dear old ex-husband.

"I better get going if I'm going to stop back by and grab some of that fresh, sweet honey." I waved off to her and hurried toward the oak tree, now more concerned than ever about Danielle's safety rather than her being a suspect.

What if Caspian was getting rid of everyone who'd made the deal go south?

The island's serenity suddenly seemed to fade as the reality of the situation set in. With determination in my step, I continued weaving through the bee farm, eager to reach Danielle and uncover the secrets that seemed to haunt her.

CHAPTER SEVEN

On my way to find Danielle's cabin, I couldn't help but try to fit going to
see Kirk in my schedule while I was on the island. It wasn't like I was
going to be able to solve this thing tonight—that wasn't the question.

The question was if I could force myself to not scratch the curious itch
I had.

There was a huge difference in the landscape as I stepped off the property
line of the bee farm and into what I'd consider more inhabited land.

A soft breeze kissed my face, carrying the sweet scent of honey and
the faint buzzing sound of bees hard at work. The sun was shining
brightly, casting a warm golden hue over the verdant landscape that
stretched before me before it would soon set. I couldn't help but feel an
overwhelming sense of serenity, as if Mother Nature herself was
hugging me.

No wonder Crissy thought the island would be a great place for the Be
Happy Spa. It felt like you were in a different part of the world. Just far enough
away from the mainland to give you a sense of awe.

I began to walk toward the island beach, following a well-trodden path that
weaved through tall grasses and wildflowers. The earth beneath my feet was
damp from the recent rain, making a satisfying squelching sound with each
step I took. I inhaled the sweet fragrance of freshly blossomed flowers. The

chirping of birds filled the air, creating a beautiful symphony that accompanied me on my journey.

As I continued along the path, I could feel the ground beneath my feet becoming sandier, signaling that I was nearing the beach. My thought was to walk toward the big oak like Kayla had suggested, but if I found the beach and walked it, there was no way I could miss the cabin Danielle had rented.

The sound of gentle waves lapping at the shore replaced the buzzing of bees, and the fresh scent of the lake air mixed with the lingering sweetness of honey. I paused for a moment to take in the picturesque view of the crystal-clear lake, its surface sparkling like a thousand diamonds under the sun's rays.

I could see the small cabin nestled in the trees, its wooden structure blending harmoniously with the surrounding foliage. The leaves rustled gently in the breeze, creating a soothing background melody that further added to the enchanting atmosphere.

As I approached the cabin, I felt the sand beneath my toes grow warmer, and I could hear the faint voice I'd recognized as Danielle echoing out of the small cabin. That's when I knew it was, in fact, her cabin.

Finally, I reached the cabin's door, which was slightly ajar, allowing the warm, inviting light from within to spill out onto the sandy path. I knocked gently and called out Danielle's name, the sound of my voice mingling with the symphony of nature that surrounded us.

"I've got to go," I heard her say in a whisper.

"Danielle? It's Roxy from the Bean Hive," I called again. "I missed you today."

There was no movement or sound of movement coming from inside.

"I wanted to talk to you about Leandar." There was no beating around the bush. "Actually, I'm guessing you know that I overheard him mention something about exposing you, then we had the emergency meeting where he wasn't happy, and now he's dead. Not that I'm accusing you, but it doesn't look all that great, and well, I'm a lawyer."

The door went from cracked to fully open with Danielle standing behind it, her hand on the doorknob.

"You're a lawyer?" she asked. There was almost a look of relief on her face. Just for a split second. Still, there was an opening for me.

"I brought donuts." I dug down into my bag and pulled out the sack, dangling it in front of her.

"Is it too late for coffee?" she asked with a simple smile. "It's not your coffee, but it's coffee."

"I love all coffee." I held out the bag. "Want to talk?"

She opened the door to the small cabin, gesturing a welcome to come inside.

As I stepped inside the cabin, I was immediately greeted by a sense of warmth and comfort. The interior was a perfect blend of rustic charm and modern convenience, with exposed wooden beams crisscrossing the ceiling and polished hardwood floors that creaked ever so softly beneath my feet. Natural light filtered through the large windows, casting a warm glow that illuminated the cozy space.

To my left, a small-yet-functional kitchenette occupied one corner of the cabin. It featured a compact refrigerator, a gas stove, and a sink with a window above it that offered a beautiful view of the lake. The wooden countertops and open shelves were adorned with colorful ceramic dishes and a collection of well-loved cookware, telling the story of countless shared meals and laughter-filled gatherings.

A comfortable living area occupied the center of the cabin, with a plush sofa draped in soft, patterned throws and an array of mismatched cushions. A vintage coffee table sat on a woven rug, boasting a stack of dog-eared books and a simple vase filled with fresh wildflowers. On one wall, a stone fireplace. I imagined how cozy and warm it would feel in here during the winter.

To my right, a small wooden ladder led to a lofted sleeping area with a low, slanted ceiling. The space was adorned with a cozy bed dressed in soft linens and a patchwork quilt that looked as though it had been lovingly handmade. A small round window in the loft allowed a gentle breeze to waft through the cabin, carrying with it the sweet scent of the surrounding nature.

Throughout the cabin, personal touches were evident in the form of framed photographs, hand-painted artwork, and other mementos that spoke of cherished memories and shared experiences. Every corner of the space exuded a sense of warmth and love, making it feel like a true home away from home.

"Wow. Kayla has really made this a great little hideaway." It was as almost as cute as my home.

"They've been great. I can't complain." She busied herself in the small kitchen, making a single-serve coffee from the maker and plating the donuts. "Would you like one?"

"No. I don't want to ruin my supper. I'm going as a guest of my mama's to the Featherstones' dinner cruise." I patted my belly. "If I can get a free meal, I'm saving the room in my stomach. But I'll always have a coffee."

"I was invited to it, until I wasn't." She sat down at the kitchen table for two and bit into the donut.

"They uninvited you?" I wanted to make sure what I thought she was saying was correct and not assumptive.

"Right after the emergency meeting, Raffery was outside looking for Leandar, and I crossed his path at the wrong time." She shook her head. "He was fuming about the development. He said Leandar should've known better and that I ruined everything. That's when he pointed at me and told me to just pack my things and get out of town. He followed it up by saying, 'You are not welcome at the dinner cruise.'"

"I'm sorry. I bet that was hurtful." I frowned and held up my hand when I noticed the first cup of coffee had brewed. "You sit. I'll get our coffees."

"Thank you," she whispered and looked down at what was left of the first of the two donuts. "There's creamer in the refrigerator."

With the creamer in one hand and the cup in the other, I placed them in front of her then went back to make myself a cup of coffee.

"I understand I'm the bad guy here." She dunked the donut in the steaming coffee. My kinda girl, I thought to myself. "The town was counting on the country club to not only provide jobs but also bring in more tourism. I let everyone down."

"You didn't. I think it's a great idea for a nature preserve like you suggested. You even went above and beyond with Alice Dee Spicer to implement something. I think tourists come to Honey Springs for the nature. Lake Honey Springs is the big draw." The cup of coffee finished brewing, and I walked over to sit across from Danielle. "When a tourist comes to Honey Springs and puts a photo on social media, nine out of ten times, the photo is something in nature. A fish they saw in the lake, a bird nesting along the beach, a crazy purple insect native to the area."

Her eyes were filled with tears as what I was saying seemed to have an effect on how she was starting to see it wasn't her fault.

"Those are the things you love. That's why you became an environmentalist, right? To protect lands but also be fair to those big developers who want to use land that's not going to hurt the landscape." Goodness, I sure was making a good case. Too bad it wasn't in front of a judge and jury.

"Now you sound like a lawyer." It was if she were reading my mind.

"No. I'm trying to be a friend who doesn't want her friend to beat herself up." I reached across the table and patted her wrist. "I admit, I came here to question you and see if you did kill Leandar. But I know you didn't."

"How do you know that?" she asked, with more relief on her face.

"I have a good way of reading people. It's my gift that helped me win a lot of cases, and I don't think you did it. But I also know Sheriff Spencer Shepard will want to question you after he gets the crime scene cleared and evidence collected. You will be first on his list." My words didn't sit well.

"I didn't do it. You just said you didn't think I did either." The frail-young-woman look had been replaced by determination.

"That's the attitude and look you need to have on your face at all times." I pointed it out to her. "And if you want to answer some key questions for me right now, I can take those to Spencer so they won't waste their time checking you out."

"I have nothing to hide," she stated emphatically.

"I think you do." I picked up the coffee and took a sip, leaving some space for my response to settle on her.

It was a technique we'd learned in law school, how sometimes dangling a carrot and then saying nothing gets you the answer much faster. No one ever liked silence anymore. It was an art to forcibly keep your mouth shut in most social situations these days. The silence made the other person uncomfortable, which by nature, made them open their mouths to talk.

"You're referring to what Leandar said to me in the Bean Hive." She was a smart girl. She knew she was going to have to tell me. "I've not always been as virtuous as it appears. A few years back, I consulted for a major corporation on an eco-friendly project. I was new in the field, and I had rent to pay."

It became clear this had to do with money, making her motive look even worse.

"I overlooked some harmful environmental practices to keep the client happy and secure a hefty paycheck for myself. If this information were to become public, it could severely damage my reputation and jeopardize my career. People might think twice about hiring me."

She ran her finger along the top of her mug. The silence had gotten even thicker than before, as I tugged my lips a little more to make sure not to say anything.

"It wasn't illegal, what I'd done. It was immoral, and I paid for it. The money I made was spent on years of therapy trying to come to terms with what I'd done." She'd pretty much put herself in her own jail over it. I didn't need to beat her up anymore. "That's when I started to really take a look at the other jobs and do more research while on those jobs. Just like this one. I could easily have incorporated that spring into a feature for the country club, but that doesn't make it right for the environment down the road."

"Even though I don't think you killed Leandar to silence him, I do need to know where you were and who you were with from the time you saw Raffery Featherstone to when you heard about what happened to Leandar."

She nodded and picked up the other donut, dunking it before she took a bite.

"That's easy." She looked away, over at the bag I'd seen her carry into the Bean Hive. The one with all her files. "I have receipts for the spa at Be Happy and drinks at the bar."

"Did you talk to anyone while you were there?" I knew it could be easy to get receipts. Not that I thought Danielle would do that or be so forward-thinking.

Let's face it—who took paper receipts anymore? I always told the cashiers to throw my receipt away, leaving an establishment without one. It was safe to say they would throw those in the trash, making it easy for someone who needed an alibi to root through the trash and find receipts for a time stamp that put them there around the times in questions.

"Yes. The owner's wife." She got up, stuffing the rest of the donut in her mouth.

"Crissy doesn't have a wife," I blurted out.

"Jessica, um..." She searched for the name.

"Ah. Jessica." I snorted, raising my chin. "Jessica is married to my ex-husband." There was a shocked look on Danielle's face when she turned to hand me the receipts. "We all have secrets."

"I'm sorry. She was very nice. I didn't meet your ex, but she was actually walking the beach after the meeting. I was sitting on the small dock." Danielle turned to look out the window.

"I didn't see that coming up." I noticed there was a little boat tied up. "Have you used the boat to go to the mainland?"

"Yes. It's not easy, but I figured it out. The development is right across the way, and when I saw all the flashing lights there, I thought someone had went over there and, I don't know, cut down some trees, trashed it." She shrugged. "Anyways, Jessica was walking the beach, and she recognized me from the meeting."

"Yes. They were investors for the development." I saw a look indicating that something had clicked in her brain.

"That's how she knew all about it." Danielle shook her head and sat back down. I looked at the receipts while she talked. "She asked me if I wanted to come back for a spa treatment at half price since they had a last-minute cancellation. I really needed it, so I took her up on her offer."

There was something fishy going on with all of this, but I wasn't sure what, so I let her keep talking.

"She even waited for me in the lobby of the spa. She said she wanted to know if her husband could use the boat to run across the lake to get their dog some food because there wasn't a ferry running. I told her I had some hot dogs back at the cabin for the dog, but she insisted the dog needed special food. I didn't see any harm in it, so I told her to tell him sure and that the keys were always left in the boat." The more she talked, the more her story played in my head like a television show. "Then she asked me if I wanted to have a drink at the bar, on the house, and I said I sure could use that too. So I did."

"When did you get back to the cabin?" I was trying to see if she knew if Kirk had used the boat or not.

"In the morning. Early. I had a little too much to drink, and Jessica let me stay in one of the rooms at the spa. I woke up disoriented, really early, before dawn, and that's when I walked back to the cabin and saw all the lights. But, like I said, I figured it was someone trashing the place, mad about what I'd discovered and said at the meeting."

"Let's go back to Caspian Blackwood." I had to get off the subject of Kirk, or I wouldn't be able to keep my cool. The man had always been motivated by money, and I had a lot of stories that could implicate him in a lot of murders he'd clearly not done, but still.

Danielle's encounter with Jessica didn't look good.

"Did you ever hear him say anything about Leandar that would give him motive to have killed him?" I asked.

"The money alone. Greed," Danielle spit out immediately. "My report wasn't wrapped up into the package deal he had with his investors. They didn't want the report done, but Caspian did. My cost alone was over sixty thousand dollars. Then he had all the other contractors out there. Even though they'd yet to pluck a piece of grass off the land, their time isn't cheap, especially when Blackwood Associates had to fly them in, which isn't easy." She snorted. "Then get them rooms to stay in. Not cheap."

"Were they paying for your cabin?" I asked.

"Yes, until a day or so ago. I went to the Realtor and re-signed a lease, knowing I'd have to be here for some questioning. It was easier to stay here than try to find something new." She told me all the answers I needed for now.

"I've overstayed. I don't even think I will make it back to the dock to catch the ferry." I jumped up after I saw the time.

"Take the dinghy boat." She pointed out the window. "It is right across the road from my house." It was a great idea, but the beach where they found Leandar wasn't high on my list of places to visit. "It would be convenient. Are you sure you won't need it until tomorrow?"

"No. I've got a good book over there to read. One of those cozy mysteries." She chuckled. "I think I'll just hole up here until I have to go talk to the sheriff."

"I can take you there tomorrow, and I'll even write up your statement." I didn't want to encourage her to go without me. Was it for her? Or was it for Kirk's sake?

I knew I could get Danielle's alibi to stick and she wouldn't be a suspect, but my mind took me to a place I certainly didn't want to go. No matter how fast I throttled the boat across the water to the development so I could cross the street to get back to my house, the new suspect in my head wasn't going away.

What if Kirk and Jessica knew Danielle was staying? They had kept Danielle occupied while Kirk took the boat over to the development. It would be like Kirk to call Leandar and get him to meet Kirk there and get his take on what Danielle said just so they could come up with a creative solution. The boat skidded up on the beach, and I jumped out to pull it up on shore, looking back across at where I'd come from.

Kirk could've easily gotten into this boat and across Lake Honey Springs without anyone seeing him. Would Jessica take part in something like that?

The last little bit of sun was visible before it started to fully set as I gave the boat one more tug to secure it on the beach, so it didn't float away until I could safely get it back to the island later.

"What is that?" I noticed something red on the edge of the boat. On closer inspection, I could clearly see what looked to be a bloody outline of a hand. I gulped. "Oh, Kirk."

CHAPTER EIGHT

We weren't expecting any more rain after last week's downpour, but I still didn't want to take any chances, so I snapped a few quick photos of the edge of the boat before I darted off into the woods between the beach and the road to cross to my house.

It was so hard to keep quiet about the bloody handprint I'd seen on the boat. The dinghy was safe, and no one but Danielle knew it was there. I wasn't about to skip the dinner cruise, even though the bloody handprint was enough evidence for me to safely say Kirk had been in contact with blood the night he'd schlepped across the lake on his secret, covert mission.

When I saw him at the dinner cruise, it was nearly impossible for me to keep my mouth shut, so I made sure I stuffed it with some crab cakes from the tray one of the serving staff was floating around.

"Tell me again why you were invited here." My hand grabbed a flute of champagne when the drink tray passed by.

"When the development went through, I saw an opportunity, and I took it." Leave it to Mama to find a loophole in a bad situation that she could turn around for the good. "That's Raffery Featherstone."

She pointed across the dining room to the man I recognized from the meeting.

"They are a big family, and if you know anything about them, you know they have a lot of racehorses on their property. I know a lot of people who knew he was going to be in a pickle," she ho-hummed, waving across the room to him.

He returned the wave with a smile and gestured for her to come over.

"I knew the deal was going south fast when Leandar Taylor came into the office a couple of days ago, saying the environmentalist was ruining everything. He wanted to know if I had any clients with lakefront property—and lots of it—they'd sell for a pretty penny." She led the way through a much larger crowd than I'd expected to see at the dinner cruise.

I'd thought it was for family, but apparently not. There were a lot of business owners I'd recognized, like the Teagardens and Alice Dee Spicer, plus Kirk.

"You're telling me Leandar was going around trying to get some land to get Blackwood Associates to look at after the natural spring was found?" I asked Mama, trying to keep up as we darted across the room.

"That natural spring was found about a week ago. It's just taken that long for the report to come back with all the findings." She planted a big smile on her face as soon as she stepped in front of Raffery. "Hello, Raffery. Thank you so much for inviting me. Let me introduce you to my plus-one. My daughter, Roxanne Bloom."

No one ever used my married name Cane.

I peeked around her shoulder and extended my arm around her to shake his hand. She wanted to be front and center.

"This is my son, Caldwell Featherstone. He got home today from college. He was going to help out with the estate sale that's not ever going to happen." Raffery groaned his disdain for the situation. "But we are all here to celebrate something, right?"

"That's right." Mama continued to smile, keeping her eyes on Raffery. "I have some really good news."

"We don't have to do business here." He tried to stop her.

"This we will celebrate." Mama sucked in a deep breath and let it go, saying, "I have secured a year's worth of hay for the same amount you paid last year from a farm over in Versailles."

366

"That is something to celebrate!" Raffery held his glass up in the air. "Ladies and gentlemen." His voice boomed across the room.

Everyone fell silent, and all eyes were on us.

"If you've not met Penny Bloom, you want to. She's done the unthinkable or unimaginable for this time of the year." He laid a proud hand on Mama's shoulder. "Not only is she a real estate agent but she went above and beyond to secure some hay for my horses for the next year at the same cost of what I paid last year. Isn't that great? Three cheers for Penny!"

The hear-hears trickled across the room before the captain of the dinner cruise came across the loudspeakers, letting us know they were pushing back from the dock at the Watershed and saying if anyone had any reason not to continue on, they should get off the boat now.

"That's a big deal your mom has done." Caldwell came up to me after Mama had ventured off with Raffery.

She was doing exactly what she'd come here to do.

Be introduced.

"Please be sure to let her know we really are grateful." Caldwell stood at least five feet, ten inches, with a lean, athletic build. He had a mop of wavy chestnut-brown hair long enough for him to tuck behind his ears, giving me a sense of a somewhat carefree appearance.

His deep-set hazel eyes conveyed a mixture of intensity and intelligence, while his strong jawline and slightly crooked smile lent him an air of approachability and made him very likable, unlike the feeling I got about his father.

Raffery, on the other hand, was well-put-together and, though my mom couldn't see it, I could tell by the way the man looked at her, and even at his own son, that he had a sense of indignation and would much rather be somewhere else now that the deal was dead in the water. Or should I have said, now that the Realtor was found dead in the water?

His Realtor. The one he could've killed.

"What are you studying in college?" I made small talk with Caldwell, who definitely had not dressed according to the dress code Penny had given me.

His wrinkled khakis were paired with a simple, well-fitted T-shirt. What looked like a trusty pair of worn-in sneakers finished off the outfit.

He definitely didn't have his father's buttoned-up style, and maybe that was what made him more approachable and really down-to-earth.

"I'm an education major. I want to be a physical-education teacher," he told me, which was exactly what his physique had told me. "Now, my dad, he wanted me to go into business. He said I could take over all of his dealings." He shook his head. "I don't need a business degree to say the investment he made with that country club was too much."

"Yeah." I frowned. "I guess you heard about that. I mean, my mom and all." I pointed out the little toast Raffery just gave in Mom's honor.

I noticed the server passing by and stopped him.

"Would you like a drink?" I offered one to Caldwell as I plucked another one for me.

"I'm twenty," he said flatly. "And I don't drink because I try to live the way I want to teach people how to treat their bodies."

"Sounds good." I plucked another one for me, making it one in each hand. "My ex is here, and..." My eyes narrowed, staring at Caldwell. He didn't give two iotas about me or Kirk. So I changed the subject. "Now, I guess you won't be moving."

"I don't live here. I came in town a couple of days ago to help get all the estate-sale items together." He had said something that stuck in my head.

"Couple of days ago?" I asked before turning to the people next to me. "Do you want a drink?" I offered them the flutes of champagne, knowing if I drank them, I couldn't be sure what I would say to Kirk. If I was going to accuse him of murder, then I better be in tip-top lawyer form because he'd be nothing less.

"Yeah. We are on summer break. I work a few summer camps at the local schools where I go to college. Mom wanted me to help out by going through things I might want, but there's nothing I want." He stuffed his hands in his pockets. "I guess we don't have to worry about that now."

"Yeah. That was bad. I mean, the other night, your dad was pretty upset about the real estate guy that died," I whispered out of the corner of my mouth. No matter what I did, I wasn't cool. So I just came out and said it. "What did you and your dad do after the meeting?"

"He was mad, and when he gets mad, it's best he goes fishing. We keep a boat down at the marina." Had Caldwell just told me his dad had gone fishing?

"Fishing? At night?" I asked.

"Jug fishing." He mentioned a type of fishing I knew well. One that you only did at night. Well, you put the jugs out at night.

He continued, "I even cut the fishing wire and hooked the end of the line as he tied them on the new milk jugs. You should've seen his old ones." He snickered.

He was talking about how you tie one end of the fishing line to the mouth of an empty milk jug, then you let the line dangle down into the water with the hook on it. The milk jug will float until a fish eats the bait and gets the hook in their mouth. The jug stands straight up in the water and zigzags around the lake all night.

"What color did he paint his jugs?" I asked because mine were painted purple, so when I went to get my jugs the next morning, I could find mine.

"His are red."

"Red," I repeated to remember to go look for red jugs, though he should've gone to get them by now.

"You didn't go with your dad?" I asked.

"Nope. He was gone all night. Well, I think he got in around four." He put his dad at the scene.

"In the morning?" I asked.

"Yes. Why?" He laughed like I said something funny.

"I didn't think anyone but me was up at that time." I shrugged so he wouldn't catch on to me snooping. "I own a coffee shop on the boardwalk."

"That's where I've seen you." He pointed at me. A look of "aha!" came up on his face. "I was in one of the home economics classes you talked to at Honey Springs High School."

"Oh. I'm sorry. I was so nervous that I barely looked at the kids." It was my way of being nice, but honestly, I never remembered seeing him. "While you're in town, you should come by and see me. Coffee on the house."

"I will. I'd love to have one of your famous maple-bacon coffees." He mentioned the most ordered drink for kids his age. "I'm not sure how long I'll be in town now that the estate sale isn't going to happen."

"You get one large maple-bacon coffee on the house. If I'm not there, you tell them to call me." I was interrupted by the loudspeaker as it screeched on and the captain let us know the dinner buffet was open for everyone to get a plate and enjoy the food.

"Are you sure your dad came in around four a.m.?" I asked before I scooted toward the dining room.

He confirmed it and said he was playing his online video game when his dad popped into his room to see why he was still awake.

Great. Now how was I going to be able to place Raffery at the scene without making his son a witness?

CHAPTER NINE

As the guests filled in the room to find their name at the place they'd be sitting, the captain gave little bits and pieces of information about Honey Springs as we passed various sites. He was talking about the island and how the bee farm was a tourist destination, pointing out how some of the decorations for the night's cruise were donations from the Noros.

I glanced around the dining area to see what Kayla had put together and noticed how the gorgeously adorned chandeliers dangling over the room cast a warm golden glow over the white linen-covered tables.

It was the centerpieces of each table that had Kayla's signature look. Stunning bouquets of flowers, reminiscent of the unique flora that contributed to the island's famous honey.

The chatter of guests filled the room, but the underlying tension was palpable.

I gripped the handle of the chair in front of the place setting with my name inscribed on the tented nameplate that sat on the fine piece of bone china. At a closer glance, I wondered if it was the famous Featherstone bone china I was going to see if I could get a few pieces of at the estate sale.

"If you're wondering"—Mama came up behind me—"because I saw your mind going a million miles a minute when you looked at the plate, it is the family china. Raffery thought it would be a nice touch to have the farewell cruise include the china before they sold it at the estate sale."

I snorted and tried not to look across the table when Kirk appeared in my peripheral vision. Instead, I focused on the waitstaff, dressed in crisp white shirts and black bow ties, navigating the room with practiced grace and offering flutes of champagne and various wines to go with the dinner buffet. The scent of the gourmet dishes being prepared in the galley wafted through the air, making my stomach rumble in anticipation.

"Gotta go to my seat." Mama patted my back before she waved at someone else she knew and darted off to find her spot.

"Roxy." Kirk gave me a hard nod from across the table.

"Roxanne," I corrected him. "Roxy is reserved for my friends."

He smiled, picked up his glass of water, and tilted it toward me, then took a drink.

"Sorry. It's just I want to know why you were on the dinghy the night Leandar was murdered," I whispered hastily so no one else could hear me and tapped on my phone to bring up the photo I'd taken of the fingerprints of blood on the dinghy boat. "And you left this bloody handprint."

In the back of my head, I also kept the jug-fishing story Caldwell had told me about Raffery and how he'd used red paint to distinguish his jugs from the others floating on top of the lake.

"What are you talking about?" Kirk looked offended, his fork in one hand and his knife in the other. He used his knife to part the flower arrangement so he could glare at me. "What dinghy?"

"The dinghy boat from the cabin Kayla and Andrew rented to Danielle Quillen. The woman you and your wife used as an alibi for what you've done." I pushed the flowers aside so we had a clear path for our accusations and war of words to fly across without any sort of obstacle in the way.

"Outside." He grabbed the napkin from his lap and tossed it on the table. "Now," he said before he shoved his chair back from the table and got up.

"Excuse me," I said to the woman next to me who had noticed the little bit of tension between me and Kirk. "My ex. We have some issues to work out."

Why I had a need to apologize to the woman was beyond me, and I beat myself up over it in my head during the entire walk outside from the dining area where I found Kirk next to the boat's railing.

"What on earth is going on with you, Roxy? You've lost your mind if you think I had anything to do with Leandar's murder, but to accuse Jessica is going over the line." He stuck his finger in my face. "Even for you."

"Move your finger from my face," I said in a very nice tone. "Are you telling me Danielle lied to me about last night's little spa-and-bar romp, and her receipts with the time stamp are fudged?"

"I'm not saying anything. I am saying I didn't get on any dinghy boat to do anything. Much less the accusations you have in that photo." He looked down to my hand where I had my phone in my grip. "Whatever it is that woman told you is not true. You can ask Jessica."

"She said Biscuit was out of his special food, and the ferry wasn't running to get you to the mainland." My words drifted off. I jerked up and looked at him. "You don't even live on the island." I gulped.

"Right. And we weren't on the island. I told you I was at home. Trust me. I was having a couple of drinks after what happened at the emergency meeting." He looked at me with his chin pointed down. "I didn't lose as much money as some of the other investors, but it was enough that it punched me in the gut."

"Do you know who else had invested in the development besides you and Raffery?" I asked.

"The Teagardens, who are here, and"—he scratched his head—"I can't think of all of them off the top of my head because it's still so frustrating. I wasn't even going to come here tonight, but I wanted to know what he was thinking and what others were saying."

"Saying about what?" I asked. "The murder?"

"No. The development. I don't know who murdered Leandar, but you and I both know from our work that there's not a short suspect list." He shook his head. "I never even figured I'd be on the list. But if they can find a new development spot, I'd still like to keep my investment."

"That's an option?" I asked.

"Yeah, if your husband agrees to it," he said.

If Patrick agrees to what? I thought, then gave my husband a reasonable doubt. He could have some information he'd not yet told me because I'd been at work all day, as he had, and I changed my plans to come here with Mama, which meant he'd not gotten the opportunity to tell me whatever it was Kirk was talking about.

"If you could talk him into it." He raised his chin. "And your Aunt Maxi. I think our pockets would all benefit from the tourism it would bring." He cleared his throat. "If you'll excuse me, I'm going to go back in and finish my supper before it gets cold. You should too."

"I've lost my appetite," I said and turned to look out over the water.

I laid my forearms on the railing and let my clasped hands dangle over the side while I looked out into the darkness off the side of the boat. There were so many things to think about.

Why on earth would Danielle lie to me? She did look very surprised when I told her Kirk was my ex, but she must have been so far deep into her lie that she couldn't get out of it, so she rolled with it.

"And I thought I was good at reading people." I laughed at myself. "You're getting rusty, kid," I said, knowing I had to do better on my next little visit to see her.

Instead of trying to make sense of it all and just keep to myself what Kirk had told me, even the concerning part Patrick might have a hand in, I ended up going back into the dining room to enjoy eating a meal off those china dishes I was never going to own.

As the evening progressed, the conversation among the guests never seemed to stray toward the topic of the golf course development. Instead, people exchanged pleasantries and shared anecdotes, deliberately steering clear of the elephant in the room. However, the occasional hushed murmur reached my ears, hinting at whispers of Raffery's possible motives for killing Leandar, the real estate agent.

It was like everyone was there to see exactly what Raffery's next move was going to be.

"Leandar had convinced Raffery to sell his farm and hold an estate sale to invest in the Honey Springs Golf Course development," Bev Teagarden told me while we were having an after-dinner cocktail, after the captain had announced that it was last call for the bar and that we were turning the boat around to head back to the Watershed.

In no uncertain way, Bev revealed that with the environmentalist's findings threatening to derail the project, some speculated that Raffery might have sought revenge on the man who had led him down this path.

While I listened to Bev lay out Raffery's motives, I sipped my champagne and observed the beautifully dressed guests laughing and enjoying the cruise on Lake Honey Springs. I couldn't help but feel a sense of unease.

"From what I hear, I think there's a new spot Blackwood Associates is looking at that'll protect at least some of our investments." Bev sipped her drink, her words only leaving me with even more questions for Patrick Cane when I got home. "Especially Caspian Blackwood."

"Why so?" I wondered why she'd say that.

"Caspian has invested all his money into the development. He was going to take early retirement, and now all his money is gone unless he finds another property." She pointed toward the windows looking into the dining room where Raffery had Mama's attention.

Chills crawled up my spine as I looked out at the lake's shimmering surface reflecting the dazzling lights of the cruise vessel. Beneath that serene facade, dark secrets churned, waiting to be revealed.

CHAPTER TEN

"I felt like a fool standing there accusing Kirk of killing Leandar when he was holding the knowledge that Blackwood Associates had already been looking for a new area to develop here," I mumbled through a mouthful of toothpaste.

"I called you a few times today and you were busy, so I didn't get the opportunity to tell you. I wasn't going to tell you on the fly because it's a big investment." Patrick walked over and stood behind me.

He put his large hands on my shoulders and looked at my reflection in the mirror above the single sink. His big brown eyes softened as his mouth curled into a tender smile. His salt-and-pepper hair was cut shorter, what I liked to call his late-spring-to-summer much cooler haircut.

"I would never make any decision without you, especially when it comes to..." I turned around to look him dead in the eyes. I knew what he was going to say, even though I'd yet to hear it from his lips.

"Aunt Maxi's house," we said in unison. I gulped while he gave me a few empathy blinks, his chiseled jaw set.

"If you aren't going to let us move into it, then we need to do something with it." Patrick and I loved Aunt Maxi's house.

It wasn't the house she was living in. It was the property overlooking Lake

Honey Springs that had the best views of any place on the lake and where she lived when I was growing up.

The house. The house that was the center of why Patrick and I had broken up before I went off to college.

Making the excuse that I'd gone to college and he was doing his thing made it easy for me to cut off the already long-distance relationship and summer flings.

During the worst time in my life, Aunt Maxi had been going through some financial difficulties. Tourism had all but stopped. The entire town needed a complete makeover, which wouldn't happen for years, and she simply couldn't afford to keep the big house.

She lived alone and found it much easier for her to sell and downsize. One problem, she sold it to Patrick's father, and honestly I thought they'd taken her for a ride. I'd held a grudge for years because I truly thought it was because they'd stolen her dream house, not that she'd sold it. She'd not told me that little bit of information. It was Patrick who did after I'd moved back to Honey Springs.

He still owned the house and was even living there. When we got married, I couldn't bring myself to live in his house, and that's why we'd decided to stay in my cabin. My sweet little cabin. I sighed, looking back over his shoulder.

"Your mom called me and asked to meet with me at the house. I asked if it was about you, and she said, 'In a roundabout way,' but wouldn't tell me. I freaked out and met her there only to find her with Caspian Blackwood, walking our property." Patrick picked up his toothbrush after I stepped out of the way so he could finish getting ready for bed.

"Mom didn't mention a word." I shook my head and picked up the hairbrush to run it through my curly black hair. I stared at myself in the mirror when Patrick bent down to spit in the sink, and my blue eyes looked so tired. Dull.

"She said she didn't want to even bring it up unless you were willing to part with it because it's a source of pain for you and her too." Patrick pointed out the knockdown drag-out fights my mom and I would have on the phone when I was staying there all those summers and she would make me come home early.

She thought it was because Aunt Maxi wanted me to stay, when Aunt Maxi never had a hand in the decision. Of course, I loved her and wanted to spend all the time I could with her, but it was my love for Patrick that kept me there summer after summer.

"What did you tell Mom and Caspian?" I asked as I left our bathroom, grabbing my robe on the way out.

"I told her I had to talk to you." He followed me out. He'd already had his robe on, and we walked down the steps to finish off our nightly ritual of letting the dogs out one last time, making the coffee so the timer could go off at four a.m., and putting out a fresh outfit in the laundry room so I could get ready in the morning.

Sassy and Pepper's nails danced on the old hardwood floors as they both anticipated going potty for the last time tonight.

Patrick and I sat down in the rocking chairs while the dogs ran off the porch. I wasn't sure if it was the actual nip in the late-spring air, the idea of me losing Aunt Maxi's house due to a big development, or knowing Leandar's killer was still on the loose that gave me a deep chill.

"Can you hand me the blanket?" I asked Patrick since the blanket was draped over the rocking chair he was sitting in.

"What are your thoughts, honey?" He stood up and took the blanket, laid it on my lap, and pushed the edges up around my legs.

"Are you tucking me in?" I teased. "Or buttering me up to agree to the development?"

"I only have your best interest at heart. I'm not tied to the house like you are. When we offered it to Aunt Maxi for supercheap a couple of years ago, she didn't even want it back."

Patrick was right.

Aunt Maxi had long since moved on and even gone on to acquire a lot more houses that she rented out for extra income and to add the boardwalk to her financial portfolio with ownership of a few buildings there. The Bean Hive being one of them.

"What did Caspian propose?" I asked.

"He said the other landowners had agreed to sell their property. Not only is his company paying top dollar, the landowners and any inherited family members will have lifetime membership to the country club," Patrick said. "It also includes all activities. Plus a pool."

"You aren't a golfer," I said.

"I might learn. It could be good for business." He shrugged. "Don't business-people like to golf?"

"I don't know. I don't. And you don't even like a pool." I pointed out the fact I could barely get him to the lake to dip his toes in, much less get his entire body in a pool of clean water.

"He mentioned something about holiday parties and even the breakfast with Santa event." Patrick was using my favorite time of the year against me.

"You dirty dog," I teased and leaned over his way to catch a kiss.

I pulled away and saw there was an inherent strength on his face. It was the look he always wore when he had a decision to make and knew it was the right decision but wasn't willing to do anything unless it was good for me.

It was the exact same look when I suggested we dress up for Halloween as a bride and groom and really get married in the hospitality room of the Cocoon Inn. The same look when I wouldn't budge on moving. The same look when the cabin caught fire and we had to rebuild, and when I had the harebrained idea of buying the building next to the Bean Hive and making a roastery.

That was our only investment property besides Aunt Maxi's old house.

"They got a twenty-seven-hole golf course planned that'll appeal to all skill levels. They will have an indoor 4k ultra-HD gold simulator that'll allow golfers to play nine or eighteen holes of some of the most famous golf courses around the world with a virtual driving range," Patrick said as he slowly rocked back and forth. "That will allow people to host golf parties indoors. They will offer golf lessons and leagues for all ages."

"It sounds like they got the whole golf thing down pat." I could admit it did sound good.

"There's an event center," he whispered. "Before you jump all over how Babette Cliff will go out of business, Caspian has already talked to her about having two event centers."

"My goodness, he's got it all covered." I wanted to be disappointed in the big development, but I knew it was growth, and we needed to continue to drive tourism to Honey Springs, or we could find ourselves in Aunt Maxi's shoes from years ago.

"Babette is on board. It's going to bring a lot of jobs to Honey Springs. Some of our citizens will get those jobs and not have to drive a few hours to the city to work." Patrick was born and bred in Honey Springs.

His entire heart and mind were invested in the town.

"Is it really the right time to do anything with Blackwood Associates?" I asked Patrick. "I mean, Caspian does have a very good motive to have killed Leandar, and the last thing we need to do is get in bed with him on a bad investment right before he goes to prison."

"I get it." He planted his hands on the arms of the rocking chair and pushed himself up to stand. The dogs were ready to go inside. "Take time and think about it. We have time. Caspian has left town, and he said he'd be back in a week. He would like to meet with you and me."

He stood over me and bent down, giving me a kiss on the top of my head.

"Are you going to bed?" he asked. The moon hung over his right shoulder, and the silhouette of the woods to the side of the house filled the landscape.

"I think I'll stay up and read for a while." It sounded good, and I was going to do that until after Patrick had gone inside with the dogs and left me out there drowning in my own thoughts.

Caspian Blackwood had left town? Did Spencer Shepard let him leave town? Had he already excused Caspian as a suspect?

Instead of wasting my time sitting outside wondering about Caspian, I knew I could run by the sheriff's office in the morning to ask Gloria Dei what she knew.

She always gave in to a good scone temptation.

CHAPTER ELEVEN

There were so many questions I had when I finally fell asleep after Patrick told me about Caspian coming to him to see if he'd be interested in selling Aunt Maxi's old house. The fact Caspian had left town gnawed at me. I didn't even get an ounce of shut-eye.

Or at least, it didn't seem like it when the four a.m. alarm went off.

My bike was still at the boardwalk and the dinghy boat was still on the beach across the road from my cabin, leaving me and Pepper to take the car.

Pepper was extra excited to be going to the coffee shop with me. The temperatures were warm that morning, and even though it was dark, Pepper still wanted to stick his head out the window.

Instead of getting lost in my head, I flipped the radio on so I could at least get into the mindset of getting the coffee shop ready to open, then I'd let myself go over all of my theories.

It sounded good, but my plans changed.

Bunny and Aunt Maxi had beaten me to the coffee shop. They were already sitting down with the whiteboard at one of the café tables, going over the clues, when Pepper and I walked in.

"We've already let the puppy out." Bunny didn't even look up from the whiteboard. She had the puppy resting in her lap and the dry-erase marker in her hand. "And we got all the donuts, quiche, breakfast pies, and coffee started."

"And the coffee station and tea station all ready," Aunt Maxi followed up and gave Pepper the treat on the table she'd apparently anticipated giving him before we'd gotten there. "I missed you yesterday," she said then talked baby talk to him. His little tail wiggled and wagged.

"How was the dinner cruise?" Aunt Maxi asked before I could even hang my bag up on the coatrack.

"You won't believe what we ate off." I took the Bean Hive apron and tied it loosely around my neck and waist. "The bone china."

"Well, I reckon they needed to get some good use out of it." Aunt Maxi cackled.

I quickly checked the industrial coffeepots I needed to take down to Cocoon Inn for their hospitality suite. They were brewing, and soon I'd need to walk them down there unless I could get one of the two sleuths to do it.

"What are you two conjuring up?" I asked and poured some kibble into Pepper's bowl and the puppy's.

The puppy was eager to follow Pepper around and happily started to eat the puppy kibble after seeing his bowl next to Pepper's.

"We are trying to figure out what on earth is going on around here. Or did you forget there was a murder?" Aunt Maxi asked.

"Did you find anything out last night?" Bunny followed her, neither one giving me the opportunity to talk before they darted questions at me.

"Did you know Blackwood Associates is looking at the house and the lakefront property to move the development to your old house?" I poured myself a cup of coffee, taking the opportunity to enjoy it while the puppy was eating.

Pepper would be fine to relax for a bit after he ate. The puppy was a different story. He had to go outside to pee every time he ate.

"And the owner, Caspian, has left town?" I asked and looked over the board. They'd not written anything else down. It looked the same as yesterday.

"Does that mean he's not a suspect?" Bunny asked, peering over her reading glasses perched on the tip of her nose.

"I don't know, but I plan on stopping by to see Gloria Dei at some point today," I told them.

"Then I better go get the apple hand pies in the oven." Bunny groaned as she got up from the table. "She's a sucker for one or two of your hand pies, but apple is her favorite. Luckily, I saw some in the freezer."

Bunny waddled across the floor, her thick black-soled comfort shoes creaking underneath her.

"Did you know?" I asked Aunt Maxi because she seemed so quiet.

"I heard some rumblings about it, and I called your mama because I knew she was going to try to get some business after Leandar died." I detected a hint of censure in her tone.

"Spill it," I told her with easy defiance.

"When I was at the emergency meeting, before you got there," she said, laying out the timeline, "I was talking to Vicky Delaney. She was telling me how she was shelving some reference books by the conference room at the library while she was working, and the Realtor Association was having a meeting. Vicky told me she heard Ursula Scott and Penny talking about Ursula calling Leandar's secretary to see what he had on the books."

"No wonder Mama has a vested interest in the property. I bet she went to all of the listings over there, which are selling for a pretty penny, and all Caspian had to do was give them a few thousand more than their asking price in order for him to buy up all the houses." I lifted the cup of coffee to my lips.

"But there's one holdout." Aunt Maxi grinned. "Patrick Cane. And that house has the best view of all the properties, including the initial development property on Lake Honey Springs."

"But why did Spencer allow Caspian to leave town?" I took the dry-erase marker Bunny had set on the table when she'd gotten up and wrote little bullet points under his name.

"It would make sense he wasn't a suspect, but with all the evidence of how deep he and Leandar were with the development, I could only imagine how much Caspian has lost. Think of the cost of all the work he's already put into it." Aunt Maxi was talking about money.

I wrote down "greed" and "money" under his name.

"Not only that, but his reputation," Aunt Maxi pointed out. "He's a man with a big ego."

"Ego." I wrote it down too.

"I also heard Caspian put all of his retirement money into this development because he had planned to move to Honey Springs and fully retire, but if the gig went south, then he had no money to retire. It would make sense for him to try to salvage something by moving the development to a piece of property that has already gone through all the environmental testing." As I rambled on and on, the thoughts in my head spilled out as to why Caspian should still be a suspect.

"If he did do it, don't you think he'd not try to move the development?" Aunt Maxi had suggested Caspian would try to get out of town as fast as he could, which he had.

"Or do the complete opposite because he thinks he's untouchable." My eyes gazed at the clock behind the counter. It was already five o'clock, and the puppy needed to go potty. "I'll be back. I have to take the coffee down to Cocoon Inn and let the puppy go potty."

"No. No," Aunt Maxi insisted and jumped to her feet. "I'll take the coffee and let the puppy out. In fact, I'll just take the puppy with me today. I have some errands to run, and then I'll stop by Central Park to let him get some exercise."

She walked over to the coat-tree.

"Can I use one of Pepper's leash?" she asked and pointed to the several on the hooks of the coat-tree.

"Of course you can." I smiled even though she was already halfway to the door with one of them clipped on the puppy.

"I'd say 'bye' to Pepper, but he's already asleep." She snickered, nodding to Pepper's bed where he was rolled over on his back with his round and full belly pointing up at the ceiling.

"You try to find out what all you can about Caspian Blackwood and Blackwood Associates." She gave me a task. "Since we did all the prep work to open this morning. You're our only shot at getting this whole thing figured out."

"Do you want Patrick and me to sell the house?" I asked her, stopping her in her tracks.

She bent down and picked up the puppy before she turned.

She stared me straight in the eye. "Roxy Bloom," she said, poking her heart. "This is where our memories lie. Not in any structure made of bricks and sticks. Right here is where I remember our summers together. If it weren't for right here"—she jabbed herself one last time before she gestured her little finger around the coffee shop—"this here wouldn't be, and you wouldn't either. And for that, I'd never go back. Sell the house."

It was her way of telling me how losing her dream house actually made her dreams and mine come true. Her dream of me living in Honey Springs as well as my dream of owning a coffee shop—and what I'd thought was a lost dream, being married to Patrick Cane.

While I went back to refill my mug, I quickly sent Patrick a text to let him know I'd like to talk to Caspian Blackwood myself. Just me and Caspian. In the end, I would give up the house, but this was my chance to physically lay eyes on and talk to the man who had a great deal of motive to kill Leandar.

On my way back to the whiteboard, I remembered all the information Kirk had told me about Danielle. It had not been lost on me. She was more of a suspect than ever, and the fact that she lied to me had lit a fire that put her on my list of people to go back and question.

As I sat at the window bar, my eyes periodically darted between the screen of my phone and the breathtaking scene unfolding outside the window. Lake Honey Springs had slowly started to come to life as the first light of dawn crept over the horizon, casting a myriad of colors across the sky. The sun began its ascent, painting the world in shades of pink, orange, and gold, its rays reflecting off the glassy surface of the lake and creating a shimmering kaleidoscope of light.

There were a few customers who came through the door. Bunny was able to handle them while I continued to search the internet on my phone for anything and everything I could find on Caspian Blackwood's personal and professional life.

The stillness of the early morning was gradually replaced by the soft sounds of the world awakening. The gentle lapping of waves against the shore mingled with the distant calls of birds as they began their morning serenade. The rustle of leaves and the murmur of the wind whispered through the trees, adding to the serene soundtrack of the awakening day.

Inside the coffee shop, the comforting aroma of freshly brewed coffee filled the air, and the gentle hum of the espresso machine provided a soothing backdrop to the peaceful ambiance. Bunny's shoes creaked as she moved behind the counter, the faint clinking of cups and saucers punctuating the quiet atmosphere.

As I continued to scroll through my phone, I delved deeper into the history of Caspian Blackwood and his company, Blackwood Associates. My fingers flew across the screen, uncovering articles and testimonials that painted a picture of a powerful, influential figure whose business dealings were not without controversy.

Caspian's personal life was as carefully curated as his professional one. He was married to a beautiful and equally ambitious woman, and together they had formed a powerful partnership. Their opulent home was a testament to their success, filled with exquisite art, luxurious furnishings, and all the trappings of wealth from what I read in a *Forbes* magazine clip where they'd been featured.

Caspian Blackwood's success as a land developer was partly due to his ability to operate in the gray areas of the law and exploit loopholes to his advantage. While not all his deals were inherently illegal, some of them were ethically questionable and skirted the boundaries of what was considered acceptable.

I continued to look out the window at Lake Honey Springs, and despite the beauty of the sunrise and the serenity of my surroundings, I felt a growing unease as I read about Blackwood's history.

Questions swirled through my mind, and I began to wonder about the true intentions behind the development of the country club and the potential impact it could have on the picturesque landscape I loved so much.

Wetlands rezoning was one of Caspian's most notorious deals that involved the rezoning of a protected wetland area.

Through his connections with local officials, he managed to have the area's environmental status reclassified, allowing him to drain the wetlands and build a luxury housing development on the land. This had severe consequences for the local ecosystem, resulting in the displacement of countless plant and animal species. Was this as illegal as it was immoral?

For each search that proved to be another strike against Blackwood Associates, there were double examples of the good the company was doing by giving back to environmental groups and even various charities.

Another controversial deal I considered shady had to do with gentrification and displacement of residents of a low-income housing complex with the intention of converting it into high-end condominiums. While the project was financially successful, it led to the displacement of hundreds of longtime residents who could no longer afford to live in their own community. Caspian had little regard for the social consequences of his actions, focusing solely on the profits to be made. Watching the video archives of the local news where this took place nearly broke my heart over the homelessness it'd caused.

But the bribery and corruption charges against Blackwood Associates had never stuck, even though Caspian was known to engage in bribery and corruption to secure deals and fast-track approvals for his projects.

There were even charges brought on the company that it claimed and accounted for lavish gifts and under-the-table payments to officials and regulators, ensuring that his projects would receive favorable treatment and bypass environmental and zoning regulations that were dropped.

"What's this?" I couldn't help but take an interest in another claim called "land grabbing" in which Caspian had been accused of acquiring land through underhanded means.

In one instance, he took advantage of a legal loophole to obtain the land rights to a small family farm that had been passed down for generations. The family was forced to leave their ancestral home, while Caspian turned the land into yet another lucrative development.

Immediately, my mind went to Raffery Featherstone.

Had there been an agreement between Raffery and Caspian? More than just Raffery selling farmland in order to invest?

The coffee shop traffic was starting to pick up, and I had to jot down all the things I'd discovered on the internet in just the short amount of time I'd sat there. Bullet point by bullet point, I listed everything I'd learned.

I took one more sip to wash away the thoughts and looked back out the window.

The sun was high in the sky, casting its warm glow on the lake. I resolved to delve further into this mystery and uncover the truth about Caspian Blackwood and his company.

The peaceful sunrise over Lake Honey Springs served as a reminder of the natural beauty that was at stake, and I knew that I couldn't stand idly by while it was threatened.

CHAPTER TWELVE

There'd been a lull between the breakfast rush and the lunch crowd, leaving me some time to take Pepper for a walk and make a phone call to Jessica. Not that I didn't trust Kirk, but Jessica would have no reason to lie.

"Do you mind watching the shop while I take Pepper for a walk?" I asked Bunny, even though I knew she wouldn't mind. "And when I get back, I want to hear all about your anniversary celebration."

She blushed. It was so cute.

As I strolled along the sun-soaked boardwalk, the vibrant midday bustle of people, laughter, and music filled the air. Boaters cruised by on the glistening lake, their laughter and cheerful conversations mingling with the distant hum of outboard motors and happy boating tunes. The weather was absolutely perfect, with a gentle breeze and a clear blue sky that seemed to stretch on forever.

Pepper trotted happily by my side, his eyes gleaming with excitement as he sniffed the myriad of scents wafting on the breeze. I held my phone to my ear, chatting with Jessica about the recent happenings at the Be Happy Spa.

"So, you're saying you haven't had any dealings with Danielle at the spa?" I asked, seeking clarification. I'd told her everything Danielle had told me.

Even the story about how Danielle had run into Jessica.

"That's right, Roxy," Jessica replied. "I didn't run into her on the beach either.

But we did have a brief conversation on the ferry ride over about a week ago. Nothing substantial, though."

"Nothing substantial" from Jessica was a loaded statement. Jessica was too nice. She didn't realize just how much she told about herself when talking to people.

As we talked, I couldn't help but feel a sense of relief that Jessica and Kirk weren't involved in whatever was going on with Danielle.

"Plus, we've never stayed overnight here. And Biscuit hasn't either." She only confirmed that Danielle had made it all up.

"Was Biscuit with you when you were on the ferry?" I asked.

"Yes, and you know, now that I think about it..." There was a pause on Jessica's end. "She did ask me about Biscuit's food because she was thinking about getting a puppy."

That part was true. I remembered Shelley and Shanda telling me how Danielle had come in there, mentioning she'd wanted to adopt the puppy she'd named Jessie.

Was Jessie short for Jessica? Had Danielle really put that much thought into it?

The boardwalk was alive with activity, and the energy of the crowd was almost palpable. Kids darted around, laughing and playing, while couples strolled hand in hand, enjoying the beautiful day.

I glanced down at Pepper, who was wagging his tail, clearly enjoying our leisurely walk.

"Oh, Roxy, I actually I need to go," Jessica interrupted. "The man is here about the raccoons at the spa. You know, raccoons have been getting into our trash, and Crissy isn't happy about having to pick it all up. I need to handle this situation."

"Of course, no problem," I said. "Good luck with the raccoon situation. I'll talk to you later."

We said our goodbyes, and I ended the call. As I looked up from my phone, I suddenly smacked right into a solid figure. I stumbled back, my heart racing, and found myself face-to-face with Raffery Featherstone.

"Raffery!" I exclaimed, my mind racing back to the red paint I'd found on the edge of the dinghy. Could he be the one who took the boat? Was he involved in something far more sinister?

His eyes met mine, and I couldn't help but search for answers in his expression. Little did I know, the encounter would be the beginning of a series of events that would lead to the unraveling of a mystery that went far deeper than I could have ever imagined.

"Thank you so much for last night. The dinner cruise was delicious, but those dishes." I gushed. "I have to admit, I was going to try to get those from the estate sale."

"That," he scoffed. We were standing in front of Wild and Whimsy Antiques, where he looked as if he was about to go in. "I really wish there'd been something to celebrate."

"Your son is home." I smiled, knowing everyone loved to talk about their kids.

"Yes. We are happy he is home, but it doesn't help us leave him a legacy, which is what my wife and I had planned on doing with the investment in the country-club development." He frowned.

The more he talked, the more he showed an even bigger motive to have killed Leandar.

"Speaking of your son, he told me about how you love to jug fish." "Love" might've been stretching it, but it gave me a way to bring up the night of Leandar's murder—or morning, however one chose to see it.

"I do. I love everything about Lake Honey Springs. So much so that I wanted to share it with the world." He was still talking about the development.

"Yeah. The night of Leandar's murder, I understand you were jug fishing," I said.

"I told you, I love it, and it relaxes me. It was after the meeting where the mayor dropped the bomb." Raffery's demeanor changed as did the tone of his voice.

It was more stiff, hard.

"Surely you knew the development was going south. Didn't Caspian tell you, as an investor, what was going on?" I asked.

"Are you kidding me?" His brows shot up. "All he would say was how everything was going to work out. I should've known when he got Leandar involved that the deal would go sideways."

"Why do you say that?" I wondered.

"Look around, Roxy." He flung his hands out. "Do you see any other land development happening in Honey Springs? We have all this lakefront property. Leandar has never—" He stopped talking and then corrected himself. "Had never gotten any deal inked. He was a good talker and could probably talk you into turning your coffee shop into some nightclub in ten minutes if he got in front of you."

"I never had to deal with him. I guess since my Aunt Maxi owns the coffee shop and my mom is now a Realtor." I was responding to the thoughts in my head out loud.

"I was hoping when your mom took over the real estate office downtown after…" He shook his head. "You know what happened, so I don't need to bring that up, but the facts are the facts. Leandar made too many mistakes and talked a good talk that he couldn't walk, which ultimately got him killed."

"Yes. He did. Back to your jug fishing." I stopped him when I saw him take a step toward the door of Wild and Whimsy. "Did you happen to use Andrew Noro's dinghy boat?"

"Why would I do that?" He snarled like it was the silliest thing in the world.

"Because it has some red paint on the edges." I gulped, not really sure if it was red paint or blood. "I saw it the other day when I used it. And Danielle mentioned it."

"Mentioned what?" He interrupted me and jerked upright, standing over me.

"She said someone had used it the night Leandar was killed, and I wondered if you might've broken down. You borrowed it." I could feel the tension coming off him as I walked the fine line between us.

"What are you saying, Roxanne?" It was never good when someone used my full name, especially when that someone was twice my size and towered over me. "Are you accusing me of killing Leandar?"

"I'm not doing anything. I'm trying to find out who was on the lake the night he was murdered, and if anyone who might've been out there saw something." I tried not to swallow or shift my eyes away from him.

"There you are!" Bev Teagarden must've seen us from inside the antique shop because she swung the door open and greeted us. "Is everything okay?" She found herself outside standing next to me and Raffery, still in our stare down.

"We are fine and finished," Raffery said in a deep Southern tone. "It was good to see you, Roxy. Tell your mama and them I said hello."

And with one hard nod, he not only walked away but also didn't answer my question.

Bev fidgeted. "Is everything okay?" she leaned in and whispered once Raffery had gone into her shop.

"It's fine. I was asking Raffery about the development. That's all." I offered her a smile to help her relax.

"Good. Isn't it a shame?" She shook her head. "But we are hoping you do want to sell Maxine's old house. It'll be so good for Honey Springs to have something new to bring in more tourism. As it is, I'm going to have to pay a small fortune for the Featherstones' bone china I was hoping to score at the auction."

"I wanted those too." My voice ticked up. "That's why he's here?" I avoided the topic of Aunt Maxi's old house.

I wasn't going to make any decisions about that property until I got in front of Caspian Blackwood.

"Yes." Bev held up both hands with her fingers crossed. "Wish me luck I can get him down to a reasonable price."

"Good luck," I told her as she turned and hurried back inside the shop. "Why is he selling the bone china if he's not moving?" I asked myself and decided to worry about that at a later time.

I had to get to the dinghy boat and run it back across the water so I could question Danielle about all of her lies.

Luckily, the day was nice, and a brisk walk would do me good if I'd not been too preoccupied by the conversation I'd had with Raffery on the boardwalk. It wasn't so much the conversation but the change in his body language that threw me off. And the fact that he needed to sell the family china now that he wasn't moving into the development seemed a little odd to me too.

Pepper was really good at being off the leash, so he ran around and sniffed the area, staying close to me.

The dinghy was exactly where I'd left it. And in the daylight, I could clearly see it wasn't paint. It was a bloody handprint.

My jaw tensed. My heart beat, and I knew what I had to do.

"Spencer, I think you need to come to the crime scene," I told him when he answered the phone. "I've got a dinghy boat here, and it sure does look like it has a bloody handprint on it."

Spencer babbled a few things about why I was at the crime scene when it was still considered a crime scene, but instead of wanting to hear about it, he then told me to forget it, and he'd be there in a minute because he was downtown, which really was about five minutes away.

The sound of hard footsteps, crunching leaves, and snapping branches were heard before I saw him, but from the time between each step, I knew it was him rushing to the beach area.

"Do I even want to know how you know this is here?" he asked, bending down to look at the print.

Pepper was excited to see Spencer. Spencer bent down to pet Pepper. Pepper sat like a good boy, and I took the opportunity to clip his leash on him.

"I'm going to tell you anyways because I think Danielle Quillen is the killer." The words fell out of my mouth as he slowly twisted his neck and looked up at me from underneath his sheriff's hat.

"I'm listening." He dragged his bag closer to the dinghy and opened it. He put gloves on his hands. He took out all sorts of baggies for the samples he was taking from the bloody handprint.

I told him how I'd gone to see Danielle and how odd it was that she'd not come into the Bean Hive the day after Leandar's murder.

"She came in every morning before that, so it was odd. You know, noticeable." I shrugged. "The day Leandar was murdered"—I prepared myself for the repercussions I was about to get because Spencer wasn't going to like that I'd kept this from him—"Leandar came into the coffee shop when he saw her sitting through the window while he passed by on the boardwalk."

"I'm listening." Spencer must've known there was a doozy coming his way. He stood up and used the tip of his forefinger to tip the hat up enough just so he could have a clear view of my face.

"He threatened to expose her if she didn't keep her mouth shut, and he was talking about the development." I tugged my lips together.

"And you felt like this was something you didn't need to tell me. I mean, there was a threat to expose something she'd done, making it a clear motive for her not to want that secret out, which would make her the number one suspect, not Caspian Blackwood." His jaw tensed, and he stared at me as if he wanted some sort of explanation.

I gave in to the awkward pause I tried so desperately not to fall for.

"You told me to keep my ears open, and I went to see her because I knew of the exchange and…" I gulped, showing my fear.

"You knew it was a bad idea. And you still did it." He shook his head. "Keeping your ears open is just that. You're good at gossip. That's why people love going to the Bean Hive. I didn't ask you to put yourself in front of a killer."

My head was stuck on me being good at gossip. Clearly, he didn't know me, and I never gossiped. Yes, there was a lot of hearsay and ho-hums going on at the coffee shop, and I admit I was listening, but I never said an ill word or lie or even participated in those conversations.

Now, if it was my immediate family, I might've opened my mouth a time or two, but never to the customers.

"You listen for any clues, like someone who is being threatened by the victim, and you call me." He was laying out the way things were supposed to go like I was an idiot or something. "Then we go and talk to the person who was threatened by the now-dead victim and had a motive."

There were a few minutes of him cursing under his breath, looking at the boat, cursing some more, bending down, and looking across the lake before he stood up, and then he glared at me.

"I'm sorry. I know you don't gossip, but this case…" He shook his head with a look of disgust on his face. "The mayor is on me about it. This was a very serious deal with a lot of investors who are going to lose a lot of money."

"There's hope they won't." I hated to mention it to him, but I could clearly see this was also on his personal radar as much as it was mine. "I have a meeting that's being set up with Caspian Blackwood to talk about selling him Aunt Maxi's old house. The land around it is filled with houses that owners are happy to sell and that has already been developed."

The land had already gone through the entire process of being surveyed by environmentalists and all that. Like I'd said, it was the best view of Lake Honey Springs.

"I know that's going to be hard for you." Spencer showed his soft side. "But it still doesn't help matters that you have been sitting on this evidence. Do I even want to know how long this boat has been sitting here? In the elements?"

"Probably not. I thought it was paint until I came back to drive it back over to the cabin Danielle is renting." I glanced across the lake where you could see the little cabin.

"Paint?" Spencer closed his eyes and clenched his jaw as if he were preparing himself to hear what I was talking about.

"Yeah. I was on the Featherstone dinner cruise the other night and Caldwell, his son…" I told him the story.

"I know Caldwell." He rolled his wrist as if to tell me to hurry along and finish the story.

"He and I were talking about jug fishing, and he mentioned how his dad loved to jug fish and told me that Raffery had just gone out the night before."

"As in the night, or morning hours, that Leandar was murdered?" Spencer asked for clarity.

"Yes. Then I thought what if this was paint, which it's clearly not." I knew it now. "Because Caldwell told me how Raffery used red paint on his jugs."

There was no need to explain to Spencer about why Raffery would paint the jugs because everyone around here already was very familiar with jug fishing.

"Raffery will be so mad if he hears you think he killed Leandar." Spencer should've told me this a few minutes ago. His jaw dropped open. "Geez, Roxy, don't tell me you confronted Raffery Featherstone."

"Okay." I shrugged and caught sight of a boat moving down the lake, going toward the beach in front of the cabin Danielle had rented. "I won't tell you."

"If you mess up this case," he started to say then turned when the boat motor got louder as it approached. "What on earth is going on?"

"That's Danielle with her stuff." I pointed my chin when I noticed Danielle, her hands full of bags and a suitcase, walking to the dock where the dinghy had been tied up. "She's leaving town."

"Who is driving the speedboat?" Spencer asked and frantically looked at the evidence he'd just collected. "This is going to have to be enough."

Quickly he gathered all the tubes, baggies, and whatever else he'd collected and threw it in his duffel, zipping it closed and tossing it in the dinghy.

"What are you doing?" I asked.

"You got photos of this, right?" He rolled up the rope that was tied to the front of the small boat, though I'd not had to tie it to anything because I'd dragged it up on the beach.

There was only one reason to toss the loose rope inside. To drive it.

"Yes, but are you going to go over there?" I asked as if Spencer standing in it didn't give me the clue.

"I'm going to go stop her from leaving." He sat down on the small bench.

When he turned back to pull the engine to life, I grabbed Pepper and hopped in.

"Get out!" he yelled over the hum of the motor. "Get out! This is official business."

I sat down next to him on the small bench and crossed my arms.

"I'm not moving. I need answers from her, too, as her lawyer." I knew that was really going to throw him for a zinger.

"Her what?" he screamed with fury in his eyes. "Please don't tell me you offered services to her."

Pepper hung over the side with his ears flapping in the wind, not a care in the world.

I stared straight ahead, not saying a word. In reality, she'd not become a client, but now I wanted answers. She'd not only dragged the entire town into this mess but also brought Kirk into it. Even though sending him to jail for a murder would be satisfying, making him the scapegoat certainly was not.

CHAPTER THIRTEEN

My heart pounded in my chest as the dinghy bounced across the water, its outboard motor roaring with determination. Sheriff Spencer Shepard gripped the handle, his jaw set and eyes focused on the speedboat ahead of us. Danielle, now the number one suspect in Leandar's murder, was making a desperate attempt to flee town with all her luggage.

"Can't this thing go any faster?" I shouted over the wind and the noise of the motor.

Spencer shook his head, his expression grim. "We're pushing it to the limit, Roxy! Just hold on!"

The wind whipped through my hair as we raced after Danielle's speedboat, which was slicing through the water like a hot knife through butter. She was supposed to be in town, cooperating with the investigation, but her sudden flight was a blatant admission of guilt.

As the distance between us and Danielle's speedboat began to shrink, I couldn't help but think back to all the signs we'd missed. The way she'd shifted the blame and motives onto others, skillfully manipulating us to focus on anyone but her. But now, her true colors were showing.

My knuckles turned white as I gripped the side of the dinghy, my gaze locked on the fleeing speedboat. The adrenaline coursed through my veins, fueling my determination to catch Danielle and bring her to justice.

"Roxy, I need you to call for backup," Spencer shouted over the roar of the engines. "We can't let her get away!"

I fumbled for my phone, my fingers shaking with nerves and excitement as I dialed the number. "This is Roxy Bloom," I said, struggling to make myself heard over the chaos. "I'm in a dinghy boat with Spencer, and we're in pursuit of Danielle. She's fleeing on a speedboat, and we need immediate backup!"

Big Bib, on the other end of the line, acknowledged my call and promised assistance. I could see Danielle glance back at us, her eyes wide with fear. The sight only fueled my determination to see her captured.

"I called Big Bib!" I screamed through the sounds of the very active chase. "He's going to jump in a boat."

I knew if I called him, he was already on the marina and would stop the speedboat faster than the local coast guards.

Spencer maneuvered the dinghy expertly, taking advantage of every opportunity to close the gap between us and Danielle. The sound of another speedboat approaching filled the air, and I knew it was Big Bib on his way.

"We've got her now," Spencer said, a fierce resolve in his voice. "She's not getting away this time."

As the chase continued, I steeled myself for whatever lay ahead. The stakes were higher than ever, and I was ready to do whatever it took to bring Danielle to justice and ensure that Leandar's murder would not go unpunished.

"What are you doing, man?" The driver of the speed boat Danielle was in had slowed. He was screaming at Big Bib.

Big Bib didn't say a word. His lips were so tight, you couldn't even see them behind his beard. He nodded back to the dinghy boat and pointed.

"Danielle Quillen, I asked you not to leave town when I talked to you the other night. It sure does appear that you're leaving." Spencer flashed his badge to the other boat driver while Big Bib steadied the speedboat, allowing the dinghy to get closer.

"You can't keep me here." Danielle couldn't bring herself to look at Spencer or me.

When the dinghy got next to the boat, Spencer swung his leg over, planting his foot on the edge of the speedboat to keep us joined.

"I'm going to have to take you in for questioning for the murder of Leandar

Taylor." Spencer reached around his utility belt and unclipped the handcuffs. "You can either come with me willingly or not."

The cuffs clinked together as he wagged them in the air.

"You didn't say anything about a murder." The boat driver looked shocked. "I have no idea who this woman is. I met her at the bee farm yesterday, and she asked if I could come take her to the mainland to catch her ride to the airport."

The innocent bystander was flabbergasted.

"Thank you. I will need you to write all of your contact information down as well as give me your license. I'll need to snap a photo of it." Spencer pointed to Big Bib's boat when Danielle got up to get on the dinghy. "We are going to have Big Bib take us to the marina."

Big Bib didn't lose his manners. He walked to the edge of his boat closest to where Danielle was standing and offered her a hand.

"If you don't mind, hook up the dinghy to the back. I'm going to need to take it in for evidence even though the bloody handprint is mostly gone from the water and the little stunt you pulled." Spencer made no bones about it. He wasn't letting Danielle off easy.

Big Bib didn't ask any questions. He did what Spencer had asked him to do while Spencer took a photo of the speedboat driver's license and had the man write down his information in Spencer's little notebook he kept in his sheriff's uniform pocket.

"I told you I didn't do it." Danielle directed her statement to me when she crossed over from one boat to the other. "I thought you believed me."

"I did until I talked to Kirk," I said flatly and moved to Big Bib's boat once the dinghy was securely tied up. "I'm guessing you didn't think I talked to my ex."

"I'm sorry. But I didn't do it. I didn't," she insisted. "And I'm going to pay you to be my lawyer."

"I knew I should've pushed you overboard when I had the chance back at the beach," Spencer said. There was no joking tone to his voice. "You might's well all come down to the station, if that's the case."

"I didn't say I was going to take Danielle on as a client." My brows knotted when I glared at Danielle to see if I could read her body language, not really sure if I could trust her.

"Just talk to me when we get to the station. I'll tell you anything you want to know," she pleaded.

Spencer let the other boater leave and gave Big Bib the signal to go.

"You want to hear what I have to say," Danielle's voice was caught in the wind, barely able for me to hear. "Caspian Blackwood killed Leandar Taylor."

That was clear.

CHAPTER FOURTEEN

"Don't say another word," I told her once we got to the marina. "I'll meet you at the sheriff's department."

Pepper had nestled himself next to her, which told me she couldn't be all that bad. He was a good judge of character, and if he was comfortable with her right now, then I was going to take my sweet pup's lead.

I assured her she would be okay and I'd be right behind them. I only had to jump into my car that was parked in the parking lot of the boardwalk.

Quickly, I took Pepper back to the Bean Hive, and by the time I got there, Bunny Bowowski had already left for the day. Shanda was at the coffee bar when I walked in, and Shelley was with a customer.

"I'd love to watch Pepper. Do you want me to drive him home after I get off?" Shanda asked.

"If you don't mind. I'm not sure how long I'll be." I glanced at the puppy. "Just drop Jessie off too."

I didn't worry about checking in with Shelley because she was upselling the customer on buying a few of this morning's donuts, but I did move around behind the counter to grab some leftovers that were probably not going to sell this late at night.

Donuts and sheriff's department paired really well when I needed to get some answers.

With the donuts and some coffee, I jumped into my car and headed straight to the department, where I found my mama already in the interview room with Danielle.

"It's about time." Mama stood up, her hand firmly planted on Danielle's shoulder. "We've been waiting."

"You couldn't've been waiting too long." I glanced between the two and put the coffee and bag of donuts on top of the table. "What on earth are you doing here?"

"I called her. She's been so helpful with everything, and I trust her." Danielle was seeking comfort from anyone she could get it from. "I know she's your mom, and I sure could use a mom right now."

"That's great, but I'm going to need to talk to my client alone." I gave Danielle a hard look before I shifted it to Mom.

"Fine. But"—Mom lingered before she pulled the bag of donuts to her—"I'll leave you with one of these and go take the rest to butter up the staff." She winked, using the sales tactic she had cultivated to perfection with clients when she was showing their house for sale.

She would come to the Bean Hive and have me give her some fresh donuts that could be heated up in the oven of the house she was selling. She claimed it made the home smell amazing and homey, a big selling point because somehow it played mind games with the potential buyers.

And she let the interested buyers have one of the just-out-of-the-oven donuts. I didn't question her, and she didn't question how I did things, so it was fine.

I walked Mama out of the room and shut the door behind her.

"I'm sorry, Roxy. I am, but I was starting to get nervous when Caspian didn't come back like he said he was going to." Danielle started off the conversation, right off the bat answering the questions I had intended to ask.

"You already know he put all of his retirement into the development, but what you didn't know was the last development he had with Leandar went south. Like over-one-hundred-thousand-dollars south. Caspian told me if this deal with Leandar didn't make up for the money he'd lost the investors in the last go-round, then Leandar would never make another deal in his life." She cried as she told me the story.

I sat there, listening.

"After you saw Leandar in the Bean Hive threatening me..." She blinked. I could tell what she was about to say might throw me a little, so I sucked in a deep breath to prepare my facial features so they wouldn't appear to be shocked. "I met him later that day, and he tried to pay me off. He told me if I didn't say anything, he'd give me the shares he invested in the development because he said he was afraid for his life."

"I thought you said earlier he had threatened to expose you for some illegal dealings." I didn't go into too much detail. She knew what I was talking about.

"It wasn't really that. I mean, yes, he had some information about what some might consider immoral business decisions, but I can assure you, I've never done anything illegal. Just like the development here." She shook her head. "They could definitely build the country club. There's nothing illegal about doing it, but it would create a terrible situation for the environment of Lake Honey Springs. Illegal?" She continued to shake her head. "No. Immoral? I'd say yes. Not the right thing to do."

"Let me get this straight." I reached across the table and filled up two glasses with the water from the provided pitcher. I picked one up and took a drink before I walked one over to her. "Leandar knew he couldn't really hurt you with the information he deemed illegal, immoral, or whatever. He ended up trying to bribe you because he knew the consequences of his actions would be murder, and from Caspian?"

I continued to walk around the room so I could get some good oxygen to my brain. It always helped me think.

"I believe so," she agreed. "Caspian came to see me after the emergency meeting. He was the one who took the dinghy boat across to the land. It was late, and the ferry had stopped running. He said he would take the dinghy over, and he did. The next morning when I woke up, it was there, but he wasn't. I figured he'd driven it back over and caught the first ferry back."

This was information I could easily get from Big Bib if Caspian did take the ferry.

"Caspian is your alibi, not Jessica and Kirk or even poor Biscuit?" I asked.

She nodded.

"Caspian knew Kirk and Jessica from their investment. I'd never had any dealings with them, so he told me to say I was at the spa if anyone asked where

I was. He even gave me the receipts I produced for you." She frowned and picked up the glass of water with a shaky hand.

"What did the two of you talk about when he was at the cabin?" I asked.

"He told me about how Leandar had messed up again. He was a mess. He was drinking and brought the liquor with him. He said Leandar was going to be a dead man, and he couldn't stop it." She closed her eyes. Large tears dropped from them.

There was a box of tissues in the middle of the table along with the water pitcher. I reached across the table and got them for her. She plucked one out when I set the box down.

"He also told me I should get out of town because this was the second time I'd written a report where the development shouldn't've been built. Yesterday, when you came by, I was already planning to leave, but you stayed too long, and I didn't get a chance to get on the ferry. After you left, I took a walk to try and think what to do. I just so happened to find myself at the bee farm where the man with the boat and his family had docked to grab some fresh honey. I asked if I could get a ride from him in the morning, and I paid for their honey." She continued to shake her head and internally beat herself up as she cried.

"Did you hear from Caspian after he took the dinghy from the dock that night after the emergency meeting?" I asked, wondering if he admitted to her how he killed Leandar, and if he did, in fact, commit the murder.

"No. Like I said, he agreed to take the dinghy and bring it back the next day. I went to bed. I saw all the lights over there that morning, and that's when I saw the dinghy boat was back. I just figured Caspian brought the boat back and got a ride." Her timeline was off. "Do you think he used it to meet Leandar at the development and then..." She couldn't bring herself to say it.

"Someone jogging on the beach found Leandar that morning. It's safe to say Leandar had only one reason to be there." It was an assumption, but knowing Leandar, there was really only one thing that would get him out of bed to go to the development, and that was money. "To talk to someone who knew enough about the development to have a new idea of what to do with the news you delivered at the emergency meeting. Someone had to entice him enough to get him there."

It went without saying that Leandar couldn't resist a deal or making a deal happen, especially after a million-dollar deal had recently gone south.

The door of the interrogation room opened, and Spencer walked in with a file. He dropped it on the table and motioned for me to sit next to Danielle. I didn't.

"May I ask your client a few questions?" he asked me as I took a seat across from her.

"Sure." I leaned back into the chair and folded my hands in my lap. "I'll interrupt if I don't think you should answer these questions, Danielle."

My senses heightened and my mind raced like it used to when I would meet clients at a police station when they were about to be charged with something. As her lawyer, it was my job to ensure she was treated fairly, and I was prepared to intervene if necessary. Sheriff Spencer took his place at the end of the table, a stern expression on his face as he flipped through a folder containing information on the case.

"All right, Danielle," he began, his tone firm but not unkind. "I need you to walk me through your evening, starting from when Caspian Blackwood came to your cabin."

Danielle shifted uncomfortably in her seat, her voice shaky as she recounted the events of that night. "Caspian arrived around nine p.m., asking if he could use my dinghy to get back across the lake since he had missed the last ferry. I didn't see any harm in it, so I agreed and helped him get the dinghy ready."

Sheriff Spencer raised an eyebrow, his gaze intense as he pressed on with his questioning. "Did you notice anything unusual about Mr. Blackwood's behavior or appearance?"

Danielle hesitated for a moment before answering. "He seemed a bit anxious, maybe even a little frightened, but I didn't think much of it at the time."

"What happened after Mr. Blackwood left in the dinghy?" Spencer asked, leaning forward slightly.

Danielle swallowed hard, her voice barely above a whisper as she continued her account. "I went back inside the cabin and spent the rest of the evening there. I didn't see or hear anything out of the ordinary until the next morning when I saw all the flashing lights across the lake. The dinghy was back."

"Can you think of anyone who might have had a reason to harm Mr. Blackwood?"

Spencer's question seemed to catch Danielle off guard, and I could see the fear in her eyes as she considered her response.

Before she could answer, I quickly interjected, "My client is not obligated to speculate on the motives of others, Sheriff."

He nodded in acknowledgment, though his gaze remained fixed on Danielle. "Very well. Did you have any prior interactions or conflicts with Mr. Blackwood or his company, Blackwood Associates?"

Danielle nodded her head. "I've worked for him on a few projects."

"Did all of those projects pass your environmental tests?" he asked.

"All but the development here in Honey Springs and another one in Massachusetts." It was the first time I'd heard her name a development in another state that went south.

"Did Mr. Blackwood lose a lot of money because of that deal?" Spencer asked.

"I can't let her answer that. She doesn't know Mr. Blackwood's company's finances. She's subcontracted by him." I interrupted again and gave Spencer a "come on" look.

"Did Mr. Blackwood say anything to you about why he was on this side of the lake or what he had been doing earlier in the evening?" Spencer inquired, his voice tinged with suspicion.

Again, I interrupted before Danielle could respond. "My client has already told you everything she knows about Mr. Blackwood's activities that evening. Continuing down this line of questioning is not productive."

Sheriff Spencer sighed, his frustration evident as he closed the folder and leaned back in his chair. "All right, Roxy, I understand. But we need to get to the bottom of this."

"Then you need to be checking with Caspian Blackwood," I said, because it was apparent Spencer had gotten a lead or some information that made Caspian the reason for him to bring Danielle here.

"Can you please stand up?" he asked Danielle. She looked at me with a bit of confusion.

I nodded. She stood up and so did I.

Spencer walked over to us, standing about four inches taller than Danielle.

"Stand up as tall as you can, please." He was at least respectful of her, and she did everything he told her, even extending her arms out to the side.

He was obviously checking her arm-length span, and I wasn't sure why, but he had to have some reason.

"That's all for now. You can go back home. Just keep your phone on you and answer if I call." He turned and took the file off the table.

"Hold on," I told her and hurried out the door after him, stopping him in the hallway. "Spencer, what was that?"

"I'm letting her go." He shrugged, tucking the file up underneath his armpit.

"What about the blood?" I asked. "On the dinghy?"

"It's not Leandar's blood type. But it could be Caspian's. I've got a call into his lawyer about talking to him. While she has been in there, we had a warrant issued to search the cabin, but the Noros gave us full permission."

No wonder I had so much time with her inside before he came into the room.

"I'm not sure when Caspian will be back in town, but I do know we found blood on the dock where Danielle was staying on the island." Spencer wasn't convinced the killer had taken the dinghy to the development, killed Leandar, and then took the dinghy back.

"You let her go pretty easy." I had to get to the root of why he'd just let Danielle go without even telling her to stay in town.

"Because Kevin gave me his final autopsy, and there's literally zero sand on Leandar except for the backside of his clothes. Not a speck on the bottom of his shoes or even inside his shoes." Spencer and I both knew that no matter how hard you tried or what shoes you had on, the heels of your shoes always kicked up sand into the back of your shoes.

"Wait." My eyes lowered. I slightly turned my head. "Are you saying someone placed Leandar there?"

His silence was all I needed to know the answer.

"There's a murder crime scene somewhere," I said, almost in disbelief.

"And my investigation just got a little more complicated." His jaw tensed. "Danielle couldn't carry Leandar or wasn't tall enough to hit him with the blow to the head that actually killed him."

"That's why you had her stand up," I said, thinking that was a really great observation, something I'd not come up against in my past life as a lawyer.

He continued to stare at me.

"What?" I asked just as my phone rang. "It's Patrick. Hold that thought."

I turned my head slightly to take his call.

"Can I call you back?" I asked him.

"Caspian Blackwood is in town, and we are going to go meet at the house. Can you come?" he asked.

"Caspian is in town?" My head swung back around and looked at Spencer. "And he's at Aunt Maxi's old house right now?"

"Are you sure you're okay?" Patrick asked with a worried tone.

"Yes." Spencer gave me the double-guns gesture with his fingers. "Go talk to him," he mouthed.

"Yes. I'm fine. I'll be there in a few." I hung up the phone with Patrick. "I don't like bringing my husband into this."

"You agreed to snoop around, and his lawyer sure didn't tell me he was in town." Spencer took his keys out of his pocket. "Ready?"

"Ready? You're not going with me." I shook my head. "No. I'm going to go by myself, and after I talk with him about the property, you're more than welcome to swoop in."

"You all good?" Mama had popped her head around the corner at the far end of the hallway.

"We are." I opened the door of the interrogation room and gestured for Danielle to leave. "I'm assuming you've missed your plane home."

I didn't know what time she'd booked a flight, but I did know that it took over two hours to get to either airport she could've flown out of, so that would put her on a late-night flight, if there was one.

"Yeah. I was taking an Uber to the airport, and I guess I can just get another one to spend the night at the airport," Danielle said, and Mama overheard.

"That will not do. You can stay with me. And what about Jessie?" Mama asked about the adoptable puppy at the Bean Hive.

"I do love him," Danielle whined before she smiled. "Do you mind if I stay the night? I'll be out of your hair bright and early."

"You will because you, my dear, are going to show up when Roxy gets to the Bean Hive, get that little Jessie, and then go home to make a good, clean life for yourself." Mama cracked me up sometimes.

I never knew when she was going to say something that made so much sense and other times make not a lick of it. The more I got to know my mom as an adult, the closer we got. Today, we'd just gotten a little closer.

CHAPTER FIFTEEN

S tanding in the once-vibrant and bustling house that used to be Aunt Maxi's, I felt a strange mixture of emotions. The large house was filled with memories of my childhood summers spent in Honey Springs, and it was where Patrick and I had first met as teenagers. I took a deep breath, knowing that selling the house was a difficult decision but necessary for the future prosperity of Honey Springs. The development of the country club would bring much-needed tourism and employment opportunities to the area.

Caspian Blackwood, the enigmatic figure behind Blackwood Associates, was there to discuss the deal and finalize the sale. His presence was commanding, and I couldn't help but feel a little intimidated as we shook hands and exchanged pleasantries. As we gathered in the living room, Caspian began to outline the agreement and the perks that would come with it.

"As a token of our appreciation for your cooperation in this project, Roxy and Patrick, you and your family will receive lifetime memberships to the Honey Springs Country Club," he began, a confident smile on his face. "This membership will grant you unlimited access to all the amenities and facilities we have to offer."

He proceeded to list the perks that we would enjoy as members of the country club. "First and foremost, you'll have access to our state-of-the-art golf course, complete with a fully equipped pro shop and a team of professional instructors. Additionally, you'll be able to enjoy our tennis courts, swimming pool, and fitness center, all maintained to the highest standards for your enjoyment."

I listened intently, trying to picture the new country club and the benefits it would bring to Honey Springs. Caspian continued, "Our clubhouse will feature an upscale restaurant and bar, where you can dine on exquisite cuisine prepared by our renowned executive chef. And, of course, the country club will host numerous social events and gatherings throughout the year, providing ample opportunities for networking and entertainment."

As he spoke, I could sense the passion and determination behind his vision for the country club. It was clear that he wanted to create something truly exceptional, and I couldn't help but feel a glimmer of excitement at the prospect of what lay ahead for our small town.

"Lastly," Caspian concluded, "as lifetime members, you and your family will receive priority access to all our facilities, as well as preferential rates for any services or events you wish to host at the club."

With a mixture of sadness and anticipation, Patrick and I signed the papers, sealing the deal and ushering in a new chapter for Honey Springs.

The house that held so many memories would be replaced by a thriving country club, and I could only hope that our decision would ultimately prove to be the right one for the community we loved so dearly.

"How about a toast?" Caspian's sly smile poked something in my gut when he pulled out the bottle of bubbly and a few glasses. "I always like to seal the deal with a little champagne."

After a quick toast, Caspian walked over to look out over Lake Honey Springs from the floor-to-ceiling windows.

As Caspian continued to speak about the country club and its potential impact on Honey Springs, I found myself captivated by his charm and charisma. He had a way of making everything he said sound like the most enticing opportunity, and I could feel myself being drawn in by his enthusiasm.

However, as I observed him, my mind started to drift back to the research I had done on Caspian Blackwood and his company, Blackwood Associates, from my laptop at the Bean Hive.

I remembered the numerous shady deals and controversies that seemed to follow him from his previous developments. There were allegations of environmental damage, financial misconduct, and even bribery. Although nothing had ever been definitively proven, the pattern of questionable behavior was impossible to ignore.

I also recalled the information I had uncovered about Caspian's personal financial situation, not to mention what Danielle had said about their past history.

From what I had gathered, he had invested a significant portion of his retirement savings into this Honey Springs project. If the development didn't go through, he stood to lose everything. This knowledge made me question his motivations even further. Was he genuinely passionate about revitalizing Honey Springs, or was he simply desperate to save himself from financial ruin?

As these thoughts swirled through my mind, I found myself looking at Caspian with a newfound sense of caution. I could no longer ignore the nagging feeling that there was more to this man and his intentions than met the eye.

Though Patrick and I had already signed the papers, I knew I couldn't simply sit back and watch the development unfold without doing my due diligence.

I needed to ensure that the future of Honey Springs was in good hands and that the community we cherished wouldn't be irreparably harmed by the development.

I smiled politely at Caspian as he concluded his presentation, all the while mentally preparing myself for the questions I was about to ask him.

I was committed to protecting Honey Springs and its residents, and I wouldn't rest until I was certain the development of the country club was truly in the best interests of our community.

"Do you have any questions for me?" Caspian opened the door all on his own.

"Yes. Why did you go to the island after the emergency meeting?" I asked.

"Roxanne." Patrick's eyes grew big as my name spit out of his mouth.

"Well? It's a valid question. I'm a lawyer, and I love Honey Springs. I think we deserve to know what he might have to do with Leandar." I shrugged and took a sip of the champagne.

"I see you have a very active mind." Caspian grinned. "There's no big conspiracy. From what I gather, I'm guessing Leandar's dealings have come back to haunt him. I thought you owned a coffee shop."

"She does." Patrick spoke up over me. "But we should go."

"No." I shook my head. "I think I will stay and find out some more answers now that we've funded his retirement."

My suspicions growing, I took a deep breath and decided to confront Caspian about the issues that had been gnawing at me. I could sense Patrick's unease as I prepared to ask Caspian some difficult questions, but I couldn't let these concerns go unaddressed.

"Caspian," I began, my voice steady and firm. "I have to ask you about Leandar's murder. It seems that you had a motive, considering the development was on the brink of collapsing and your retirement was at stake. Can you explain your relationship with Leandar and why some people might think you had a reason to want him gone?"

Caspian's confident demeanor faltered for a moment, but he quickly regained his composure. "Leandar and I had our differences, but I would never resort to violence. Business is business, and sometimes things don't go as planned. That doesn't mean I would ever harm someone."

I pressed on, unwilling to let him evade the question. "What about the threats your investors made against Leandar if the deal fell through? I heard from Danielle that you mentioned, in no uncertain terms, that Leandar's days were numbered."

Caspian's face flushed, and he shifted uncomfortably in his seat. "Those were just words, Roxy. I didn't mean anything by it. People say things in the heat of the moment, but it doesn't mean they'll act on it."

Out of the corner of my eye, I could see Patrick fidgeting, clearly anxious about the direction the conversation was taking. But I couldn't stop now. I needed answers.

"What about the scratch on your arm?" I asked, gesturing toward the visible mark. "And the blood we found on the dinghy? How do you explain that?"

Caspian hesitated before responding. "The scratch is from the dingy accident, nothing more." He laughed as if he were having the memory. "I'm not a boater, and I had a few too many drinks at the bar at the Be Happy Spa with one of my investors."

Was he talking about Kirk?

"I knew Danielle had the cabin, so I walked down there and asked her if I could use the dinghy to get across the lake. She didn't mind at all, but I couldn't untie it right. I scratched my arm on the wood post, and the blood dripped down my arm."

He pulled his sleeve up a little to show a full gash that was still looked pretty raw.

"I sat in the boat and was a bit dizzy. I'm sure it was from the booze. I held on to the boat on both sides to steady myself so I wouldn't flip. Eventually, I slipped down into the boat and fell asleep." He didn't even drive the boat. He never left the dock. "I got up sometime during the middle of the night and headed back to the dock at the bee farm where I hitched a ride back with the ferry guy."

I could feel Patrick trying to interrupt, but I ignored him, my focus solely on Caspian and the mounting evidence against him.

"Big Bib?" I asked, knowing he'd be able to tell me. Big Bib never forgot a face.

"Beard, overalls, really plays the part of mechanic." Caspian observed but did not realize Big Bib was not an actor playing a part. He reached down into his pocket and took out his phone.

He hit the screen like a text had come in.

"I've got to go. It seems like your sheriff is also very interested in what I was doing the night Leandar died. I will leave."

Despite his attempts to explain away my questions, I couldn't shake the feeling that something was off. I knew I needed to dig deeper, gather more information, and uncover the truth about what had happened to Leandar.

The future of Honey Springs and the safety of its residents were at stake, and I was determined to get to the bottom of it, no matter the cost.

CHAPTER SIXTEEN

As Patrick and I returned home to our cozy cabin, the sky was awash with the soft hues of dusk. We entered the living room and settled down on the couch, the warm glow of the fireplace casting flickering shadows on the walls.

Sassy and Pepper wagged their tails and jumped around us, excited to see us home after our tense meeting with Caspian at Aunt Maxi's old house.

"All right, you two," I said with a chuckle. "Let's get you outside for a potty break."

Patrick held the door and ushered Sassy and Pepper out into the front yard, where they immediately began sniffing around and exploring.

We stood there for a moment, watching them play and enjoying the fresh air as the sun dipped lower in the sky, casting a warm golden glow over everything.

When the dogs were content, we called them back inside, and I headed into the kitchen to prepare some snacks for us to enjoy. I rummaged through the cabinets, gathering an assortment of crackers, cheese, and sliced meats to create a small charcuterie board.

As I arranged the snacks on a wooden platter, Patrick grabbed a bottle of wine from the rack and began to uncork it.

"Here, let me help you with that," I said, taking the corkscrew from him and expertly freeing the cork from the bottle.

He grinned at me, his eyes twinkling with amusement. "You've always been the wine expert in this relationship."

"And coffee expert." I smiled and gave him a quick kiss.

With the bottle uncorked, Patrick fetched two wineglasses from the cupboard while I finished arranging the snacks. We carried our impromptu feast into the living room, setting everything down on the coffee table before settling onto the couch.

Patrick's expression was a mix of concern and frustration as he turned to face me. "Roxy, I can't believe you confronted Caspian like that. What if he really had killed Leandar? You could've put yourself in serious danger."

I sighed, feeling both guilty and defensive. "I know, Patrick, but I couldn't just sit there and not ask the questions that needed to be asked. We needed to know the truth about Caspian's involvement."

His eyes softened, but the worry remained. "I understand that, Roxy, but I can't stand the thought of anything happening to you. I love you so much, and the idea of losing you... It's unbearable."

I felt tears prick at the corners of my eyes as I reached out to take his hand. "I love you, too, Patrick, more than anything. I promise I'll be more careful in the future."

He pulled me into a tight embrace, burying his face in my hair. "I just want to keep you safe, Roxy. You mean the world to me."

As we held each other, Pepper jumped up onto the couch and snuggled between us, wagging his tail and seeking our attention. We laughed through our tears, the tension between us dissipating as we focused on the love and happiness we shared.

Patrick gently tilted my chin up, his eyes locked onto mine. "I'll always be here for you, Roxy, no matter what."

I smiled, my heart swelling with love for this wonderful man who had been my rock through thick and thin. "And I'll always be here for you, Patrick."

As our lips met in a tender, passionate kiss, the sun dipped below the horizon outside our cabin window. Our love shone brightly in the midst of uncertainty and fear, a beacon of hope and strength to guide us through whatever challenges the future held.

As Patrick and I sat on the couch, entwined in each other's arms and surrounded by the love of our little family, we began to discuss our shared love for Honey Springs.

"You know, Patrick," I said, my voice soft with affection, "I can't imagine a better place to call home than Honey Springs. There's just something so special about this small town in addition to me meeting you here."

He nodded, his eyes taking on a distant, dreamy quality. "I couldn't agree more, Roxy. The sense of community, the natural beauty, the charm of our little shops and cafés... It's all so incredible. Even growing up here, I never had the urge to move away."

"I just hope that the development of the country club won't change Honey Springs too much," I mused, my brow furrowing with concern. "I mean, it's bound to bring more tourism and employment opportunities, which is great, but I don't want our town to lose its soul in the process."

Patrick hugged me tighter, his warmth reassuring. "I know what you mean, Roxy. But we'll do everything we can to preserve the essence of Honey Springs. We'll work with the community and make sure that any development is done with sensitivity and respect for our town's history and traditions."

I smiled at his optimism and determination. "That's one of the many things I love about you, Patrick. Your commitment to our town and its people is so inspiring."

He brushed a strand of hair from my face, his eyes filled with love. "And I love your passion for justice and your dedication to protecting the people of Honey Springs. Together, we'll make sure that our town remains the beautiful, welcoming place we know and love."

Patrick's phone rang.

It was Franny, Patrick's secretary.

"Wonder what she wants so late." He had a funny look but accepted the call. "Hey, Franny. I've got you on speakerphone with Roxy here. Is everything okay?"

"Okay? It's more than okay!" she screamed. "Patrick! Roxy! I'm so sorry to bother you after hours, but I just couldn't wait to tell you the news!" she gushed.

"What's going on, Franny?" Patrick asked, his curiosity piqued.

"We got it! We got the bid for the new country club! Cane Construction is going to build it!" she exclaimed, barely able to contain her excitement.

Patrick's eyes widened, and he exchanged a thrilled glance with me. "That's incredible news, Franny! Thank you so much for letting us know."

"Yeah, Franny, this is fantastic!" I chimed in, my heart swelling with pride for Patrick and his team. I had no idea he'd even put in for the bid. "We really appreciate you calling to tell us."

Franny's voice softened, but the excitement was still palpable. "I just couldn't wait until tomorrow. This is such a huge deal for Cane Construction, and I wanted you two to know as soon as possible. Congratulations!"

"Thank you, Franny. We'll celebrate this accomplishment at the office tomorrow," Patrick promised.

After saying our goodbyes and ending the call, Patrick and I looked at each other, still processing the incredible news.

"Can you believe it, Roxy?" Patrick asked, his voice filled with wonder. "Our company is going to build the new country club. This is going to be huge for us!"

I reached over and squeezed his hand, my eyes shining with pride. "I knew you could do it, Patrick. This is going to be amazing for Cane Construction and for Honey Springs."

We clinked our wineglasses together, toasting our success and the bright future that lay ahead for our town and our business. With love, determination, and a shared vision, we knew that we could help shape Honey Springs into a thriving, vibrant community that would continue to grow and prosper.

But in the back of my head—and it stayed there though I would further investigate later—was it me, or was it just coincidence that we'd just met with Caspian, sold Aunt Maxi's old house to him, and confronted him about his possible involvement about Leandar's death, and *then* Cane Construction got the bid at this hour?

It would go right along with the information I'd found on the internet about Blackwood Associates's shady deals.

CHAPTER SEVENTEEN

I stood behind the counter at the Bean Hive, the early morning sun streaming through the windows and casting a warm golden glow over the lake outside.

The aroma of freshly brewed coffee filled the air, its comforting scent promising a perfect start to the day.

Danielle was coming in this morning to pick up Jessie before we opened. She'd made it official that she was going to adopt the cute pup and take him home to live with her.

It was funny how friendships formed. Though she didn't live in Honey Springs, we'd been able to form a bond between us in the most unexpected of circumstances. It was a friendship I was sure was going to last.

I had already gotten the adoption papers ready, so when she came in they were ready for her to sign. Jessie knew something was up. He was prancing around all by himself, not following Pepper like he'd done since Louise had dropped him off. It was a sign he was ready to be the dog of his own domain.

"It looks like we are all out of leads." I sat little Jessie's bag of toys and the packet Louise Carlton had left for him when she dropped him off to be the featured animal from the Pet Palace.

"I can say my time here in Honey Springs has definitely been one to remember." Danielle looked a whole lot better than the last time I'd talked with her.

"Now that the new development doesn't require me to do any more environmental testing for Blackwood Associates, I think I'm going to find a different job."

"Oh yeah?" I had a pit in my stomach from signing the papers for Aunt Maxi's house over to Caspian Blackwood for the new country-club development.

It was good. I had to remember that it was best for Honey Springs. There was more lakefront property and beach than any old development. It was the development that would help spur more tourists to visit here, and it was going to be a great way to show off our gorgeous little part of Kentucky.

"What do you have in mind?" I asked her and tucked the official adoption papers under my arm as I got us two cups of freshly brewed hot coffee.

"I'm not sure. Where I live, we have the ocean, mountains, and forest, so I'm sure I can find something there," she said. "You should come visit. I think you'd like it."

"Where do you live?" I asked.

"It's a small town out west called Holiday Junction." She picked Jessie up and nuzzled him. "He is going to love all the walks. We even have a dog that's the mayor. Mayor Paisley."

"A dog?" I snorted.

"Yes, but I'm thinking Jessie might give her a run for her money next election." She winked. "Where do I sign?"

She put Jessie down so she could sign the papers to make it official.

As Danielle signed the adoption papers, Jessie wagged his tail excitedly, his little body practically quivering with joy.

Pepper was going to miss having Jessie around as a playmate at the Bean Hive, but seeing the love and happiness on Danielle's face made it all worthwhile.

"Roxy, I just wanted to thank you," Danielle began, her eyes filling with gratitude. "Not only for being my lawyer when Spencer thought I killed Leandar, but also for your friendship. You stood by me when so many others turned their backs."

I smiled warmly, my heart swelling with pride and affection. "That's what friends do, Danielle. I'm just glad we were able to prove your innocence."

As we shared a quiet, heartfelt moment, a sudden blur of movement outside the window caught our attention. A man sprinted past on the boardwalk, his pace steady and determined. Danielle watched him go, a thoughtful expression on her face.

"You know," she said, her gaze following the runner, "that guy runs by here every day. He even stopped to chat with me once. He mentioned something about the land development Leandar was involved in and how it had ruined his family."

"Oh really?" I got up and tried to look out the window, but the runner was gone. "Where did you run into him?"

"The little antique store down the boardwalk. He was bringing the owners some of his family's bone china. The owners were so excited about it." She had to be talking about Caldwell Featherstone.

"Did he tell you why he thought Leandar had ruined their family?" I asked.

"He wasn't talking to me. He was telling the owners how they still had to sell the china in order to get hay for their livestock or something like that. I overheard them." She looked around and said, "You know, the china he brought in would go great with your décor."

"Yes, it would." I kept to myself how I had planned on buying that china at the estate auction that never was, but I couldn't keep to myself who he was. "I bet it was Caldwell Featherstone."

"Any relation to Raffery Featherstone? One of the golf course investors?" she asked and took the last sip of coffee.

"His son." I tried to recall the conversation I'd had with him on the boat that night, but the sun was up, and the first customer was at the door, waiting for me to unlock it.

It was Bunny's day off, so it was just me in the Bean Hive this morning, which meant any notion I had to go question Caldwell about what he'd said in passing to the Teagardens was going to have to wait until the afternoon staff came.

Even when Danielle and Jessie left, she didn't take with her the thoughts I'd gotten when she ID'd the runner.

What if Raffery Featherstone really did kill Leandar? He had a very shoddy alibi with the jug fishing.

The more the morning dragged on, I started to recall some of the conversation about how Caldwell knew the time because he was playing video games online with buddies. Not realizing it, he really did put his father at the scene of the crime.

A shiver ran down my spine, realization dawning on me. Could Caldwell be the real killer?

I might have just stumbled upon the key to solving Leandar's murder.

There was only one way to find out which Featherstone had killed Leandar, and that was going right back to the Featherstone farm and doing a little more snooping around, this time without Spencer.

CHAPTER EIGHTEEN

Before I went, I decided to take all the knowledge I was armed with about Caldwell's little visit to Wild and Whimsy, thanks to what Danielle had told me. I decided to stop by the antique shop to talk to Beverly Teagarden myself to see what she had to say about the conversation.

The one sure way to get Beverly to open up was to make and take her one of her favorite breads that just so happened to be in season: honeysuckle-infused bread. We in Kentucky called it Appalachia summer bread.

I'd already made the honeysuckle syrup when the honeysuckle trees had bloomed in early spring. It was a tedious job to pick all the flowering buds and boil them down to the syrup, but it was one of those things I did on Sundays when I took advantage of the coffee shop being closed during the winter and early spring months.

Since it was the lull time between the lunch rush and the afternoon customers, I was able to prop the swinging door between the coffee shop and the kitchen open. I couldn't risk the health department coming in and shutting me down, so I had to work fast.

I grabbed all the dry ingredients off the shelf and put them on the kitchen workstation before I went to the refrigerator for the wet ingredients.

Since the bread was a staple in my life growing up due to the fact that we had so many honeysuckle trees, I was really good at eyeballing the ingredients instead of going straight from the recipe.

With my oven set on preheat, I retrieved the stand mixer from one of the shelves underneath the workstation and started to add the flour, baking soda, oils, salt, buttermilk, lemon zest, eggs, and the final touch—the homemade honeysuckle syrup.

With everything all married together, I put the mixture in a few glass bread-baking dishes and placed it in the oven.

It didn't take long before the sweet aroma of the baking bread, infused with the delicate sweetness of honeysuckle, brought back memories of countless summers spent in Honey Springs, surrounded by the gentle fragrance of blossoming flowers.

It was Aunt Maxi's recipe that was baked into my head and beloved by all.

The tantalizing smell of the bread mingled with the rich, earthy aroma of freshly ground coffee beans, creating an irresistible blend of scents that permeated every corner of the cozy kitchen. The familiar smell of butter and sugar caramelizing in the oven filled the air as the bread baked to golden perfection.

As I inhaled the delightful medley of scents, I felt a wave of contentment wash over me.

The kitchen was my sanctuary, a place where I could lose myself in the simple pleasure of creating delicious treats for others to enjoy and forget about why I was making the bread in the first place.

Still, Leandar's murder wasn't too far buried in the back of my head.

While the loaves of bread baked, I made sure everything inside the coffee shop was stocked so the Riddle twins didn't have to worry about anything. I'd even had time to get the morning industrial coffeepots ready, which was now on the afternoon employees' list of things to do.

It wasn't too long after the timers for the oven went off that the twins got there for their afternoon shift, allowing me to leave a little earlier than normal.

"Afternoon!" Beverly greeted me as soon as the bell over the door chimed and she recognized it was me. "You better not walk any further unless you've got something in your hands."

I lifted up the bag with the Appalachian honeysuckle bread in it.

"Do you think I'd do that to you? Especially if I've got a loaf of Appalachian honeysuckle bread you love in here?" I wagged the bag as I walked through the store to the check-out counter where Beverly was using the handheld pricing machine to stick the price on some of the new antiques they'd gotten.

I set the bag on the counter.

"How are Savannah and Melanie?" I asked and looked around the shop to see if they were there. "I do have a couple extra mini-loaves in there for them." I winked when I saw they weren't around.

"Do we have to tell them?" she joked. "And Dan is outside working on the awning, so when you leave, don't tell him about these either."

Beverly had already taken one out and bit into it, humming happily with each chew.

"I didn't see him when I came in." I would've noticed since I'd walked right under the awning where the sign that read Wild and Whimsy dangled down.

"There's a few rusty bolts where he had to screw the awning on the tin roof," she muttered under another bite. "He probably had to run to the hardware store."

"Ah." I nodded.

"So." Beverly gave me the side eye. "What are you doing here this time of the day? And with my favorite seasonal bread?"

"You know me all too well." There was no pulling the wool over her eyes. "Two things. How much for the Featherstones' bone china?"

Beverly laughed.

"And can you tell me about the conversation you had with Caldwell Featherstone when he dropped off the china?"

Now, that threw her for a loop.

"Why? Is Caldwell in trouble?" she asked.

"No." I shook my head. "I'm doing a little double-dipping with Spencer by keeping my ear to the ground if I hear any information and also representing Danielle Quillen, the environmentalist in town, as a suspect in Leandar's murder. And she happened to mention how she overheard Caldwell in here talking about his family."

"You know kids." Beverly pooh-poohed the conversation. It was her way of not getting involved or gossiping. "Caldwell was talking to me and the girls. They are the same age and went to high school together."

"I know. He said he remembered me from teaching their home economics class that time." I laughed.

"Anyways, I'd asked him about how his parents were doing with selling, and that's when he said they'd decided not to sell because Leandar's little scheme messed them up." She used the word "scheme," which was very interesting.

"Scheme?" I asked to make sure.

"You know kids. I'm sure he'd heard it from Raffery and was just repeating. But when I asked about why he was bringing the china in, he said his mom told him they needed the money because they'd not gotten enough hay or feed for the horses since they thought the new owners would take over." She tsked and frowned.

"Were they having financial problems?" I asked.

"One of my girls said she'd heard they had a hard time paying the mortgage, so when Blackwood Associates was looking for investors, Caldwell told her how Raffery had jumped on it. Not only would selling the farm give them enough to invest, but also the cost of a small townhome at the country club would be paid off, as well as a lifetime membership to the country club." Beverly didn't know it, but what she just told me gave me plenty of motives and reasons for Raffery to have killed Leandar out of anger.

"That's too bad." I shook my head, keeping my thoughts to myself. "How about the price of that china?"

Beverly never gave me the price. She said she'd let me know, and I'd have first option to buy, which I fully intended to do.

There was one more person I needed to visit before I went home for the night.

Raffery Featherstone.

As I drove along the old, winding roads in the late afternoon, I couldn't help but marvel at the beauty of the Kentucky countryside. The Hill Dairy Farm, with its gently rolling hills and lush pastures, was a testament to the bluegrass region's rich agricultural heritage. The sun cast a warm golden light on the fields, making the vibrant green grass appear to glow with life.

Eventually, I arrived at the Featherstone farm, an impressive estate known for its prized racehorses. The sprawling property was undoubtedly worth a fortune, but I knew that maintaining such a place came with considerable costs. When the development deal fell through, the Featherstones found themselves in dire financial straits—at least, that's the conclusion I came to after visiting with Beverly Teagarden.

She'd confided in me that the Featherstones were struggling with mortgage payments, which was why they were hosting an estate sale. The sale of their belongings would allow them to purchase a nice condo within the country club, offering them a more manageable lifestyle.

I was there to talk to Raffery Featherstone about his potential involvement in Leandar's murder. His late-night jug fishing put him at the scene, but with the discovery of a second murder location, I needed to find out where Raffery had been right after the emergency meeting where the development was voted down. Had he killed Leandar in a fit of rage?

When I arrived at their home, Caldwell, Raffery's son, let me in.

"They aren't here. I think they went to the bank to meet with that developer." Caldwell stood inside the entry.

In the background, I could hear the sound of muffled voices. Was Raffery there and Caldwell covering for his father?

After all, Caldwell was the gamer.

"Do you know how long they will be?" I asked and moved past him to look into the other room where the noise was coming from.

"No," Caldwell said. "I'll go grab a piece of paper from Dad's office, and you can write a note. If you don't, I might forget you stopped by."

Caldwell left the room. I heard someone over the earphones attached to the gaming console, yelling for Raffery to play.

Picking up the earphones, I listened for a moment.

"Raffery, man, come on. You're going to get us killed," one of the other players said, confirming they thought it was Raffery playing, not Caldwell. This revelation didn't make sense to me at first, but the pieces began to fall into place as I continued to survey the room.

I had been transported back to the dinner cruise when Caldwell had told me how he was playing video games in the middle of the night and early morning when Leandar was murdered and his dad had come in from jug fishing.

Was it the other way around?

The other gamers continued to yell for Raffery to move in what appeared to be a game where they all played together in order to advance. I picked up the remote.

My eyes fell on a small amount of what looked like a smear of blood on the corner of the remote control where the fatty part of the thumb would lay.

I scanned the room and noticed a baseball bat in the corner.

It suddenly became clear to me that Caldwell was the one who had hit Leandar on the head right here in this home.

It was possible that he'd taken Leandar to the beach to be found. It was Danielle who had ID'd Caldwell earlier when he was jogging past the Bean Hive.

He'd called the sheriff, pretending to have stumbled upon the body while out running.

As the chilling truth dawned on me, I realized I needed to confront Caldwell and uncover the full extent of his involvement in Leandar's murder. I couldn't let an innocent man take the blame for a crime he didn't commit, and I was determined to see justice served.

I took a deep breath as I approached Caldwell, my heart pounding with a mixture of anxiety and determination. It was time to confront him about Leandar's murder, and I had to know the truth.

"Caldwell," I began, my voice steady despite the storm of emotions swirling within me, "I need to talk to you about what happened the night Leandar died."

He tensed, his eyes widening in surprise and fear. It was clear that he hadn't expected me to discover his secret.

"I know you were the one who killed him, Caldwell," I continued, watching as his face turned pale. "But I also know that you didn't mean to do it. I believe you thought he was an intruder."

Caldwell stared at me, his eyes filled with a mixture of relief and desperation. "Roxy, I swear, I didn't mean to kill anyone. I was just playing my video game, and when I saw his reflection on the TV screen, I panicked. I thought someone had broken into our home, and I was just trying to protect myself and our house."

His voice trembled, and I could see the weight of his guilt and fear pressing down upon him. "I didn't know it was Leandar until it was too late," he added, his eyes brimming with tears. "I didn't know what to do, so I took his body to the lake, hoping it would buy me some time to figure things out."

As I listened to his confession, I felt a swell of sympathy for Caldwell. He had made a tragic mistake, driven by fear and a desire to protect his home and family. It was clear that he was haunted by his actions, and the burden of his secret had become almost too much to bear.

"Caldwell," I said gently, "you need to come forward and tell the truth. It's the only way to start making things right. I know you didn't mean for any of this to happen, but it's important to take responsibility for your actions."

He nodded slowly, tears streaming down his face as he finally surrendered to the weight of his guilt. "You're right, Roxy," he whispered. "I'll tell the truth. I just hope everyone can understand that I never meant for any of this to happen."

As I stood by his side, ready to support him as he faced the consequences of his actions, I knew that the road ahead would be difficult for both Caldwell and the entire community of Honey Springs. But I also believed that through honesty, understanding, and compassion, we would find a way to heal and move forward together.

But I knew we had to call Sheriff Spencer Shephard.

I took out my cell phone, dialed Sheriff Spencer's number, and waited for him to pick up. "Sheriff, it's Roxy. I'm here with Caldwell, and he has something important to tell you."

I handed the phone to Caldwell, whose hands were trembling as he took it from me. He hesitated for a moment, taking a deep breath before speaking. "Sheriff Spencer, it's Caldwell Featherstone. I... I need to confess something."

There was a pause as he listened to the sheriff's response, his eyes flicking to me for reassurance. I gave him an encouraging nod, urging him to continue.

"I was the one who killed Leandar," he admitted, his voice cracking. "But it was an accident. I thought he was an intruder when I saw his reflection on the TV screen. I panicked and hit him with a bat. I never meant for any of this to happen."

Silence filled the room as Caldwell listened to Sheriff Spencer's response. It was clear that the sheriff was taken aback by the confession, but his voice remained calm and professional as he instructed Caldwell on the next steps.

After a few more minutes of conversation, Caldwell hung up the phone and handed it back to me, his face etched with a mixture of relief and anxiety. "He said I should come down to the sheriff's department right away to make an official statement."

He paused for a moment, his eyes pleading. "Roxy, would you come with me? I don't think I can face this alone."

"Of course, Caldwell," I replied, placing a comforting hand on his shoulder. "I'll be there with you every step of the way."

We left the Featherstone home and headed toward the sheriff's department. But as we walked side by side, I was reminded of the power of truth, compassion, and support to help guide us through even the darkest of times.

As Caldwell and I entered the sheriff's department, Sheriff Spencer and Caldwell's parents were waiting for us. Spencer must've called them to let them know what Caldwell had confessed to.

Spencer's expression was a mix of sympathy and professionalism. He gestured for us to sit down in a couple of chairs across from his desk, and we obliged.

"Thank you for coming in, Caldwell," he began, his voice firm but gentle. "It takes a lot of courage to face the consequences of your actions, especially when they've had such tragic results."

Caldwell swallowed hard, nodding in acknowledgment. "I know I can't undo what's happened, but I want to do whatever I can to make things right."

Spencer nodded, his eyes meeting Caldwell's. "First, we'll need to take a formal statement from you. I'll ask you to recount the events leading up to and following Leandar's death, and we'll have a deputy transcribe your words. This statement will become part of the official record."

Caldwell nodded, his hands fidgeting nervously in his lap. "Okay, I understand."

"Once we have your statement," Spencer continued, "we'll need to investigate further. This includes gathering any additional evidence, speaking with witnesses, and corroborating your version of events. We'll also need to consult with the district attorney to determine the appropriate charges."

Caldwell's eyes widened with fear, but he didn't protest. "I'll cooperate fully with the investigation," he promised.

Spencer softened his expression slightly. "I appreciate that, Caldwell. And remember, you have the right to legal counsel throughout this process. I recommend you get in touch with a lawyer as soon as possible to ensure your rights are protected."

Caldwell looked at me, his eyes pleading. "Roxy, would you consider representing me?"

I hesitated for a moment, weighing the gravity of the situation. Then, I nodded. "I'll do my best to help you through this, Caldwell."

With my support, and the guidance of Spencer, we began the difficult process of addressing the consequences of Caldwell's actions. Although the road ahead was uncertain, we were committed to seeking justice and healing for all those affected by this tragic event.

CHAPTER NINETEEN

The next day was difficult for Honey Springs.

One of our own was dead. Though Leandar Taylor was shifty at times, he was still ours. And one of our own was his killer.

I recalled standing in the Featherstones' living room the day before and talking with Caldwell after he'd been given the appropriate charges, the shocking truth about Leandar's murder finally becoming clear.

Caldwell had come home from college early, unaware of the events that had transpired during the emergency meeting. He had been at home, immersed in a video game with his headset on, completely oblivious to the world outside.

Leandar, having not yet received Raffery Featherstone's emails and voice-mails about removing the farm from the market and canceling the estate sale, had used his key as the Realtor to enter the house and check if it was ready for the upcoming event.

When no one answered his knock on the door, he went inside, unknowingly setting off a tragic chain of events. Raffery and his wife hadn't gone straight home after the meeting, so they had no idea this had taken place. When they did get home, Raffery did go jug fishing, just like Caldwell had told me.

Caldwell, startled by the unexpected intruder, caught a glimpse of Leandar's reflection on the television screen. In a moment of panic, he dropped the game remote, grabbed a nearby bat, and swung it with all his might, striking Leandar in the head and killing him instantly.

Overwhelmed by fear, Caldwell hastily transported Leandar's body to the lake, where he later called the sheriff, pretending to have stumbled upon the body during a nighttime run. When he returned home, his parents were there, but they had no idea what had transpired. Caldwell had carefully concealed any signs of the incident, replacing the bat and resuming his video game as if nothing had happened.

But he hadn't noticed the small amount of blood that had transferred from his hands to the remote, a crucial piece of evidence that I had spotted when I came to confront Raffery about the murder. It was that seemingly insignificant detail that had allowed me to put the pieces together and uncover the truth about Caldwell's involvement in Leandar's tragic death.

As I stood behind the counter of the Bean Hive, reflecting on the devastating series of events and the lives that had been forever changed, I felt a mixture of relief and sorrow.

We had finally solved Leandar's murder, but at what cost?

The weight of the truth weighed heavily on my heart, a stark reminder that life could be irrevocably altered in the blink of an eye and that sometimes the most heartbreaking truths lay hidden beneath the surface.

I took solace in knowing the Bean Hive was more than just a place for people to enjoy coffee and delicious treats; it was a haven where people could come together, share their thoughts and emotions, and find support in one another. It was a testament to the resilience and strength of the Honey Springs community that, even in the face of tragedy, they were able to rally together and find solace in each other's company.

As I continued to serve my customers and listen to their stories, I was reminded of the importance of human connection, especially during trying times. People from all walks of life found their way to the Bean Hive, united by their shared experiences, grief, and hope for healing.

In the weeks that followed, the Bean Hive became a beacon of light for the people of Honey Springs. The laughter, tears, and heartfelt conversations shared within its walls spoke to the power of community and the unbreakable bonds that held us together.

Through it all, I found my own sense of purpose and fulfillment in providing a space where people could find comfort and healing. The Bean Hive had become more than just a coffee shop; it was a symbol of the enduring spirit of Honey Springs, a place where people could come together and face even the darkest of times with hope, love, and unity.

As I glanced around the coffee shop, my eyes fell upon Aunt Maxi, Patrick, my mama, and Bunny, all engrossed in a lively conversation about the new development of the country club. Their excitement was palpable, and it was clear that they believed the project would bring about positive change and prosperity for Honey Springs.

Not only had they posted the building plans for the development in the courthouse for everyone to see, but also they'd decided on keeping Aunt Maxi's house for the main building of the country club where events could be hosted.

After all, it had the most beautiful view of the lake and was a grand place to have an event.

However, as I observed their animated discussion, I couldn't help but feel a twinge of uncertainty.

The country club would no doubt boost tourism and create job opportunities, but at what cost? How much would Honey Springs change in the process? Would the tight-knit community I had come to love and cherish still retain its charm and warmth, or would it be transformed beyond recognition?

As I pondered these thoughts, I realized that change was inevitable and that progress often came with its own set of challenges. Yet it was in the face of change that the people of Honey Springs had always displayed their resilience, adapting and coming together to ensure the well-being of their community.

With the Bean Hive as a cornerstone of the community, I resolved to do my part in keeping the essence of Honey Springs alive and thriving, even as the town embarked on a new chapter of growth and development.

I stood behind the counter, using a wet towel to clean and dry my new Featherstone bone china. Beverly Teagarden had sold it to me for the price she could've gotten if she'd sold it in the store.

I couldn't help but think about the one thing I knew for sure.

The Bean Hive was more than just a coffee shop; it was a place where people could gather, connect, and find comfort in the simple pleasures of life, like the aroma of fresh honeysuckle bread wafting through the air.

And no development would change that.

THE END

If you enjoyed reading this book as much as I enjoyed writing it then be sure to return to the Amazon page and leave a review.

Go to Tonyakappes.com for a full reading order of my novels and while there join my newsletter. You can also find links to Facebook, Instagram and Goodreads.

Macchiato Murder, book 13 in Killer Coffee Cozy Mystery is now available on Amazon. You don't want to miss this Halloween edition to the series that'll keep you guessing until the end. Keep reading for a sneak peek!

Chapter One of Book Thirteen
Macchiato Murder

The spirit of Halloween wafted through the coffee shop, filling hearts with excitement. Neewollah Festival, our town's annual, beloved celebration of all things autumn, was in full swing.

As the morning sun bathed the boardwalk in a gentle glow, I soaked in the magic of the season seeping through the café walls. The cozy atmosphere spilled out with the laughter of friends who were walking in the door of the Bean Hive Coffee Shop.

"Good morning." I greeted them as I did every single customer who walked through my coffee-shop door. "Y'all enjoying the festival activities so far?" I asked and ushered them to a table near the front of the coffee shop so they could enjoy their morning coffee with the amazing views of Lake Honey Springs and the fall colors that had painted the trees wrapping around the lake.

"Of course, they are going to the festival." Eleanor Blackthorn sidled up behind me. She reached around me and put a flyer on the table. "And I sure hope you come to Hollow Manor."

Eleanor, our spirited historian, had her sights set on breathing new life into the old farm mansion on the outskirts of town. She had a knack for exaggeration, often spinning tales of mythical creatures and haunted happenings. The running joke was how you had to take whatever Eleanor said and cut it in half to get to the truth.

And after she'd inherited the old mansion and told everyone in town how she was going to get it in the historic registry, everyone, including me, had our doubts.

We were all surprised when she did put together a plan and worked over the last few months with Babette Cliff, an event planner who owned All About the Detail.

"We have something for everyone." Eleanor had a flair for being over the top. Even more than my aunt Maxine Bloom.

And that was saying something.

Eleanor had a wild mane of silver-streaked hair that seemed to have a life of its own. She truly embodied the word "eccentric." Her wardrobe was an explosion of colors, patterns, and textures, with flowing skirts, mismatched socks, and an array of whimsical accessories. Each piece she wore told a story, reflecting her free-spirited nature and love for all things unique.

No wonder she and Aunt Maxi had been lifelong friends. When I was a child and visited Aunt Maxi every summer, one of my favorite activities was going to visit Eleanor with Aunt Maxi. I would sit and listen to her tell big tales about the town's history and folklore. However, she often added her own imaginative twists to the tales, weaving elaborate stories of mythical creatures and supernatural happenings. At least, that's what Aunt Maxi would tell me when we'd get back in the car and I'd be daydreaming of all the stories Eleanor had told me.

"You have to get there early today and pick a pumpkin from the Pumpkin Patch." She pointed to the flyer that listed all the activities for Hollow Mansion. "There's a carving station that's open until five p.m., then you can take your pumpkin over to the judging tables. The winner will be announced at nine p.m. after the big magic show."

"Thank you," I interrupted Eleanor politely. "Let me get them caffeinated so they can participate today."

It was my way of not disrespecting Eleanor as one of my elders but still making sure my customers were taken care of.

"What can I get you started off with?" I asked and didn't bother writing down what the four of them had ordered, mentally repeating their order in my head as they gave it to me. "While I get your orders made, you're more than welcome to check out the menu."

I pointed out the four large chalkboards that hung down from the ceiling over the L-shaped glass countertop.

The first chalkboard menu hung over the pie counter and listed the pies and cookies with their prices. The second menu hung over the tortes and quiches. The third menu before the L-shaped counter curved listed the breakfast casseroles and drinks. Over top the other counter, the chalkboard listed lunch options, including soups, and catering information.

"We have a variety of homemade pastries today, and you can read those over the first chalkboard. As you can see, they are all holiday themed for the festival," I told them and smiled as I pointed out the tasty treats. "You check out the list, and I'll be right back."

Wicked Witch Cupcakes were very rich chocolate cupcakes topped with vibrant green buttercream frosting and a candy witch hat garnish that one of the twins, Shelley and Shanda Riddle, had thought up when we were brainstorming about what we could offer to go with the coffee. They were amazing young women who worked at the Bean Hive after school, on weekends, and on holidays.

Spooky Spiderweb Donuts were fluffy donuts drizzled with a delicate white glaze in a spiderweb pattern, adorned with a chocolate spider that was so darling.

Pumpkin Patch Pies were mini hand pies with a buttery crust and a hint of pumpkin spice, sprinkled with cinnamon and nutmeg, and shaped like tiny pumpkins.

Haunted House Brownies were truly decadent chocolate brownies topped with black icing to resemble a spooky haunted house, complete with ghostly marshmallow shapes.

Shanda's favorite was the Monster Mash Cookie that she'd come up with. It was a colorful sugar cookie decorated with edible monster faces, featuring googly eyes and mismatched icing. Out of the two, she was the more creative when it came to decorating.

Then, for our more traditional customers, we offered what we were calling the Graveyard Cheesecake Bars, a creamy cheesecake bar on a crumbly chocolate cookie crust, topped with cookie tombstones and gummy worms.

Then I turned our usual macarons into Candy Corn Macarons, delicate, almond-flavored, and filled with a sweet, candy corn-flavored buttercream, capturing the iconic Halloween candy's colors.

Of course, Bunny had to put her two cents in because she loved my homemade cinnamon rolls. They were easy enough to make into Vampire Bites, where I drizzled a little bloodred glaze on top for a delightfully spooky twist.

I kept the scones the same because they were already perfection, if I had to say so myself. We just changed the name to Witch's Brew Scones and then paired them with our Witch's Brew Coffee blend.

We had something for everyone, and coming up with all of it made this year's festival even more fun.

As I left the table with their coffee order in my mind, Eleanor continued right where she left off.

"The last time the Hollow Mansion was open was over fifty years ago when the then-owners had a Halloween party with a magician. Only the curse of Hollow Mansion killed the magician, and it's been haunted since." I heard her and looked over my shoulder to see the reaction of the customers.

Eleanor's eyes, bright and sparkling with curiosity, held a hint of mischief and a touch of mystery as she continued to tell them about the old wives' tale that'd never been proven.

Her hands twisted in the air, and her eyes seemed to dance with an inner light, making me think she really did believe the old run-down mansion was haunted.

Her voice, as she spun her tales and shared her ambitious plans, was filled with enthusiasm and an infectious energy that had drawn the customers in.

"She's bad for business," Bunny scoffed when I walked behind the glass counter, where she was boxing up a few of the Spooky Spiderweb Donuts. "She sounds crazy." Bunny's brows knotted. Her gray hair, parted to the side and cut at chin length, framed her worried face.

"She's harmless," I said to keep the peace. "Look at them." I tossed a chin toward the group as I started to make the murdery macchiato concoction, which was literally the basic macchiato with a festive name change for the holiday. "They are enthralled by her story."

"They are enthralled by her crazy." Bunny lifted her crooked pointer finger up to her ear and started to gesture the crazy sign, making me laugh. "It's your coffee shop. I'm just here to help out."

Bunny Bowowski had been what she called "helping out" since the first week I'd opened the Bean Hive. She and her best friend, Mae Belle Donovan, were my first ever customers that'd made it a morning ritual to hold their gossip session in one of the few café tables that dotted the inside of the cozy shop.

Many times I'd sit at one of the two long window tables with stools butted up to them on each side of the front door while they sipped and gossiped, just waiting for more customers to come in.

It was a time during the revitalization of the boardwalk and Honey Springs itself where the Southern Woman's Club, along with the town council, had spent a lot of time and effort to grow the economy by putting money into tourism.

Luckily, Aunt Maxi owned the building, and the recent tenants had a restaurant that'd folded, making it easy for something like the coffee shop to move right on in.

I'd found myself at that same time building my new life as a recent divorcee, where I'd fled life as a lawyer to find comfort in the one place that had embraced me like a warm, fuzzy blanket.

Aunt Maxi's and this little lake town.

Though I wasn't from Honey Springs or technically grew up there, every summer as soon as my dad's car would cross the county line, I felt like I was coming home. I was a kid, but I knew my feelings. Every year when summer was over, it felt like a part of my soul had been ripped out of my body.

So naturally, when my soul needed healing for me to live again, I found myself in Honey Springs, opening up a coffee shop and reconnecting with the then-teenage boy I'd fallen in love with during the long, summer lake nights.

Patrick Cane.

"See? Look at her." Bunny smacked the back of her hand on my arm, flinging the crooked finger back to Eleanor, who had found another group coming in the door to hand her flyer to. "Crazy with a capital C. Did you hear me?"

"Yes. I heard you. But I was thinking back to when I was a kid, and I could sit and listen to Eleanor for hours." I shrugged off Bunny's concern. She made quite obvious by her *harrumph* that she didn't like my response.

"Like I said, I'm only here to help you out," she said again and handed me a small serving tray for the drinks.

"Then you don't want this?" I turned and plucked an envelope with her paycheck in it from the stack next to the register.

"I didn't say that, now." Bunny snapped it out of my hand, folded it, and put it in the apron she'd tied around the waist of her housecoat, her usual dress attire even though we had uniform shirts with the Bean Hive's logo on them.

With the drinks on the tray, I headed back to the customers where they'd decided to enjoy their coffee without anything to eat.

As I made my way around the bustling café, I engaged in lively conversations with our other patrons, eager to ensure their every need was met.

"Is there anything else I can get for you?" I asked, my voice filled with genuine warmth and hospitality. The laughter and animated chatter echoed against the walls as friends gathered to savor moments of connection in the midst of their busy lives.

I picked up some paper wrappers and empty cups along the way, tossing what I could in the trash and the recycle bins as I made my way over to the fireplace.

"You just tell him to move if he's bothering you." I pointed to Pepper, my furry schnauzer companion, who thought of the coffee shop as his second home.

The customers didn't mind him all snuggled up next to them as they sat on the couch letting the fire warm them.

I quickly stacked the coffee magazines and holiday-themed books along with a few nonfiction books about Honey Springs on the coffee table that I'd purchased from Crooked Cat Bookstore at the far end of the boardwalk.

I picked up the magazine with the fall decoration photo on the front and quickly flipped through it. I loved to get decoration ideas for the Bean Hive and my little log cabin.

"See anything you like in there?" Loretta Bebe asked in a singsong Southern drawl as she snuck up behind me.

"I do like how they arranged and stacked the different colors, shapes, and sizes of pumpkins on this front porch," I said and showed her the photo. "Thanks for the magazine drop-off."

"It's my pleasure. I like to flip through them and then spread the wealth." Loretta wiggled her brows. "And I brought some new ones that are already showcasing Thanksgiving. Can you believe it?"

Stacks of gold bangle bracelets rattled down on her wrist as she plunged her hand into her pocketbook and took out another pile of magazines.

"I wanted to make sure I dropped these off before we head down to Florida for a few weeks. We are going to see Elliot." She was referring to her son.

"That's so nice. How is he?" I asked and put the Halloween-themed magazine back on the coffee table before I took the stack I'd save to put out next month.

"You know, he's Elliot, but it's Birdie we are excited to see." Loretta smiled. She looked around. "Oh! Eleanor is here." There was excitement in her voice. She shoved her hot-pink painted nails into her short black hair, making it stand a little taller. "She's early," she said. "But if you want to get a few of those fancy pumpkins from that photo, you need to come to Hollow Manor. Eleanor has them."

She winked before she excused herself.

"She's a one-woman show," I muttered and picked up the poker to stoke the fire and then put another log on.

"Can I get you anything?" I asked several customers as I walked over to the coffee bar to make sure it was stocked as the morning rush continued.

All of them said they were fine, but I believed in making sure they were catered to. After all, this was my passion, not to mention my livelihood.

The coffee bar had six industrial thermoses with different blends of my specialty coffees as well as one filled with a decaffeinated blend. The coffee bar had everything you needed to take a coffee with you. Even an honor system where you could pay and go.

With it all cleaned and ready for the next round of pay-as-you-go customers, I made my way over to the opposite side where I had a tea bar for our tea-drinking customers.

We offered hot tea and cold tea with a nice selection of gourmet teas and loose-leaf teas. I loved having the antique tea pots from Wild and Whimsy Antique shop, which was also on the boardwalk. The pots were not just a decoration, but customers could enjoy their own pots by making them to their liking.

As I walked past another group, Eleanor's voice rang out, regaling them with her grand plans for the mansion's transformation. She painted a vivid picture of a place where the spooky reputation would be embraced, inviting them to experience the thrill of a magician's spellbinding tricks within its aged walls. The excitement in her voice was palpable, but beneath it all, a sense of unease gnawed at me.

Loretta stood next to her, offering approving head nods.

Glancing around the bustling coffee shop, I caught Bunny's critical scowl. Her silent disapproval spoke volumes, a reminder of the tensions that lingered between Eleanor and some of the townsfolk. Though the smiles, the chatter, and the aroma of steaming coffee filled the air, there was an unsettling feeling that something wasn't quite right.

I, too, had had my own encounter with the mansion. Something Patrick and

I had never talked about since the one afternoon when we were seventeen and decided to see if the tales Eleanor had spun back then were true.

A shiver ran down my spine. The same shiver that'd happened all those years ago after Patrick and I took off running away from the old mansion.

Though I told Eleanor I'd cater the coffee for the big finale tonight, I still couldn't help but think about what secrets hid in the shadows of the mansion.

I couldn't shake the feeling that our cozy autumn haven was about to be thrust into a chilling journey where nothing would be as it seemed.

After all, I'd never stepped foot on the mansion grounds since I'd run away.

Little did I know that returning to Hollow Manor would awaken more than just memories.

Macchiato Murder is now available to purchase or in Kindle Unlimited.

RECIPES FROM THE BEAN HIVE

Maple Bacon Coffee
Hot Honey Almond Milk Flat White Recipe
"Appalachian Summer" Bread

MAPLE BACON COFFEE

Ingredients:
   6 strips bacon-for the syrup
   1 cup pure maple syrup-for the syrup
   1 cup whole milk
   2 oz espresso
   ground cinnamon, for garnish

Directions:
   Make the maple bacon syrup:

1. You can bake the bacon at 425°F for 15–17 minutes, until crispy.

Or you can microwave the bacon or fry it. All of them are fine. I like to bake my bacon because I like it to bake evenly.

1. Transfer the bacon to a cutting board, blot with a paper towel to absorb any excess grease, and chop.
2. In a small saucepan add your chopped bacon and the maple syrup. Bring to a boil over medium-high heat, then reduce the heat to low and simmer for 15 minutes, or until thickened slightly.

3. Remove the pot from the heat and let it sit for 15–20 minutes.
4. Strain the syrup and reserving the bacon bits for the later when you top the coffee.

Make the maple bacon latte:

1. Add milk to a milk frother and set to the steam setting. Steam until hot.

If you don't have a frother, you can warm the milk on the stove in a small saucepan over medium-low heat, stirring occasionally, until beginning to steam. Use a handheld immersion blender, blend on low speed until frothy.

1. In a coffee mug, stir together the espresso and 2 tablespoons of maple bacon syrup.
2. Pour in steamed milk until the mug is ¾ full, then top with foam.
3. Garnish with some of the bacon bits and a sprinkle of ground cinnamon.
4. Serve immediately. Enjoy!

HOT HONEY ALMOND MILK FLAT WHITE RECIPE

If you're looking for a delicious twist on your daily cup of coffee, try this hot honey almond milk flat white recipe.

Ingredients

1 shot espresso or strongly brewed coffee

2 teaspoons honey

½ cup almond milk

Cinnamon for garnish

Directions:

1. Add the espresso and honey to your desired mug and stir to combine.
2. 1 shot espresso,
3. 2 teaspoons honey
4. Froth the almond milk.
5. Pour frothed almond milk over the espresso,
6. garnish with a pinch of cinnamon

"APPALACHIAN SUMMER" BREAD

For the honeysuckle simple syrup:

1 1/2 cups fresh honeysuckle (Lonicera periclymenum) flowers
1 cup unbleached, non-GMO cane sugar
1 cup of filtered water

Bring 1 cup of water to boil in a small saucepan over medium-high heat. As soon as the water boils, add 1 cup of sugar and stir to dissolve. Turn heat off and add in honeysuckle flowers. Cover the saucepan with a lid and let this infuse while you move on to making the cake.

When you're ready for your honeysuckle simple syrup, strain the mixture through a fine-mesh sieve. Compost the honeysuckle flowers and reserve 1/3 cup of the syrup for your cake. Transfer any remaining syrup to a glass canning jar and store it in the refrigerator for 2-3 weeks. Use it to sweeten herbal teas, drizzle ice cream or other desserts, or to sweeten your summer botanical mixed drinks!

For the pound cake:
1 1/2 cups of unbleached all-purpose flour
1 teaspoon aluminum-free baking powder
1/4 teaspoon baking soda
1 teaspoon fine-ground sea salt

2 tablespoons of Honeysuckle Simple Syrup, plus 1/3 cup reserved

1/3 cup of buttermilk (or plain yogurt)

2 tablespoons of freshly grated organic lemon zest (or 18 drops of organic lemon essential oil)

1 cup of unbleached, non-GMO cane sugar

1/2 cup of avocado oil

2 eggs

Preheat the oven to 350 degrees. While the oven is heating, butter and flour a 9×5 loaf pan.

In a small bowl, combine flour, baking powder, baking soda, and salt. Gently whisk to combine, and set aside.

In a large bowl, combine sugar, oil, and lemon zest (or essential oil) and whisk until the mixture is smooth. Whisk in the eggs, one at a time, until combined. Finally, add buttermilk (or yogurt) and honeysuckle simple syrup, and gently whisk to combine.

Next, slowly incorporate the dry ingredients into the wet ingredients, whisking as you go to keep the batter smooth. Scrape down the sides of the bowl until everything is well incorporated.

Pour the batter into the prepared loaf pan, tapping the pan on the counter a few times to remove trapped air bubbles. Bake for 45-60 minutes, until a knife or toothpick comes out clean.

When the cake is finished baking, let it cool in the pan for 10 minutes before inverting it onto a cooling rack. Carefully turn the cake right-side up on the cooking rack and place a tray or dish underneath. Poke holes in the top of the cake (getting close to the cake edges) with a knife, skewer, or toothpick, and brush 1/3 cup of honeysuckle syrup over the cake. Feel free to reuse any syrup drippings caught in the tray under the cake.

Lastly, top the cake with a sugar glaze, and set it aside to allow time for the honeysuckle simple syrup to absorb, allow the glaze to slightly harden, and give the cake time to cool.

For the sugar glaze

1/3 cup of non-GMO powdered sugar

1-3 teaspoons of water

Add 1/3 cup of powdered sugar to a glass measuring cup and slowly drizzle a small amount of water into it, adding 1 teaspoon at a time and stirring with a spoon, until the mixture is smooth.

Drizzle the mixture back and forth over the top of the cake, allowing it to run down the sides.

BOOKS BY TONYA
SOUTHERN HOSPITALITY WITH A SMIDGEN OF HOMICIDE

Camper & Criminals Cozy Mystery Series

All is good in the camper-hood until a dead body shows up in the woods.

BEACHES, BUNGALOWS, AND BURGLARIES
DESERTS, DRIVING, & DERELICTS
FORESTS, FISHING, & FORGERY
CHRISTMAS, CRIMINALS, AND CAMPERS
MOTORHOMES, MAPS, & MURDER
CANYONS, CARAVANS, & CADAVERS
HITCHES, HIDEOUTS, & HOMICIDES
ASSAILANTS, ASPHALT & ALIBIS
VALLEYS, VEHICLES & VICTIMS
SUNSETS, SABBATICAL AND SCANDAL
TENTS, TRAILS AND TURMOIL
KICKBACKS, KAYAKS, AND KIDNAPPING
GEAR, GRILLS & GUNS
EGGNOG, EXTORTION, AND EVERGREEN
ROPES, RIDDLES, & ROBBERIES
PADDLERS, PROMISES & POISON
INSECTS, IVY, & INVESTIGATIONS
OUTDOORS, OARS, & OATH
WILDLIFE, WARRANTS, & WEAPONS
BLOSSOMS, BBQ, & BLACKMAIL
LANTERNS, LAKES, & LARCENY
JACKETS, JACK-O-LANTERN, & JUSTICE
SANTA, SUNRISES, & SUSPICIONS
VISTAS, VICES, & VALENTINES
ADVENTURE, ABDUCTION, & ARREST
RANGERS, RVS, & REVENGE
CAMPFIRES, COURAGE & CONVICTS

MOTHER'S DAY MURDER
A HALLOWEEN HOMICIDE
NEW YEAR NUISANCE
CHOCOLATE BUNNY BETRAYAL
FOURTH OF JULY FORGERY
SANTA CLAUSE SURPRISE
APRIL FOOL'S ALIBI

Kenni Lowry Mystery Series

Mysteries so delicious it'll make your mouth water and leave you hankerin' for more.

FIXIN' TO DIE
SOUTHERN FRIED
AX TO GRIND
SIX FEET UNDER
DEAD AS A DOORNAIL
TANGLED UP IN TINSEL
DIGGIN' UP DIRT
BLOWIN' UP A MURDER
HEAVENS TO BRIBERY

Magical Cures Mystery Series

Welcome to Whispering Falls where magic and mystery collide.

A CHARMING CRIME
A CHARMING CURE
A CHARMING POTION (novella)
A CHARMING WISH
A CHARMING SPELL
A CHARMING MAGIC
A CHARMING SECRET
A CHARMING CHRISTMAS (novella)

About Tonya

Tonya has written over 100 novels, all of which have graced numerous bestseller lists, including the USA Today. Best known for stories charged with emotion and humor and filled with flawed characters, her novels have garnered reader praise and glowing critical reviews. She lives with her husband and a very spoiled rescue cat named Ro. Tonya grew up in the small southern Kentucky town of Nicholasville. Now that her four boys are grown men, Tonya writes full-time in her camper she calls her SHAMPER (she-camper).

Learn more about her be sure to check out her website tonyakappes.com. Find her on Facebook, Twitter, BookBub, and Instagram

Sign up to receive her newsletter, where you'll get free books, exclusive bonus content, and news of her releases and sales.

If you liked this book, please take a few minutes to leave a review now! Authors (Tonya included) really appreciate this, and it helps draw more readers to books they might like. Thanks!